The Angel of

Part 1

Shining House

The Angel of Subjugation – Part One

The following book is fictional and brought to life by the author's imagination. Any resemblance or parallel to real people, living or dead, as well as any real places or events is purely coincidental.

Chapter 1:
Maelstrom of the Past

A chill wind grazes my face as my eyes finally open. I don't need to be yet fully conscious to recognize that my situation is… ugh, to describe it as "dire" would *greatly* undersell it. My eyes fight the piercing glow of the sun to witness the travesty I barely escaped with my life. The small vessel that just hours ago I had been the prisoner of is now a barren, broken husk that clings to the rocky spires that had so nearly grinded me into paste, sticking out from the thunderous, crashing waves like a sore thumb. Half of it is lost to the depths whilst the other half displays its sorry self for the entire world to see, with the last of the embers that had engulfed it pathetically withering away atop its decrepit mast. Bits and pieces of its exterior are dispersed through the waters, and a lucky few have even ended up on the beach with me. A support beam here, a piece of an engine there… what hideous decoration. My sister always wanted to visit a beach; laying her eyes upon this travesty would swiftly change her mind.

My back and outstretched arms have become all too acquainted with the soft but cold sand that makes up this small beach - where rocky hills enveloped by trees form natural walls for this sandy enclosure - and my legs are dangerously close to where the tide has climbed. Had I ended up much further down, I would have faced a rather humiliating death, but I should count my blessings that I managed to survive in the first place.

Now, what would my esteemed mentor do at a time like this? It's an easy enough question to ask, but an exceedingly difficult one to answer when bereft of his company. A man of infinite wisdom, infinite resourcefulness, infinite pragmatism; an idol to everything a man ought to be. He would easily jump up to his feet, shake off the sand like a drenched dog and walk his way back home merrily, his journey pathed out before his eyes even opened. But I'm not that. Despite absorbing years of his teachings, I'm as out of my depth on this one as any common man on the street; I'm in the middle of a completely unknown land with only the clothes on my back. All I can do is hope I stumble my way into a solution. In a way, I'm glad he isn't here to watch me embarrass myself the moment I'm off his leash.

Not wanting to waste any more time, I begin to bend my legs and push my hands into the ground when-

"*AAACK!*"

I'm sent tumbling back to the ground as a strong jolt of pain shoots up my right leg; said leg crashing into the sand only exacerbates the problem. After my tumble, I can do little else but lay there with burdened groaning in place of the incessant screaming I have nary the energy for. Once the pain begins to withdraw, I raise my head to identify the source: a shard of wood, lodged into my right shin while just barely penetrating its front, and I have no doubts my disastrous attempt to get back on my feet had enabled it to burrow even further within. Worse yet, the wound has begun bleeding anew. I can't afford to let this problem fester, and so I get to work removing my cloak and then shirt, recalling as much of Saki's scant teachings as I can. The dark blue cloak Kyrie gave me for my birthday is unfortunately damaged, with cuts and rips dispersed throughout the beautiful fabric – not beyond repair, thankfully, but it still troubles me greatly, as it's all I have of her at this moment. However, the priority at this time is its internal contents, and as I scramble through its contents I am pleased to discover my serrated knife still in its scabbard, as well as a pen contained in a small, buttoned pouch.

But within this same pouch is a possession not of my own: a strange, small doll with buttons for eyes. It has many strands of stringy brunette hair protruding from its head and is wearing a robe of blinding white. Where and how did this end up in here? I've certainly never seen it before. Did it belong to that bastard on the boat? If so, I'll take some glee in robbing him of his possession, even one as... strange as this. I ought to just cast it to the sea like a worthless stone... but there's an uncanny familiarity to it that I can't pin down, and this is all the justification I need to return it to my pocket. Perhaps this act of theft will invoke yet more bad luck upon me, but it's the only revenge I can enact at this time.

Once again hard set on the task at hand, I remove the lock that covers and tightly secures the knife's hilt, taking it into my right hand, and begin hacking away at my shirt, producing some makeshift bandages from the ordeal. I set the bandages to one side on the sand with the pen atop them, and take a long, hard look at the oozing wound. This will be far from painless, but... well, the alternative is slowly bleeding to death, and I at least have enough of my wits left to determine which is preferable. Besides, Kyrie will personally hunt my ghost down if I perish to a problem so pitiful. After bracing myself for the pain, I grasp the thick end with my right hand and pull it downwards with as much force as I can muster. The sharp pain is barely tolerable but in just a few seconds, the shard of wood is removed, and my hand falls to the floor, limp from the exertion.

Once my blood obscures the gleam of the sun on my thumb, I force myself back into action, covering the wound with the bandages - taking care that any parts that made contact with the sand don't come close to it – and securing it in place by rotating the pen despite the dull, aching wishes of every muscle in my arms. The terrible tourniquet is complete, if not particularly effective. If by some miracle I end up ten years in the past, I'll stop at nothing to find myself of the time and force him to pay more attention to Saki's teachings.

With the dismal self-doctoring complete and my vision mostly cleared, I can finally absorb more of my surroundings. In addition to the rocky walls at my left and right that reach maybe 30 meters into the sea itself, I look behind me to discover I am closer to the upper edge of this beach than expected, being met by a dense forest with sparse hints of ice and snow forming along its perimeter. A foreboding path leading into abject darkness lies within its centre, laying behind me as though setting foot in there is an act of tempting fate itself. Will I be eaten by a wild animal the moment I set foot in there? I don't fancy sitting on this beach for the rest of my life, so I have to take my chances, two functioning legs or no. I put back on what remains of my shirt in addition to my cloak and force myself onto my legs. Just standing up proves to be painful, let alone continuous walking, but I summon the strength to power on through the path's opening regardless.

My eyes growing accustomed to the harsh sunlight proved to be short lived once I limped into the forest, as the dense oak trees are making a commendable effort to prevent any and all sunlight from highlighting this doomed soul's plight - this has made it exceedingly difficult to assess the physical damage I've suffered, but I can at least make out that my prosthetic thumb has been twisted slightly, maybe by 30 degrees or so at its central joint. It's producing an unsettling sensation in my nerves now that I'm aware of it, but it's not exactly *painful,* per se. I'm not particularly bothered by the lack of light; the subdued gloom in addition to the lack of any sounds aside from the irregular chirping of birds affords me some time to ponder as I navigate the linear path.

While I should be devoting my speculation to who exactly abducted me and for what purpose, I can't help but worry about my family I left behind in Ford; I was thankfully separate from them whilst I was accosted, but if my survival at the cost of my abductors' lives is learnt of, I can only hope they aren't targeted for retribution. Confirming their safety is of utmost priority, but that begs an even greater question.

Where am I?

I have no idea how long I was held in that ship for before my escape, but surely I remain in Morosus still? A trek across even half of the country would take weeks, if not months; the idea of ending up in another country only complicates the issue by orders of magnitude, due in no small part to the ongoing war between Morosus and Ennui.

My pondering is brought to a swift halt once I reach a fork in the road: a stone path to my left, with unlit and (formerly) Tenkite-powered lanterns atop poles roughly half my height running parallel across each side of it – a dirt road to my right, still muddy and wet from the rain in which I had made my unceremonious departure from the ship. Thinking the solution to be obvious, I look away from the dirt road and begin taking a step towards the stone path. My foot is not even able to make its first footstep before I'm frozen by what I find before me: A... cobra, coated in black with white stripes breaking up the stygian tedium, emerging from the bushes.

...a cobra, *here*?!

My foot touches the ground once again as its full body emerges, coiling into a circle at the left edge of the path some ten meters away from me and slowly opening its maw, inviting me into its digestive system. From this distance, I'm certain I've seen a cobra such as this one before- no, I'm certain this is the same one I saw in my childhood; the black and white pattern of its face is an exact match. A chill runs down my spine, and while frozen in place, I can only blink as I await my fate – and then she appears.

"Why, oh, why, Vega? Why look at my precious with such disdain in your bright little eyes?"

Sitting on the tree stump right next to the cobra, she speaks down to me in an accusatory yet mocking tone with her exposed back facing me and her hand beneath the cobra's chin, gently tickling it with her right hand as its expression changes from disdain for its prey to joyous glee... at least, as gleeful as I imagine a snake can look.

"My serpentine darling is bestowing upon thee a gift, and I beckon you to regard it with open arms."

Her presence explains to me in an instance the cobra's familiarity, and with her demand made, she finally turns around to face me, crossing her legs in extravagant fashion as her devilish, childishly elated grin looks exactly as it did all those years ago. With more for me to witness than just her face this time, I can finally affirm that my saviour is as suspicious-looking as she is appealing to the eye, adorned in a crimson dress that reaches down to her ankles - with sparkling golden trims at its edges and little coverage of her ample breasts. Her asymmetrical skirt reveals a pair of legs that tread the earth with only a pair of brown sandals, in stark contrast to the blood red nails found on the appendages of both her feet and hands. None of this seems out of the ordinary, until you

8

look at her hair… or the lack thereof; she's completely bald, with only a spindly silver tiara in place of hair. A small image of a snake eternally coiling in a circle lies inside the gem that rests within the centre of the tiara.

All of this is present and accounted for, but there's something else that catches my eye yet – across her chest is a gruesome scar, reaching across the entirety of what she exposes of her upper chest. It looks faded but deep, and stands out strongly from her fair skin. I can't say for sure if this is a newly acquired wound or if I simply never noticed it before, but I'm leaning towards the latter given its seeming age. Either way, her very presence is difficult for the eyes to process; had I not met her in my early youth, I would be eyeing her with substantial suspicion, as would any sane man.

"Who… who are you?"

"Who am *I*?" she says haughtily as she raises her cobra-coated arm to her face, stroking the head of the critter in question with her finger, "My dear, there's one thing you ought to know about this world: knowledge is only as powerful as those who can hear of it. And yet, as a battered little boy *and* with your tongue constricted in such a manner, you pursue that which you cannot share regardless?"

…in retrospect, my question really was thoughtless. Considering I can't even so much as *write* about her, let alone speak of her, who am I to pursue anything from her?

"But I'm feeling generous. What good is it to step in on your behalf and leave you with no name? Not that *I* would lose sleep over the matter, of course." she continues, much to my shock, and daintily strolls ever closer to me with each set of cryptic words to leave her mouth, "The inhabitants of this world have called me by many names. All of them long lost to time, of course, but names carry power, and an alias too to a limited extent. Cacophitas, Anta-Rakamos, many more you will never find in a history book…"

My mind is telling me to remain steadfast, but my body is insisting otherwise; I've been pacing backwards as she approaches, and now my back is against a tree whilst she pushes forward yet. The sensation is suffocating, much like our first meeting; her presence alone is far more overpowering than the dreadful tunnels of the Basin.

"But my true name is Sihan-Perseli. Commit my name to memory if you must, for you obviously cannot chronicle such a thing."

Having answered the question I now wish never left my lips, she at last backs away, maintaining an unclear expression.

I'm completely unsure what to make of it. Sihan-Perseli... I can't construe meaning from such a strange name, and further yet why she would provide it to me. Is she trying to... tell me something? I certainly can't share it or make any real use of it. Is she... *tormenting me*?

"W...why did you tell me that?!"

"You *did* ask me." she says with a yet more gruesome smirk, "Anyway, I am certain it requires no explanation from myself, but for clarification, whatever choice you intend to take at this moment will result in..."

SWOOSH!

"...your certain death~"

Her final words are accompanied by a spear materialising into her hand as she runs it hair-raisingly close to her throat. I no longer have any idea if she genuinely means to warn me or decided to stomp on my face as I entered another spot of bother.

That being said... if she held any ill will towards me, I would have died before I even saw ten years of age. With no reason to doubt the sincerity of her warning, I reluctantly accept her words, but the continued silence as to her intentions, her origins, her... anything is as aggressive as ever, perhaps moreso now that I'm not a frail little boy anymore. If she had never showed up again, I could have chalked her up to being an imaginary friend or a childhood guardian angel. Now that she stands here before me again, in the flesh and very much real, all I can do is wonder what ulterior motive she holds; I don't fancy dancing to the pull of any puppetmaster's strings, no matter their allegiance. Regardless, I have no idea when we shall meet again, so I'll take any chance for answers I can get.

"If I could get you to produce a name, is there any chance you could tell me what it is you want of me? I enjoyed leading a simple life; if you've some grand ambitions for me, then our wishes align not."

I keep myself reserved and calm as I pose the request, doing my best not to let the anxiety pour into my words like a busted fountain. The smirk on her face doesn't even finish forming before the regret sinks in.

"I have shared everything that *you* are at liberty to know of, Vega"

Ugh... while I'm frustrated that she remains tight-lipped as ever, I also can't help but feel utterly defeated by my own ignorance, especially in matters pertaining to my life or death. It would be avaricious to demand more from a woman who saved my life, but she's really leaving me to grasp at straws in a most tormenting manner. She may well be the only entity in all the world who could befuddle Kyrie through words alone.

Satisfied by the bewildered look on my face, she at last perks up and snaps her fingers.

"That cloak looks good on you! Until we meet again~!"

Upon the utterance of her cheery farewell message, I rush forward as fast as my wounded leg will allow, begging her to stop and reaching out my arm towards her, hoping to grab onto anything; risking a cobra bite is little deterrent from gaining at least a small facet of the answers I've sought for ten years now. Sure enough, a few meters away from her, I am forced to blink by the wind rushing into my eyes, and she disappears along with her pet before my eyes open once more. An ugly scowl scrawls itself across my face; what would I have even done if I *could* have reached her? Slapped some answers out of her? In a state such as this? What a miserable exchange; all I can do is obey her warnings had march along the dirt road, uncertain of what future Sihan-Perseli has waiting for me.

It takes roughly an hour of walking through the dirt path to catch a glimpse of civilization once more: as the trees recede, giving way for the gloomy grey clouds to look down upon me once more, I catch a glimpse of a mountain – not a particularly large one, but an impressive sight nonetheless. I'd sooner see this on Ford's horizon than the Skyspur and the grim memories stapled to it. The mountain is shaped in a distinctive way, as if reaching its arms as wide as it can to swallow up as much of the little village in front of it as possible, and even from this distance I can see a tower of red and white standing by its lonesome at an elevated lot of land beneath the central peak, with a single wooden bridge connecting it to the rest of the settlement below, rendered slightly harder to see by black smoke with an origin closer to me but yet unseen. The distinctive red and white bring to mind a certain place: Tenryuu. But... surely I can't be *that* far from home, right? That would imply my captors somehow snuck through the raging naval war taking place between Morosus and Ennui, a naval war just as violent and dreadful as the warfare one finds on land.

Seeking confirmation, I pick up the pace, rushing forward as the makeshift tourniquet unravels and becomes one with the wind, but the still pressing pain in my leg is completely overshadowed by a single, dominant feeling: dread. Maybe I ended up in one of the more obscure corners of Morosus, maybe I somehow missed this very distinctive mountain on every map of Morosus I've ever seen, maybe my way home won't be agonizingly long, maybe, maybe... no... it's useless. The gold sign at the entrance arch of the village confirms every one of my fears; it proudly states the name of the village I face at this very moment: Dias. And this isn't just any old village in Tenryuu, not at all; the machinations of whatever fate or god is pulling my strings have sent me to the village of my mentor: Mahro Katsuragi.

My feet feel heavy as I force myself through the opening to the village, though despite my current predicament, I can't help but take a moment to observe the beautiful little abode I have wandered through the entrance of; each and every building's exterior stays true to the red and white colour scheme found at its upmost establishment, as does the entrance arch with its two pillars meeting above my head. Each building stands out for their great volume, largely exceeding those seen in my hometown of

Ford, and their shingled roofs presenting a wide spectrum of shades of red, most of which are now adorned with blue, ovular lanterns to commemorate the arrival of winter. Judging from the signs denoting a blacksmith here and a clothier there among others, the entrance leads directly into a business/industrial sector. The entire scene is complimented by a layer of ice dressed across the canopies of these buildings, though the slowly gathering rain seeks to put an end to such natural decoration. Even the weather has an ill sense of humour.

Not that the rain particularly bothers me after swimming away from my certain death, but it acts as a cue to head deeper into the heart of Dias. As bad as my circumstances are, it's long been a dream of mine to walk the streets my mentor calls home; I wish my first visit were not so abrupt or unanticipated, but I'm in dire need of a silver lining, and this is exactly it.

As the rain begins to fill the cracks in my stony path, I pass by a cramped-looking guard station within the entrance plaza to see nobody inside of it. I suppose living in a part of the country largely free of war affords a little more flexibility in matters of security, but I still feel ever so slightly uneasy without a reliable guy like Ringo watching our backs... I can't help but wonder if he's running himself ragged trying to resolve my sudden disappearance, the poor old geezer. Guess that gives me more cause to hurry up and send word to the folks back home. The thought of Kyrie and Tsubasa crying themselves to sleep, not knowing whether or not I'm even alive... impalement is less torturous.

Seating myself on a bench beneath a tree for some very necessary rest, the next course of action is materializing somewhere in my clouded mind: if I've been directed to the village of my mentor, somebody clearly wants us to have a chat and work this whole mess out together. And he'll no doubt pull through; I've watched him slay an unimaginable abomination with my own eyes – arranging a return journey should be nothing for such a monolith of a man.

My only problem, albeit a colossal one, is that Mahro never mentioned any details about his home beyond the name of his village; my only recourse is to ask around for details while keeping an eye out for either Mahro himself or Matra. Of course, his other daughter or his wife may also be around, but I know nothing of Myra or Minami beyond their shared hair colour with Matra and given that I'm already the stranger in a strange land, I don't fancy getting thrown in a jail cell for approaching random women on the off chance they might be my master's other daughter or his wife. The rain shows no sign of slowing down, so I have no excuse to be sitting down here myself; given that I've spent some hours lying on a beach and plodding through a muddy forest, an impromptu shower should do me more good than harm.

It doesn't take a genius to figure out that a family of four aren't going to reside in the industrial sector, so I take my leave from the area and head inward with haste, soon arriving at the town centre. At the town's centre lies an expansive patch of grass, with two rings of stone surrounding a fountain with a stone statue of a nude woman standing in a sterile pose atop it, no doubt a mythical or historical figure of high importance to the natives; out of respect for the locals I'll refrain from ignorant shots in the dark as to her identity. Next to the base of the fountain, a structure with two large wheels on each side houses some sort of mobile restaurant, though the climate is sending the queue into a frenzy to hurry up and return home. The indescribable mixture of pleasant delicacies wafting towards me from the mobile restaurant would no doubt compel me to march helplessly into the queue were I not so lacking in time or funds. Speaking of... *shit!* I just remembered my wallet was taken by the bastards on that ship after they abducted me; I hope they didn't get a chance to waste it, but I would rather that money be in my pocket and food be in my stomach.
Sourly disappointed and reminded of my encroaching starvation, I walk past the foot of the fountain just in time to watch a crowd almost universally clad in white and red robes dispersing. Most are walking in the same direction as me, towards a large array of buildings looking similar to the area I just left but without the abundance of signs and attempts to extract Sera from wallets. I opt to follow the crowd into what I hope is the residential district, heading forward as fast as my tortured right leg will allow. As I

14

approach the mass of people, I attract the odd strange look from men and women alike. Whether it's due to my being a foreigner or looking like a breathing, shambling corpse, I couldn't say. Mahro made me well aware of his people's general distrust for outsiders, but I'm certain my physical appearance isn't doing me any favours. I'm not particularly self-conscious either way; it's no use rushing back to the beach for a bath when attention is best devoted to looking for Mahro or Matra.

But while I'm here, making some observations about my temporary company should be inoffensive at worst. First of all, Mahro continues his streak of being proven objectively correct about everything (come on, I'm tooting your horn, show yourself already you bastard) as I notice that indeed, many of the women are both imposing in height and fairly well-endowed in comparison to those of my home country, and are not shy about showing off both their stature and their beauty to the rest of the world. The men too are as a whole well-built and carry a dominating aura, though the contrast is not quite so pronounced in their case. A frequent sight among the males is a scorching red dragon adorning the back of their robes, looking ready at any and all times to reduce me to ashes. While their subject matter is shared, each robe provides its own unique dragon illustration, and I'm stared down by an army of red dragons, all disputing over the best intensity with which to roast me – the gods of weather may be all that prevent me from ending up a well done steak in the middle of this street. The females, on the other hand, appear more prone to decorating their backs with... cats. Not a ferocious "cat" such as a tiger, but rather little kittens who couldn't hurt a fly. The disparity is so jarring I can't help but snort in amusement, drawing yet more suspicious glances from some nearby residents. The people of Tenryuu have a special intensity in their glares; in a stark betrayal of everything Ringo has ever stood for, I ought to exercise some caution in my mannerisms.

The most important observation to make, however, is that no familiar faces lie among the crowd. Right as I'm just about ready to curl into a ball and give up, a pleasant smell forcefully invades my nostrils; it turns out that as I turned the corner along with the slowly shrinking crowd, I unknowingly entered a market district, full of stalls for all sorts of food. Mostly delicacies of the Tenryuu people, namely an awful lot of fish and the associated infinite number of ways these people could come up with to devour them. I have no money to offer these people but perhaps I could get an answer or two as a freebie.

I wait patiently, leaning over the seats of a small stall calling itself "River King" as I watch the small ripples in the green curtain separating its back from its front ebb and flow. It's a long shot but I'm not unconvinced that anybody serving here for a decent amount of time would know every face in the area off by heart. Sure enough, a charming young lady soon emerges in a pink shirt and black apron, looking ever so pleased to see this half-dead foreigner. I have no interest in declaring her apparent pleasure to be artificial or prolonging an interaction with a customer who has no money to offer, and so I throw out my question as she leans against the counter, before she has a chance to spew out a sales pitch.

"Miss, I am terribly sorry but I am not here for business. I am desperately searching for a man called Mahro, do you happen to know where I can find him?" I ask sheepishly.

At first she just stares in disbelief - I bring my hands away from the counter and scratch the nape of my neck with my right hand as the silence festers, and the strong aroma of her rose-tinted perfume is doing little to help. She ultimately sighs in disappointment, but at least she isn't chasing me away with a sharp utensil as I slowly came to dread these past few seconds.

"That man would sooner eat raw mammal, fur and all, than anything with even a hint of fish. An odd duck, that one. I have no idea where he lives but I suggest paying a visit to the Head Enforcer's office, darling. Turn left at the end of this road and you'll know the building when you see it, he should be able to help."

Her smile looks painful as she points to the end of the road I was already traversing; it seems Mahro has a bit of a reputation even in his own town for his strange proclivities.

"Thank you. Sorry to disturb you." I say as I rush away to follow her directions, breaking eye contact before I can see if she hates my guts for wasting her time and not even having the decency to pay for it.

As I turn the corner in pursuit of the Head Enforcer's office, being met by a completely empty street, the rain begins to intensify once again. Before the rain can cloud my vision any further, I catch a glimpse of a familiar sight: the bridge leading to the sole building sitting in front of the mountain's central peak; this street in particular is where the mountain's presence is by far the most pronounced and noticeable, and I stand there for a moment to take in the sight, with the wide waterfall emerging from the rightmost peak and blending into the river running beneath the bridge proving to be particularly enchanting. I can't say ending up on the other side of the world was worth the pain and strife of getting here, but I can at least rest assured that I won't go home devoid of stories to tell.

At last I reach the Head Enforcer's office - located only about 20 meters away from the bridge and identified by a fairly direct "Enforcer's Office" sign above the door - and begin ascending the stone steps, only to be greeted by a sign kindly informing me that "only the dead or dying may knock". Undeterred by the living status-based discrimination, I raise my hand and prepare to knock on the door when a pair of wet, loud footsteps erupt from the steps right behind me. In a hurry, I turn around to discover a cloaked man staring up at me with a cold, vacant look in his one eye and a mangled mess in place of his other. His hands are withdrawing from his pockets but remain concealed within his cloak, and his legs are widened, ready to cut off any attempt to run. He clearly means trouble, but I can't afford to get caught causing it here. I just have to endure whatever he throws my way...

"Well, what do we have here? I've been fishing all over the world, let me tell you, my little'un, I've plucked fish from lakes you can't find on any map I ever heard of and I'm certain I ain't never seen a catch... like... *this*..."

The stranger steps up to me with a voice so intense and rough that a blind man would think he's speaking with a rock weighing his throat down. Almost his every tooth is black, barely distinguishable from the first fish I ever tried to cook, and the stench emanating from it proves that the cover *can* serve as a prelude to its contents; I can barely stare him down without wanting to gag, but this is the last moment at which I want to display any kind of weakness.

"What's with that look on your face, boyo? You lose your Mommy? Well, I dunno about you, but standing around here is no good, no sirree! Being the kind gentleman I am, I'll help you look for her! I'll even be so gracious as to offer you the clothes on my back!"

With a feigned look of solemnness, he raises the side of his filthy cloak towards me with his left hand, tittering as he brings it in front of my face, before dropping it like blazing coal and keeping his finger pointed towards my face.

"So come on, where did she lose you, little boy?"

A thick silence ensues, and our mutual gaze of abject hatred intensifies by the second until the stranger brings his pointing hand to the wall next to me, obscuring most of my vision with his foul, beaming mug. In addition to his sickly skin, he reveals a pair of two gold teeth on his bottom jaw, looking awfully tacky and excessive to the extent that I have to hold back the urge to punch them out here and now.

"Aaaaaah, that's right! She's burning down there, isn't she? The big man downstairs is having all sorts of fun with her body, doing all those dirty, disgraceful things I wish I could've done to the bitch while she was still kicking. You have fun suckling on her cold, dead tits when it all wrapped up, boy? Or did you like 'em warm? I'm not judgmental, keheheh~"

What the law says is meaningless now; this shitbag undoubtedly carries ill intent, and if his disgraceful attitude towards my late mother isn't solid ground to knock him out cold, then his threatening aura and physical proximity are more than enough reason for me to act. Uninterested in how exactly he knows about my family history, I prepare to retaliate by balling my fist and...

"Know your place!"

As he says this, he delivers a punch to my gut too fast for me to react, forcing me against the door to the Head Enforcer's office.

Now I'm just being sloppy. With a sickening snicker, the stranger bends down to run his mouth forevermore.

"This is where you belong, kid: under my boot, impotent and useless. Now... if they get their hands on me the man in that building is gonna drag my ass down to the capital. But for a catch like this... hell, what wouldn't I risk for that? When I'm done making you squeal like a piggy, for all the shit *you* put me through, maybe I'll even take a little stroll down to... I don't know, *Ford*, maybe? Your buddy Pat's in bad need of a piss, and old Stephanie's grave is looking reaaaal dry! Then I can give her some company, if you're picking up what I am so graciously putting dow*AAAH!*"

His bloviating is interrupted by my headbutt, sending him tumbling down the steps and landing face first on the stone road. I'm more than a little dazed now but I eventually regain my balance. The vile creature cowering before me is struggling to stand again, coughing and wheezing as he makes the effort. I remain in place, reluctant to kick even this disgusting weasel while he's down. My strike was cathartic, but I shouldn't escalate it further; I don't wish to shed blood within my mentor's very own home, and I don't need whatever trouble that would cause getting in the way of a path home through his efforts.

But my hesitancy evaporates, becomes utterly incorporeal, once I witness what is scrawled onto the man's arm: a tattoo of a wyvern. And this is no ordinary wyvern tattoo...

...it's the insignia belonging to the Band of the Wyvern.
...this...
...this can't be!

Julius told me, with absolute certainty, that they had been destroyed, exterminated even! So *WHAT* is this bastard doing here, with that garish tattoo scrawled on his arm?! When confronted with a sight like this, all I can think about is my mother's death and the role played in it by these bastards; all of the security and stability brought about by his clan's supposed end is unravelling in mere seconds. My head feels like it's been forced onto an uncomfortably fast rotisserie.

I storm towards him with no further hesitation, filled with an overwhelming desire to wring his neck as the artificial fingers occupying the spaces of those I lost all those years ago begin to throb furiously. Beating the stuffing out of him won't bring back the security I've enjoyed for these ten long years, and it may well cause an ugly stain on my relationship with Mahro after I drag this bastard through the street by his hair until his arms and legs go numb, but it's the only way I can personally enact some small revenge for that *miserable* day.

Before I can reach the second step, I'm alerted by a creaking sound from above me, and by the time I turn around a new assailant's foot is mere centimeters away from my left shoulder and it lands with great force before I can react, sending me tumbling back to the street and smashing my right leg into the bottom step. As my mind starts to go numb from the resurfaced pain and limitless fury, I bring my hand behind my cloak, discreetly unlocking the scabbard for my knife and pulling it out with a reversed grip before Pat enters my sight once more. The odious bastard rests on his knees above me with a knife in his hands, as his companion stands with his arms folded a few meters away. Even in my rain-coated, dazed vision, I can tell the knife is about 10 centimeters away from my face; I can't afford to slip up now, given that any mistake here is going to result in parts of my brain ending up with steel in their place.

"You piece 'a shit! If you wanna die that fuckin' badly I'll gladly send you to He-*AAAAAACK!*"

Seeking to cut the chatter, I swiftly pull out my knife while Pat continues to monologue incessantly and shove it straight into his gut, tilting my head as far to the right as possible and getting away with only a light cut to my cheek as he tumbles forward and drops his weapon. There's a light stinging in my left cheek, but it's nothing I haven't dealt with before. Before his buddy can jump in and subdue me, I grab Pat's knife with my free left hand and launch it at him, missing my throw but sending him into a panic.

Seizing the chance, I tear the knife out of Pat's gut and turn him around for use as a human shield – this being the only reason I haven't killed him here and now - whilst his assistant, obviously inexperienced in the ways of combat, is scrambling for Pat's knife and uttering all sorts of profanities under his breath. He turns back to me, knife in hand, to see my knife at Pat's throat.

The brawl seems fairly decisive in my favour; Pat's clearly the leader of the two, and to put it into terms favourable to Kyrie, a pawn isn't going to dare strike a man holding his king hostage. I'm ready to negotiate a surrender, but it's at this point that I hear a rush of footsteps from my left. Fearing more assailants, I turn to see a darkness-cloaked figure skulking towards us from an alleyway between two buildings opposite the Head Enforcer's office; the body shape appears to be that of a young woman, but I have no means by which to determine if she's friend, foe or even looking to get involved in the first place.

"Stop it! *Stop, you fucking idiot!*" my foul-mouthed captive cries out, thrashing his arms around like a wild animal.

Wondering why he's crying out, I turn my head back to his pawn charging towards me, preparing to plunge his knife into my head. I begin pressing the knife against Pat's neck, the hostage in question wincing in pain, but this does nothing to deter my attacker. My eyes widen in dread; I've made a horrible miscalculation, and I'm in nowhere near good enough shape to deal with the fiery mess I've been flung into. If I'm to die here, my only option is to take Pat with me...

Though before he can get close enough for me to carve a cavernous wound into Pat's neck, a crossbow bolt flies from my left into the man's right eye, followed by another one hitting his right arm and a third bolt flying past him into the wall of the head enforcer's office, all in the span of a few seconds. The first shot is enough to instantly kill him and he collapses to the floor with a loud, bloody crunch, his grip on the knife staying firm. It's a mortifying sight; the bolt protruding from his head with slimy viscera coiled around its shaft makes me *extremely* glad this third party was on my side.

"What the *hell* is going on here?!" a commanding voice booms from inside the Head Enforcer's office, and the door soon flies open.

Stepping outside his door with his hand shielding his eyes from the rain, the man looks in my direction, seeing me there with my knife still at Pat's throat and looking awfully confused by the whole ordeal.

"For the love of..." he says as he stares daggers at my hostage with a laboured groan, "Is the other guy a friend of yours?"

"Yes sir. My father's student."

That voice... there's absolutely no doubt, that's Matra. The Head Enforcer (whose name has been mentioned by Matra but currently eludes me) storms over to us and tears a now limp, shocked Pat from my grasp, and as much as I would like to use this newfound freedom in arm movement to wave hello to Matra and have a nice chat about what we've been up to since we met, the intense bleeding in my leg as well as the blows I sustained in the fight cause me to fall back in exhaustion once the fight dies down. I hear nothing from her, but a moment later I can feel myself being raised from the ground.

"Nice work, but just... get him to your dad, fast. He looks more like a corpse than the guy whose eye is slung out the back of his head..." the Head Enforcer says with a nervous chuckle.

Matra begins panting heavily as she struggles to bring me to her torso and walk across a path completely unfamiliar to me. I can't see her face, but I hope she can still smile at a time like this; from the brief time I spent with her, the sheer optimism emanating from her broad smile was contagious.

That being said, I won't be smiling anytime soon; the minute or so of walking that follows is greatly disorienting – assisted in no small part by the sound of rushing water filling my ears - and I can feel my consciousness badly waning, kept alive only by my wish to hear my mentor's voice again. It's a mercy that Matra doesn't speak a word the entire time, as much as I desire to hear her voice further yet.

"Matra, who's this gu- wait a minute, Vega?!"

Mahro's voice is the last thing I hear before I fully lose consciousness. Above all else, I at least got what I wanted most...

I at last wake up, this time in a home completely unknown to me. It only feels like I've been asleep for a few hours, but the stern look on my mentor's face at the foot of the bed - infrequently exchanging words with an unseen observer to my right - as well as the dark sky outside the window right behind him suggests that I may be slightly underestimating in that regard.

Once he at last notices I'm slowly re-entering the realm of the living, he leaps into action, rushing to my side and pushing his hand into the pillow next to me as he watches for any sign of life I have left in silent dread. From here, I can make out that he looks... tired. Dreadfully tired. Not in exhaustion, but as though he's perpetually disdainful of life itself. The shadows beneath his eyes are nearly as large as the eyes themselves and his hair is beginning to lose some of its vibrancy, inching ever closer to grey instead of black. Mahro's worries are assuaged by the time my eyes are at last fully open; he retreats to his previous position, sighing in relief and wiping the sweat from his brow, upon which I at last see his two daughters.

Matra is uncharacteristically intense but composed, crossing her arms and closing her eyes as she breathes in the stale air through her nose, whilst a shorter but similar looking young lady – no doubt Mahro's youngest daughter Myra – is staring at me in abject confusion, and she appears to be hiding behind her older sister. I, too, would be bewildered if my father and sister dragged this scruffy looking stranger into the house and threw him onto their bed as if I were just an old drinking buddy who was too inebriated to tell the road home from my own arse, but I suppose her surprise is mirrored by my own; rather than the casual and revealing clothes she spent her impromptu trip to Morosus in, Matra is wearing a lifeless black blouse and thick red overalls that reach up to the lower side of her chest and cover the entirety of her legs – the overalls are burdened by a bevy of scruffy pouches.

In a blinding contrast, Myra is robed in elegant white and pink silk, all of it remaining translucent save for her chest and the area surrounding her waist whilst prominently baring her navel – she looks utterly unperturbed by the dreadful chill that has come to fill the air around this time of year. I guess it runs in the Katsuragi family?

Matra's eyes finally open to awkwardly meet my own, though the brief glimmer of relief in her eyes is quickly torn away as her attention diverts to her father.

"See, he's fine. We can finally get some answers."

Her behaviour seems... strange. She doesn't necessarily sound dismissive of my situation, but definitely seems somewhat detached and blunt, expressing none of the exaggerated emotion I've come to expect of both her and her father. Already, what should be a momentous, triumphant occasion is boring a chasm in my stomach.

"I understand my student *far* better than you do, believe me, I'm perfectly well aware of how tough he is. It's just... I can't imagine he's ended up on the other side of the world with not a Sera to his name by his own free will. Am I correct to think that?"

Much to my relief, he's not lost one bit of his wit; I nod with as much strength as I can muster without straining my neck, but it quickly becomes apparent that his disposition is eerily similar to Matra's. The dark bags under his eyes suggest his issues aren't just contained to this conversation. Either way, I by far have more explaining to do, so I'll hold off on prying into their circumstances.

As the blinding brown walls and intense stares from all parties in the room leave me to ponder, one single, significant question is pounding the forefront of my mind, and it is soon repeated by my mentor, as if he can read me like a book.

"How in the world *did* you end up here?"

Chapter 2:
A Quaint Corner of the World

I wish I could say that all of the memories I have of my mother are cheery, full of joy and taking place against the backdrop of a bright beaming sun and a flowery meadow for all of us to frolic about in without a care in the world. That I grew up knowing nothing but love and companionship, forging bonds of steel with everyone around me and helping prop each and every person in the little village of Ford to greatness. But alas, the truth isn't so mercifully idyllic. I still treasure my earliest memory whilst loathing to think of it; it's a reminder of the life I led in an age long past, and a mirror into a world where my life took a dramatically different and less painful course.

This particular day started with me waking up in abject darkness – disturbed only by a thin ray of weak, early morning sunlight entering through the curtains that I was much too short to reach - on the floor of my bedroom, with the thin pink blanket belonging to my mother doing very little to separate me or Altair from the discomfort of the rock-hard floor.

Speaking of Altair... where was he?! Normally my slothful older brother would be lying right next to me, subconsciously fighting for more than his fair share of the much more comfortable but still not too spacious white blanket belonging to the two of us alone. And yet, he had taken the initiative to wake up before me? Something didn't add up, and so curious little me stood up in my favourite pyjamas, adorning me with a smiling puppy at my chest, and fumbled around in the darkness until I at last pushed against the door leading to our bedroom.

What I saw next greatly surprised me: Altair was sat at the table in the centre of our living room, wide awake and enthusiastically reading through a thin book about a knight and his shining sword, while my mother was hard at work cooking breakfast for the two of us, with the bubbling and bursting of oil and the sweet smell of food causing my stomach to rumble. As if alerted by the rapturous sound of my stomach, the two of them turned to me with a smile, and their greeting came in unison.

"Happy birthday!"

Indeed, this day – July 2nd 578 AR - was my third birthday, and my mother put down her utensils as she walked over to me, picking me up and raising me uncomfortably high into the air, but the gleeful smile on her face made objecting to her actions impossible. My mother's name was Stephanie, and I distinctly remember that she was wearing a heavily stained white apron over a loose, sky-blue blouse, complimented by a charming, cherry blossom-coloured skirt reaching down to her ankles.

Her lengthy brunette hair reached around her shoulder and emitted a pleasant scent of shampoo that intensified as she brought me closer. If it weren't for the ends of her bony arms poking out of her blouse, one would find it difficult to tell that my poor mother was noticeably emaciated, having often neglected her own need for sustenance. It's not as though we were so run down as to not be able to afford food for the three of us; the little village of Ford, located not a mile away from the western coast of Morosus, was a place where food was as plentiful as raindrops in a monsoon, and therefore affordable in equal proportions. No, instead, my mother seemed to take displeasure in the *act* of eating; she would eat cake delivered from the heavens itself with the same difficulty as chowing down on bugs pulled from some filthy corner of a cave, always looking ready to throw back up anything that entered her digestive system. She went to great lengths to hide this in front of her children, but Altair was more than astute enough to observe this aberrant behaviour towards the end of her life.

My mother sat me down at the table's end, giving me a premium view of our living room for the special occasion; this was the only room in our home aside from mine and Altair's bedroom as

26

well as the cramped bathroom located right behind me, therefore my mother got her good night's rest on the faded but intact black sofa resting against the wall to my right - with a currently unlit lantern resting above it. The entrance to our home, secured from outsiders by three locks, sat to its left.

To my left was a dedicated kitchen, providing all the tools and facilities my mother required to ensure mine and Altair's needs were accounted for. A series of cabinets were tucked between the wall and the ceiling, with the sole cabinet left open containing a half-empty sack of sugar. And what laid before me, blocking the view of the room's sole window, was a small stack of wrapped gifts – no prizes for guessing their recipient.

"Happy birthday, bro." Altair repeated his greeting as he stood up in front of me, raising my right hand with his left and high fiving me with his free hand.

Once our breakfast reached its conclusion and I had been fully clothed in a white vest and blue shorts along with Altair, my mother looked at the time and reacted with panic.

"Let's hurry, boys! You don't want to keep a young lady waiting!"

My birthday gifts were set aside for the time being – I was disappointed about having to wait, but confident that I would find the opportunity later in the day, my only show of protest emerged as a dull groan.

My mother unlocked the hardy front door, shifting her key between the three locks and opening it slowly as she gazed attentively at the outside world. Once the door was fully open, she beckoned us to exit after her, and from our diminutive bungalow - coloured in a similar shade to my mother's blouse - resting near the top of a hill, I laid my eyes on the wonderful sights of Ford, a sight I'll never forget nor become tired of.

Most apparent when gazing upon such a scene were the rapids on the eastmost side of the town, surrounded by rocks too steep to ascend and too tall to traverse in the opposite way without breaking one's legs. These rocks served to separate Ford from the rest of Morosus, save for a path through the forest on the entire other end of the village from us.

The rapids converged into a steady river running through the centre of the village and separating Ford into two distinct halves; while the half from which I emerged was where you found homes and recreation, the other half was rife with both farmlands, where hard working men and their machines prepared for the upcoming harvest season, and a mass of factories and workshops, all running at varying levels of capacity and spewing stygian smoke into the skies.

Neighbouring these factories was a network of living quarters carved into the rocky walls, and many were seen waiting for motorized black platforms to come and go between their homes and the surface (despite our better living space, such a home looked cosy in its own way, I thought). The sole link between these two halves was a formidable bridge providing space for two lanes of vehicles as well as side paths for pedestrian traversal – though the vehicular lanes saw exceedingly rare use.

If you had told me at that age that Ford was the entire world, I would have readily believed you; at an age where the mind was filled with play and little else, I could have endlessly adventured through the dense forests or capered between the cluttered alleyways littering the streets for all eternity and savoured each and every second of it as though I had just tried cake for the first time.

Would I still find joy in such simplicities had my childhood not been cut so abruptly short? It's a hard question to answer, but a harder one to stop pondering.

So what was my mother's purpose on this day? I'm not sure what I expected, but as the library resting a few minutes' walk away from our home came into view, my eyes sparkled in wonder.

"Listen, my angels, Mommy's going to help the young lady with her work in the library, so I need you to be good little boys, alright?"

Altair and I agreed without hesitation, though Altair looked bemused by our destination, and she raised her head once more with a proud smile.

As we walked along the street's footpath, a handful of the village's residents emerged from their homes, mostly men young and old, equipped for what was no doubt dangerous but important work in Ford's industrial half. My mother greeted an elderly gentleman tending to the weeds in his front garden - Mr. Redgrave if I recall correctly. He waved back at her with all the strength his frail old arms could muster, looking ever so grateful that anyone would give this old man the time of day.

Our stroll concluded once we reached the library itself – to say it "towered above" its peers would be a stretch, but it certainly stood out among the normally-sized lodgings it neighboured, if not for its size then certainly for its colours; amidst the sea of conserved, lightly-coloured housing, this library stood alone with a mix of bold black for its walls and deep crimson for its roof and the steps leading into the textual ether. The door appeared to already be slightly ajar, and with a spring in her step, my mother brought the two of us inside, closing the door behind us with a firm boom that reverberated through the space we had just entered.

What I witnessed upon entrance - after the closing of the doors put an immediate end to the sound of chatter and machinery permeating the streets that had almost become white noise by this point - was a deceptively cramped library considering its exterior, but I was wowed nonetheless; immediately before us laid four circular tables each with four chairs, all with red cushions to rest one's posterior on. The number four appeared to be something of a theme here, as that too was the number of rows in which the spotless wooden shelves were compartmentalized, each with their own ladder that could slide up, down, left, right, however one pleased… provided you were an adult, of course, as indicated by the very heavy handed sign at the edge of the third row to the right declaring 'ANY CHILDREN CAUGHT ON THE LADDERS WILL BE REMOVED'. Opened square windows to our left and right provided the only view of the outside world one could obtain within the confines of this library, and each was much too high for me to reach without assistance or elevation.

"*Ku-ku-kuuuu~!* Welcome, one and all, to my domain!"

Both Altair and I were sent into a head-shaking frenzy trying to identify its source of the strange voice – my mother's gaze remained rooted to the ladder in front of her, having already found the culprit.

"Good morning, Kyrie."

At last, the young lady descended from her ladder by sliding in a stop-and-start manner, during which I finally found her and pointed my finger towards her with an excited yell. She leapt down from the third rung and barely stuck her landing, and she looked at the three of us as her hand reached for the nape of her neck. She was an extraordinarily attractive young lady, wearing a baggy white shirt with the characters for "Love" and "Victory" printed boldly upon it in deep crimson.

Whatever attempt she was making to endure the sweltering summer proved to be fruitless; if her pale, phantom-like skin wasn't a solid indication of her weakness against the heat, the sweat drowning every square inch of her visible skin was the definitive killing blow.

Most curious, however, was the comically large hat atop her head; with an ultramarine hue and its tendency to envelop her eyes in reaction to even minute movements, it seemed ever so slightly too large for her, but she wore it with such pride that it became the defining trait of her appearance, and it mixed well with the dark purple hair that she had braided into an elegant ponytail.

"What do you think, Miss Vadere? Am I not the... the most wicked, most beautiful, most elegant witch in this quaint little corner of the world?!"

Kyrie posed enthusiastically as she awaited our mother's appraisal – Altair couldn't help but burst out laughing in ridicule, while I was enamoured with her motions.

"You look fantastic, my dear. Though... was there not a costume associated with the hat?"

I could almost hear Kyrie's heart shatter as my mother's question blasted it into fragments, though she made her best effort to continue laughing once she snapped back to the real world.

"*Ku...ku,* I'm afraid I was untimely in informing the providers of such goods of my needs, and thus... it sold out."

With each passing word, we could observe more of her soul leaking out of her body.

"Though despair is not the path I seek to traverse just yet, dearest Stephanie, for I have been treated to the utmost priority once production resumes once more."

"And when will that be?" my mother innocently asked, not expecting Kyrie to lock up once more and looking awfully concerned when that is in fact what happened.

"...next year..." Kyrie mumbled before swiftly turning around and proudly marching to the back of the library with renewed vigour. "But enough talk, let us present your offspring with their accommodation, my treasured apostle!"

All of her long words did an amazing job at confusing both me and my brother but given that I was mesmerized by her hat and her charming manner of conducting herself, I had no objections to more of her company.

We at last reached a small room at the back of the library, belonging to Kyrie. I was surprised to learn she had her own room, and even moreso by the actual contents of it, as a significant portion of it was dedicated to memorabilia of a cute-looking witch character, sharing a hat with the curious librarian herself; tapestries depicting all sorts of colour schemes and dynamic poses were assembled across the entire wall to my left, a shelf bolted into the wall in front of me displayed no less than five delicately sculpted figurines of the witch in question, and the walls were coated in a mesmerising pattern depicting the wondrous and colourful cosmos above our heads.

The room was not much larger than the one belonging to me and Altair but contained far more furnishings of note in comparison, first among them being a decently sized cloth wardrobe enveloped in black as well as a handful of her used clothes atop it and divided into three horizontal segments by zippers. The last items of note were her plain black bed, tucked into the corner to my right opposite her wardrobe, and the unusually low table, cloaked in a square cloth that reached the floor on all sides and rested upon the purple carpet.

The table itself - in contrast to its unassuming size - may well have had more objects on it than our entire house; a strange, bulky screen with two buttons below it, a stack of esoteric books of unknown origin, a pot filled with pens and pencils, a pink purse, three bottles of perfume, an unopened cardboard box roughly the size of an average novel and... a sealed plastic bag full of dry strips of meat?

"Ah! My apologies, I shall return momentarily!"

Kyrie raced out of the room, holding the plastic bag I had just noticed and looking awfully embarrassed to have left it there, though I was confused more by its purpose; by the time she returned with a small stack of books in her arms, the question had already eluded my little brain.

Kyrie placed the books on what little free space remained atop the table and clapped her hands together as she sat down on her knees at the side of the table nearest to the door. Altair and I sat down with our legs crossed opposite each other, with Kyrie to my right, while my mother faced the librarian with her legs pressed against her chest.

"There is time yet before the library is officially available for public access, so please, may I be entrusted with the names of these two *gentlemen*, dear Stephanie?" Kyrie asked as she bowed her head, to which my mother hummed in approval and beckoned Altair to speak.

"I'm Altair, Miss...?"

"Kyrie Pyre, my lovely." she divulged her full name as she playfully ruffled Altair's short, golden-brown hair, before turning her attention to me, "And you, my adorable companion?"

I had no idea what 'adorable' or 'companion' meant at that time, but I could intuit that the time had come for me to speak.

"V...Vega."

"Well, the two of you have wonderful names! As if handpicked by Melodias herself!"

Her hand relocated itself from Altair's head to my own, sifting through my mass of black hair with her fair-skinned fingers; the sudden display of physical affection unsettled me at first, but after a few seconds, I came to feel comfort in the warmth of her hand, in much the same way Altair had, and I looked up to find her innocently smiling at me. For all of her exotic behaviour, she felt just as welcoming and loving as my own mother.

Before we could get to know each other better however, Kyrie hopped to her feet in dramatic fashion, and my mother followed at a slower pace.

"But alas, the two of us must momentarily depart!"

Kyrie made the announcement with a faint glimmer of sadness in her voice, bringing the back of her palm against her head to exaggerate the misery.

"While we're out, please be good and don't mess with anything, okay? We've left some books for the two of you and we'll come and check on you, so no naughty stuff, okaaaaay?"

She patted the stack of books she had brought into the room three times, and then four times, before standing up at last and exiting the room with my mother, and the two of them waved us goodbye, which we energetically reciprocated.

A few hours passed, and aside from my mother popping her head through the door a handful of times to ensure we weren't up to no good, all that happened was me and Altair reading through the stack of books Kyrie had brought to us, all of which were simplistic picture books befitting of boys our age... not named Altair.

"Uuuuugh, I'm *bored*!" he cried out, carelessly dropping a book about caterpillars on top of Kyrie's purse and rushing to his feet.

His eyes scanned the room in pursuit of anything more interesting to engage with, before locking his gaze on Kyrie's wardrobe and rushing towards it with speed akin to the tiger I was reading about the great adventures of. Without hesitation or mercy, he began pulling the wardrobe's lowest zipper as far to the left as his arm could take it before the latter third of the fabric flap collapsed towards the floor.

"Vega... co-come here!"

Altair beckoned me towards him in amazement until I frustratedly acquiesced; I was fairly engaged by the saga of Tango the Dancing Tiger, but my brother's bewilderment was enough to draw my attention.

As Altair stepped to the side, I finally saw what had generated such amusement in my older brother: within the lowest compartment was a neatly organised pile of women's clothing, and it goes without saying that they belonged to one Kyrie Pyre. I was perplexed by just how much the clothes of women deviated from my own; the shelf contained a series of short skirts and undergarments, which drew incredible amusement and interest from my older brother. Most of her undergarments were a plain white but the rare crimson exception added some visual variety to our illicit observation.

Rather than being amused, I grew exceedingly nervous that my brother's escapade would drag me into hot water with him, and so I futilely reached for the zipper as my head rushed back and forth between it and the door.

"We're going to get in trouble!"

Seeing that I was on the verge of tears, Altair at last took mercy and returned the zipper most of the way to its rightful place before we could be discovered. I walked back to my spot with a strong sigh of relief while he chuckled at my expense, transitioning into yet another bored groan halfway through.

"Well there's gotta be *something*…" he mumbled as he prowled around the perimeter of the table, looking for anything of interest.

I continued with my reading after the third cycle of watching him walk around the room in desperate search of anything that wasn't reading or a ticket to trouble, and at last reached the conclusion of Tango's tale: Tango dominated the dancing ranks and became a veritable celebrity among the people of Vana, the country located directly to the northeast of Morosus; I spent the next year believing the story to be in fact biographical due to the mention of a real country, a belief which Kyrie would proceed to shoot down and then immediately regret once the diabolical truth caused me to tear up.

"Aha!" Altair cried out as a machine whirred to life on the table, moments after I literally closed the book on Tango's story.

Concerned once more that Altair would be getting us into trouble, I hastily dropped the book and rushed to the opposite side of the table, fully intending to tell him off once more but instead finding myself enchanted by what sequence of events my older brother had set into motion; the bulky machine on Kyrie's table was now alive, with its screen divided into five black strips separated by dazzling white lines. A girl riding atop a broom (at least according to Kyrie later that day; to me and Altair she looked like an incomprehensible mass of squares) rested at the bottom of the centre lane, also rendered in a bright white, as circles of a matching colour slowly descended from each lane.

A timer built into the machine counted down from 60 right above the screen, and once the witch passed through the first ring to descend the middle lane, a score of 1 showed up at the very top of the screen itself. A simplistic jingle following the same rhythm as Kyrie's patting earlier that day was the cherry on top of this marvel.

Both of us were rendered utterly awestruck. Altair quickly pressed one of the buttons – bearing a faded right arrow – and the witch moved to the lane immediately to her right; as if a light bulb had gone off in his head, Altair started dancing to the game's tune at once, shifting the character between lanes in pursuit of the rings.

There was yet another twist waiting for us, however: every 15 seconds, the game would speed up by roughly 50%, throwing off Altair's rhythm as soon as he had settled into it. He made all sorts of combative noises as the timer ticked down evermore, and once the timer hit zero, Altair had ended up with a score of 11.

"Ha! Bet you can't beat *that*, bro!"

For all of my big brother's qualities, he's never been the humble type. With an overwhelming urge to wipe the cocky smile off of his face, I took his place, and after he pressed a button on top of the machine the game reset itself to zero, with the timer granting me a fresh 60 seconds to prove my superiority.

I most certainly had trouble with the latter half, once the speed reached unfathomable levels and Altair's taunting grew louder and louder – were I the cynical type, I would have suspected his volume to be an intentional distraction tactic. But under normal circumstances, not even the deaf would describe Altair as 'quiet'. As the game neared its conclusion, I secured my narrow victory with two points I happened upon through dumb luck, by that point hammering each button with reckless abandon.

"12?! *No way* I'm letting you win!"

Altair nudged me aside with a little more force than he probably intended until I shuffled over, and it was his turn once more.

And so the cycle repeated, for a good long while at that, with the final scores and the tension mounting with every click of the two buttons. Once my stomach finally began to rumble for want of food, I had reached a peak of 18, while Altair capped his newest attempt off with a jaw dropping 21.

"Woohoo! Take that, Vega! Nobody can defeat me! *Never!*"

"*Kuku! Nobody*, you say?"

Altair and I were both horribly shocked by the sudden voice, and we turned around to discover Kyrie sitting at the edge of her bed, leaning towards us with a devilish grin.

"H-how long have you been there?!"

Altair raised his hands away from the device that had sucked up so much of our time and quickly shuffled towards the wardrobe; he raised a very good question, given that we had neither seen nor heard the door opening whatsoever.

"Long enough to ascertain that thou shalt not emerge from this room unscathed." She answered. For the entire time I've known Kyrie, she's always been good at pushing my buttons; this was merely the first fanning of our competitive flames.

She took her seat before the contraption, conjoining her fingers and cracking them as our utter destruction loomed. Once the jingle started anew, a demon of speed festered and erupted from her soul.

"Come, Tsubasa! Let us do justice to thy grace and greatness!".

Before the timer could even reach 45, she was on the cusp of surpassing my high score with ease, and she kept up with every successive increase in speed, keeping up with the final act at a level of competence surpassing that of me or Altair tackling even the very first. Her fingers bolted up and down with blinding speed, her breathing intensified by the second and her face drew uncomfortably close to the screen. By its conclusion, both mine and Altair's high scores had been buried beneath a colossal 134, leaving us both utterly speechless. After breaking out of our lengthy daze (and following an impressive amount of self-aggrandizing from the victor) we emphatically swore vengeance, to which Kyrie merely repeated her gruesome cackle, as if eagerly looking forward to the day we could surpass the master herself.

My mother's time at the library for that day came to its end once Kyrie's father, Frederick, returned from the industrial half of Ford at last; he was a very tall and sturdy-looking gentleman, but Kyrie chastised him for the dirtiness of his overalls, fearing the library's floor would soon match them. We spoke with him little before departing, but he seemed friendly enough, if ever so slightly tipsy. I wish I had grown closer to old Mr. Pyre before his untimely death, even if he were oft too inebriated to register my presence. Kyrie gleefully waved goodbye to us as her father embraced her, concluding the first of many joyful days in her company to come. Once we returned home, I finally got to open my gifts: A brown sun hat with a pair of cute dog ears decorating its top, a colouring book themed around animals and last but not least, a plastic model of a black Morosus tank with moving treads. I had no idea what a tank even *was* at the time, but pushing it around on the floor certainly pleased my little brain.

After many hours of playing around without a care in the world, bedtime soon approached. No more than five seconds after I had been put into my pyjamas, a rapid series of knocks came at our door, starting with three and following with four. My mother opened the door to find Kyrie – now separated from her hat - bowing down and raising a wrapped box towards my mother, who graciously accepted it.

"I forgot to tell you but... happy birthday, Vega!"

After I thanked her, she hastily waved goodbye once more and within a blink she was gone, leaving the darkening sky in her wake. She had bought a blue watch for me, which I took great care to never leave the house without until the day it could no longer fit around my wrist; for how little time we spent apart, the idea that a reminder of that esoteric young lady would remain forever with me was heart-warming. Given the blue cloak I never leave home without to this very day, maybe I never really did change all that much...

Chapter 3:
An Idyllic Life

And thus, life proceeded peacefully. A few days a week, my mother would bring us along to the library to assist Kyrie whilst Altair and I sat in her room, reading through the contents of the library that the librarian picked for us and tap tap tap tap tapping away at her addictive little game, being usurped near the end of each day by Kyrie the Destroyer. Altair peeked inside her wardrobe once again not long after our first visit, only to be disappointed that the "grand treasure" (his words, not mine) had been relocated. I however exerted a great sigh of relief, knowing that my brother's course in life had been corrected.

Over the course of the next 15 months, we came to learn much about her family's circumstances; her mother, Jackie, had been called upon to perform vehicle maintenance for the Morosus Armed Forces, due to growing turbulence between my home country and our much-loathed eastern neighbour, Ennui. Her father Frederick volunteered to assist in the farmlands in her place, with his absence from the library increasing as harvest season reached its peak, leaving a void my mother was all too happy to fill.

Any other visitors in the library were exceedingly rare, more often than not an elderly gentleman here and there who came to pick up or return a book with hardly a sentence being exchanged, but every so often, whilst leaving the library, a young man with shaggy blonde hair would be standing outside of the library, being invited inside by Kyrie not long after we descended the steps; our formal introduction would take place upon Kyrie's 17th birthday on October 21st, the year after our first meeting.

My mother had dressed the pair of us up in the most presentable and formal-looking clothes we had on hand: a blue shirt and trousers for Altair, and a white and red patterned shirt along with black trousers for me.

We made the journey down to the library with Kyrie's gift from the three of us in my hands, only to be met by the most curious sight once we arrived at the foot of its steps; Kyrie was diligently peering at the sky through a pink spyglass whilst sitting elegantly atop the library's highest step. In spite of the chilly autumn winds, she was dressed in a red camisole and skirt, which, if it were any shorter, would have exposed her undergarments for all of Ford (and Altair most troublingly of all) to see. Her peculiar choice of clothing clashed against the season's woes with such intensity that she drew more than a few odd looks from onlookers of the village, but she was too absorbed into whatever she was looking at to react or even notice.

"Good morning!" Altair yelled, hoping to shock her out of her trance, but the watchful birthday girl was utterly unperturbed.

It was at this point that I dreaded she had been magically turned into a statue at an unfortunate time and place, though we were soon caught off guard ourselves by the sound of wings flapping. Kyrie at last parted her eye from the instrument, leaping to her feet in enraptured joy and speeding down the steps.

Once her bare feet at last shared a stony surface with the three of us, a blindingly white creature came soaring from the skies, landing before Kyrie with elegant grace and revealing itself to be a white dog with majestic, falcon-like wings that now retracted to beneath its stomach. And the wings were not all that stood out about this magnificent creature whatsoever, as hiding behind its adorable, fluffy head and its stud-like black eyes was a harness carrying a decently sized wooden box with the name "Sanzu" on its side, though the ease with which Kyrie removed and then raised it from the dog's back suggested its contents were light enough to invoke little in the way of burden on its back, much to my relief.

"Oh, how I've waited for this day! At last, the stars of fortune align!"

Her energy was and always has been infectious; I couldn't help but smile and anticipate seeing the box's contents as she skipped and jumped around like a restless hare.

Kyrie raised the box above her head as she celebrated uproariously, drawing even more concerned looks from the few bystanders that lingered around. After simmering down, she at last set the box at the top of the library's stairs and pulled a strip of meat out from a bag that sat beside it, quickly feeding it to the dog as she gently stroked its back.

"Oh thank you, canine courier of the stars! You've chosen an incredibly good day to make a girl happy!"

Even though we had come here to celebrate Kyrie's birthday, the entire scene had pushed that purpose entirely to the back of my mind, and I was *dead set* on only one goal at this point in time.

"Ca- can I pet it?!" I asked with bated breath.

My begging was itself much too characteristic of a dog but she nodded with a grin, nudging the dog towards me until it walked the rest of the way on its own volition; it finally stopped right in front of me, and was roughly equal to me in height, but I couldn't have been happier as I placed my hand on its head and shifted my hand from ear to ear, giggling the entire time.

I only stopped once its pink tongue bolted from its mouth to layer my right cheek in saliva - leaving small fragments of meat in its wake – and the dog at last turned around towards the empty road, ceasing its barking before we bore witness to its takeoff. We waved the wonderful doggy farewell until the heroic courier that would come to soar through my dreams for the rest of my youth at last became one with the clouds. With the encounter having come to an end, we at last remembered our original purpose for being there and following a brief countdown (and cheek cleansing) from my mother, our next words arrived in perfect unison.

"Happy birthday!"

Kyrie escorted the three of us inside the library after graciously accepting the box from my hands, and as she rushed to her room to store her acquisitions, we were left in an awkward silence, sharing the room with Kyrie's parents: Jackie and Frederick Pyre, who were sat next to each other at the rightmost table.

"Mornin' to ya!" Frederick greeted us once he at last pulled his uncomfortably close gaze away from the book he was reading, titled "The Book of Blossoms"; it had been some time since our last encounter, but his volume was noticeably higher to a jarring extent.

"Fred, volume!"

"With all due respect Jacqueline, my sweetie, I dunno how the friggin' hell you could work 'round all those machines all day and all night for all your life, they give me a bloody headache!"

"What about your ear plugs?"

"Whassat? Eat bugs? How's that gonna help me, ya wammal?!"

"How in the blazing hell did the military let you handle a gun, exactly? Even the meekest munitions blast the socks off of any tractor!"

Mrs. Pyre utterly gave up on the conversation with a burdened sigh, diverting her attention to us instead.

"Thank you all for coming. I wasn't sure if I would make it back on time, but I can rest assured my treasure would've had some fine company regardless."

Mrs. Pyre walked towards us and shook my mother's hand; once it came time for me and Altair to reciprocate, I was stunned by how coarse her hand felt in comparison to my mother and Kyrie, as if I were wearing a glove made of cardboard, and a shiver ran down my spine, to which she chortled.

"Well, you're more like Kyrie than you look, young man!".

The comment proved to be grimly prescient, but at the time I could see the same matriarchal affection in her demeanour possessed by my own mother; the fact that such a kind woman has spent most of my life in distant military service is a great shame.

"How *does* it feel to see your little one outgrow you, Mrs. Pyre?" my mother asked, with a curious glance towards Altair and then me.

"Please, call me Jackie, and let me tell you, I feel like a fragile little fossil, that I do. I watched a tank explode like any seat Old Quazzy ever sat on and set half the camp's field on fire, and that didn't rattle my bones nearly a quarter as bad as coming home to see her standing nearly a head above me!"

"*Kukukuuuuu!*"

As Mrs. Pyre raised her hand to roughly Kyrie's height, her voice erupted from an unknown place within the library, though this place was not unknown for long as by now, we were more than familiar with Kyrie's hiding spot of choice: the ladder nearest to us, which she began to slide down with unflinching and concerning speed.

"Welcome, mortals, to the cherished demesne of the fabled sorceress of dreams! The darkening skies recede from thy presence, the gaze of the moon gleams with cosmological power once more! Let this reunion mark the ascension of the bringer of darkness and champion of the mythical arts, Tsubasa Euriclytes Pandemonia!"

Her introduction was topped off by a majestic pose, with her hand covering her face and her eyes icily peering from between her fingers, and the whole ordeal provoked enraptured applause from everybody present, save for poor old Mr. Pyre who was still trying to figure out what she had even said. Kyrie had emerged in a brand new outfit identical to the one worn by the character who made up much of her room's decoration, but now I could discern the finer details of the costume in question.

In addition to the hat we rarely saw her without, she now appeared before us in a body suit that appeared ever so slightly loose for her at this time, but that she would grow comfortably into over the next year. It covered much of her torso in a dominating cobalt, save for her breasts and buttocks which took on an alluring black in its place. Her dazzling legs were left barren save for the black boots that reached just below her knees, complimented by short white heels, and the final component to bring it all together was a bracelet on her right arm, with a red talisman hanging beneath it.

Kyrie gratuitously soaked in all of the praise directed her way until a series of slow but strong knocks at the door sent us all into silence – in truth, it sounded more like somebody bashing it with their shoulder. My mother took on the responsibility of allowing this newest guest inside, and in walked the shaggy-haired young man, dressed only in black and grey while struggling to carry inside a large metal box, as his right hand propping it up at its bottom also clung onto a disposable camera. After placing the metal box in the centre of the nearest table and sending a vicious vibration through the walls and floor, he unleashed a groan of great relief and wiped the immense sweat from his brow with the sleeve of his coat, before placing against the wall a black bag (about as large as me at that time) that hung from his shoulder.

"Happy… Happy Birthday, Kyrie…"

Even beneath the strain of hauling so much on his person, his voice had a strong, earnest tone to it – it was difficult not to quickly take a liking to him.

"Thank you, Jules!" she exclaimed, leaning over the table and staring at him as she hopped like a room full of bunnies, "Did you get to see the stage show?"

This "Jules" fellow replied by underarm throwing the disposable camera to her, which she caught between her thumb and index finger with a grin.

"I'll take you to print them later, we haven't long gotten back. I take it our other guests are the Vadere family?"

He looked curiously at the three of us as Kyrie verified his observation.

"It's a pleasure to make your acquaintance. The name's Julius."

Rather than offering his hand, the young man simply bowed down in front of my mother. She was about to introduce herself when Kyrie let out an ear-piercing shriek and rushed over to him, probing his head and shoulders around with her hands.

"How the hell did that happen?!" she cried, revealing to us all a dark bruise on the nape of his neck.

"I was sparring with Mahro again. He gets a little rough when he gets into it, *heheh*…" he said as he scratched his chin.

"Don't '*heheh*' me! What if that idiot carved your head clean off?!"

"You think we spar with the real thing? Bloody hell Kyrie, a little wooden stick never killed a man."

She attempted to summon further protest but ultimately conceded, instead kissing him on the cheek and bringing her arm around his shoulder, taking care not to touch his bruise as they sauntered towards their seats.

"I've never understood your obsession with this... witch, sorceress, whatever she is, *but*..." Julius' sentence was interrupted by a short yelp from Kyrie, and I caught a glimpse of his hand retracting from her butt back to her waist immediately after, "...that looks good on you."

Now that all of the attendees had arrived, the party engaged in full swing. We shifted and shuffled around as the day progressed and Kyrie's parents made regular trips to the kitchen and back, returning from lands unknown with a variety of cakes and alcoholic drinks (the latter obviously being prohibited for me and Altair, much to our annoyance).

By midday, Altair, Julius and myself convened around Kyrie to watch in awe as she assembled what he had brought her: a device similar in size to the one found in her bedroom. Putting the thing together proved to be a decently lengthy process; the table swiftly became a mass of empty plates and tired tools. My mother joined Mr. and Mrs. Pyre outside for a discussion of their own while this symphony of steel and scraping played out, and after 5 minutes of Kyrie fumbling around, she and Julius got to talking about the latter's recent holiday as my brother and I gorged ourselves on all sorts of delectable cakes.

"So, my dear, how was thy stay in the eastern land?"

"We made effective use of our time there. Barely got my map of Shigan drawn out before we left, and I had to cut a corner or three, but at the end of the day I got what I wanted out of it." he answered, sounding noticeably uncertain, and he leaned closer to Kyrie's ear before continuing, "Though... look, I'll fill you in when there aren't kids around, but long story short, Mahro's been looking into some *grim* shit."

"*Ugh,* I asked about *your* time in the country. Spare me the details of whatever trouble that oaf's liable to drag thee into, and refrain from involving thyself with it!"

Kyrie took up a yellow screwdriver, securing the device's screen in place with a screw in each corner as she spewed further venom at this Mahro character under her breath – if I knew him as intimately then as I do now, I would have furiously fought in his corner, pushing back against her gross misuse of the word 'oaf', for he is anything but.

Julius sat back on his seat and crossed his arms, as if embarrassed to have even brought Mahro up at all.

"Uh... well, I stood atop the peak of Mount Melodias and screamed my lungs out, is that exhilarating enough for your tastes?"

"And what did thee scream about, dearest? Thy eternal devotion to thy beloved back home?"

"All the parts of you I want to touch."

Julius' remark earned Kyrie's finger poking at his neck wound, but even such lax force was enough to produce an awful screech.

"Hold it, hold it! I just want to hold your hands! What did you think I meant, woman?!"

"I know precisely what thy remark pertained to, bastard dog of lust."

"If you want to know what I really said, I said... well, nothing really. I just yelled like my soul was exploding, wanted to make myself heard by all the tiny people walking around Dias, you know? Wanted to leave behind a legacy as 'that weird guy who screamed from the top of our mountain', for what that's worth."

"And what was it like, seeing the world from such a vantage point? What grasp did the trees hold on the blue sky? Could you see our home from up there? Was the feel of the chilly mountain breeze exhilarating or did it lock thy face up, akin to a malfunctioning automaton?"

Kyrie sounded more and more excited with each question she posed, eventually halting her progress on the construction altogether as she turned to Julius, awaiting answers.

"...very far, no, and for the love of Melodias, use words that any of us can understand. I definitely think you would like it there."

"How about you take me one day, then? As much fun as it is being cooped up here, a little taste of the world beyond these walls would be refreshing~"

"I'll try and get Dad to pull some strings, love, but in the words of our eastern friends: One can craft wishes from Sera, but one cannot craft Sera from wishes."

With a sigh that emitted a strange cocktail of disappointment and optimism, Kyrie returned to her craft, and while I was more focused on watching Kyrie assemble her newest plaything than the conversation at hand, Altair was quick to pursue the topic further.

"Did you go there on your own?"

Julius looked back at my brother like he was stupid, until he recognized that he was talking to a five-year-old.

"Ah... no, mate. My dad went along with me; I couldn't possibly prepare myself for a trip up a mountain without screwing *something* up. Kyrie might call him every foul name under the sun, and he's probably earned half of them, but make no mistake, he's at least half of the reason Ford stands so proud to this day!"

He obviously expected some sort of applause from the children who knew nothing of Ford's politics or history, and hastily slumped back in his chair when that was not what he received.

"So how's about your daAAAAAAAAAGH!!!"

Julius' seemingly innocent question was sharply cut off by a loud stomp and his earth-rending scream.

"Kyrie!! What was that for?!"

"Don't bring that up."

Her sternness was out of left field and far more alarming than whatever Julius was about to ask. Altair and I shared confused glances amidst the awkward silence, though as my brother seemed right on the cusp of pressing Kyrie for an answer, the front doors flew open and an icon of drunkenness stumbled his way inside.

"Hello kids, you get your... tinker winker... whatever thing working yet?"

Mr. Pyre was... to be frank, shitfaced, and he slumped across the table as though about to fall asleep before ever getting an answer; a verbal answer proved to be needless, as immediately after the end of his sentence, Kyrie shoved a thick battery into the back of the machine and tapped a button atop it to bring it roaring to life.

And what a life it displayed, immediately demonstrating its power over the prior machine with one noticeable, earth-rending innovation: colour. Gone were the days of stark white on dull black, representing that which could only be identified by the likes of Kyrie, as even from the introductory screen, we were treated to rich reds, dazzling blues, the nostalgic greenery of nature and the grey of the clouds enveloping the sky. Not even a single button had been pressed yet, and already the lot of us were completely wowed, even the normally stoic Julius.

"Ye gods! How far these machinations have come in these five short years!"

Kyrie immediately took to selecting the second option presented on the screen by utilizing yet another innovation: one of the two thin sticks protruding out of the front of the device, each next to a set of three buttons.

"Woah, two people can play?!"

After confirming his observation to be true, Kyrie shuffled across in her seat in order to allow Altair to sit next to her for the first game of many to come that day.

As we cycled between players, I made some further observations about the game once it finally started, and immediately I was shocked by how much more it could do than the little machine in Kyrie's room; I almost felt bad for said machine, given that this newest rendition surpassed it with such magnitude that I have no doubt it gathered dust in some cupboard somewhere for the rest of its days, seeing less human contact than a monk confined to a subterranean cave. This brand-new game allowed movement in any direction one pleased using the stick, though Altair took some time to wrap his head around the buttons being used for shooting rather than movement, and the first match ended in a swift victory for Kyrie.

Julius was next to be mulched up and annihilated by her, but he held his own decently well, shooting the robotic enemies descending from the top of the screen and sending rocks to Kyrie's side in a vain attempt to crush her. Much to his dismay, her aptitude with the game swiftly skyrocketed, and she sent storms of magical power back at him with unparalleled frequency and intensity, wrapping up their duel in just over a minute.

At last, my first turn afforded me a proper look at the game, and I discovered a rather colourful cast of characters; the first and most recognizable among them was this Tsubasa character Kyrie had a strong affection for, though I was locked out from selecting her due to Kyrie staking her claim at blinding speed. My alternatives proved to be interesting in their own right: a giant girl carved from stone, a gun-toting waitress in green, a scissor-wielding young girl with short, dark hair covering her eyes and most bizarrely of all, a bespectacled secret agent with pistols attached to her legs. While I was too caught up wondering how such a combat style could ever work, my time to select ran out, and I was locked into the secret agent. My first game commenced, and it ended somewhere between that of Julius and Altair's own. I managed to land a hit on Kyrie with the hail of bullets that flooded her screen shortly before my demise, to which she reacted with great astonishment – she really put her all into pulverizing the pre-pubescent.

The rest of her birthday continued in much the same pattern, though Kyrie was graceful enough to sit out voluntarily on occasion, just to allow us boys to combat each other. Our matches lasted about as long but the competition was much tighter, and Julius was met with defeat at our hands more times than he was comfortable with, openly bemoaning his disdain for such "toys" before lining back up for another turn moments later.

Our parents continued their own conversation as best they could whilst drowned out beneath our fierce yelling and tapping, in addition to the addictive jingle emanating from the machine the entire time. No less than fifty duels had taken place before the sky began to darken, and my mother at last initiated our exit.

"I think we had best give our friends some... time alone, boys!" she said as she uneasily walked towards us, taking me by the hand and walking to the library's front door as Altair followed behind me.

The remaining inhabitants offered their goodbyes as we waved back and stepped onto the streets of Ford once more; we were not alone in the streets for long, as Kyrie and Julius soon bolted past us in the opposite direction from our home, with the camera he had given her firmly grasped in her hand.

"We've but five minutes, my dearest! Let us charge valiantly to our rendezvous!"

"Repeat that last sentence in a language I can understand, woman!"

As I watched them rampage towards Ford's other half, I could only begin to imagine what kind of life I was looking to lead with company like that.

From Kyrie's birthday on, we became very friendly with Julius, blissfully unaware of the crucial role he was soon to play in our lives. He would regularly enter the library even while my mother was working, providing a strong impetus to part with the educational books Kyrie was handing to me and my brother with growing frequency, no doubt at the request of my mother (it's worth noting that we grew to spend more of our time in the library itself, under the watchful eye of our matriarch as we ingested more of life's valuable lessons).

He put up a fairly stoic front but every so often - as we fiercely competed in game after clicktastic game, racking up more and more absurd times chronicling our feats of endurance - I could see a glimmer of juvenile glee in his reddish-brown eyes; I think it's a safe assumption that we considered each other good friends by the time his father's 55th birthday arrived on August 14th, the year after our formal introduction.

Much of that day was spent within the halls of the library with neither hide nor hair of Julius having been spotted, with the general assumption being that he would spend the day exclusively with his father – not that we would have begrudged him for doing so - but once our stomachs began to make ever so tiny tremors, and the idea of procuring some food was entertained by Altair, Julius casually walked through the front door. Kyrie was delighted to see him and rushed over to embrace him, and it was at this moment that a man me and Altair had yet to meet walked inside.

"Oy there tadpoles, pleased ter meet the lot 'a ya!"

The older-looking gentleman offered his hand to me.

"Name's Ringo, kiddo!"

As I shook the old boy's hand, the difference between Ringo and his far quieter son was immediately distinct; Ringo's skin was of a noticeably darker complexion, no doubt a result of tanning as indicated by his far lighter shoulders and upper chest, made visible by the plain white tank top shared with his son. Whether he maintained astounding standards of health, or his unusual complexion did a marvellous job of obscuring the wrinkles and creases of age, he in no way looked like a man celebrating his 55th year in this world, his inexplicable virility bolstered by his carefree demeanour.

"Happy birthday, Old Man Marshall!"

Kyrie haughtily crossed her arms as she greeted the old ma-

"Call me an old man one more time, lass, and your tongue will taste the bed of the river!"

Kyrie was undeterred yet, and she chuckled nefariously before imitating his gesture with malicious intent, listing off insult after insult in an addictive melody.

"Geezer, codger, coffin-dodger, senior citizen, greybeard, cave dweller, ancient, old-timer, gramps—"

"Gramps? Jules, ya din't tell me ya knocked her up, boy!"

Ringo interrupted Kyrie's seemingly unending list of pejoratives and raised his palm towards his son, who reciprocated with a high-five much to her annoyance

"Let's drag her to Saki, she'll tell ya if it's a boy or an adoption form!"

"He has done no such thing yet, you..."

Kyrie realised her mistake immediately after it had occurred and tugged her hat down in embarrassment, but it proved to be too late nonetheless.

"Yet? *Yet?* Well, get on with it! I can only dodge my coffin for so long, lass!"

Ringo's deriding laughter continued seemingly forever as me, Altair and my mother could only watch in astonishment, but after a prolonged and unamused silence from Kyrie, he finally brought himself back to reality.

"Anyway, I din't drag wee little Jules here to make me a grandpa - yer can learn to poke a hole in yer own time, little missy – but instead he had a funny lil idea fer our... let's call it our boys' day out!"

The heads of everybody in the room perked up at this announcement, and a nervous, cautious excitement mounted as we awaited what in the world this "idea" would turn out to be.

"You two, so long as your mother permits it, would you... like to come fishing with us?" Julius asked, looking uncharacteristically sheepish.

Altair looked more enthusiastic about Julius' proposition than I, and while I was uncertain about exploring the world beyond my house and this library we were sat in, my mother looked more concerned about the proposal by orders of magnitude.

"Mr... Marshall, is it? I wouldn't at all like for the boys to head that far beyond our home; it's an awfully unsafe world out there, after all."

"But Moooooom!" Altair cried out, though he was soon silenced by a stern glare.

Ringo wasn't content to give up at the first hurdle however, and stood in a commanding, upright manner as he made his case.

"Miss Vadere, I understand yer concern. Life hasn't been kind ter ya and even in the coziest 'a corners these days there's some villain out ter mug ya. But cooping these pair up ain't goin' ter do much good if the past comes back ter bite ya in the arse, is it? A boy who knows nothin' 'a the world beyond books will a boy forever remain."

Our mother's reluctance began to wane at a surprising speed, considering both how vocal her opposition had been just moments before and what we would soon find out about what "the past" ultimately held in store for her.

"Besides, yer lookin' at a man with 25 years 'a military experience, yes, a whole 25, count 'em on your fingers, my dear! If I can't take care of yer lil boys, what was any o' that worth, may I ask?"

The old man stood before us with immense pride, but something about his words confused silly little me.

"Hang on, we only have ten fingers!"

"Exactly! Yer can't measure the greatness that stands before ya, tadpole!"

"Yeah, 25 years of sitting on a wall and waiting for things to happen, what a stellar military career." said Julius.

As Ringo's fist nearly sent his tittering offspring into next week, my mother at last acquiesced, granting Ringo and Julius her blessing to bring us to the river but *absolutely* no further. Though I was reluctant, his remark of "A boy who knows nothing of the world beyond books will a boy forever remain" stuck out prominently in my head, as if tailored to claw at a weakness I was not yet cognizant of. In the end, I joined in on the escapade, anxious but also slightly excited to grow as a person; how could I expect to look after my mother later in life if I wasn't up to the task of fishing, after all?

Our "training" began before we even laid hands on a fishing rod, as Ringo passed up on his share of the three blue bags resting outside the library's front door (citing his birthday boy status as an excuse), leaving Julius to carry the heaviest of the lot, hauling on his back – in addition to the black bag he was rarely seen without - the largest container housing the rods themselves as well as a large box-shaped object that could barely fit inside it, whilst Altair and I each took a smaller bag, hauling the replacement components and bait respectively.

Our trek took us through the main street of Ford's residential district, which looked largely identical to what I was accustomed to between my home and the library, and our journey remained a straight road up until we were standing at the foot of the great bridge in its centre. As we made our way there, Ringo greeted all of the few people who crossed our path, and they reciprocated with gestures of friendliness bordering on reverence; despite Julius' mockery, Ringo appeared to be very well-regarded by our fellow man.

I assumed we would be crossing the bridge until Ringo directed our attention to a dirt road off the beaten path between some pine trees, down which we found the riverbed, and it proved to be an interesting locale, if ever so slightly... unsettling; while our dirt path led us to a grass-coated part of the river's edge, where sunflowers bloomed unperturbed and with great radiance, directly to our right and leading beneath the bridge was a mass of white, perfectly round (save for man-made imperfections) and featureless stones that nevertheless rested at the same angle and height as the grass upon which Julius had begun to set up our activity for the day. It was something both my brother and I had never seen before, given that our only observations of the river had come from our home that was now obscured by the trees that enveloped our path here, and so I decided to press the greatest artifact of them all for more information.

"Mr Ringo... why are there stones there and grass here?" I asked, unsure where to direct my finger.

The old man cackled loudly, with a tint of... *evil*, even.

"Quite the tale ter tell ya there, son. Let's take a seat before yer skeleton pops out yer mouth, ay?"

With his promise of answers to come, we placed our bags down and sat across the wide grassy patch as Julius finished assembling the two fishing rods, placing one at his side and passing the spare to his father.

Ringo elaborated on the tale as he affixed a thrashing worm to his hook.

"Well, I don't expect the two 'a yer ter know all tha' much 'bout our humble li'l abode, but this hasn't always been under the rule 'a Morosus, as a matter 'a fact. When I were a wee boy, we had the odd grumble with Tenryuu here and there. Hard ter imagine nowadays, given we're good pals with the lot now, but since we're on the cusp 'a Morosus' eastern coast, they annexed this little village once upon a time, and I'd argue fer the better if I may be perfectly honest; they were responsible fer the nice big bridge right beside us, ya see, not ter mention much 'a the industry still going on today.

"However, ter say it were all sunshine, rainbows and bellydancers would be 'bout as close ter the truth as calling an apple a cucumber, my merry tadpoles! The new management musta pissed off ol' Terryn upstairs, 'cause not even a year after the eastern lads took over, *bam!*, they had a plague on their hands, and it took little in the way 'a prisoners, I'm told. Men, women, little'uns, they all dropped like flies, and so whatever was left of the eastern boys came up with this *genius* plan: they'd take all the dead little boys and girls, bury them next ter the river, and then cover their graves in stones, as any civilized man does with the dead, ay? Something 'bout an old ritual supposedly, but I don't think yer need me ter tell ya it did squat. Zilch. Jack shit. Eventually the new management fled with their tails between their legs ter Mot and got driven back outta the country anyway not too long afterwards. So, how's about it, tadpoles? Fancy digging up some 'a them stones fer a li'l grave hunting?"

Altair and I were left speechless, and while I can't hope to speak for my brother, I was mortified by the thought that lying right next to us could be a mass grave of children, with only a layer of rocks dividing us from them – I eyed those stones with suspicion forevermore, waiting for the day a skeleton would emerge from the earth, clawing after me for treading upon its resting place.

"Oy, pops! You plan to throw that thing before you crawl into your coffin?!" Julius shouted, at last breaking the mortifying haze.

Ringo chuckled as he looked once more at the worm still wriggling on the hook of his rod. He flippantly cast it into the river's centre, and it didn't take long for Ringo to begin running his mouth again.

"Oy, kid! Ya plan ter put a ring on yer gal before *you're* in a coffin yerself? Ain't got no use fer ya if ya ain't goin' to carry on me legacy!"

"Wh-What's this now? What's that got to do with anything?!"

"Just saying, tadpole, yer can't stay as merry li'l playmates forever. One day ya gotta find yerselves somewhere *other* than a... box of books, ya know?"

"So what's your point?"

"My point, tadpole, is that day in, day out, yer fling with her is a bit... samey. Each day ya run there after work, ya come home and when I ask if anything interesting's going on, well... either yer

55

hiding quite the *extraordinary* life or there's not much 'a note going on."

"So. What's. Your. *Point?*"

"Listen fer a moment, won't ya, tadpole? What I'm tryin' to say is that lasses are like scatterbrained li'l kids, they crave change and excitement; if ya keep things like this forever, she'll be bored 'a ya, and *whoosh*, off she flies ter the more exciting avenues of our woefully short little lives."

"You clearly don't know her very well, pops; she could spend every second of every day she has left in this world among those dusty old books and find euphoria in all of it up until she's on her deathbed. Please, refrain from projecting your unfaithfulness onto my darling, she is not so fleeting with her affections."

Ringo's answer... never came. The remark sent him into an unusually quiet and ponderous state, and I could see a bead of sweat running from Julius' forehead. That being said, before the atmosphere could end up too heavy, a harsh tug on Julius' fishing rod sent him leaping into action with mechanical efficacy; a silvery-green little feller that was about half as long as I was tall soon hung from the end of the rod, and Julius quickly catapulted it into the box that hosted an ice-cold world of its own within its confines.

"Bloody hell, you'll never let me catch up, will ya?!" Ringo jeered with a hearty laugh, though his pride came through very clearly – even the embittered Julius couldn't help but smile.

"Listen, tadpole. I get it if you're nervous. Terryn knows I was shittin' meself in the buildup to popping the question. But ask yerself one question: What's the worst that can happen, eh? Worst case scenario is ya just have ter try again later."

"Would the worst-case scenario not be the end of our relationship altogether?"

As Julius raised an eyebrow at his father's optimistic assertion the disgusting maggot was left to wriggle uncomfortably close to my face – I could picture a scenario in which Julius clumsily dropped it into my mouth, and the sickening mental image of the bug's taste sent a shiver or nine down my spine.

"Mate, if the gal were so sure she never wanted you as a hubby, yer wouldn't still be together now, would you? Besides, if popping the question is enough fer her ter break it off, I hate ter break it ter ya mate, ya weren't gonna last long anyway."

With his father's insight obtained, Julius finally freed me from the clutches of the devilish maggot's… existing, and with a single hum, he took to educating me in the practice of turning the marine into meals.

As time passed, Julius and Ringo would assist me and Altair respectively in learning the art of fishing; Julius took great care to guide my hands through the process in depth and assist in pulling any catches away from their habitat, while Ringo more or less left Altair to his own devices beyond his verbal explanation unless my brother happened upon a particularly feisty marine creature.

As the next hour slowly ticked by and the cooler filled with fish of all shapes and sizes. I was under the impression they were all still alive since their eyes remained open, until Julius' shocking revelation that fish do not, in fact, have eyelids. Ringo and Julius would name the types as they were extracted from the river. The diminutive, vacant-eyed Nene coated in grey. The bear-toothed Grau, snarling and gnashing as we dragged it from its habitat. The charcoal-scaled Barbadur, piercing its captors with its glaring red eyes. I bore witness to many things curious and all too concerning that day.

The most exotic, however, and a surprise even to the seasoned fishermen among us, was what they referred to as a "Glassnymph": A curious specimen coated in mirror-like scales that reflected the world around them with astonishing clarity. Julius noted its ability to blend into the water extremely well and produce a high pitched whine when captive as mechanisms against its natural predators. Unfortunately, such creatures were rendered utterly unfit to consume by said scales, tasting like glass as much as they looked the part and requiring extensive, professional effort to make edible, therefore after reaching for a camera in the bag I had carried there, Julius took a picture of the glassnymph before releasing it into the river once again.

"It's a shame we didn't have any bags on hand, pops; I would've quite liked it as a pet." Julius said as the fish seamlessly blended into the current.

"Yer ain't havin' a fish tank in *my* home, little one! Last time we tried that, we had ter replace the damn floor!"

Ringo's "little one" (who stood a head and a half taller than the old man) slumped back in dejection.

"So, boyo, how's that stint with that nurse working out? Ya cheated on yer lass yet?"

Still irked by their earlier conversation, Julius only responded with an icy but vitriolic glare, as if he were about to jump to his feet and give the glassnymph a human companion for its travels.

Being the brave little interrupter I was, I decided to pose my own question, if only to avert an argument.

"What's your job, Mr. Ringo?"

"You can just call me Ringo, buddy, and I'm... well, I do lotsa things 'ere in the middle 'a nowhere, but a lot 'a the time yer'll find me atop that there gate, yer see?"

Ringo pointed towards a firm stony wall in the distance, with its peak barely eking out above a large warehouse in the farmlands. Atop it I could barely make out two armour-clad men performing stretches in near-perfect harmony, and I giggled at the sight. Ringo sounded far less amused.

"These bloody kids drop everything and start prancin' around like little girls the moment I scoot out the door, it's astonishing, I tell ya. Anythin' more than a pin hittin' the floor is gonna spell the end of us if our fate's left in their hands!" Ringo yelled, crossing his arms in a huff.

But for all his jesting, the old man proved to be awfully prescient.

Our fishing finally came to an end about three hours later, at 4:15pm according to the blue watch which could barely fit around my wrist by now; I was saddened by the idea of no longer being able to make use of Kyrie's gift, but I committed myself to clinging onto it forevermore, like a sacred treasure, even when it had long outlived its usefulness. By that time, our stomachs were trembling with such might as to shake all of Ford, and the four of us rushed back to the library, following the same arrangement of who carried what with the exception of Ringo hauling the now significantly heavier cooler in his hands; Julius by far got the sweetest deal, given that he was relieved of the weight of said cooler, and he was the only one to enter the library not utterly drenched in sweat from the uphill ascent. It was once we finally took a seat next to my mother and Kyrie that Ringo broke out into song,

> "Oh, Mrs. Pyre
> Crank up that fire
> And out of this fish
> Oh, produce us a dish
> For that is my wish
> Come... uh, grab this fish!"

Despite his surprisingly fitting voice, the manner in which he flubbed the conclusion as well as his banal lyrics earned him little in the way of applause, accompanied only by the creeping realisation that Mrs. Pyre hadn't even been present for 10 months.

"I... I sing better with a couple drinks in me, you hear me? So c'mon, chop chop! The men in the house need feeding!"

"I guess the responsibility may fall upon myself, given that I am the only female Pyre present, though a missus I am not."

"Kyrie, darling, if you require my help, you need only ask." my mother said with a smile.

Kyrie answered with a silent but grateful nod, sending the two of them to the Pyres' kitchen with the cooler grasped firmly in Kyrie's hands.

The conversation between the four of us pertained to our exploits on the riverbank, up until the girls returned with platters full of fish and boiled potatoes a little under an hour later. The once bluish-grey marine creatures were now grilled meals for us tyrannical humans to enjoy, with a tantalizing aroma I'll never forget for as long as I live, and we proceeded to feast with great gusto, having waited so long for the day's meal.

Altair and I were prone to occasionally dropping bits and pieces on the floor, but my mother assured both us and Kyrie that she would thoroughly clean up afterwards; Kyrie's fondness for cleaning up after meals was on par with her aptitude for cooking said meals without a helping hand. Regardless, once this grand dinner came to its conclusion and our bellies were sufficiently stuffed, we offered our thanks to the chefs, who gracefully bowed and soaked in the admiration. We expected the day's events to end there, but Julius had one more surprise up his sleeve, standing up with a sly smirk directed at his father, as if to taunt him.

"Kyrie..."

His utterance was quiet but confident, and for not a single moment did his gaze avert from the love of his life. Keeping his eyes locked on hers, he brought a slim box out of his pocket – his hands were subtly shivering despite his outward confidence, but even Ringo could only watch in stunned silence as his next words erupted like thunder,

"I value our time together in this world more than any possession, than all possessions even. I truly believe, in the depths of my heart, that the two of us were put in this world for the purpose of holding one another's hand, and of enduring each and every hurdle life throws our way. You complete me in more ways than I can describe. Therefore, I would be honoured if you would take my hand in marriage."

The entire room was shocked into silence as we awaited an answer from Kyrie, who was sweating with such frequency that her forehead served as the world's most bountiful wellspring of sweat. But with no hesitation beyond a single gulp, she accepted unconditionally, and the rest of us cheerily celebrated the development. Once the two had a moment to themselves, Ringo patted Julius' back with such force I half expected to see the latter's spine erupt from his mouth. Rather than returning home before the sun could set, my mother opted to wait for Mr. Pyre to return, solely to witness the look on his face; I unfortunately fell for the temptation of sleep before we could break the news, though apparently his jaw all but crashed through the floor that Mother had just made spotless.

Chapter 4:
Crushed Beneath the Feet of Dragons

Despite Julius' successful proposal, the wedding never actually materialised for a very long time, given that both of them insisted on Mrs. Pyre being present for the occasion – from what I recall, she could only take three months' leave at a time every two years at a minimum, and even then her ability to take absence was contingent on her division's circumstances. A particularly busy period for Mrs. Pyre turned this into three years in this instance. The self-imposed requirement and its consequences proved to be disheartening, but we otherwise went about our lives as usual.

Julius, in between trips to the rest of the world with his father, managed to secure long-term employment with Saki, our village's well-esteemed if enigmatic nurse; I hadn't met her myself up until after the events I'll momentarily describe, but her most controversial trait among our small circle was her strange crimson eyes. Kyrie's room evolved – a cynical mind would describe it as a regression, but I digress – alongside her duties in the library as Mr. Pyre spent more and more time in the fields, now being charged with procuring additional texts from around the world.

This peace persisted until shortly after my seventh birthday (whereupon I received yet another watch from Kyrie once my previous one could no longer be worn by yours truly), and Kyrie at last received word from her mother that she would be arriving in Ford, the tail end of September being the earliest date she could give. The library erupted with joy and celebration, and plans were immediately made to secure our apparel for the occasion, with my mother reluctantly planning to take myself and Altair to the clothier the next day, albeit under the supervision of Ringo. It seemed like a day as normal as any other, until Julius made a request of me.

"Hey, Vega, little buddy, I uh… left my bag in front of the Basin, is there any chance you could do me a favour and fetch it?"

The Basin – the very name causes me great displeasure, but I knew little of it then besides its entrance lying in the cliff face beyond the forest surrounding our district of Ford. Regardless, I was happy to help my good friend - though my mother held a different opinion on the matter.

"And you wish for my little boy to go there alone? Are you *really* too busy planning a wedding to do it yourself?"

Julius needed little time to process her answer, given that he shared his father's aptitude for assuaging her paranoia.

"It's only a minute's walk from your house, Steph, and I think that kind of life experience will do your little man here some good. None among these streets would dare offend my father by acting upon him, irrespective of their opinion of you or your children."

My mother protested no further, though her sneer gave off the distinct impression that she let the scheme slide more to placate Julius than out of genuine approval.

She wished me well, promising that cooking would soon commence, and thus I was on my way, with a flock of pitch-black birds soaring over the library right as I stepped outside. I can't help but imagine that they were watching me, serving as a prelude to the catastrophe to come.

Now I was off in search of the Basin; an abandoned mineshaft, a relic of a time before my own, where excavating the underground's bountiful goods was done by more primitive means. There was little in the way of minecarts and automation, but instead thousands of man-hours from back-breaking manual labour is what bore fruit in the days of the Basin. Not that its interior mattered much to me, for I was merely heading there to pick up a bag sitting in its entrance. The way to the Basin was not too dissimilar to the path we took to the river that divided Ford in two for our fishing expeditions (which irregularly continued after our introduction to the activity, and fluctuated greatly in outcome). The Basin rested as the final destination of a simple dirt path through a small patch of trees located between my own home and the library; the edges of the path were faintly engraved with vehicle tracks within the sunken trails of earth, a testament to the prosperity the Basin once enjoyed even in its final days. The air carried a stagnant smell that made me feel as though my nose had been blocked, and aside from irregular, ominous chirping from the few winged denizens of the forest, there was nothing to fill the void of silence that permeated through the entire path. But I minded the silence not, as I welcomed the opportunity to see the world outside my home or a library without the constant background noise that I was all too familiar with in the streets of Ford.

    With little else of note, however, I arrived at the Basin's entrance, and it was a fairly unexciting entrance at that. The only sign of its existence was a wooden arch grafted into the sky-rending stone walls, leading into an endless and mesmerising darkness. A thin dirt path trailed off towards the area of the forest I had emerged from, but it was almost entirely reclaimed by nature. As I grasped the bag that leaned against the left side of the arch, I rightfully began to wonder what in the world Julius was even doing here – if I had to make a guess now, he was more than likely working out or training in relative isolation; he told me numerous times that doing so in the presence of others was distracting, and this was by no means a bad location to claim a moment's silence.

    Then the silence was erased by an *ear-shattering boom*.

    The sheer magnitude of the sound sent my ears into a spiral of sharp pain, and I couldn't bring myself to move my hands from them for several seconds. By the time I turned around, I discovered a colossal cloud of black smoke coming from the direction of Ford's front gate, reaching higher into the air than I ever could have imagined. Already I could hear voices screaming, soon to be backed up by a symphony of discordant gunfire, and my distance did little to nullify the reverberating pain inflicted on my eardrums.

    But I had little time to concern myself with these sounds, as the next development posed a much more immediate danger to me; in the right corner of my eye, I watched as an abyssal beast leapt from the rocky cliffs surrounding Ford and onto the roof of a house which I could just barely make out above the trees. Even from this distance, it appeared so pitch-black that even the sun that proudly beamed down upon us could not deliver an ounce of salvation to this wretched beast I would never forget – an unsightly abomination, with teeth as sharp as swords, as though its maw alone could chew through an entire building with not even a chip. Its... 'paws' resembled a grotesque fusion of a dog, a predatory bird and a human; its texture and fur coating matched that of our beloved canine friends, but its appendages were as long as an adult human's, and each transformed into a piercing claw by their end. Its tail was thin but stretched nearly as long as its own body, and it was whipping around like an all-consuming tornado of darkness.

Upon its landing, it gripped the surface it had landed on and split the sky with a guttural, raspy roar that eclipsed even the explosion in its volume, and by the time I could bring myself to even look at it once again... its gaze was locked on *me.*

I didn't need to be up close and personal, or even particularly wise, to know exactly what its deep stare meant: It was after me, and it acted upon its objective with haste, leaping off of the roof and somewhere into the thin patch of trees separating us. In a panic, I threw Julius's bag onto the grass and bolted inside the Basin, having absolutely no plan for how to walk out of this situation in one piece. My footsteps boomed like thunder in the vacant darkness, and I struggled to stay upright as I tripped and stumbled over all sorts of rocks and minor obstacles. Everywhere I looked there was only shadow, taunting me as I remained trapped, unable to fight off its suffocating omnipresence within these halls. Minutes seemed to pass; the halls appeared to grow ever tighter and constricting, confining me with the grisly thoughts of becoming the monster's meal, until I at last caught a glimpse of a golden light in the corner of my eye. Confused but far more terrified by the harmony of rapid, reverberating pattering following behind me in the distance, I bolted straight towards the light.

It turned out that the light was originating from behind a door, one of many that littered each side of this thin corridor, but this particular door was located at the stone-carved corridor's end.

The door handle was just barely visible, reflecting the light that emerged from a crack in the door; I all but lunged for it, swinging the door wide open and leaping inside before slamming it shut once more.

I couldn't even begin to entertain the delusion that I was safe before I realized that the light had in fact disappeared; I was left in abject darkness once more, sending me into a frenzy as I torturously searched for salvation before catching my foot on an unseen object and tumbling into a large pile of mining equipment. Short cuts and stabs littered my back, and I was awfully fortunate to avoid any serious damage at that moment. That being said, the pain was a bit much for me to bear at such an age, and I rolled my head back as the sound of footsteps emerged once more, this time slowed down and periodically pausing, taking great care in its hunt to ensure no stone went unturned.

"*Little...one...*"

The voice caused me to raise my head in shock; where had this voice come from, and who had spoken these words? The room I had tumbled into was barely even large enough to contain a single grown adult in its current state, let alone when combined with a clumsy child. My answer was one I needed not wait long for.

"*Little one... my apologies if I frightened you.*"

It was at this point it finally clicked: this... beast was *talking* to me, with a deep, guttural and yet... heartfelt voice. An animal with the ability to talk was utterly unprecedented, even moreso than its apparent familiarity with me.

"*I truly cannot believe five years have passed. Your scent, it is as vibrant as it was when your infantile hand first stroked my back with such eagerness. If my nostalgic reverence for such a time has caused you distress, I can only offer my most sincere apologies, and I would do it without end if you demanded so, my Lord.*"

Have I really just misunderstood this creature? Was its arrival and that massive explosion just a coincidence?, I naively began to ponder.

Truth be told, I was almost tempted to stand up and face it once more, having been charmed by its seeming benevolence and sincerity, and the thought of opening the door to witness this beast up close was a tempting one. But sure enough, I was rendered unable to act upon such a desire when a cold sensation slowly crawled up my right arm, delicately coiling around it, and once it had enveloped my right arm, it finally appeared right before my eyes: a snake. I was too shocked to move, too paralyzed to scream, too deep in abject fear of yet another horrifying encounter that I could do nothing but close my eyes, waiting for my death.

"Open your eyes."

An authoritative female voice rang out within my ear, but this time, I knew exactly where it was coming from before I even looked upon its source once more: the snake itself.

There was a faint golden glow emanating from its otherwise pitch black eyes, illuminating the black and white skin surrounding its head but nothing else, and all it had to bestow upon me beyond that was yet more commands.

"The beast pursuing you is true in heart; it desires not to harm or kill you, but it is merely a pawn, playing to the tune of its masters, using its reverence for you as a carrot on a stick. Your position is that of leverage, not one of powerlessness. A mighty man sees opportunity within such imbalance."

Kyrie's... wordiness had done much good for my verbal comprehension, but I was still left perplexed by what exactly the snake was implying in terms of my next course of action, leaving me stuck in an uncomfortable stare with the slender serpent until, with a hiss of what I can only assume to be annoyance, its head retracted from before my face and rested atop a long wooden pole beneath my right hand. It painstakingly crawled up the shaft of this weapon until its head came into full view: it was directing my attention to an awfully rusty but no doubt sharp spear, nestled beneath a small layer of pickaxes and primitive drills. Its presence among these mining tools thus confused me; it was as though the spear had been placed there explicitly for this situation, for I could think of no other application for such an item in such a place. Obviously, whatever was being done here in years long past was well beyond my childish interpretation of a big tunnel where men smacked the walls with pickaxes all day, but as my hand grasped the hilt of the spear, my pondering was cut short by the creature's voice once more.

"Little one... your location is not unknown to me now. Your scent... it is one I shall never forget; whatever false name the apostate consort has bestowed upon you cannot erase our bond. So please, come quietly, and let us return to life as it once was; why cut yourself off, why retreat to this... desolate village, wallowing in poverty and weakness, when your family is waiting with open arms, willing and able to grant you a life beyond this... mediocrity? Spending one's life in such a place is simply not sustainable when destiny holds far more in store."

My... family?! The light scratching against the door did nothing to nullify the confusion that now overwhelmed me completely and utterly; the only family I had ever known was my mother and Altair, yet this beast, whom I had never laid eyes on and had no knowledge of whatsoever, claimed to not only know the rest of my family but reside among them? A harsh hiss and the scraping of a tongue against my ear snapped me out of this train of thought, upon which I realised my grip on the spear had loosened.

"His words must deter you not, regardless of his attachment to you. Take this weapon and put an end to this ordeal with haste, lest both yourself and this creature live to see horrors beyond your imagination. He will not leave without you, whether you will it or not."

The conflicting words and thoughts in my head had made me extraordinarily hesitant to act upon a beast of no malice; I began to feel awfully guilty as its soft whimpers could be heard with increasing volume from behind the door. On the other hand, I had no idea what this snake was capable of doing to me, and the dagger-like stare in its eyes acted as yet more pressure, threatening to snap at me in an instant. Unable to stand its stare for much longer and in fear of retaliation if I acted against its wishes, I begrudgingly took the spear into my hands, tearing it from the pile, and pointed it towards the door in front of me, at the place in which I estimated its head to be. An affirming nod and short hiss followed to approve of this placement.

With a heavy heart and a silent apology to the creature, I forced the spear through the door with as much force as I could muster.

"UAAAAAAAAAAAAAAAAAAAAAGH!"

The rusty but nonetheless steel end of the spear tore through the door like fire through a dry field, and the creature's screech, while deafening, was the confirmation I needed to know I had landed my hit. Said scream, however, proved to be greatly to my detriment, as while my head recoiled in pain and my hands firmly grasped the spear yet, the beast's maw reflexively came crashing down upon my left hand multiple times, mangling my thumb as well as my index and middle fingers.

The pain shot through my entire body like a bolt of lightning, and I all but froze up as it reverberated through my every bone and muscle. Once the initial paralysis wore off I finally let go of the spear, and I tumbled backwards in much the same fashion as I had earlier, this time too absorbed by the earth-rending agony localized within my fingers to care about whatever was digging into my back. The creature continued to make all sorts of gruesome sounds as it thrashed around, and I could hear the spear crashing into walls and splintering apart by the second, until eventually it died down. I was so pre-occupied by confirming its death that I had not yet noticed the absence of my serpentine co-habitant, and what I witnessed upon opening the door did nothing to jog my memory of that particular detail; the beast was laid out on the floor in front of me, its head maybe half a metre away from where the door reached while fully opened. Even within the darkness, I could make out that it was looking directly at me, not with anger or retribution... but with sorrow.

"Why...? Please... tell me, who made... you do this, Hu...mani..."

And thus, the creature perished, failing even to eek out its final words, while I could only sit there and watch in silence as its blood oozed from its mouth and its dying gurgles and choking battered my ears. Once its blood touched my feet, I snapped out of my daze and collapsed backwards, shocked at both the hideous pain clawing at my hands and what I had just been driven to do. Regardless of my own fears or this thing's intentions, I had just taken the life of another creature, something my mother was very exhaustive in telling me and my brother not to do throughout the years. She emphasised sparing the life of anything up to and including the smallest of spiders, and abhorred violence in all its forms. Could I face her with this kind of blood on my hands, even if it occurred for the sake of my own survival?

"Concern thyself not, young one. By tarrying your innocent hands with the blood of this beast, you spare the bloodshed of millions more."

A familiar voice rang out in the scant darkness, and I only noticed at this point that my back was resting against... a woman's legs? I scurried towards a wall in a panic, abusing my poor fingers the entire time, as she walked towards the dead creature, stepping on and then kicking its corpse with a gruesome smirk.

"I would normally ask, nay, *mandate* that one eats what they kill. But for an abomination such as this... well, such torture is best reserved for only my most bitter enemy."

As she said this, I looked up to discover a face belonging to a strange, bald woman, her sharp face illuminated by a golden light emitted by a spear in her right hand; it was constructed entirely of an indeterminable metal that no doubt made it appear far stronger and more durable than my utterly shredded tool of warfare.

"Now then, you may not know of it, but your fate concerns much more than just the little village of Ford. Let us make haste and ascend from this dreadful darkness."

For the entire duration of our return trip, as I grasped my left hand in a desperate but ultimately futile attempt to curb the sharp stinging caused by that beast's biting, the stranger (who would later state her name to be Sihan-Perseli) appeared unconcerned by my plight, instead maintaining her hold on the shining spear as it lit up the surprisingly twisted return trip; I'm uncertain how I managed to evade so many small rocks, old minecart rails, all sorts of hazards I should have certainly caught my foot on during my escape, but maybe all was according to her "plan"? I can't begin to process what in the world she was talking about even in adulthood, but divine providence guiding me across this path can't entirely be ruled out. Unable to remove the pain via the grand medical advancement of "grasping the hurty spot very tightly", I attempted to divert my mind away from the pain by questioning my questionable guide.

"What are you doing here?"

"Just doing my duty."

"Your duty?"

"Yes, my duty. There isn't wax in your ears. Adults aren't fond of being made to repeat themselves, and most won't be so courteous as to warn you first."

The tone of her voice did not at all adjust to match the severity and harshness of her words, leaving me confused as to whether or not she meant a word of it. Put off by her attitude, I abandoned that specific line of questioning in favour of another.

"Who are you?"

"I am the culmination of my memories and experiences"

While it *was* an answer, it was much too literal; as much as I would have liked her to have dropped the veil of obfuscation in favour of some real answers, my first query proved to me that such an effort would stretch well beyond the realms of futility.

Indeed, she seemed to be deriving far too much fun at my expense, as her devilish grin only intensified.

"Don't be so untrusting as to believe I find humour in your circumstances, Vega; I only find the peculiarities of childish inquisition to be… funny, is all."

What a sadistic woman.

Our trek eventually brought us outside of the Basin once and for all; out of the Basin, into the fire, so to speak. The previously clear blue sky was shrouded in black smoke as an inferno raged through the quaint little town of Ford, though the fire itself was contained to the industrial half much to my relief.

Undeterred by the smell of smoke wafting in my direction and the demonic skies, I broke into a dash, hoping to get back to the library and discover that Mother, Altair and everybody else was unharmed, but my return journey was brought to an abrupt halt by two words from within the Basin's darkness.

"Forgetting something?"

And indeed, my legs had just barely avoided tripping over Julius' bag, which I had come here to collect in the first place. Despite everything that had happened, it would have been audacious of me to return without it considering it was my entire impetus for being there, plus I didn't want my hand to end up mulched with nothing to show for it. Grasping the handle in my good hand, I turned to the entrance of the Basin to offer my thanks... only to discover that Sihan-Perseli's light had faded, and the pitch blackness lying within was all that could provide any answer from this point forth. Confused but glad to be alive at all, I shelved the matter in a corner of my mind and made haste in my return to the library.

I only reached the halfway point of the forest path when I at last met a familiar face: Julius. Except Julius was sprinting towards me with blinding speed, completely and utterly uncharacteristic of somebody that was oft docile in his motions to an amusing degree – the most life I had ever seen from him before this point was during his proposal. Before I could get a single word in or properly process what I was witnessing, his arm coiled around my waist and he all but dived behind a row of bushes to my right, grasping my mouth with his left hand to avert all the screaming I would have done thanks to my own left hand's nasty collision with the floor. Tears could barely begin to well up in my eyes before the justification for his bizarre behaviour emerged: a band of furious footsteps followed his trail some ten seconds after, and the exchange between them made it clear that they weren't here to ask what I wanted for my birthday.

"Where has this fellow gotten off to? We saw him just seconds ago!" an older, meek-sounding voice exclaimed, joined by a symphony of stomping.

"Patience, my elder! He's obviously hiding, as any *coward* is swift to do when cornered! A *real warrior* will stare down even his certain death with grace, and dignity! A victory claimed by *dirty tricks* leaves only a permanent stain on a man's soul, and his pride!"

The far more boisterous voice did nothing to draw Julius out; indeed, his grip on me only intensified.

"And you believe it wise to alert him to our presence, knowing we possess not the territorial advantage? Your passion must be tempered yet by wisdom. Now settle down and keep your eyes open. First we send this kid to the black gates, then we look for Humanitas, understood?"

"...yes, my elder."

The heaviness of my breathing and whimpers died down soon enough, upon which Julius released his grip over my mouth and sternly brought his finger to his lips. He took a hold of the bag I had thankfully brought along with me and launched it into the path once he confirmed neither of our pursuers were looking in our direction, whacking one of our assailants and sparking confusion as well as angry jeers bemoaning his "cowardice".

Taking advantage of this confusion, he rose from the bushes with the swiftness of a bee as he pulled a knife from inside his coat, and the battle that followed was so short-lived as to be unremarkable; I was disturbed by just how quickly his victory occurred, as if life-or-death situations were as natural to Julius as breathing. It's safe to say that by the time he took my hand once more, guiding me back to the library as he tirelessly averted my curious gaze from the dead bodies he left in his wake, my perception of Julius was the most radical change to have taken place yet on this very, very tumultuous day – this meek friend of ours was almost... *assassin-like* in his conduct, and it was all that saved us from our early graves.

But I would have found any action necessary if I could finally reunite with my mother by its end. Maybe this just wasn't our day, and we were in the wrong place at the wrong time; maybe we would get back to the streets and all of the disorder would be cleaned up by now, and everybody would be waiting at the library, a little shaken by the excitement but looking forward to the rest of our days together. This delusion would prove to be woefully short-lived.

By the time we emerged into the streets of Ford once more, Julius didn't even bother attempting to shield my innocent eyes from the fallout of the ongoing attack; while the streets nearest to us remained relatively untouched by the carnage as of yet, the same could not be said for the rest of Ford, with the frequency of bodies lining the streets accelerating once one looked past the bridge at the village's centre – the bloodshed followed an unnerving osmosis, and I couldn't help but dread that the carnage would soon spread to where we stood.

There was not too much damage done to the structures of the village, however, as the vast majority of the factories and homes stood solid still, albeit with more than a few fires having started and ended. If anything, this only amplified my dread; combined with the conversation I had overheard in the forest, I could only draw the conclusion that wanton destruction was not the goal of whoever had done this. No, they were after... *me*.

"Whatever happens, do exactly as I say, down to *every* stroke of *every* letter."

Julius' usual dry wit had utterly evaporated amongst the fiery nightmare; whatever had emerged in its place was far more calculating, and driven only by a desire to emerge from this hell that had descended upon us.

As soon as we settled into an alley between the Pyres' library and somebody else's home, Julius brought us to a stop. Setting his bag to the ground, he withdrew a small first aid kit from his pocket and hastily wrapped my left hand in bandages. Whatever was in the bandages stung badly enough for me to want to scream, but his hand kept my voice from erupting.

The bandage was barely complete before our attention was drawn to the sounds of men screaming and shouting from inside the library, Mr. Pyre most prominent among them. The old man was screaming all sorts of profanities as he fought to keep yet more of these foul people away from his daughter, as well as the rest of my family. If my silence weren't critical to my survival, I would have proudly cheered him on, but Julius broke into a cold sweat as he listened to the battle unfolding.

"Shit... there's too many of them..."

Amidst his mumbling, Julius at last revealed what had been kept in his bag for so long: an extensive, single-barreled weapon resembling a shotgun, but with a colossal arrow-headed projectile in place of shells. Julius took a small container the size of his thumb and coated its barbed tip in the yellow substance inside, taking great caution to not get it on his own skin or mine.

The sounds of fighting subsided, up until Mr. Pyre was launched through the window behind us with a loud crash. Julius was as startled as I was but placed his hand around my mouth once more before I registered the awful truth: Mr. Pyre was dead, covered head to toe in ghastly gashes and ugly bruises. With how long he had spent holding off his attackers, it was impossible to tell just how much of the blood on him was his own, but either way, the toll that this unknown group's pursuit of me had taken not just on me but the people I held dear was beginning to crush me, and Julius' iron grip was the only thing keeping me from keeling over in despair.

"Don't look, buddy. Mr. Pyre's somewhere... better now..."

Julius turned me away from the grisly sight, but the subdued throat clearing and scant few tears landing on my hair made it clear as day that this stone-cold side of Julius was by no means unaffected by the loss. All he could do was consider his next move as we watched what unfolded next, obscured by the shadows.

"*Die! Die! Rot in hell, you pieces of shit!*" a high pitched wail erupted from the library as its front door flew open, and the screams continued further as Kyrie was dragged from the library and thrown to the stone road about ten metres away.

Soon followed Altair and then my mother, who were far quieter but no less terrified. The people dragging them out of the library were all adorned in similar clothing: loose robes of pure white, oft save for the blood and wounds earned from their scuffle with the late Mr. Pyre. These weren't your average gang of thugs looking for a payday; there was a degree of professionalism and order to their terror. Altogether, there were about five of them standing outside the library, though the unamused scowls and grimaces indicated that there were more among them prior to Mr. Pyre's intervention.

"Excellent conduct. For you to have found Castitas with such swiftness is commendable... but alas, it seems the other little one is not among them."

That bold, authoritative voice emerged from a little further down the road than we could see – it was low enough to be mistaken for a beastly growl, and I could only recoil in fear just from the sound of it.

Once he finally strolled into our view, we witnessed a monolith of a man, towering above his underlings by orders of magnitude; the thick black beard and moustache did absolutely nothing to hide his rage as he walked up to my mother, pressing his finger into her forehead.

"Reveal the location of Humanitas to me, at this instant, lest your punishment maintain its severity. Your transgression of absconding carries the punishment of death… but in my eternal generosity, I am willing to compromise; return to me, as my consort, and you can join us in paradise. You will bear more children yet, and they will know no strife, no evil, no sin. The path I am graciously bestowing upon you is one only a fool would refuse - given that I would never choose a fool to mother my children, I eagerly await Humanitas' whereabouts."

The most off-putting part of his appearance, however, only came into view once he briefly stopped talking, his finger still at my mother's head: *his chest had what looked like a giant, blue, pulsating eyeball attached to it, with tendrils reaching across its entire breadth!* Who… who *was* this man?! It was clear as day that my mother was at one point married to or at least romantically involved with him, and yet I had been definitively told by my mother, at every turn imaginable, that my father was dead, his ashes having long been scattered to the wind. A father's role was to protect and nurture his children, as Mr. Pyre had done to the last; why would my own so callously orchestrate such bloodshed?

Nevertheless, he was referring to me with the very same name that the beast I had slain was attempting to call me in its dying breath. The words that left his mouth were slowly tearing apart a world I had spent my entire life in, and yet my mother's silent acceptance of his words as the truth, with not a word of protest, was all that was needed for the entire web to crumble. Julius was equally dismayed by the revelations so casually being extolled by this stranger, with a disgusted and confused look on his face as the weapon in his hand shook.

"Mahro... what the fuck? What evil has descended upon this world...?"

Julius and I could only watch in blinding bewilderment as this bastard struck my mother with the force of a hammer using his fist.

"TELL M-"

"He's dead! He died on the way here, ended up in the forest and..."

"DO YOU THINK I AM STUPID?!"

The deranged bellowing was followed up by a sharp slap to my mother's face – I was ready to tear away his neck with my teeth like a primal, mindless beast, and Julius' grip was all that kept me from getting myself killed or taken away that day.

"It sickens me to have once called you my wife."

With my mother's refusal, the monolithic man looked over at Altair and Kyrie, no doubt waiting for them to spill information on my whereabouts. Being met only with the pained and deathly afraid looks on their faces with not a single word to join them, he placed his hand firmly on my mother's head, pulling her hair back so that the two made firm eye contact.

"He has been seen here; we *know* he is here. Our eyes see *all*. You know this, and yet you lie as easily as you breathe. Humanitas will be recovered, whether you co-operate or not. As for you... I can imagine nobody less deserving of paradise."

The moment he concluded his speech, the eyeball on his chest began to squirm, with its blood red pupil darting in all directions one can imagine, and coinciding with its fit came the sound of freezing; starting from the hair, my mother's body was slowly transformed into *solid ice*, and she choked, gasped and reached for her throat before her hands too became solid. Julius recognized what was about to happen well before I did, and as the leader was passed a two-handed hammer by one of his servants, Julius turned me 180 degrees, shielding my body and keeping me tightly in place as the sound of ice shattering erupted in my ears.

Altair and Kyrie's screaming, Julius' repeated commands to not look, all of it was drowned out as I furiously tried to deny the truth in my own head; what if a window had just happened to smash at an unfortunate time, and a hero was here to save the day as I cowered in fear, driving away the evil infesting our humble little village? Anything, literally *anything*, would be an improvement over what was so obviously the truth, but by the time Julius released his grip over me in reaction to rapid gunfire coming from some indeterminate distance away, all I could do was collapse onto the floor, staring at the wall of the library; there was no need to verify.

By the time I raised my head once more, ready to cry and wail, the sounds of gunfire and bloodshed had died down. In their place, a dark figure stood at my feet, breathing heavily with his hand against the wall and thankfully obscuring the sight of my mother's corpse.

"Hu... Huma... my... son..."

I couldn't believe it - the voice most certainly belonged to my mother's murderer.

With an anguished scream, I scrambled backwards, failing to find my footing and banging my already scrambled left hand into Mr. Pyre's corpse as the murderer took a few agonizing steps towards me, upon which I noticed the projectile from Julius' weapon stuck in his hip; its effects caused him to falter more and more with every step, until he crumbled to his knees and was held up only by his right hand as his left futilely reached towards me.

At this point, Julius emerged once more, racing through the alleyway and kicking this vile murderer onto his back. As he got on his knees, he ordered me to look away, an order I hastily complied with.

"You! You... would spit in the face of the Angel herself?! Have you no idea just *what* yo-!"

The man's bellows were cut off by a sharp punch from Julius, sounding powerful enough to shatter both his hand and his target's jaw. Julius said nothing in response, delivering a few more attacks to disable him until he could only produce sputters.

What followed next was a series of sounds I'll never forget, for as long as I live: behind my back, Julius slowly and painstakingly tore the eye-shaped object from the man's chest, and the repulsive sound of its stem tearing through flesh was joined by the bearer's ceaseless screams of agony. Julius himself was greatly exerted by the task but never let up, never once relented or stopped to gather his breath, and he cursed the murderous bastard in every manner and tongue he could fit into such a brief span of time, abandoning all manners or notions of kindness as he exacted his revenge. He was feral and violent in a way I had scarcely imagined a human being could possibly be.

Some thirty seconds passed before the screaming and tearing at last ceased; I turned around to discover both of them drenched in murky red blood, with Julius holding the eyeball-like object as its tendrils furiously thrashed around, leaving shallow cuts on his face while retracting back to the core of this... thing. Once its fit at last subsided, it resembled a flower, though with a pulsating blue eye in place of a stigma and docile but still eerily alive tendrils for petals. The stem was formed not of flora but of fauna, being comprised of a sharp, hollow but firm bone with a jagged edge.

As Julius collapsed onto his back, grasping onto the fleshy flower and panting, I did much the same, once again focusing on the intense pain in my hand. All of my questions about my lineage, my mother, this... *thing* that Julius had extracted from my father's chest, they were all too much to bear. Overwhelmed by the physical and mental burden of this truly awful day, I rested my head against Mr. Pyre's body and allowed my consciousness to wane at last.

Chapter 5:
Incompleteness

The aftermath and specific details of this event were explained to me in excruciating detail further down the line, but I'll provide a summary here: a group identifying themselves as the Band of the Wyvern, some bearing tattoos of either a wyvern or the character for the word itself, launched an assault on this little village in the middle of nowhere. Arriving by boat a few miles from Ford, their forces were ill-equipped but composed of at least 100 members, with the entirety of their numbers eliminated in combat with soldiers and armed villagers.

Unknown to everybody beyond myself, Altair, Julius, Ringo and Kyrie was that the fodder were merely a distraction; through the chaos, their unnamed leader rampaged through the village of Ford in pursuit of me and my family, swiftly cutting down all who dared stand in his way with a silver sabre. Apparently the cruel manner of death he delivered to my mother had been reserved exclusively for her.

As the beast pursued me deep into the Basin, my mother's location was narrowed down and surrounded, though not before Julius snuck out through a window to find me. After a furious battle with Mr. Pyre left three of their members dead, this led to the horrific scene I bore witness to in the streets of Ford. While I was thankfully spared the sight of watching my mother die, Altair was afforded no such luxury, and he spent many a sleepless night from then on haunted by what he had witnessed.

The first day after this awful event began with me waking up in a blindingly white room, with an upbeat, melodious whistle soothing my eardrums from behind a grey curtain. The reek of blood and sweat that I had become reluctantly accustomed to had all but vanished, and the sterile air of the clinic was like a bundle of the most ripe flowers in all of Morosus in comparison. Yawning and dazed, I raised my left hand to rub my eyes... which is when I noticed that my thumb, index finger and middle finger had been replaced with shining metallic appendages.

In complete horror, from both the unexpected replacement and my inability to yet move these new fingers, I yelled out for help, desperate to know what had been done to me. Instantly, the whistling intensified, increasing in volume whilst maintaining its soothing aura, and the grey curtain surrounding me retracted to the leftmost side as my wailing died down, revealing a white wall surrounded by blank space and introducing me at last to Saki.

"At last, you rise. I do not expect your dreams to have been pleasant but rest assured - you are safe once more." she said, resting her hand on my head.

In reality, I don't think I had dreamed at all – at the very least, any dreams I may have had must have been so innocuous or unremarkable as to not be worth commenting on – but I had no desire to act like a pint-sized smartass when I was too focused on the woman standing before me; in an utterly perpendicular contrast to the gruesome events of the prior day, and the death and violence I had been unceremoniously thrown into the midst of, she was elegantly adorned in a black dress that tightly fit around her body, emphasising each and every curve the gods graciously granted her, combined with a neat, grassy green tabard that reached from her neck to her knees and was adorned in the image of purple flowers across its perimeter. Such clothing was utterly foreign to me - in a rather literal sense, considering that she hailed from the eastern country of Tenryuu. The thin black glasses resting in front of her sharp but delicate eyes brought the look to completion.

Were my description to end there, you could walk away thinking little of her. But behind those glasses laid a perplexing and mysterious sight; each of her soft eyes was an intense, bloody red, with pulsating pupils surrounded by a slow, murky vortex of even darker red. The sclera enclaving her pupils was pitch black, devoid of detail. Such anomalous eyes sent a shiver down my back the first time I witnessed it for myself, but what frightened me far more was what had become of my own flesh.

"What... what happened to my fingers?!"

Saki sat next to me atop the bed and lightly gripped my left hand, fidgeting with the artificial appendages I had obtained. While the warmth of her hand was a welcome surprise, given that my fingers were no longer flesh and bone, the sensation still felt... alien. It was harrowingly similar to the chill that follows scraping the snapped end of a pencil across a desk. Even if I couldn't see what they had been replaced with, I would have had difficulty discerning just what they were touching. I was left stunned in a confused silence, wondering how in the world I could ever get used to such an impairment until she leaned in closer to me with a welcoming gaze.

"You'll learn how to use them properly with time. Whatever happened to them caused such great damage that returning them to a healthy state was impossible, even for me. It would be wise to offer your thanks to Julius next you see him; he proved to be a great help during your surgery."

The instant she mentioned Julius, the events of the prior day crashed into me like a tank bursting through a wall. My detour into the Basin, that strange woman, these violent cultists, and most of all...

"Where's my mom?!"

I begged Saki for an answer, struggling to accept that what I had been witness to the prior evening was anything other than a horrible, twisted nightmare; her tight grasp around my shoulders and her hand running through my hair did next to nothing to prepare me for her next words.

"She's... gone. To a place where nobody can hurt her anymore."

I spent the next few days recovering in the clinic and explaining to Saki just what had happened to me on that day. It went seamlessly up until I tried to bring up my saviour, Sihan-Perseli... only for not a single word to leave my mouth. I tried arduously to describe or even allude to her, but the intensity of my efforts only constricted my tongue harder, as if a snake truly were tightening around my throat.

I want to find her, I thought, *I want to know why she saved me, and only me.*

As Saki's look grew ever more concerned and the futility become ever more obvious, I instead claimed to have stumbled my own way out, releasing the stranglehold on my tongue as if it were never there. She was suspicious, of course, and the curious look in her eye betrayed exactly what she was thinking – *you're not lying, but there's a piece of the puzzle you're not telling me.* She would've been well within her right to grill me for elaboration. But she instead chose a different path.

"In the end, you escaped with your life. That's all that matters." she said with a smile, and the curtains slowly closed as she left me to my own devices.

Further down the line, once I was released from her clinic, I went so far as to try and write the truth down... but my hand was stayed with much the same unexplainable reluctance. Not once did a good night's sleep come to me – exacerbated by my strange inability to discuss the woman who had saved my life - and what little rest I got was now plagued by nightmares, the details of which I've long forgotten save for the horrifying image of my mother's head imposed upon that black beast as it chased me through a seemingly endless abyss, for hours and hours at a time.

The evil dwelling within my dreams made me cherish my waking hours far more; I came to learn quite a few things about this enchanting nurse in between regular checks on my motor functions and general health: Saki was just barely a month older than Julius, at the age of 21, and had spent most of her life among an isolated community in a mostly uncharted crevice of Tenryuu, identifying themselves as the Shrouded Anemones. Isolationist communities were hardly rare, according to Saki, but this particular society harboured a unique quality: Every member of the clan was born with either one or two aberrant eyes, so long as they were conceived within the colony and were born to a mother possessing such an eye.

And their peculiar peeper was by no means exclusively cosmetic; through these eyes, one could see human skin as translucent, granting them an intricate insight to the workings of our bodies with none of the risk involved with cutting somebody open. The opacity of people's skin varied from person to person, but Saki's eyes could perceive human skin as almost entirely transparent, according to the nurse herself. Therefore, she concluded that her talents lay in healthcare, but with no room to hone her craft among the Anemones – many of whom had arrived at an identical conclusion - she ultimately left behind her family to pursue this occupation, well aware that self-imposed exiles were never welcome there again.

Incidentally, Saki also exposed me to a fact about my own brother I was entirely unaware of: at an early age, Altair had been diagnosed with colour-blindness, exercising great difficulty in differentiating between the colours green and red. It made perfect sense in retrospect, but I was still confused by the idea of how one could struggle to differentiate the two (which proved to at least be a better understanding than my initial reaction of *He can't see red?!*)

How Saki came to end up in Morosus, as well as how she procured the finances to start the clinic in the first place, were not yet disclosed to me, but over the next three days, I had grown rather fond of my nurse. She always made sure to stay by my side as I at last went to sleep each night, gazing into my eyes with a longing but caring look.

But inevitably, the end of those three days saw Saki discharging me from her clinic, the prosthetic fingers very much there to stay, and she invited me to write my own name on her list using my left hand. I was reluctant, but having had no affinity for one hand over the other up to that point and even to this day, I ultimately resigned myself to the fact that I would have to live with this. As I messily scrawled my name onto the sheet, it occurred to me that I had grown somewhat accustomed to the replacement appendages by this point and was slowly gaining adeptness in using them, though I had become no less repulsed by the sight of them; every time I so much as glanced at them, I recalled the mangled face of the beast that had pursued me in vivid detail, as well as the intense dread I experienced with every second more I spent in that godforsaken place it had chased me into. But for as much as I despised them... I would have gladly given up the rest of my digits if it could have somehow saved my mother's life. The wound bore twice as deep with nothing good to show for it.

"If you have any trouble with them, please don't hesitate to talk to me; I take pride in my work, and I don't want you walking around with your fingers *or* your underwear in a twist, alright?"

The nauseous sensation of my metallic fingers scraping with the metal handle of the front door threw off my ability to fully digest her request, but I nodded regardless.

After a brief embrace from behind by the nurse, I was allowed to leave the clinic at last. One would ordinarily wonder why a child of such stature would be allowed to walk into the streets alone, three days after a major attack that had left at least 60 out of a population of roughly 400 dead, as well as countless more assailants. The answer to this question was right behind the clinic's front door: Julius was waiting for me, crossing his arms and leaning against a wooden column to my right.

"Good morning, buddy. We've been waiting for you."

What followed his greeting was a slow stroll through the busier half of Ford, during which I saw many, many bodies in the streets covered by large black or white sheets, with those covered in black being painstakingly hauled into trucks that could fit no more than five of them. While the members of the Band of the Wyvern who perished that day were taken elsewhere for an unknown but presumably unceremonious process of disposal, the slain villagers were afforded a much more commendable departure, as a patch of farmland burnt up during the attack was converted into a graveyard, and there were many a grim look on the men's faces as they dug graves for family and friend alike. I couldn't help but wonder if my mother and Mr. Pyre had already been buried, but it was a curiosity I dared not sate.

Beyond the converted land I could see that many of the homes carved into the rocky walls surrounding Ford had vibrant green wreaths hung up on their front doors, commemorating the lives of those who perished in the attack. The same rang true for when our feet at last treaded upon the residential district itself.

Julius, however, looked relatively undisturbed by it all, occasionally looking down to me and offering the same reassuring look as always now that the danger had died down. I was incredibly unsure of what to make of his behaviour; he had acted with incredible pragmatism and initiative when our lives were at stake, but just three days later he was the same as ever, as if nothing had ever happened? I couldn't reconcile his apparent indifference, and he only took one look at the twisted grimace on my distrusting face until we at last crossed the bridge and took a detour to our familiar fishing spot. As quiet and serene as ever, this river and the bank surrounding it may well have been the only parts of Ford not forever stained by the Band of the Wyvern.

"Got a lot on your mind?" he asked as we took a seat on top of the soft grass; I was sat some three meters away from him, feeling great unease but glad to at last see nature once again.

That being said, there was far too much on my mind, as a matter of fact, much of it contradictory or of subjects I was too scared to broach with Julius. Where was Altair? Who were these evil people? Why did that man claim to be my father when my mother had told me, consistently, that he was long dead? Did Julius just stand by and let my mother die? Was he hiding a deep bloodthirst beneath a veneer of friendliness and companionship? Was-?

"It looks like I'm right then, you're still trying to process all of this..." we finally locked eyes as he interrupted my train of thought, and then after a deep breath he continued, "First and foremost, Altair and Kyrie are safe. Your brother has barely spoken a word since that day... but physically, they're unharmed."

The news of my brother and Kyrie's safety brought some modicum of relief - the first in many days - and I let out a sigh of relief.

But the next words to leave his mouth were preceded by bowing his head in shame.

"And second... I'm deeply, sincerely sorry that I didn't save your mother. I won't make excuses; up until my dad arrived, I was

85

too scared to act. If he too had perished or arrived too late, I have no doubt I would have just stood by like a coward and let them run off with Kyrie and your brother. My old man deserves your thanks a thousand times more than I do, and I suggest you offer it next you two meet."

He was beginning to sweat and fidget with his fingers as he confided in me; many of the same mannerisms and behaviours he displayed during his fight for our lives were emerging, but I could in no way interpret them as a show of bloodthirstiness. He was as vulnerable as he had ever been, not at all confident that he did everything in his power to protect us.

"I don't expect things to just stay how they always have. Every time I lay my eyes on you, I remind myself of how much you... no, how much all of us lost that day. Not just your mother, but also our friends, our family, all of the good people who've spent their lives here. When I look at how much good my father's done for this village, even in its darkest hour, I can't help but feel like a failure in comparison."

Following his explanation came a lengthy period of silence, within which I gazed down at my left hand; every word Julius had just said - about being reminded of his failures and everything we had lost as a community – gave me the perspective I had sorely lacked during my recovery; what did three of my fingers matter when many times more lives had been lost?

"There's obviously more of this story to tell, but at this present moment, my only desire is to make things right. While they're now utterly defeated and gone, this so-called 'Band of the Wyvern' made up only one force of strife in this vast, vast world we pour our blood, sweat and tears into. I can't abandon you, not after everything you've endured, and there is no way in Hell that Kyrie would allow me to do such a thing even if I were heartless enough to catapult you into vagrancy."

I could tell Julius was preparing me for a big revelation, but he began to sound far more upbeat as he leapt to his feet and then stood proudly before me, his hand outstretched.

"I can never aspire to be half the guardian your mother was, nor can I ever demand that you truly forgive me for my cowardice, but I ask that you... come under our wing, so that we may help the people of Ford emerge from the ashes, stronger and more resilient than ever."

What he was propositioning by this point was crystal clear: he was inviting me to live under the care of both himself and Kyrie. His words had done much to break down the lingering bitterness and doubt I had festered towards him, but this final, utterly sincere and selfless gesture, which no doubt spelled the end of much of his world-faring, was the catalyst that allowed me to look at him with a newfound understanding and respect. Even if I had any other alternative, I was by no means reluctant to take up his offer, and so our hands united at last.

It's just unfortunate that ten years later, he may be forced to eat his words in regards to our attackers, considering my recent encounter with a very much alive Band of the Wyvern member – if put in my damp shoes, would that pragmatism and precise, calculated execution emerge once more, knowing his work went incomplete? I'm sure he would have handled it better than me. But I would never wish my circumstances upon him; he has just as much - if not more - to lose than me.

My first steps into the library as an adopted member of the Pyre family was met with an uproarious cry from Kyrie, who raced towards me and raised me into the air with the speed of a hurricane. Were it not for her ample chest cushioning me, she may well have crushed me to death, but I couldn't object to feeling her warmth once more, and the lively energy emanating from her every gesture was a much-welcomed contrast to the stale clinic I had spent three days idling in.

"How relieved I am to discover thee in pristine condition! Hath thou eaten well? Did thy nurse treat thee well? Did-did you get enough sleep?!"

I was unable to answer her hailstorm of questions before my face was buried in her sternum, presumably to hide the tear or 15 that she was shedding. After what felt like an eternity, I was finally released and placed back on the floor, upon which Kyrie looked up at Julius as she wiped her eyes on her sleeve, breaking out into a smile. While I was very glad to see her happy once more, especially since her own father had died on the same fateful night as my mother, there was a pressing question I couldn't put off any longer.

"Where's Altair?"

"He's asleep in my parents' room, little one. Please, exercise caution with your brother, his condition is rather volatile, given the horrors he- well, I'll not aggravate thy troubles. Once Julius' father is free from his duties around the town, we'll make arrangements for the two of you to receive proper accommodation within this building, darling. For now, my parents' room shall have to do. Hopefully this ugly matter shall be remedied before Mommy Dearest arrives..."

She concluded the topic on a sour note; I could tell from her lip biting and grimacing that her thoughts were consumed by how her mother would react to the news that her husband, a family friend and countless others had died for no good reason, and by villains in pursuit of *me*, no less. Perhaps I was better off losing a finger or three than being charged with delivering such awful news.

Kyrie hoisted me up and carried me to the centremost table with not quite the usual spring in her step. She sat me down in her lap, clutching onto me for dear life, while Julius made his way to the back of the library for a purpose that would soon become apparent. My arms wrapped around her own, and I took solace in the long-devoid warmth... but I couldn't ignore the hideous sensation coursing through my left hand. So much as grazing her arm with my prosthetics caused my arm to jolt in disgust.

In the meantime, I took note of the library's condition. The window Mr. Pyre had been launched through remained broken, though it had been boarded up in its entirety and the floor beneath was thoroughly swept clean of glass. Meanwhile, there were multiple large cuts and dents in the bookshelves and tables, though nothing had been damaged to the point of utter destruction or collapse. A pile of wooden shards and torn up books gathered in the corner of the room, poorly concealed by a wide, ancient looking broom that reached above my head while seated. On the leftmost table lay a small pile of flowers surrounding a framed photograph of Mr. Pyre standing upright in its centre.

"I have no doubt he would have been proud of you, darling."

Kyrie's gaze was also transfixed on the table, and she rocked back and forth, stroking my hair all the while, until Julius at last returned, a pen in one hand and a piece of paper in another. His hand was flying all around him the moment he sat down, intently focused on this single task as if his life depended on it.

The final stroke of his pen came some two minutes later, putting an end to the furious scrawling that had filled the room for so long.

"What are you writing, lovely?"

Julius' intense stare morphed into one of unease as he looked back up to his fiancé with an onerous sigh.

"I'm writing a letter for Mahro. Considering what we've seen first-hand, and how much of what he said has unfortunately come to pass, I'm hoping he can make his way here for further investigation of these... what did he call them... Screaming Roses? And if he doesn't object, I'm hoping he can teach the boys a thing or two about self-defense. Of course, it all depends on his family circumstances, but with any luck..."

Julius' train of thought derailed before his sentence slowly came to a halt, akin to a battery exhausting its last morsel of power. He quietly stared down at the sheet of paper with a grimace; whether he was checking for mistakes in a particularly dour mood or contemplating just what kind of request he was making of this Mahro character, I haven't the answer. Either way, I was more perplexed by what exactly this 'Screaming Rose' was; its name brought to mind the... thing Julius had ripped from my father's chest, so I was more or less just trying to confirm a hunch, but Kyrie piped up before I could pose my question, releasing one hand from my waist and pressing one down on the table as she took a deep breath.

"Julius, darling, please, I love you, from the deepest depths of my heart... but I cannot see what inviting that... that *loathsome twat* is going to accomplish! I'm not at all fond of his "training", whether it's applied against thyself or these fastidious young men, and if he's so invested in these Rose artifacts, just transfer the one in your possession to him! If need be, I can arrange for Sanzu to deliver it with haste so please, desist entertaining the notion of bringing that man and all his troubles to a village that's seen enough!"

Kyrie's desperate plea reverberated around the entirety of the library, with her disdain for this 'Mahro' seeping from every syllable. I couldn't help but wonder, just what evil deed had this man done to earn such hideous scorn from a woman I cherished so greatly?

"Sweetheart, are you still this upset over a strawberry?"

...excuse me?

Julius must be pulling my leg, there's no way she can be this scornful over a piece of fruit, I ignorantly thought to myself, and I awaited the truth of the matter from Kyrie herself.

"Stealing it on my birthday, from my own cake, no less, and then making a show of it before my entire family! Relegate him to the deepest confines of prison and obliterate the key!"

Her words struck like thunder as she threw her hand to the skies, and I was beginning to wonder if it was she who instead belonged in *my* lap.

"We're dealing with matters of life and death, Kyrie. We can't dictate these matters over long-distant misdeeds of fruit. It's been nine years, get over it."

Her objections founded on a childish grudge having been rebutted, she could only pout as she offered a reluctant agreement to his arrangement, though he was not yet ready to hold his tongue.

"Besides, I think you'll come to find the two of you are far more alike than you recall. I could even go so far as to make the argument that you took more than a few cues from the man after all, despite your utterly petty grievances."

She looked as if she had swallowed a lemon whole upon hearing this. While she was well beyond having any grounds on which to protest, she gave her pithy reply her all, "Why not go off and marry him instead, if I'm just some inferior facsimile of the brute?"

Julius was swift and decisive in his answer.

"Polygamy is illegal, sweetheart."

Later that day, as Julius headed off to leave his letter in the hands of a cross-continental courier, Kyrie took it upon herself to bathe me. The bathroom was located directly adjacent to Mr. And Mrs. Pyre's bedroom, a confusing location to my little brain, so used as I was to each room being accessible from a central hub.

The room itself was not too dissimilar to the one in my former home, with its floor layered in black vinyl and the walls coated in a combination of white ceramic tiles for the lower half of the walls and a blank layer of light grey paint occupying the rest of the space. The most obvious difference came from the bathtub's placement in the middle of the room as opposed to along the edge of any wall, along with its curtain.

"Summon me when thou art submerged!" Kyrie yelled from behind the closed door.

Entering the bathtub… it was by no means an arduous task, and one I had performed all too many times, but there was a stark difference this time around. Not only did entering one Kyrie and her family had made much use of feel awfully alien, but my newly attached fingers made a terrible scrape against the ceramic edge of the tub as I tried to place a firm grip on it. Indeed, the sound threw me off so greatly I was barely able to avoid tumbling in headfirst, and the scalding water my hands found themselves in soon after only exacerbated the discomfort felt in my artificial appendages.

Hearing the commotion, Kyrie entered of her own volition. Not even this occasion could get her out of her much-beloved costume, but she had at least removed her hat and returned her hair to its free-flowing default state as opposed to the braided ponytail she was rarely seen without. By the time I fully turned around, ready to face her, she had taken a stool and sat at the bath's edge, staring at me nervously.

"Um… Saki said your fingers should be okay in the water…" she said quietly as she rescued my tortured hand from the depths, toying with the metallic appendages. "I must say, for how terrible the circumstances that led to such replacements are, they most certainly look… what's the word… *cool*, I guess?"

As she released my hand with a beaming smile and it sank into the depths of the shallow bathwater at last, I couldn't help but sneer in disagreement with her assessment; I couldn't have despised the sight of them more, and if given the choice, I would have petulantly insisted on going without three of my fingers if it meant ridding my body of this permanent stain. Everything they touched felt simultaneously numbing and overwhelming, even if only in its numbness. Sifting my hand through something so commonplace as water produced a spine-chilling sensation, as if they were being forcibly dragged through the depths of a swamp. Retrospect makes the childishness of such a school of thought obvious, given that three stumps on my left hand would have been just as hideous, but I digress.

Struggling to come up with any further subject to discuss, Kyrie nervously reached for a bottle at the bath's edge, pouring its lavender-scented contents into my scruffy hair and slowly running her wet hands through it.

"Who's this Mahro guy, Kyrie? It sounds like you hate him."

My inquiry manifested out of the lack of any other topic to bring up, but I immediately suspected that my tongue would have been better off held. Kyrie simply chuckled and shook my head lightly, though.

"I was merely being facetious, my darling. For all of my accusations and jeering, he's a respectable man, and he's been a friend of Ringo ever since... perhaps the age I find myself at now?"

I can't help but feel as though she wasn't being entirely honest and was instead backpedalling on genuine grudges after what Julius had told her earlier that day, considering how profusely she protested the idea of his presence. But desiring not to argue over something so inconsequential, I produced another question in an effort to shift the conversation.

"How is Ringo? Did he get hurt?"

"He's fine, dearest. He wasn't working at the time, so fortunately he was spared from that ghastly explosion. It's an awful shame for the young men who were there; they never stood a chance."

Her speaking concluded alongside her treatment of my hair, and she hoisted me up to sit along the bath's edge, but she gasped in shock and almost lost her grip as she was at last privy to the cuts and stabs littered across my back; expecting a shocked demand for an explanation, I instead felt her finger dancing across my back, inciting a small tingling sensation as it trickled across each bump and crevice across its expanse.

"What garish marks, my precious. I won't ask you to relive what happened that day, but I can promise you this: These marks, these imperfections, they will fade away with time. There are many things a good night's rest and a plaster won't get rid of, but things like this, marks that leave no scars, they teach us that our situation can always get better, that we can heal. And we will heal, Vega. You, Altair, Julius and me. The village of Ford can never be 'normal' again, nor should we try and force it to be. Nay, we'll make our own happiness, even if we must claw and grasp at it until our fingers are raw and our legs are creaking."

As she leaned down to conjoin my hair with her chin, her arms wrapped around my chest, she concluded her declaration with as much cheer as she could extract from the depths of her heavy heart, "Does that sound like a plan?"

Needless to say, I was conflicted; Kyrie was the only person left in my life that resembled a mother figure whatsoever, and thus made for the only logical hand to hold through the tumultuous journey of life. But she could never replace my mother no matter how hard she tried. That being said… this was a reality we were mutually cognizant of. Kyrie wasn't trying to replace her, and thus to consider the matter as if that were her intent came across as an inherently wrong approach as I mulled our conversation over - acting as my guardian didn't alter anything about the Kyrie I knew and loved.

With a deep breath and the image of my late mother concealed behind my eyelids, I nodded firmly.

The night concluded with Kyrie drying me off (while putting considerable effort in to not lay a single glance upon my body) and carrying me into her parents' bed, placing me down next to my snoring brother and stroking my face before she left at last, closing the door behind her.

As the last light of the hallway was subdued, I rolled over towards my brother, troubled yet by thoughts of my mother and those evil Band of the Wyvern people. The cloth of the blanket enveloping me felt as alien as the water that cleansed me, as its fibers caught themselves between the nuances of the metallic appendages. But for the first time in what felt like years, with the Band of the Wyvern having been completely eradicated, I could at last look to the future with optimism, confident that while its cost was immense, the worst part of my life was at last behind me.

Chapter 6:
King of Strangeness

The next few weeks were spent adjusting to our unprecedented situation; Kyrie and Julius gradually became accustomed to their duties as adoptive parents, and the former would frequently invite Saki over during her days off to better teach her how to cook, more often than not with disastrous results but occasionally producing a diamond among the desolation. Julius was by no means happy to see much of his fish reduced to cinders when they could have been perfectly fine pets within the fish tank he installed into the library's main hall, but the single docile Grau that had made its home there as of Mahro's arrival managed to force a smile out of the still mostly mute Altair with its curious motions and snarling.

For as little joy as it was, I was proud that anything good had happened to him at all – between his astonishing loss of appetite and tendency to stare into nothing, among other despondent behaviours following our mother's death, any small facet of positivity re-entering his life was a milestone worthy of celebration. On the contrary, I could not yet find joy in my new appendages – I was slowly growing accustomed to how they intruded on my sense of touch, but I couldn't see them physically as anything other than a harsh metal stain on my hand.

Three weeks after the dreadful assault, the graveyard containing my mother, Mr. Pyre and every other victim of the Band of the Wyvern's attack was officially complete, and so we all went to pay our respects, save for Altair, who was physically repulsed by the idea of viewing our mother's grave. While I had slowly come to accept Kyrie and Julius as my guardians, my heart still ached with sadness as I read out the words "Stephanie Vadere" in my head, still in abject shock that these words were inscribed onto a tombstone.

It stood to me as a representation of all of the years of experiences and love we should have shared, that were instead cruelly ripped away. Regardless, I believed I had come to terms with her passing and offered one final goodbye, hoping she was watching me from the heavens above and able to receive it.

In the weeks following that, I joined Julius and Ringo on a few of their expeditions, and whilst Ringo looked awfully tired from running around town, lending his hand to anybody who sought it for weeks on end, the fires of Ford could never burn away his passionate grin.

It was while we were out on one of these trips - a week after Julius at last received a reply from Mahro confirming that he would indeed be coming to our village - that we had a curious, if not all that remarkable encounter along the riverbank. As Ringo and Julius took on their usual conversations, "Kyrie" this, "old man" that, and as I watched the leaves of the trees turn from vibrant green to a deathly brown, I began to doze off and look to my left... only to come face to face with a young girl holding a white rock up to my face with both of her hands cupped as though she were making an offering, sending me wide awake as I tumbled from my chair in shock.

As I looked up once again, the girl bent down towards me, persisting in her offer, but I was more intrigued by the young lady herself; she can't have been any more than five years of age, and the dark tone of her skin solidly surpassed Ringo's complexion - yet it was entirely natural, providing a powerful contrast with her unkempt but unrestrained silver hair that flowed delicately against the building winds. Whilst her red dress was tattered but otherwise spotless, her black shoes and socks were stained with dirt, much of it dry and seeming at least a few days old. Her emerald eyes locked with my own in earnest, and not once did she blink as we stared each other down until yet another, much more imposing figure walked behind her.

The man standing behind her bore a similar skin complexion but had nowhere near the friendly outward demeanour of the little girl in front of me; his body was adorned in a black robe covered with blood red patterns resembling veins, tied together with a white sash around the circumference of his waist. His head remained upright as his eyes bore down on the two of us, revealing a pair of crystal blue eyes beneath his narrowly open eyelids. The most outlandish part of him, however, was what I noticed last: On his back rested a *colossal* thin sword with a black hilt (in an outlandish contrast to the pink heart-shaped ornament tied to its peak), while the blade remained concealed within a same-coloured sheath, and the weapon reached about two thirds as high as this man who towered even above Ringo.

"Ya have some business, stranger, or are ya just here to scare the skin off 'a little boys?" Ringo asked as he effortlessly tore a flailing Nene away from its habitat.

"I have done nothing and shall do nothing to earn your ire. I was told I can find one Ringo Marshall sitting along the edge of this river, plucking nature's treasures from the veins of this world." the stranger said, glaring down at the diminutive old man.

"We've had enough trouble with strangers as of late, so forgive me if we're not takin' the presence of a Pegasus man all too warmly, especially with a thing like *that* on yer back!"

Ringo was understandably aggressive, and the manner in which he tossed his prize into the cooler reflected so.

But the old man was quickly put on the defensive once the sword-bearing stranger clutched the hilt of his blade, though not to cleave poor old Ringo in two, much to my relief. Instead, he drew the hilt far forward enough to present a small pink ornament affixed to its end by a string, and the stranger sighed lamentably.

"Whatever trouble it may bring I shall embrace, for I would sooner separate myself from this world itself than from this sword. It's... a memento."

"Well then, it's no use standing around lookin' at girly charms if yer've bona fide business ter discuss. Take a seat, Mr...?"

"I see no need for formalities. Call me Damian. I should warn you, I'm no storyteller, but I hope to regale my situation with due respect for your time, Mr. Marshall."

Over the next half an hour or so, this Damian fellow took my seat, introducing the young girl as his daughter, Amara. She pulled me towards the rocky patch of the riverbed, and we passed the time by stacking stones until they collapsed; bleak entertainment, but entertainment nonetheless.

Though Amara uttered not a single word during that time, she at least responded positively to being called by her name – I repeated it more than a few times, if only to see *somebody* smile again in the once merry village of Ford. As for their purpose in speaking to Ringo, their journey was an interesting one.

Well before I was born, the Pegasus Isles, a collection of twelve islands far to the northwest of Vana, were rocked by seemingly perpetual political turmoil; some decades prior, during Tenryuu's attempted conquest of Morosus, a particularly violent storm sent one of their military vessels careening into the island they would soon name Akaga, though the natives of the Isles, Damian being among their descendants, insisted on using its original name – Kara-Mea. During their ship repairs, a group of intrepid soldiers wandered around the island, eventually finding themselves within a system of caves. And within these caves? Tenkite. Many, many rich veins of Tenkite, the bread and butter of Tenryuu's military dominance.

Their reaction was immediate and predictable – the ship soon left, and returned as one among many carrying a legion. Not of soldiers, but of slaves taken in combat with Morosus and Vana, as well as their drivers. A small society formed close to their landing area, blissfully ignorant of the natives living within the forests of Kara-Mea. But this ignorance lastly very shortly once Tenryuu started claiming its bounty; the natives were discovered, and their demands to leave the island were met with force. The fighting was fierce and constant, but the natives of Kara-Mea stood no chance once Tenryuu's warships arrived, a small military force trained on tales of savage natives throwing bricks through their windows in tow.

Within the next few years, Tenryuu would force their way through each island in their path, eventually claiming five of the twelve as their own. But beyond the Pegasus Isles, Tenryuu's conquest was falling apart as quickly as it had started up – with the seemingly miraculous discovery of Tenkite within Morosus and

Vana, those that had played the underdog in this global brawl were swiftly able to turn the tables, at last matching their cockily undermanned assailants in technology. As Ringo put it, *the dragon shaggers fled wit' their tails 'tween their legs!*

But that left Tenryuu with a large problem: what in the world were they to do with the Pegasus Isles? Terms of ceasefire were already being drafted before the men stationed within the isles learned much at all about the ongoings of the outside world, and the news were met with panic; the soldiers and slave drivers rushed to their vessels and scurried away, leaving their former slaves behind, directionless but unchained. An agreement eventually formed between the two sides residing within the isles: they could co-exist, out of necessity more than friendship. Though actors on both sides of the veil were less than happy.

The veneer of peace lasted a few decades, up until Damian's early childhood. Each society progressed in parallel, begrudgingly drawing advancement and inspiration from one another. The former slave colonies learned to live without perpetually checking over their shoulders for Tenryuu's return, and the natives were on the brink of forgiving their "guests", despite their lack of culpability. But one notable incident set the powder keg alight: the violent and forever unsolved death of a young native girl, her body having been found bound and rotting in the forests of Kara-Mea. Blame was thrown around by and towards men of both factions, and it took less than a month and the loss of one life for decades of begrudging peace to escalate into the Pegasus Secession War; the natives wanted the intruders gone, and the intruders sought to finish the job their drivers had started.

Damian was an active soldier in the Pegasus Secession War, fighting on the side of his own people. Prior to his service, he had been romantically involved with a young woman by the name of Reveka, who was born of a native woman named Shurava and an unknown man of Vana heritage. After many years of fighting and bloodshed, it all proved fruitless; tiring of the perpetual stalemate each side found themselves in, a ceasefire was at last reached, with even the most virulent and militant amongst both sides tiring of the needless warfare.

After months of negotiation, eight of the twelve islands that composed the Pegasus Isles branched off into the Kurro Dominion, Damian's home of Rhoda - the largest of the islands - being among them. The remaining islands were incorporated into the Minas Union, and an uneasy period of healing ensued for both sides. Damian returned home after three years of fighting, unsatisfied that his fighting had amounted to very little but ready to embrace Reveka with open arms once more, only to discover that she had long vanished, leaving behind a daughter he never knew about in the care of Damian's father.

After a hasty investigation, Damian determined that her disappearance coincided with the departure of another individual by the name of Tadeas who was spoken of with great contempt, apparently having been a thorn in Damian's side well before he departed for war. This individual had made his way to Morosus, and thus utterly devoid of any other lead, Damian pursued him with Amara in tow. Ringo derided his choice to bring his daughter along on such a pursuit, but Damian remained adamant that Amara would stay well out of harm's way, even if this prolonged his quest by an incalculable length of time.

As his story developed, I couldn't help but be fascinated and slowly draw more of my attention towards his retelling; events of such a grand scale sounded straight out of a story book, but I was hearing all of this from a man who was there to witness it firsthand. It opened my eyes to the fact that even beyond Ford, there was a whole wide world operating on its own whims, independent of whatever may have been happening in Ford... and thus, the chilling realisation that despite the tragedies we had endured, there was an entire world beyond our village that did nothing to help us. Amara's infectious joy as she treaded the exotic riverbed was what ultimately salvaged my mood at that moment.

His story complete, Damian posed his request, "Now, good sir, have any individuals by the name of Tadeas or Reveka come to your attention? I have it on good authority that their journey across the seas ended not too far from the little village of Ford."

Unfortunately, Ringo, despite his comprehensive knowledge of Ford's inhabitants, was entirely unaware of any individuals by the names of Tadeas or Reveka, living or deceased. Regardless, he offered to pull a few strings and arrange for Damian and Amara to travel to Titan, Morosus' enormous capital, but Damian politely refused, insisting that he knew the lay of the land well enough. And with Ringo's offer rejected, Damian took his leave, bringing Amara into his arms as our very last stone tower crumbled.

"Farewell, young man. I am disheartened to see such promising young men suffer so greatly, but you will be stronger for it. Nothing hardens the heart quite like tragedy."

With his last words spoken, Damian at last walked out of Ford forevermore, cradling Amara in his arms as his words left me awfully confused. Either way, I was more dismayed by the loss of a playmate, especially one I had no confidence I would ever see the cute smile of again.

And we would indeed prove to never meet again; their slow stroll across the bridge above us was the last we would ever see of this imposing warrior and his daughter. I can only hope he got the answers he so desperately sought, if he isn't still hopelessly pursuing them, that is.

Indeed, on the same day as our encounter with Damian, yet another foreign presence welcomed himself into our lives, and this one would prove to be far more long-standing, not just in my life but Altair's too.

As the sky was no less than an hour away from turning red at last, I was sat in the library with Julius and Altair. In my hands lay the Book of Blossoms I had caught Mr. Pyre reading so long ago - it was a fairly schlocky romance novel all things considered, and I dropped it once the main character's girlfriend... became a tree? The exact details elude me, but I found it stupid even at seven years of age.

Altair, as reclusive as ever, was trying in earnest to read through a book on geography, but his attention was constantly drawn away by minor sounds, such as birds chirping or footsteps outside the front door.

Julius was reading something in his lap, no doubt something strange or erotic – I happened upon one of his preferred texts some years later and... I still don't quite know how to describe just what was emblazoned on my sorry eyes. I'm grateful that he was at least shielding our innocent eyes from it, but I feel as though there were better times and places for it...

Otherwise, all seemed perfectly normal until an ever so faint stench of sweat filled the air. I wrote it off, thinking it to be a result of the heat causing one of my companions to sweat a great deal more than me...

Then a voice began reading a line in my book from behind me.

"Thus, oh so *profuse* is my *adoration*, my dearest, for I would part the *seas* and rend the *heavens* if it would unite us for *one moment more!*"

Assuming the voice to be Julius, I looked up to... see him remaining yet in his seat but looking in my direction.

Huh?

Then who could this voice have been?

With a tingling sensation of dread, I slowly turned around... to meet a black-haired, hazel-eyed man hanging upside down. He was suspended in the air by a chandelier, and his coat drooped all the way to the floor.

I was beyond speechless, and before I could scream out in shock or assess what wild animal had wandered into the library, he rocked the chandelier forth with incredible speed and launched himself into the air, performing all manner of flips and spins and rotations before landing perfectly at the centre of the table on both legs, facing me with crossed arms and a smug grin.

"Evening, buddy. Name's Mahro, meased to pleat you. Mind if I join in on book club?"

He didn't bother to wait for an answer before he dropped down to one hand and launched his foot into a plain white book next to Julius, bringing his wild spinning to a stop atop his elbow just in time to catch the book as it ricocheted off of a shelf and landed in his hand, to which he mumbled something which seemed to embarrass Julius an awful lot.

Mahro was dressed in a manner that seemed counter-intuitive to his schizophrenic manoeuvres, adorning himself in a long grey coat that covered his spine, shoulders and the sides of his sleeves in emerald-coloured zigzag motifs. His trousers were a firm black, held in place by a white belt that was then overlapped by a crimson belt (the utility of having two belts has still never been explained to me). His chest was covered by a flimsy looking dark green vest that emphasised his impressive musculature, while a bandolier containing short knives and several small containers was stretched across his centre mass.

Julius awkwardly chuckled to himself while Altair and I could only sit there in complete bewilderment, wondering what black magic he had performed to enter the library completely unnoticed – the front doors were as loud as an entire flock of birds suddenly taking flight on both its opening and its closing.

As he jumped up to his feet, remaining on the table yet, this line of questioning was brought to a halt by a thick book titled 'How to Make Friends and Win Hearts' flying straight at the back of Mahro's head, only for him to spin around in an instant and deliver a powerful jumping kick. The optimistic tome crashed through the boarded-up window in the same manner a bullet would chew through paper. The perpetrator of the textual assault turned out to be Kyrie, who had positioned herself atop the rightmost table, also without making a sound.

"Hey Strawberry Sunshine, how's it going?" Mahro asked.

'Eyes That Never Open' was launched at him next, which he deflected back towards the shelves with a thunderous slap to its front cover. The violent winds released by his slap almost knocked me backwards entirely.

"The taste of that little thing is still ripe, you know? Its fleshy interior, those... seed... things..."

Soon came 'Awe-Inspiring Agriculture', which was answered with an astonishing aerial axe kick that 'gently' relocated it to the table on which Mahro stood.

"I know you're Queen of the Strawberries, but such sourness is ill fitting of you, Kyrie. Let's catch up a little, it's been fifteen years!"

Kyrie's finale came in the form of not one, not even two, but *three* books all being consecutively launched at Mahro. This wild man was not even slightly deterred by the rapid fire; before I even had a chance to read the books' titles, he launched himself into the air, violently rocking the table we were sat upon, and ran through the air using the books as stepping stones until he landed with a somersault behind Kyrie. By the time each of the three books landed in front of Julius in a perfect stack, Mahro had already grabbed Kyrie by the leg and was suspending her upside down above the edge of the table, nonchalantly whistling in a fast pace as she thrashed around violently, before going limp in resignation once her beloved hat fell beneath the table.

"Attagirl! Your violence cannot deter the greatest weapon of them all: stronger violence!"

From the moment we met, he was already a dispensary of... *unique* life lessons.

Mahro lowered Kyrie slowly, only releasing his grip once her head reached the ground; her prolonged moan was an immediate and undeniable admittance of defeat.

"You really haven't changed a bit, have you?" Julius asked.

"To change is to conform to destiny, my good friend. And if you ask me, destiny can do one!"

His grand antagonism towards the idea of destiny itself sounded ridiculous given his jovial tone – I suppose it would have sounded weightier if it came from a bitter madman dressed in all black and wielding a sword taller than Mahro himself.

Nevertheless, his hawkish eyes were next drawn to me as he leapt onto our table yet again, this time landing with a squat no less than half a metre away from my face.

"Can I get a name from you, my friend?"

Mahro extended his hand towards me, and I provided my name as our hands joined and he shook it with dominating force.

"Vega, eh? So the other one must be... ah, what was it... Pithopopholes?"

Mahro turned to face Altair, likely expecting an angered outburst. Instead, Altair merely offered an unamused stare before retreating back into his book.

"Pithopopholingles it is!"

"Oy, Mahro, how's the family?" Julius asked.

Mahro delicately extracted a photograph from an inside pocket of his coat and showed it to Julius, who clearly didn't regret his request.

"I can see why you're so proud!"

The photograph was then shown to Kyrie (who couldn't hide her admiration even while maintaining her flimsy veneer of vengeance), then an indifferent Altair, and last of all to me.

Against a barren green backdrop, I could see a rather short but voluptuous woman dressed in white and proudly displaying her medium-length blood red hair. Her arms were wrapped around their daughters, both of whom shared her hair colour and fashion sense. The eldest of the two was beaming with confidence and crossing her arms, while her sister looked terrified by the prospect of existing within any photograph at all but still gave a forced smile her all, albeit with her eyes closed. I didn't say anything in response, but I could see why he was so proud; I found all three of them adorable, and despite taking greatly after their mother, his daughters absolutely inherited his eyes. *I hope one day I'll marry somebody as beautiful,* I thought as he returned the photograph to his pocket.

"I'll be checking back on them every year or so while Jules and I sift through the peculiarities of this cataclysm you lot were handed on a plate, but I insisted on having something to look at whenever I get lonely; it beats crying myself to sleep!" said the most masculine man in the room.

From this point on, Mahro too would take up residence within the library, though the lack of any spare bedrooms forced him to make a bed out of the library's left-most table. This proved to be a bewildering sight when I woke up early the next morning, perturbed by Altair's mumbling as he slept. By the time the library was opened to the five other people in all of Ford who actually set foot within it, his bungled bed dressings had been unceremoniously shoved into a cupboard along with the rest of his possessions – all of which were contained within a large bag roughly half his height.

As my watch struck half past nine in the morning, me, Altair and Julius met him once more behind the library. Resting against the black wall of the library was a series of wooden weapons: a staff roughly my height, a one-sided hand axe and a flail.

The most curious part of this whole scene, however, was Mahro himself; he was wearing a pair of goofy, translucent glasses each bearing a black spiral, complimented by an absurdly sized pair of buck teeth protruding from his mouth. He was drawing doodles along the edge of a blackboard using white chalk, and the extravagant 'How To We ꝑ apon 101' written upon it as well as the sheer quantity of silly depictions of the library's residents suggested he had been at it for some time. I didn't take too kindly to being drawn with jagged teeth like some sort of wild animal, but I was spared the horrible depiction reserved for Altair; Mahro's depiction of his face landed somewhere between a capybara and a hamster.

"Morning, morning, everywah! ...everywah! Every- damn it!" Mahro's attempt at an introduction ended with him tearing the fake teeth out and launching them into the forest behind our library, never to be seen again... thank goodness.

"Good morning! Apologies for the technical difficulties, but the turbulence is long distant now, my compatriots!"

Julius sat down on the chair he used for our fishing expeditions against the library wall, grinning in excitement over what was to come – up until then, he had only ever smiled in such glee whenever Kyrie went off on one of her stranger tangents. The writing was on the wall.

"It's my understanding that I'm here not just for business; Julius here wants me to show you weaklings how to hold your own in a scrap, and I think that's an awfully valuable lesson to teach. I'm honoured to be given the responsibility."

Mahro followed up the introduction with a mocking curtsy towards the two of us, which I obviously found more amusing than Altair.

"That being said, I've no experience teaching children other than my own daughter – and she staked her claim on crossbows from the instant she met eyes with one. Ah, she really is her father's daughter. I wonder if she's still bawling her eyes out; in retrospect, a month to us old guys is like a year to you young'uns, but Daddy's going to visit before she kno-"

"Get on with it! What do you want us to do, already?!"
Altair screamed with the greatest volume we had ever gotten out of him since the Band of the Wyvern's attack, but Mahro appeared more impressed than annoyed by the audacity of my brother.

"Ah, have we our first challenger after all? Your vigour impresses me! Pick your weapon, Ponpokopi, and let us see where you stand in the tournament of champions!"

As Mahro struck a dramatic pose, taunting Altair to come closer, my brother grabbed the wooden axe in a huff and rushed towards our teacher. Altair was preparing his first swing with such intensity that I could hardly look, terrified that we would end up with yet another body to haul to the graveyard. I watched with one eye between my fingers as the axe launched straight down towards Mahro's upper chest... only for him to casually sidestep and whistle with his hands behind his back as Altair pathetically flung himself onto the grass. Julius could barely contain his humoured snort.

My brother was determined yet; he painstakingly brought himself back to his feet, glaring at Mahro with bloodlust in his eyes as he grasped his axe with both hands. He rushed forward once more, aiming for a horizontal strike this time, and all of his power was channelled into this definitive, killing blow. But yet again he whiffed as Mahro casually dropped onto his elbow with an amused grin, and this time the wooden axe went flying from Altair's grasp, crashing into the library's wall right above Julius' head and shattering into pieces.

"Well, it's certainly one of your lessons, Master Katsuragi." Julius said dryly as he brushed the flakes of wood from his hair.

"Why thank you, disciplined student, for the reminder!" Mahro answered with surprise as he brought Altair to his feet once again, "Vega, Ponpokona, I would appreciate being referred to as 'Master Katsuragi' from this point on – Katsuragi's my family name, for future reference. Are these terms agreeable, or is another round of whooping Pippalopadopolous in order?"

"I get it, Master... King... Rag!"

Altair stormed off in annoyance, taking a seat next to Julius now that his weapon of choice was in more pieces than Ford had ever had inhabitants – Julius offered a few whispers of reassurance as his hands combed through Altair's hair, calming down my brother somewhat.

I could read the room... well, field perfectly well: it was my turn to take on Master King Rag. Therefore, I went for the only remaining weapon that made sense to me: the staff.

It was no spear, given that both of its ends were entirely blunt, but it was a decent stand-in for the only weapon I had any experience wielding. I adopted an identical stance to my first experience, with my left hand firmly grasping centre mass as my right hand trailed behind, and I rushed towards our mentor, aiming for his stomach. Much like my brother's initial attack, it was intercepted by a nonchalant sidestep, and he mockingly shrugged once I turned around for another attempt. The second rush connected with Mahro's palm, and I at first assumed it to be my victory until I continued running forward, and the end of the staff facing me crashed into my own abdomen.

I dropped the weapon as I keeled over in a fit of coughing, which is when Mahro walked over and knelt in front of me to offer his input.

"Julius told me about what happened to you in the Basin, and I'll be the first to tell you that any experience is valuable experience."

Mahro buried the end of the staff into the ground before he delved into the meat of his lesson, staring me down still behind those ridiculous glasses.

"But what you're doing is treating a bomb like a book; their only similarity is the letter they start with. A spear strikes with one point, delivering decisive attacks on those caught lethargic or unaware. But in an open confrontation such as this, your opponent is neither lethargic nor unaware, according to a very reliable and handsome source - me! Think outside the box a little more, Vega; with no defined point of strike, what you're instead left with is endless possibilities!"

Endless possibilities… the term sounded awfully dramatic for a wooden stick, but I understood the gist of what he meant; when there was no definitive method of attack, there was no wrong way to use it. As I stood up once more, I pulled the stick from the ground, slightly exhausted but with the staff in my hands once more, wielded closer to a sword this time and with my right hand now positioned above my left, provoking an unsure look from Mahro.

Before he could raise any questions, my attack began anew, this time consisting of a series of slow but long-reaching horizontal swings. Mahro was able to outpace it by walking backwards, but he looked impressed nonetheless.

"Combat prowess is intertwined with adaptation and mixing up one's attacks, but the bare essentials are not to be neglected either! Keep it up!"

He ducked and weaved around my attacks, and these evasive manoeuvres continued for at least ten seconds until he raised a palm in the weapon's path, knocking it out of my hands.

It was as he took a moment to gloat with his hands raised in the air that I grasped the weapon with only my left hand and swung in a clockwise motion towards him; he barely quit his gloating and looked back at me in time to dodge once again in awe, and the staff shattered the garish plastic glasses to pieces as it crashed into its rim.

Julius and Altair stood up in surprise and my brother cheered on my victory over the evil Master King Rag. I imitated our Master's smug gesture, gloating and soaking in the praise until the Master himself grabbed me by my leg from behind, suspending me precariously in the air as he had done to Kyrie – in an instant, an immense sensation of doom gripped my entire body.

Once he shook the staff out of my grip, he launched himself off of the ground and with an incredible barrel roll of his own he sent me flying through the air, rotating with unbelievable rapidity. Every full rotation of my body through the fall breeze knocked more and more wind out of me, and I was almost too scared to breathe lest my lungs take in too much and burst.

Right as the dread of crashing into the floor and rolling into an even worse fate set in, Mahro caught me perfectly by my collar and set me down on my feet once more, though I was barely still able to stand after the ordeal. The entire world was a blurry mess for a good ten seconds after, and once I at last looked up at Master Katsuragi, he had raised the staff well above his head.

Before I could process what was happening, his chanting began.

"*Part* the seas! *Rend* the heavens!
"Through matter thin and matter thick!
"By blunt brutality or sword's prick!
"Deliver this *demon* to the *pits of oblivion!*"

Completely shit scared he was going to cave a chunk of my brain in out of retribution, I cowered as the staff began to lower, until it at last crashed into my cranium.. with a thud I could barely register.

"Consider this your victory, my esteemed student: there are men three times your age who haven't so much as singed a hair on my head!" he declared as he threw the staff to the ground, snapping his fingers as they transitioned into a confident thumbs up.

I couldn't help but wonder what he was thinking; he had definitely done worse to me than I could ever have dreamt of inflicting upon him, as my lungs would have readily testified. And yet, he looked down at me with intense pride for so much as grazing an article of his clothing; a man who had only met me just days prior exuded an air of fatherly pride, in much the same way Julius did. Beneath his sheer strangeness, I found him remarkably approachable; to this day, I feel that there was no better teacher for my brother and I in all of the world. Perhaps our strange lives demanded a stranger teacher yet. And thus, through our first lesson, the initial link in a long-standing bond had been spectacularly forged.

Chapter 7:
Primordial Fancy

Our first few months learning under Mahro passed quickly, and a lot happened in that considerably short span of time, most prominently among them Mrs. Pyre's brief return at the beginning of October; she was horrified to learn of her husband's death as well as the desolation that had descended upon Ford as a whole but was not at all displeased by the fact that me and my brother had now taken up residence in her home. Ringo took some time out of his busy schedule to renovate our new home, allowing it to accommodate all five permanent residents – Mahro was unfortunately left with a table on which to rest his weary bones, but the window repairs meant that the chilly autumn draft could no longer harass him throughout the night. He even took a... liking to it, I dare say.

Speaking of Mahro, in between our lessons, he spent an awful lot of time behind closed doors with Julius; the specifics of their work remained a mystery to me until my teens, but I was at least aware that they were in active pursuit of any further sightings or experiences with Screaming Roses.

Kyrie was usually left to look after the two of us on her own whenever Julius and Mahro were hard at work, and she better adapted to her duties as a guardian now that Mrs. Pyre had shown up to provide some wisdom. Mrs. Pyre proved to be the substantially better cook during her short-lived visit, and every male in the household silently clamoured for it forevermore once she at last returned to military service.

But the most astonishing movement of all came from Altair; he was still somewhat quiet and prone to shut himself within his own world, but he eagerly awaited every lesson with Mahro – my older brother finally had a bit of drive and vigour in him after enduring so much. Not to suggest that I myself was idle; a new breed of competitive spirit festered between the two of us, which the slowly decaying village of Ford increasingly failed to provide.

But fate took a strange turn around that time, beginning with an unexpected proposition one otherwise unremarkable morning. Kyrie and Julius' wedding had been set for December 18th, exactly two weeks after this point, but Kyrie suddenly came to a realization as the five of us (herself, Julius, Mahro, Altair and me) settled down for breakfast.

"Julius! Have our cherished young boys' suits been arranged yet?!" she asked as she all but leapt from her seat.

As shocked by the revelation as the rest of us were, Julius almost choked on his toast, though h was fortunately still entrenched enough within the realm of the living to answer once he finally swallowed it.

"Uh... I'm afraid not. I went to ask the old boy next to Saki's place yesterday, but it turns out he buggered off to some other village for a month, something about 'family affairs'"

"And you only found it pertinent to inform me of this development *now*?! Are we to fabricate such apparel from the blankness of space itself?!"

"We're not quite doomed yet, Strawberry Sunshine." Julius answered, "Mot is just half a day's walk away, and an old friend of Dad runs a clothier there. According to the old man himself she's practically tireless in her craft and hasn't left that building unopened for decades; we can have this whole matter resolved by next week."

"Are there no other means than walking? This is a matter of great urgency, my dearest! Why not buy... an automobile?!"

"Well, unless you want to divert every Sera we have left into obtaining a mode of transport we'll use approximately once per year, and set aside yet more funds for maintenance, new parts, Tenkite fuel and of course security so as to not let some lowlife piss away all of our hard-earned money... I think walking is all we have."

By the time Julius was half done, Kyrie had already slunk into her chair, utterly defeated.

"But what about our darling boys? Do they not need to be measured to determine the best fit for their attire?"

"Who said we'll leave them behind?!"

All of our eyes turned to Mahro, whose feet had planted themselves on the table and whose owner looked incredibly proud of himself.

"Julius, you know the drill: let's get these boys some experience in the field!"

"Wait, you mean leaving Ford?!" Altair asked excitedly.

Kyrie appeared primed and ready to leap across the table and strangle our boisterous mentor to death when the door suddenly opened, and in walked none other than Saki herself, wearing a white coat with a fur hood over her uniform.

After a shiver and a deep breath, Saki produced a key from her pocket and tossed it to Julius.

"Your father told me I could find you here, not that I should have expected anything else, you busy little bee. If I may be so audacious, what exactly are you discu-?"

Saki was stopped dead in her tracks by her first sight of Mahro, who was now dancing daintily atop the table to taunt our adoptive mother.

"Greetings, the name's Mahro Katsuragi! I take it you're my student's diligent boss, then! Considering what a quality man he's made of himself, I ought to thank you for taking up the reins in my stead! Perhaps the lads and lasses of Tenryuu are natural born mentors, eh?"

"I'm... flattered?" Saki meekly answered as the two clasped their hands and bowed to each other.

Mahro later elaborated that this type of greeting was largely exclusive to his home country, but at that present moment, he was preoccupied with showing off his family photo to his new friend.

"Morning, Captain. Mahro was suggesting we bring the boys on a field trip to Mot to procure their suits for the wedding, but... I'm not sure I can make time for that; our wedding is just two weeks distant, and I've procrastinated on the matter more than I care to admit."

Saki looked up from Mahro's family picture in his hand as Julius finished speaking, upon which a light bulb went off in her head.

"Why not send me in your place? I trust that you are more than able to look after my clinic on your own for a few days, whilst your betrothed will be no more than a few minutes away."

"You just fancy yourself an adventure, don't you, Captain?"

"True, I'm not *that* selfless; even I can find that place stuffy on occasion and spreading my wings for once sounds fun! That, and I believe I can lend my own aid as a teacher, given my profession of seven years."

When the opportunity of adventure presented itself, Saki was... bizarrely proud and boisterous. For a moment, I pondered if it was instead her twin sister who had entered the library.

"Then it's settled!"

Mahro excitedly launched his chair towards the roof with the back of his foot, holding his tongue until one of its legs landed on his pinkie with impeccable precision.

"I take it nobody here objects?"

For a while, nobody said a word; I had my own reservations about ever setting foot outside of the village, since we had already seen enough destruction within Ford itself. Our mother's death was still fresh in all of our minds, most of all Altair's. It was up to me to break the silence.

"Will we be in any danger?"

"*Hah!* Danger?! The wildlife and shrubbery between here and Mot are as threatening as... as a fluffy little dog, Vega! A puppy's bark would wound you more than anything prowling between here and there! Besides, you'll have the greatest guardian in the universe watching your every motion! What's there to fear, my friend?"

"Well, we've got you too, Mr. Katsuragi! You'll make a worthy sidekick!"

"Thank you, Nur-"

Mahro's face stiffened as the real meaning of Saki's words dawned on him.

"Lesson fifteen, boys: a woman's tongue is far more vicious than any dog's bite! Should trouble assail you, let her shout them to

114

death! With this ultimate technique, your safety is all but guaranteed!"

I live with Kyrie, I'm more than aware, Master King Rag, I oh-so-desperately wish I had answered.

And so, it had been settled: the four of us were to depart for Mot the very next morning.

The following morning, just as the sun was finally rising from its slumber, our party departed from the gates of Ford and was quick to detour from the stone path leading into our village. We had spent the last hour trudging through a mostly uphill forest path stuffed to the brim with dead trees, and the entire forest was coated in a layer of snow from the night before which reached up to my ankles at its worst, while the air clawed away at our faces with its bitter frost; whatever god of nature was looking over us at that time had a sick sense of humour.

Fortunately, most of us were dressed appropriately for such terrain, as Saki wore her white coat from the previous day on top of a red sweater and dark blue hiking trousers, whilst me and my brother wore matching costumes consisting of a thin but densely layered coat with white neck warmers, as well as black wool hats and legwear.

The only real way to differentiate us aside from our height was through our gloves; while the nurse in our company was going without, she provided the two of us with pairs of our own – blue for me, and green for my brother. What brought me comfort was not their shielding me from the elements, rather their obscuring of my hands; whatever small discomfort the gloves brought to my artificial fingers was overwritten by finally ridding my eyes of such blights for the time being. If they were not so incompatible with everyday tasks, I may well have never removed them.

Mahro, however, remained in the outfit he was very rarely seen without – if I were not at all concerned about the very awkward conversation that would be sure to follow afterwards, I may well have checked on him while bathing just to be sure his coat didn't follow him into the bathtub.

"We're nearing a cliff's edge! Hope it still looks how I remember it... well, all this snow's in the way, but I assume you've the wit to understand what I mean, my friends!"

"More wit than you, old man!" Altair shouted back, grinning like an idiot.

"*Hahahah!* My wit is not yet in the negatives, Panpokolondous! I'm afraid you're on your lonesome there!"

Altair was no longer grinning like an idiot, though I most certainly took up the mantle at his expense.

Anyhow, despite hauling along a large bag full to bursting with the utterly unknown, Mahro was keeping up far better than the rest of us, and even Saki's breathing was starting to strain. Sure enough, no more than a minute had passed before Saki paused a few metres behind Mahro, who my brother and I stood next to as we at last got a full view of the world beyond our village.

Around three miles in front of us, Mot's iconic and forever vibrant Skyspur – a thick tree boasting a height well exceeding any that most had ever seen in their lives, and home to Mot's entire commercial district - towered above the withering trees that surrounded the town. The snow that had become an all too familiar sight mounted in intensity the higher one laid their gaze upon the Skyspur, though the town beneath it was by no means untouched.

But the path from there to Mot was itself daunting; we stood atop a vast valley largely devoid of trees beyond a thick path running between each of the valley's ends about a mile ahead – itself marking the end of the two steep walls closing off the valley's edges - within which small animals could be seen darting around. Beyond that turbulent milestone rested the valley's most defining landmark: a giant rock pile free of snow, its peak reaching half as high as the elevation between our current position and the valley's surface.

Truth be told, it was such an overwhelming sight that my knees began to tremble; I had never seen the world beyond Ford, and I was stunned to see the magnitude to which Mot utterly dwarfed my home. For the first time, I felt... *small.* Neither weak nor insignificant, but at last truly cognizant that my home and by extension the people in it were just one small factor in a grand, amazing existence beyond my imagination. For the first time in my life, curiosity towards the world outside of Ford jolted through me.

"Ah, nature's treated Old Man Amos' place with the same non-existent grace as it did those nine years distant. As the river of time flows forevermore, Morosus remains... locked in the past."

Mahro's observation was met by bewildered looks from all three of us, but before any of us could ask what in the world he was rambling about, he had already taken off like a giddy child, leaving us to sluggishly follow him through the dense snow. It was as we passed the downward path leading into the valley that he at last returned, holding a large wooden panel beneath each arm – they had been torn from a building that had accumulated years, if not decades of disrepair, and housed much more cobwebs than comfort.

How he carried them back with such swiftness while also hauling that heavy bag was beyo- actually, no, this was Mahro; the man could run across water whilst cradling the moon in his arms.

"Saki, you take the littlest one. Paipopaipopaipo, with me!"

With militaristic efficiency, we assumed said positions atop the panels. Upon Mahro's whistle, he *instantly* soared down the snow-covered path with Altair screaming in excitement the entire way, whereas Saki - after a brief pause of bewilderment – followed suit with significantly more restraint. This proved to be one of the few instances where perhaps I preferred some measure of distance from my outlandish mentor; the bitter wind was battering my face even at this subdued speed and I spent the entire ordeal in a state of rapid blinking, but Altair no doubt had it exponentially worse, as the sea of snow flying in their wake all but obscured the pair of them. The warmth of Saki's body provided the only relief from our own furious barrage - I believe it's worth pointing out that she felt noticeably warmer than Kyrie, and her heartbeat was far higher even while idle; I asked once if it was related to her strange eyes, a query which she neither confirmed nor denied. As we slid to a halt at the base of the slope, we found great amusement in the sight of Mahro half-buried beneath a snowy mound that Altair was lying face down next to, both of them groaning and mumbling under their breaths.

After our little escapade, the four of us were trekking through the valley at last. As the sun towered over our heads, Altair raised a very pertinent question.

"Did you bring any food? I'm hungry!"

Mahro looked behind at my brother, intensely staring him down, until he broke into an uproarious laugh.

"*Bring* any food? Not at all, Pomegranate!"

"*Ehhhhh?!* Then are we going to starve to death?!" Altair cried out, clutching his stomach as though its entire contents were draining through a sieve; I too was shocked by the revelation, and Altair's mention of the subject caused my own stomach to rumble.

"Take a look in those trees, boys; it's within these that our next meal dwells!"

With his next course of action declared, Mahro withdrew a crossbow from his bag, grinning with childlike glee; the rest of us looked to a small patch of trees conjoined to the valley's left wall, seeing within it a herd of brown mammals with thick torsos and thin, uncanny heads bearing black snouts and ears. They didn't seem much like a pleasurable meal at the time, but Mahro's glare of great gluttony assured me that he knew what he was talking about.

"Those Ateria make for fine food, from personal experience. Nurse, would you and Vega kindly set up a camp here whilst I give Pompokolin a lesson on procuring his next meal?"

Saki nervously nodded in agreement, and after collecting a pouch of crossbow bolts from within, he tossed his bag to her, which she just barely managed to keep off of the snowy floor. Altair and Mahro soon rushed off towards the woods, eager to hunt, leaving the two of us to try and construct the camp with no guidance.

Gently placing the bag on the floor, the first item Saki extracted looked like an overly ornamented umbrella; it took a good minute or so of tinkering with this strange item before I twisted its bottom, fearing I had broken it, only for the rest of the foundational rod to extend all the way to the floor. Saki raised it to its peak, where it reached up to her neck, and then buried the base into the soft ground beneath the snow. About five more minutes passed and by this time we had at last opened up the top of the rod, which spread surprisingly wide into the shape of a rounded square, and planted the end of each metal bar extending from its top within the snow. The first of two tents had been laid down and the next followed suit in swifter fashion, adjacent to its predecessor.

"By the heavens, he ought to have at least given us some guidance!"

With a groan, Saki planted her posterior onto the snow - thankfully, Mahro had already procured some firewood and placed it inside his bag before we departed. After a short period of rest, I assisted Saki in taking about half of the firewood from the bag which was sorted into a pile in front of the tents.

"Eh? What's this, a lighter?" she asked as she pulled a small, irregularly shaped blue device from one of the many pockets within the bag, turning it around and inspecting it before raising it to the air for a test.

Upon pulling the trigger, what was unleashed was not fire but *lightning* - it reached as high as the Skyspur itself and the erupting boom could no doubt be heard from both Mot and Ford. Saki was barely able to still stand from the shock while I covered my ears, wondering why in the world Mahro would possess such an object – it was clearly an accident waiting to happen. Fortunately, I held onto my ears long enough for Saki to repeat her action in the direction of the firewood, setting it alight in an instant. Preparations had been arduously completed, and Saki rushed inside the first tent, smiling blissfully as she laid on her back.

"Can I come inside?" I asked, to which she heartily nodded.

I was able to walk around inside it, needing only to lower my head in order to enter the peaceful, cherry red interior, but I sat down in front of Saki in need of rest for my legs. A silence supplemented only by the crackling of the fire and the stench of smoke remained unbroken for a while as our eyes struggled to meet, ending only when Saki asked me a rather sudden question.

"How's your hand, Vega?"

Her question came quite out of nowhere and I shuffled in discomfort, my hand being a subject I wished not to discuss or even dwell on. But in my adventurous mood, I decided to answer bluntly:"It looks horrible and everything I touch feels nasty. I would rather have no hand."

"Aww, really? I tried to make those fingers look as nice as I could!"

It should have been obvious, but learning that she had in fact created them was both surprising and enough to make me feel ashamed about the attitude I had just shown towards them.

"I'm sorry." I said, avoiding her eyes as best I could.

"There's no need for it. I understand how much the memories associated with them must hurt. That being said, have you considered anything I could do to lighten the burden on your mind when the time comes to replace them?"

"Replace them?!" I cried out, "Will you have to rip these off?!"

"You'll be asleep for the procedure, of course, but yes: at your age you're growing at an exceedingly fast rate, and I suspect the need for replacements will arise even within the coming months to match the rest of your hand."

Learning that these were not the last fingers I would have to familiarise myself with was dismaying; I was still troubled by the whole ordeal leading up to and the product of the replacement itself so the thought of an incessant cycle of replacement every few months or so, specifically for the part of my body I despised and wished to be rid of most of all, was by no means pleasant. My silence was all Saki needed to understand my worries, and the subject was dropped there and then. Disliking the sterile silence that followed as a consequence of my own sulking, I decided to pry a little into my nurse's life.

"Do you miss your family?"

"… I… I do, I do." she said with a look of stunned surprise, "I'm sure Koga has grown up to be an upstanding gentleman even without his big sister, though I wish I could be there to watch him. It might sound selfish, and it well and truly is, but I couldn't put up with a place such as that; for everything it's cost me, and for all of the troubles I've ended up in the thick of because of it, I could never give up these precious experiences accrued from living in Ford, or these opportunities to help those in need."

Her smile was betrayed by the hint of sadness in her eyes. I really had no idea what to say to the idea of leaving one's family behind; considering my own mother had passed just months before now, it was hard not to equate a death in the family with fating oneself to never meet them again. But in my case, I had Kyrie and Julius to fall back on in my moment of greatest need; a void my mother's death had left was soon filled, not in her exact shape, but close enough to invoke the same comfort – Saki's family were on the other side of the world, likely to never meet her again, and from what I could tell she had nothing in their place. I couldn't help but feel that somehow, despite the lingering discomfort of my circumstances, she had ended up with a worse deal than me, even if she had faced less in the way of overt tragedy or heartbreak.

But our conversation was brought to a swift end by the very loud arrival of Mahro and Altair, who dumped two freshly made Ateria corpses near our fire; their proud grins quickly wiped the melancholic thoughts from my young mind, and my stomach trembled like the most tempestuous of volcanoes.

"Apologies for the wait, my friends! Let us thank the gods for this feast!"

As the sun continued to descend ever closer to the horizon, Mahro educated the three of us on how to make an animal's raw meat safe for consumption; I found myself rather grossed out by the process of skinning the Ateria at first, but by the time we were undressing the second, I mostly got over my aversion to it. Mahro took responsibility for cutting up the animals with the butcher knife kept in his (seemingly infinite) bag, though we were allowed to watch as he explained the process. Soon enough, the chunks of Ateria had been placed in a makeshift rack above the fire, and we were each taking bits and pieces to consume for ourselves. Altair and Mahro wolfed down their shares with unrivalled gusto, whilst me and Saki took our time in comparison, savouring the well-cooked meat. Following a few games of tag between me and Altair, our party packed up the tents, snuffed out the flame and proceeded with our journey.

Trudging through the snow proved to be as arduous as ever, and by the time we emerged from the other end of the streak of trees running between the ends of the valley, the sky was decorated with streaks of red, stunning me into silence as I gazed upon it in amazement. Seeing it within my own village was one thing; watching the sun close its curtain on our world for that day, as I stood among the vast expanse of nature itself, was immeasurably more exhilarating.

"Let's see how far we can proceed before the stygian grace of darkness eclipses our world once more..."

Mahro dramatically brought his index finger to his forehead as he appeared to be in deep thought – in reality he was goofing around as usual, given that he could find a way to make the reading of a children's book sound grand and imposing.

"H-hello..."

The soft whimper stopped us dead in our tracks before we really got going once more – Mahro deducted that the voice came from behind the giant rock pile, and soon enough, a skinny woman who appeared to be in her early twenties emerged from the left side of it.

She was pale as a ghost, perhaps even moreso than Kyrie, and her long silver hair was entirely dishevelled. She had brought with her nothing beyond a single thin layer of black clothing and clutched her stomach as she winced in pain. Saki rushed over to her and began inspecting her body for any damage, revealing nothing much to the nurse's relief. Despite the lack of physical damage, the woman looked utterly bereft of life and she keeled over into Saki's arms not long after, her ragged breathing remaining her only sign of consciousness.

"We ought to set up at the end of the forest for tonight; she requires our aid, and we'll be in Mot tomorrow regardless."

Mahro's idea remained uncontested, and Saki brought the young woman into her arms as us men got to work setting up camp once more.

By the time the sun had set, the five of us were sat around the newest campfire, feasting on yet more Ateria that Mahro had hastily hunted and prepared. Given the urgency, it didn't taste quite as good as my first experience with it, but our guest treated it as cuisine of the highest order, as if it were the first bite she'd had to eat in a decade. After we brought the food to a swift end, the woman at last spoke up.

"Thank you all... I wasn't sure what... I would do."

She was soft-spoken and reserved, her voice as mesmerising as her hair that glinted like precious jewels beneath the moonlight.

"Not a problem, lass. Is there any chance you could enlighten us on what you were doing in the middle of this valley, dressed like it's the summer solstice?" Mahro asked.

"Ah... I was making my way to Ford when all of a sudden the snow... came upon me, and as you can see, it hasn't turned out well, *hah*."

"At least you're taking it in stride, lass. Could we get a name?"

"My name... what would you want *that* for?"

"I'm no lady, but I wouldn't fancy being called 'lass' from dusk til dawn. Besides, if you're not hasty Peripompalotes over there will make up a name far worse than whatever your parents could conceive!"

"Go to hell, Master King Rag!"

Beneath the resultant giggling from the rest of us, the woman sat there yet, grimacing before she at last gave in.

"Eden. That's my name. I hail from the town of Creviss."

Creviss... to this day I know little about it; all I could tell you is that Creviss is a small town, decently well-off considering its size, and it resides not too far from the coast of Morosus, not unlike Ford. Though it lies at least a good handful of miles away from our humble home, and travelling from one to another at winter's worst was far too taxing a journey for the ill-equipped.

"Well, you're awfully lucky we were around, Eden." Mahro said, "One can never undercalculate the calamities at risk on any day, not even for an act such as walking. Mahro is the magnificent moniker belonging to yours truly, and my invaluable companions are Saki, Vega and Peristopholes."

"It's Altair, Master King Rag!"

"It's practically identical!"

Altair looked all but ready to leap to his feet and clobber Master King Rag (see also: fail miserably and return to his seat with a pout, repeating history once more), but what Eden said next, after she spent a moment too long gazing into Saki's peculiar eyes, would prove instrumental and all too telling.

"Mahro, you say? Why, perhaps the forces of fate are indeed at work; for the past month, I've been making my way to the little village of Ford, and who else untangles me from the final hurdle than the man I've been seeking all this time?"

"*Oy*..." Mahro answered, looking rather grim, "I'll have you know I would sooner perish horribly than plummet to the depths of infidelity!"

With a smile, he produced the photograph that the rest of us were all too familiar with – Eden appeared uniquely disgusted by it, in a way Kyrie couldn't even mimic facetiously.

"You're well aware that wasn't what I meant. I wish to speak with you on another matter: the Roses."

At last, Mahro appeared to be taking the matter somewhat seriously, putting his photo back into his coat.

"If that's the case, we'd be best off speaking about the matter when we're with Julius; I don't fancy having to reiterate any new revelations you may offer forth."

"It's not as though I have any revelations to offer, per se, instead that I'm merely interested in helping you pursue the topic; where I hail from, most who have even heard of such an artifact write it off as a fabrication, a myth invented by madmen who want to wrap the hysteria of the public around their fingers. Then there's me. Maybe I'm the strange one but I can't help being fascinated by the matter." Eden answered.

"Fascinated, eh...?"

That particular choice of word soured Mahro's mood – he had the perception to back up his strength, and it was clear he knew how this conversation was to proceed well before we reached its inevitable conclusion.

"I suppose it is fascinating, though not in any good way..."

Mahro's unenthusiastic opinion on the matter seemed to set Eden off – buried beneath her graceful voice from then on was a sprouting seed of contempt.

"Is the one in the possession of your party not the only one of its kind?"

"Who said *we're* currently in possession of it?"

Eden's tongue froze. Her eyes began to dart between us, and she stammered horribly as she scrambled for an answer. Saki began to take particular note upon observing this behaviour and leaned forward, maintaining an inquisitive gaze on the young lady – I'd learned firsthand that she was an intensely good judge of authenticity, so any lie on Eden's part was unlikely to go unchallenged.

"You-- a man of your strength would never leave such a thing to be defended by the people of Ford, would you? What happened to that little village has been the talk on everyone's tongues for months now – if you could help it, you wouldn't leave such a prize there to be helplessly plundered in your absence, correct?"

Once Eden at last answered, Saki's look turned decidedly more uncertain – her eyes narrowed, but it was difficult to distinguish if Eden's answer had left her confused or suspicious. Mahro stared daggers into the young woman's eyes as he mentally picked her answer apart – a shiver ran across her entire body, and it certainly wasn't incited by our climate.

"You... have a point! How that same intuition of yours got your sorry self in these circumstances is an enigma to me!"

Following our mentor's lead, Saki leaned back with a quiet sigh, though she kept an eye trained on Eden as she drank water from a small cup that had laid at her side.

"Um... thank you?" Eden answered with an eyebrow raised.

"Eden, it may be pertinent to inform you that I witnessed another Rose in my homeland, firsthand. It died with its bearer, at my hands no less. We've received reports of them being seen or found in Vana and other parts of Tenryuu, with those thankfully being in good hands. I would ideally also wish to be rid of the one we possess, but even if we had known of its seeming indestructability at the time Julius obtained it, it's proved far too critical to our information gathering to dispose of."

"Indestructibility? Now... now hang on, did you not say one died with its owner?! What prevents the destruction of an isolated Rose?!"

"That's the *only* way to erase them. Crushing, fire, grinding to paste, plucking all of its putrid petals one by one, calling it mean names, none of it serves as a permanent solution; it always finds a way to reconstitute itself, no matter what, unless bonded to a human heart. And once it's in that heart, that's it; either you die when it's torn out, or it dies with you."

"I see... either way, why would you be so quick to destroy such an artifact? With the great unknown lies great potential..."

Eden was cut off by quite possibly the most foul sigh to ever leave a man's mouth, courtesy of Mahro.

"On how many occasions do you think I've heard such a notion entertained?"

"I... I just wish to know if, rather than destruction and chaos, such instruments could be used for... for the sake of good, of health, of... making dreams come true."

"No. *No.* Don't even bother dreaming of such an outcome. It's patently ridiculous. I'm not sure how you heard from us but I doubt you've read much of what we had to say, because I've stated outright to all of our contacts that such a thing is unlikely, if not outright impossible. I've *seen* it, Eden; these Roses, it's as if they're... imbued with their own desire to bring malevolence, and they infect whoever becomes their host with a lust for carnage. For those with evil and hatred in their hearts, such a transformation may not be necessary or particularly noticeable, but I've seen one of these things transform a perfectly good man into a monster that rivals the despicable bastard ruling over Ennui."

"But are these not rare artifacts with little known of their properties or possibilities? I hardly find one case out of one to be an exhaustive summary of their potential."

"Alright then, tell that to these boys; some old bastard leading a merry band of wanton murderers marched into their village and killed their mother right in front of them, using the strength imbued by one of those *things*, and his company sent much of the town to the afterlife with her. Realistically, we're at two out of two. Is that enough of a sample, princess?"

The mention of my mother made both my brother and I uneasy – I couldn't so much as begin to understand why anybody in the world would pursue the same monstrous entity that had helped bring upon Ford the worst day in its proud history.

"Dragging the tragedies of little boys into this? Is that the best you can put on the table?"

"What would you know about tragedy? You're a little girl playing adventure, seeking a prize you know nothing of even as the world tries to save you from yourself. Stick to whatever cushy life you currently lead – you'll be better off."

"You--!"

Eden clenched her fists and gritted her teeth as her stare cut straight through Mahro – I half expected her to try and punch him in the face, but she at least retained the self-control to not get herself killed *just* yet. After several seconds of shaking on the spot, she at last calmed down, looking up with a vacant smile.

"Fine. First thing tomorrow, I'll make my way home. Will that please you, Mister Katsuragi?"

"It would be better for all of us if we never meet again after tomorrow, Eden. Return home, and think no further of this."

And thus, the topic was not brought up again for the rest of the night. Saki and Mahro talked in hushed voices inside one of the tents, while Eden stayed firmly before the campfire, gazing up at the nearly full moon with wistful wonder in her eyes. As me and Altair joined her there later into the night, becoming ever so tired, she at last spoke again.

"It truly is a shame, boys. Your teacher could be denying the world great progress and triumph with his arrogance; if only he weren't so set in his ways..."

"But aren't those Rose things evil?" Altair asked.

"For all of his talk about 'imbuing with malevolence', your mentor sure is quick to imbue an awful close-mindedness into his students."

127

I was stunned by her hostility – my brother had earned a lot of venomous responses during our time with Mahro, but an innocent question such as that by no means earned it.

"Why are you talking to him like that? He just asked a question."

My question came rather thoughtlessly, though she appeared to take the berating in stride, leaning back onto her arms and staring back at the moon once more. The strong winds filled the silent void as she drowned in contemplation, until she looked upon us once more, appearing to be a lot happier.

"Boys, have you ever heard a story about a girl called Luna?" she asked with a muted smile.

"Eh? What's that got to do with anything?" Altair asked.

"Campfires are where stories are exchanged, are they not? However, I can't say I'm surprised if the story is unknown to you; it originates from my home of Creviss, though I can't testify as to its reputation beyond its walls. I sincerely hope you find it thought-provoking.

"The story starts with a little girl called Luna, of course. For all intents and purposes, a perfectly normal eight-year-old, living with her mother and father... until the day she set a single foot beyond the barrier of her village, upon which she wandered into the forest and forever lost her way back. She slowly trudged through the muddy forest for days, tripping over sticks and banging her feet on stones the entire way, until she arrived on an encampment within the woods: one belonging to the werewolves. Luna was deathly afraid of werewolves; her parents – nay, the entire village – had told her the werewolves were to be feared and scorned, perhaps even *exterminated*. Nobody ever lived to tell the tale of meeting a werewolf, she had been led to believe. What they showed her, much to her surprise, was compassion and love, and the werewolves adopted her into the village.

"As the years passed, Luna began to find purpose in her once dry life, becoming a hunter queen of the forest as she slowly adopted more of the werewolves' physical features – her ears became fluffy and triangular, her teeth shaped into fangs, and from the bottom of her spine emerged a fantastic black tail. By the time she had become 20 years old, she at last departed from the werewolves' village, unable to return to the home she had spent 12 years in once she stepped beyond the forest's boundaries but eager to show her parents just what kind of transformation she had undertaken.

"But what she found in place of her old village was a pile of rubble – smoke and dying flames clouded the ruins, as though her chance of reconciliation had just barely slipped through her fingers. Right as she was about to give into despair and become one with the flames, the Wolfmother emerged from behind her, with the entire rest of the pack she had come to love right behind her. *We can make this right*, the Wolfmother told her, *what we have here is little more than ashes, but we can sculpt them into something better, something ever more enduring. For centuries we have languished and grown lazy; now is the time to restore the good name of us werewolves.* And so, the werewolves built a great, everlasting village atop the ruins of Luna's former home, and she lived to the great age of 145, long enough to see man and werewolf become one at last."

For a moment, Altair and I were left in a daze, perplexed by the tale in both a narrative and allegorical sense. After several seconds of no noise other than the slowly declining winds, Altair at last posed the most important question.

"Werewolves can build?!"

"*Ha*, I suppose that's one lesson you can take from it. But to me, it means a lot more. And I hope it means something to you too. Good night."

With her story told, the silver-haired woman entered the vacant tent, and remained within for the rest of the night.

Eden's curiosities notwithstanding, our first night outside of Ford proved to be peaceful; I can only wish this nocturnal peace had remained consistent.

Chapter 8: Indomitable Glare of the Full Moon

The next morning, after consuming what remained of last night's Ateria, we at last arrived in Mot as the sun passed its midday peak. After being granted entry by the town guards, Mahro at last turned to face the still very cold but substantially more energetic Eden.

"I suppose this will make for our farewell, lass. Can you find your way back home?"

"I have friends here, Mr. Katsuragi. I shall be fine." She answered through gritted teeth, taking her time as she strolled away.

The four of us couldn't help but watch with a mutual unease as she walked towards the corner to our left, intermittently looking behind her and swiftly looking forward once more once she realised our gaze remained unbroken.

"As a nurse, I ought to be concerned for her wellbeing, considering the circumstances of our meeting… but she struck me with a truly ugly sensation." Saki said in a low voice – and she spoke for all four of us, "Let us hope this is the last we see of her, for I fear what may come of a reunion."

I sincerely wish that *had* been the last we saw of her. But fate was not so kind.

"Well, boys, what do you think of Mot?" Mahro asked with glee once Eden behind a corner, as if his memory of her and its unpleasant baggage disappeared alongside her, and at last I got to absorb the sights of the curious town of Mot in person.

The Skyspur itself was the obvious standout feature of the town, towering extraordinarily high into the blue sky and being home to at least 50 different buildings, at least from what I could see from the ground, but even more amazing yet was its presence throughout the entire town; everywhere we walked, the ground was coated in thick roots that stretched all the way to the Skyspur, and these roots had been meticulously shaped and constructed into footpaths with raised borders that Altair and I were raring to balance across like tightropes.

At every turn, in every nook and cranny, the town's identity was prominently displayed, with each house being constructed out of the Skyspur's dark brown wood and decorated with vines and vibrant green leaves, exuding the town's character far more than the currently snow-laden Ford ever could. Vehicles were obviously unable to traverse the roads of Mot, but every path was still packed with both the inhabitants of the town and its visitors, the latter often staring up at the Skyspur's peak in awe, and after 10 minutes of walking the roads that guided us with intricate but meticulously organised tree roots, we arrived at the foot of the sky-rending flora itself.

"By Melodias' name, this thing's even taller than last time!"

Mahro directed us towards the peak of the Skyspur – it reached well in excess of 800 metres into the sky, and I could hardly believe such a thing existed even as I stood at its base.

What fascinated me even moreso was what rested on the monstrous tree itself; wrapped around its trunk was a grand spiral of firm wooden steps that continued in perpetuity, disappearing into the leaves of the Skyspur's top quarter, and there were no less than 15 platforms that branched off of the steps into distinct areas, each supported by one of the Skyspur's colossal offshoots. As we stood there in awe, we were approached by a... walking tree?! At first I was shocked and backed up against Saki, believing yet another monster had emerged and was trying to clobber us, until I looked up to discover a face belonging to a vibrant looking young lady.

"Heya! How can I help you, beloved guests?"

We couldn't help but watch in bewilderment her hands danced around in symmetrical fashion, jostling around the fake leaves and branches covering them.

"*Hahahah!* Greetings, young lady! Any chance you could point us in the direction of a clothing shop, owned by an old ha- nice old lady called Kon? These young men require suits for the loveliest of occasions: a wedding!"

"Ah, a wedding?! In that case, we'd better rush to the eighth floor!"

"Eighth?! How in the deepest shadows of oblivion does she haul her hind up there day in and day out?!"

"Oh, the days of living quarters being exclusive to the ground are long behind us, Mr...?"

"Katsuragi. Mahro Katsuragi, Your Treeness."

Mahro slicked back his damp black hair in an attempt to show off – it spontaneously erupted into a mess once more, much to his chagrin... and the amusement of everybody else.

"Right, Mr. Katsuragi... and *please*, call me Sonia instead. Nowadays, it's common practice for small, family run businesses on the higher floors to integrate their living quarters into their place of work."

"Ah, I see. I haven't visited this place in some fifteen years, Sonia, but consider me impressed; maybe Morosus isn't so stuck in the past after all."

"Fifteen years?! Wow, I wasn't even born then!"

Sonia stared up at Mahro in amazement, curiously inspecting the walking relic in front of her... Mahro, however, was not amazed, and he slowly turned his head towards us with an expression no word could even begin to describe.

"I'm old, aren't I?" the 35-year-old man asked in abject doom and gloom.

Despite her short-lived involvement in our tale, Sonia would prove to be an invaluable asset to our journey. It was on this day Saki discovered she had a fear of heights after all, and she spent the entire journey hugging the trunk of the tree and mumbling in fear, despite a firm metal fence being installed at the side of the stairs for its entire length. Not to toot my own horn at Saki's expense, but I never had such an aversion to heights, so I was able to concentrate perfectly fine on what Sonia had to say as we continued along the path.

"Ladies and gentlemen, here we are at the first floor! Here's where you find our ever-frenzied convenience services selling all sorts, not much in the way of specialized establishments, but I'll never say no to the sizzling sandwiches of Sam's Settlement!"

What catchy alliteration; for as stilted as her delivery was, it certainly stuck in my head for some time after.

"And coming up on our second floor, here is where you'll find accommodation at one of our iconic hotels, painted in an enchanting black; if you're in need of rest or romance, there's no better place in all of Morosus!"

"Hang on, why are the hotels not on floor one?!" Altair asked.

Sonia leaned down towards the two of us, her arms still raised, to deliver an explanation: "The guys running this place, they uh... never thought we would have this many people, so they just turned the game rooms into a bunch of hotels a few years back."

As... *bizarre* as it may sound, I was not so used to being talked to only with language typically expected to be within a child's understanding - my company up until now had largely consisted of Kyrie, Mahro and everybody else infected by their verbosity...

...but I was *more* confused by the idea that anybody would ever get rid of any establishment dedicated to games, let alone a whole district of them! The peons could sleep on the streets, damn it!

"Anyway, my friends, let us continue forth!"

Sonia stood upright once more and walked forward, high... tree fiving a fellow guide (a slightly older looking girl of a tanned complexion) as they crossed paths.

"Floor three is where the treasures of Mot are distributed; want a shiny necklace, or need the perfect ring for your ideal girl? You'll find all of that here, my lovelies!"

As I glanced in the direction she was pointing, I was utterly stunned to see a diamond ring advertised in a store window at 5000 Sera... *at a discount.* For reference, Julius once told me that the machine he gifted to Kyrie (and that had been used so extensively by this point the buttons were bereft of colour) cost him 150 Sera, whilst the eccentric librarian herself once bemoaned the price of a large bread roll rising from 3 Sera to 3 Sera and 4 Lin (10 of which are equivalent to a single Sera). *That last zero HAS to be an error!,* I thought to myself; with time came the stunning realisation that yes, diamonds *are* that expensive.

"Floor four, I'm back for more! As you can see, this area, along with floor ten, is reserved for the staff of Skyspur Services; I have the utmost confidence you would do no such thing, but please don't interrupt the staff as they take their ever-valuable breaks – n- not that I need one of course!

"Floor five, a deep dive! Here's where things get practical; in need of a tool, or perhaps even hunting equipment! Let Skeet's Shack guide you in the path of robbing nature's beautiful creations of their lives, or hammering in a nail!"

The glee in her voice as she described the snuffing out of these creatures' lives was a bit offputting, but it was obvious to me even then that she was playing the matter up for dramatics. I wasn't lacking decency such that I would grandstand to our very helpful guide over something so trivial.

"Floor six, where rivers betwixt! This is where you can obtain catalogues detailing what our friends in Tenryuu and Vana are selling, as well as purchase some of those goods yourself or place orders with Sanzu!"

"The- the one with flying dogs?!" I asked in starry-eyed amazement.

"That's the one! I think those dogs were called... Cladio?" Sonia informed me.

Cladio... I'm not sure I found the name entirely fitting, but I couldn't have been more ecstatic to finally have a name to attribute to those majestic beasts. Come to think of it, it's a wonder Kyrie never informed me of such a name; I find it hard to believe a custodian of the world's most obscure knowledge would be caught unaware of such a fact so I can only assume she never found it pertinent to inform me for whatever reason.

"At the seventh floor, knocking on oblivion's door! You won't get a shop, but you can certainly get a chop at our high-quality gyms and physical activity courses! Maybe there's a hidden dancer in all of us!"

"I concur, Sonia! I haven't spent decades training this body for nothing!"

Before we could collectively scream at him to not proceed under any circumstances, Mahro broke into dance, contorting his body in such alien ways that the words to describe what he was doing fail to present themselves. He continued for about ten seconds, drawing bewildered looks from every single other human being nearby, before he snapped back to a normal standing pose, entirely unfazed by the strange looks. I couldn't help but look at him in amazement; not for his actual dancing (it was awful) but for the sheer temerity of doing so at the drop of a needle. Even the most alienating of behaviour became endearing when performed by Master King Rag.

"I'm... i-impressed, Mr. Katsuragi!"

"Thank you, my friend! I'm usually chased off by a barbaric mob, so a little appreciation for the art of motion was due, methinks!"

Altair nudged me with his elbow as we carried on with our ascent, offering a particularly insightful critique of Mahro's act.

"Master King Rag stinks at dancing! He should stick to the lame jokes."

"Lame jokes such as *your existence*, Paradoximum?"

While he was no doubt being facetious the suddenness and the fact that he heard Altair at all sent my brother jumping out of his skin.

Sonia rushed forward to the front of the eighth floor, as did the rest of our party, before she resumed her duty.

"And last stop on your journey, I presume, is floor eight! Got a tear in your tie or some suits to buy? This is the place to be!"

Now that we were at our actual destination, I paid significantly more attention to my surroundings; standing before us was a thin walkway to the eighth floor, which spanned at least 50 metres in width and double that in length. There were three different stores – one in its left half, another in its right, and Dragon's Fleece standing at the opposite end from us - the eponymous red dragon atop its entrance stared us down, as if challenging us to enter. Perhaps a bit over the top for a clothing establishment, but it made for the most interesting sight on the Skyspur.

In the centre laid a small park, with three dark wooden benches laid out in much the same way as the stores themselves, each resting against a giant trough just barely shorter than me that were filled with all sorts of exotic plants I was nowhere near botanically literate enough to identify from a glance. Even from the entrance to the floor, their sweet scent was unmistakable, and a welcome contrast to the stale wooden odour that I had become all too familiar with in the prior 10 or so minutes.

"Thank you very much, Sonia. You've been an invaluable asset to our conquest!"

Mahro passed a 10 Sera paper note, which she accepted with a gleeful smile before awkwardly storing it inside her costume somewhere around her chest, battling viciously with her branch-laden arms the entire time. Our farewells were exchanged before she departed for the higher floors as our party walked towards Dragon's Fleece.

Our first steps into Dragon's Fleece were as bizarre as they were mesmerizing; while the interior was lavishly decorated with spotless wooden walls coloured like the feathers of a phoenix and the floor was coated in a pattern resembling the scales of a mighty dragon, the scene we walked in on was... something else.

"I will ask you again: *where* are my glasses?!"

An old lady - dressed in green with a black apron and barely any taller than me - bellowed as she looked up into space, clearly aiming for but missing the significantly younger woman in white robes, adorned with the same crimson dragon that gazed upon us outside of this establishment.

"Mother, must I repeat myself? The object of your desires rests upon your head."

The young woman brought a smoking pipe to her mouth in frustration once she divulged this esoteric knowledge; she was indeed right, as the old lady's glasses were placed atop her head.

"Don't play coy with me, Little Miss 'I Studied Philosophy In Creviss And All I Got Was This Lousy Clothing Job'!"

"It was Tourism I studied, you saggy old bitch!"

Before long, the argument devolved into all sorts of colourful insults Kyrie would wash my mouth out with soap for repeating. It ultimately reach a point where even Mahro's patience was tested, and he dropped his heavy bag to the floor with a booming thud, alerting the two storekeepers to our presence at last. The old lady at last brought her glasses in front of her eyes while the younger lady hastily dusted herself off and stood before us with her hands curtly conjoined.

Her tone was... less than enthusiastic

"Welcome to Dragon's Fleece. I am Kei, and I work with my mother, Kon. We aim to deliver the highest quali-"

"It's alright, you can save us the spiel. My good friends have testified as to your authenticity, and I only befriend those with nothing but truth and dignity in their hearts!"

"You won't find a friend in us then; a lump 'a coal's got more grit in it. Just who *are* these 'friends', if I may be so presumptuous as to inquire?" she asked, leering at Mahro from the veil of smoke.

"Funny you ask, as our trip here pertains to a wedding for one of the old boys involved. The name Julius Marsh-"

Mahro's explanation was cut off by Kei *snapping the pipe between her fingers*, and its bisected remains plummeting to the floor reverberated with the violence of a bomb.

"That name... for the love of Melodias, please, do *not* utter that name in front of Mother! She tells the horror stories of that boy in vivid, surreal detail even to this day! I cannot verify the authenticity of any of her... bestial ramblings, but under no circumstances is his name to be spoken, understood?"

I was utterly lost on why Kon held such unerring disdain for Julius, as was the rest of our party, but Mahro sounded no worse for wear.

"We're here for suits, miss."

Not too long after, Kon at last emerged from the back of the store, batting a curious eye at Kei as she hurriedly swept the remains of her pipe into a corner but concerned more with attending to our party at long last.

"So, who's taking this old lady for a ride?"

The first round of measurements took place with Mahro taking the old lady for a ride (whilst begrudging his having arrived in Morosus without his wedding suit), whereas Altair was attended to by Kei. Saki and I took a seat in the lonely entrance as everybody else relegated themselves to the back of the store, stifling our laughter as Mahro very loudly derided Kon's use of a stool, and the insult match that followed was no less uproarious. Part of me was tempted to ask Saki what exactly she thought of Eden; she was an astoundingly good judge of character, perhaps even moreso than Mahro, and so it was rare for her assessment of one's character to emerge in such a vague fashion. But the matter had left us all a bit uneasy; the minutes of silence that I instead opted for proved to be preferable.

As those uneasy few minutes came to an end, an amused Kei and a proud looking Altair emerged whilst the elders emerged soon after, upon which Kei at last brought me to a small cubicle concealed by a crimson curtain. Uplifted by my brother's confidence, I strolled into my destination nonchalantly, sure that this brief respite would make for an upgrade over the dull silence.

Her first words were commanding and concise.

"Take off your clothes."

My initial reaction was one of shock; I couldn't help but be baffled by what her intentions were, exactly. Was I ready to be a father? Could I raise any substantive moral objection to convince this devilish predator to let me go? As the questions and the dread mounted in equal measure, Kei cackled in amusement.

"Ah, fear not, the underwear may remain. I'm already engaged."

I sighed in relief, knowing a very morally dubious relationship transcending shopkeeper and patron had been narrowly averted. I slowly obeyed her commands and dropped my clothes to my side, and my shirt had barely scraped the surface of the ground before she wrapped white measuring tape around my chest. The cold, deathly touch of her hand sent a shiver through my entire body; being used to Kyrie's energetic warmth by now, the contrast was even more shocking to my system.

"What a muscular young man you are. I'm all too used to having to wash this tape clean of whatever gunk the stubby little ones who normally find themselves here keep in those hideous folds, but were I of a superstitious mind, I would refrain from relieving this tape of whatever energy you've imbued it with. I bet you're the talk of all the girls in Ford, hm?"

Her admiration sounded sincere, but the topic gave me food for thought in a way she most certainly didn't intend; it was rare I interacted with anybody outside of the library, let alone girls, but I'd definitely shared a cute glance or two with the odd girl entering the library with a parent, before their guardian hurried back out of the door, likely not to be seen again for another month.

Or… ever again, given the people of Ford's propensity to up and disappear whenever the circumstances proved unviable. In fact, it would be appropriate to say that was the most likely outcome out of all that presented themselves. It was tough to reconcile that earnest praise could possibly remind me just how lonely the village of Ford had become.

"Aaaaand we're done!" said Kei stood upright once more, playing with the tape between her fingers, "It appeared you had a lot on your mind, so I wished not to interrupt; I know better than to interrupt one who is thinking of the fairer sex~"

It was apparent that Kei had an eye not just for my physical attributes, but also for my state of mind. After noting my relevant measurements on a whiteboard ,on which Altair's were also written, she turned to me with a gleeful smile.

"Follow your heart, Vega. You miss every fish you don't try to catch."

The meaning was obviously metaphorical, but I was more caught up by its literal implications: from the heights of the Skyspur, I had seen not one lake or body of water within a mile of Mot at the very least.

"How can you fish from up here?"

Kei burst into laughter at my query, embarrassing me a great deal.

"I'm not sure, how can a bird use a toilet?"

"They can't...?"

"You've got it! I haven't felt the grip of a fishing rod in my twenty years of life. Perhaps the talk of fish is best reserved for those with experience."

"Then-then we can make a fishing rod that reaches the sea!"

"*Keheh~* I suppose I'll leave that invention to you, O Divine Marine Master Vega!"

I enthusiastically accepted the responsibility; in my naïve little mind, Kei would one day know the joy of fishing from the Skyspur, even if it took until my last rancid breath at an ancient age.

Money and the promise of suits ready by tomorrow's noon exchanged hands, and after some brief farewells, the four of us were at last on our way, stepping out of Dragon's Fleece to find the last embers of the red sky dying out, and the full moon could not even wait for its eternal nemesis to fully slumber before its glare dominated the sky once more.

"Ahh~ Much like the ever-pillaging demons that haunt the darkest crevices of this world, so too must the sun sleep beneath the indomitable glare... of the full moon."

The rest of us couldn't help but find his proclamation ridiculous – a great deal of tittering occurred behind the towering man's back.

"But enough dallying, friends, for we've a hotel to procure!"

With his declaration, we were on our way. Our destination was the second floor, home to all sorts of temporary lodgings, though we would only reach the height of the fifth floor before trouble struck once again.

"Mr... Mr. Katsuragi!"

A familiar but breathless voice bellowed from behind, and bolting down the now mostly dormant steps was Sonia, covered in sweat and dressed in casual black clothing as opposed to her floral form.

"There's... there's a big problem!"

"Hold your tongue for a moment and catch your breath, lass."

Sonia all but collapsed against Mahro's chest, and he stared down at her with a hand on her head as she recuperated her stamina.

"Now, what's this problem you speak of? Anything short of the world ending is hardly a problem for a man of unmatched calibre such as myself!"

"I'm sure that's true, but I simply *must* tell you; an unruly gang fancying themselves vigilantes and numbering no less than eight brutish looking men was moments ago wandering these steps, asking around for you and carrying these scary-looking weapons!"

"What's this? This is one of my good days where I *haven't* had to clobber anybody yet! What the bloody hell's someone picking a fight with *me* over?!"

"That's not all, Mr. Katsuragi; there's this woman among them, white-haired, skinny looking, a look of malice in her eye, and they claimed you had done all sorts of awful deeds to her in your travels here, things I could never imagine you ever doing in your life!"

"You've put a concerning amount of trust into me, but you're right, little lady. I don't think the words exist to describe my bewilderment."

For the first time in the months me and Altair had been under his tutelage, Mahro appeared genuinely pissed in a way a training fumble or childish defiance of his instructions could never reproduce, and he didn't need to say a word for the prime suspect behind our predicament to become obvious.

His glare was cut short by the sound of rushing and metal clattering and jingling; in one swift motion, Mahro placed his bag in Sonia's hands and shoved her towards us as gently as he reasonably could, ready to face the crowd of attackers that was emerging from the spiralling stairs above. The lot was as unkempt and uncharismatic as Sonia's brief description had implied: most of the nine green-clad men present were overweight or otherwise out of shape, carrying primitive weapons that had clearly spent more years as decoration than minutes as tools of warfare, among them fancy-shaped but impractical swords, wooden clubs with leather grips and axes with edges as blunt as Mahro's sense of humour. The group mostly circled Mahro as he stood unimpressed against the trunk of the Skyspur, with the shortest among the men, a stubby fellow with a spindly beard and dusty curved sword, keeping a firm eye on me, Altair, Saki and Sonia from behind his comrades.

The mastermind behind our situation barely revealed herself at all; Eden stood with her back against the Skyspur's trunk, barely within my view, and she glared down at Mahro with an uncomfortable disdain in her eyes, seeming to pay no heed to the rest of us.

"Can I help you, fine gents?" Mahro mockingly asked of the gang of men who clearly weren't here for directions to Dragon's Fleece.

"Oi, you's that Katsugari bloke!"

The fattest and most bone-headed of the group stepped forward to a symphony of weapons clanging together and flabby chests enduring a jingoistic beating from their owners.

"The Pervert Prince of... actually, I don't give a rusty fuck what pile 'a goat shit you learned your manners at! Here in Mot, however, we believe very firmly in our manners, that we do! So we don't take it *too* kindly when some... pompous prick such as yourself hops a border or seven and preys on our lasses. We're a hospitable people, you know? We ask for very little beyond refraining from rapin' and plunderin'! Are all your people like that, or is there a reason you's hanging where you don't belong?!"

"Eden! We rescued you from the consequences of your own stupidity and this is our reward?!"

142

Unfazed by Mahro's anger, Eden meekly looked away, feigning despair and discomfort.

"*Oooooh*, that makes it okay, then!"

Another member of the crowd piped up, this time a man who landed more towards the middle of the road in terms of the group's weight distribution (though still overweight by any reasonable metric).

"You heard it boys, feed a lass some Ateria and you can rip her dress off and plunder her carnal treasures all you please! Well then, sorry to bother you, off you pop, tata!"

Rather than a much-welcomed departure, the group devolved into mocking laughter. Indeed, they were all so deep in applauding their own tact for derision that they were stunned to open their eyes once more and discover the first speaker lying on his back, his nose bloodied and his tongue hanging out in a complete daze. Mahro had unleashed a weapon from inside his coat that both me and Altair had never seen before, and was confidently swinging it in a perfect circle by the time he held the group's attention captive once more.

The weapon was an awfully simple one on paper, consisting of roughly two and a half meters of rope with a thick metal sphere tied to one end of it. You would have to be a madman to take on swords and axes with such an instrument, I thought. But I was overlooking one very significant detail: Mahro Katsuragi is a man whose madness was and always has been paralleled only by his utter brilliance. Such a weapon seemed almost quaint for a man with such an enormous presence, and enormous was what the fight to follow would end up being. As I shared uneasy looks with Altair, Saki and the woefully frightened Sonia, the vigilantes at last snapped back to their senses and descended upon Mahro like kings on cake.

The only king among them, unfortunately for the mercenaries, was Mahro; while they flailed around their antique weapons like toys and exercised absolutely no adeptness in combat, Mahro was an uncontested force of nature. His seemingly ill-fitting weapon proved to be to his advantage as it continuously coiled around and launched itself from his body with every swing he performed, and his attackers were busted and bruised more and more with every elegant kick and arm motion that sent the tempestuous steel ball crashing into them. The inept vigilantes would be deterred by a close call only to rush headfirst into its whiplash as Mahro at last uncoiled it from around his limbs, punishing their inexperience with a broken nose or rib. Even motions that appeared counter-intuitive, such as coiling the rope around his own neck, always ended up serving some purpose, be it to deter or set up momentum for a stronger attack. There was not a single wasted or miscalculated move throughout his entire performance, and whether the vigilantes attacked on their own or in numbers, Mahro would always drive them back into the frightened, shuffling semi-circle. Eventually even the creepy little bastard who had been fixated on our circle of non-combatants was dragged into the fight by his compatriots, and he made his less than graceful exit moments later as he flew into the metal railing and the top of his sword's blade snapped before it buried into the stairs, having accomplished nothing.

With Mahro sustaining zero injuries and slowly but surely disabling each attacker one by one, we took this as our cue to retreat to the fourth floor and call upon the Skyspur security upon Sonia's suggestion. For a moment, I sighed in relief, believing Mahro would resolve the whole situation single-handedly, and deliver Eden the justice she so strongly deserved. But...

"UAAAAAAAAGHH!!"

We turned around to discover Sonia screaming in pain, pierced through her abdomen by the broken curved sword. As we watched in a panic, Sonia dropped the bag entrusted to her by Mahro and keeled over it with her hands clutching her wound, revealing Eden to have been the one who assailed her. After slowly drawing the sword out from the catatonic young girl, she hastily shoved Sonia aside with her foot and hurriedly searched the contents of the bag as she pointed the sword towards Sonia's neck, shaking it with intense trepidation as her eyes darted between the bag and the three of us, who could only stand there helplessly. After several seconds of fumbling, she at last produced the object of her desires from one of the bag's pockets: the Screaming Rose.

It made sense for such an object to be here: it was obviously better off in Mahro's care than Julius', given that one was significantly more adept in the defense of his own life as Mahro was *ably* demonstrating just metres away. Despite this, I could still hardly believe my eyes as Eden brought the writhing monstrosity's eye to meet her two own, a gruesome smile forming as her clutch tightened. Keeping the sword pointed towards the three of us, she walked backwards before dropping the weapon and breaking into a sprint towards the heights of the Skyspur. Saki was immediate in tending to Sonia's wound, paying absolutely no mind to pursuing Eden and pulling a first aid box out of Mahro's bag with a swiftness comparable to the man himself. Altair and I could only watch her tend to Sonia, terrified that we may have witnessed a real murder, until Mahro finally approached, a mountain of unconscious vigilantes left in his wake.

"It was Eden, she ran up the stairs with the Rose!" Saki hurriedly informed our mentor.

Mahro was bewildered, looking between all of us as the questions visibly mounted beyond reason, but he took off in pursuit of Eden without a word. This entire miserable scene, the quiet mutters of a bleeding Sonia, Mahro's boisterous confidence disintegrating in a matter of seconds after Eden's betrayal of our goodwill, the hideous reek of sweat, blood and whatever else these self-righteous champions of Eden had had whacked out of them... it awakened something horrible and violent in my soul. As I at last caught sight of a blunt axe with its tip sticking out of the ground, as if tempting me to take the weapon up as my own, I decided for the first time in my life that I was ready. Ready to kill somebody, and that somebody would be Eden, for all of the hardship her lying had brought upon not just our group but also an innocent bystander – a bystander who shown us genuine kindness and guidance, no less. I'll admit it was an extremely stupid idea, but after what had happened to my mother and what Sonia was currently enduring, I determined that I had done enough skulking around in the shadows as others fought these battles for me. Steeling myself for what I was convinced I had to do, I rushed over to pull the axe from the ground and charged up the stairs as fast as my legs could carry me to confront Eden, paying no heed to the protestations of Saki and my brother.

The stairs had largely been emptied by now, as a result of both the now pitch-black sky and our brawl scaring off whatever few bystanders yet remained, and so the trip to the top of the Skyspur was an exhausting but uneventful one. As I emerged into the top platform, and laid witness to the sky for the first time in hours as the branches finally receded, I had almost collapsed, and was leaning against the axe for support as I recuperated my strength; Mahro's training had done wonders for my physical limits, but the length I traversed up the Skyspur would have been arduous even across level ground.

The top platform was by far the most expansive on all of the Skyspur, being composed of two rows of ascending seats that reached 200 metres in front of me on each side. In its centre rested a large rectangular stage with a flight of stairs running up the centre of each edge, and the entire area was constructed out of the Skyspur's pristine wood and painted in amber and green when the natural colour was deemed not to suffice. The otherwise empty space of the stage's perimeter that was otherwise not filled with stairs instead prominently displayed a multitude of flowers, identical to the ones seen on the floor where Dragon's Fleece had made its home. On the distant stage stood a dark figure, with yet another standing a few metres away from the foot of the stairs that stood opposite me. How the Skyspur could even sustain the weight of this floor alone, let alone in addition to all sixteen other floors, completely baffled me, but I was too consumed with exacting vengeance on Eden to think much of it.

As I finally regained the will to power forward, I could make out that the figure on the stage was Eden, as the powerful moonlight behind her starkly outlined the feminine shape of her body. However, she had keeled over and was gripping at her chest with a burdened and continuous groan; the moon was at last released from the grip of the dark clouds once and for all, which illuminated her enough for me to realise that she had removed her clothes, which littered the surface of the stage.

But the far more concerning development was that the Screaming Rose was plunged directly into her heart, and its eye was beginning to violently dart around. While I would normally have been averse to the sight of nude women and turned my eyes in self-righteous prudishness, given my age, I was so intent on delivering punishment to this wicked liar that I marched forward with my eyes locked onto hers, more than ready to strike her in a moment of apparent weakness as she glared back at me. My vision was so narrowed on the object of my hatred that I didn't notice Mahro whatsoever until my advance was abruptly cancelled by his firm but sweaty grip on my arm, and he wrestled the axe out of my hand before shielding me with his body.

"If you go near her, you're dead!"

I was angered by his apparent non-committal to hunting down Eden and became more and more fierce in my attempts to dodge the barrier he had turned his own body into... until the Rose began pulsating.

A translucent and unevenly spherical miasma of blood red began to expand and retract from the frenzied eye of the Rose as Eden fell back and began seizing up, writhing in agony as the pulses intensified. The wooden stage beneath her began to deform and bend, and before long the wood began to splinter and fly in great volumes in all directions. The flowers caught within the pulses began to shrivel up and die, until each and every petal among them was decrepit and corpse-like.

But the most grotesque transformation of all was reserved for Eden herself; The first and most obvious deformation came from her hair, which turned from a hypnotic silver to an abyssal black as it extended beyond reason and unevenly wove itself throughout her entire body like hundreds of needles. Her limbs tore and contorted as they forcefully extended, taking on a gangly appearance as her hair concealed and fortified the grotesque end result. Her nails transformed into razor sharp claws that glistened ominously beneath the daunting moonlight, much like her teeth that had also sharpened to a horrific degree. Ten years later, I am still left utterly bereft of words to truly describe what kind of mangled creature was coming to life before us.

The pulsating came to a stop alongside Eden's transformation, and she dug her claws into the deformed flooring of the stage as she slowly brought herself to her feet. She glared at us with bloodshot eyes, and my resolve shattered like glass; were they filled with adrenaline and life, or murderous intent for the obstacles standing before her? I could never tell you the answer to that, as the instant Mahro's hand raced into his coat to reach for a weapon, Eden's retreat commenced with haste; she turned 180 degrees in an instant, building up speed as she ran to the edge of the stage, and with one last leap that crushed the base of the stage beneath her legs, she flew over the metal rail that marked the end of the Skyspur's peak platform, descending into the darkness that was now her domain.

Chapter 9:
Calm Between Storms

The trip to Mot had resulted in an unmitigated disaster; while the clothes for Kyrie and Julius' wedding had been obtained, Eden had repaid our goodwill with pure evil, leaving us devoid of the Screaming Rose whilst posing an unknown but seemingly insurmountable threat. That horrific thing I witnessed the birth of atop the Skyspur came to haunt my dreams for some weeks after, and a good night's sleep became something of a rarity. Sonia's injury was too severe for even Saki to tend to with any real degree of efficiency, and the last we heard before our departure from Mot was that she would likely spend the rest of her life confined to a wheelchair – nothing short of a ticket to misery in a place so vertically inclined as Mot.

As noon struck, and our clothes were ready at last, we were soon rushing out of Mot's front gate, reluctant to look back at the town that now stood as a monument to our first and most significant failure. A cursory investigation into Eden's whereabouts had turned up nothing, and Mahro left Mot alongside us with a grim expression I could never have imagined just a few days before. For the first time, this avatar of confidence and enthusiasm looked utterly bereft of any solution to what ailed us; the prospect of innocents coming to harm as a result of his failure seemed to bore away at him, despite his efforts to bury his discomfort in front of my brother and I. For the entire journey we were looking over our backs for any hint of Eden returning for further retribution whilst very few words were exchanged outside of Mahro bemoaning how in the world he would explain the entire situation to Julius, up until we finally returned to the large rock pile that stood as one of the valley's landmarks. We were all quite hungry by this point, and so Mahro took this as his opportunity to teach me the art of hunting whilst Altair joined Saki in constructing the tents and preparing a campfire.

As we laid down on our stomachs, looking upon a pack of Ateria inhabiting a small grove, I gulped in anticipation, expecting the hefty-looking crossbow in Mahro's hands to soon be in my own. But before that could happen...

"Why did you follow me yesterday?"

I froze as I looked into his eyes; Mahro had confronted me with a question I was deathly afraid of honestly answering. I had already told myself that following Eden with no supervision or plan for what to do against a woman with such a wicked heart was stupid and shameful, but I wished more than anything for Mahro to have forgotten about it and become too wrapped up in the aftermath to ever force an explanation out of me. His eyes told the whole story; he wanted to hear an answer, and he wanted to hear it from my own mouth.

"I... I wanted to... hurt her. Like she hurt somebody else."

In my mind, I knew an answer of such extremity would only raise concern from my mentor. Nevertheless, his narrowing eyes suggested that he could read between the lines, and I looked away in shame, bracing myself for a scolding over my flagrant disregard for human life... though Eden was human no more.

"And did you have any kind of plan to do that? A heroic, good-hearted young man such as you stands little chance against those who will obfuscate and trick their blades' way into your heart. You were better off leaving it to me; if she had chosen to attack us rather than flee, having to protect you would have impaired me greatly."

"...I'm sorry."

"No need for verbal prostration, my friend. At the end of the day, we made it out in one piece. If you're going to start making mistakes, you're all the better off if it doesn't cost you an arm and a leg. I didn't end up losing *quite* that much, but rest assured, I got myself into far worse trouble during my youth, and walked away in much worse condition."

"But Sonia got hurt-"

"And that's not your fault. What happened to the poor girl is awful – if I found out anything even half as bad as that happened to my girls, my soul would never rest until the culprit was buried deeper than Queen Tsutsu. But you had nothing to do with it. If you want to blame anybody, then allow me to take responsibility for this mess. Even if it takes weeks or months or years, I'll make sure Eden is dealt with."

Mahro soundly washed away the tinge of guilt I felt over Sonia's predicament, though the bitter desire to have done something about it remained yet. I couldn't bring myself to blame him either, given that he had put his own neck on the line just to keep the lot of us safe.

"Anyway, that's in the past, and it's my burden to carry from here. Take this."

At last, he placed the crossbow into my hands – the powerful weight of a weapon such as this clouded my head with a sense of both awe and dread, matching the responsibility that had been entrusted upon me.

"Now, close your left eye and place your right just around... here."

He shifted my head around slightly, until my right pupil was lined up with a small notch on the other end of the crossbow, behind which laid the torso of an unaware Ateria as it loudly munched on a mixture of grass, snow and ice.

"When your next meal's in your sights, you ought to aim for centre mass – the head is oft too small a target, and even if a body shot doesn't put it down there and then, rarely will it get far."

With the pull of the crossbow's trigger, I proceeded to take the life of an animal for the second time; the Ateria stumbled for only a few seconds before it collapsed, its peers scattering like shredded paper in the wind – I can only wonder if Mahro intended to desensitize me to the act, in preparation for another encounter with Eden or those who would wish us harm, but deciphering that man's true intentions was as feasible as keeping a Cladio as a house pet.

The brief window into my unknown saviour's mentality on eating what one kills also came to the forefront of my mind; I could only wonder how far her obvious reverence for the lives of animals extended to us silly humans, and whilst I doubt she was quick to engage in cannibalism, I can't say for sure she would have approved of my eagerness to exact retribution against Eden. Then again, if she felt so strongly about it, she very well could have shown up again to correct my path. Engaging in these types of hypothetical exercises was fruitless anyway, since we didn't meet again for ten years, but they plagued me for some time regardless.

After a night spent in the ruins of Old Man Amos' house, we arrived back in Ford, entering the library at about 8am to find Julius, Kyrie and a visiting Ringo sat down for breakfast. Kyrie was quick to rush over and hug both me and Altair as if it were the first time we had seen each other in four years rather than four days, but Ringo and Julius could tell immediately that something was wrong; Mahro's summary of the trip commenced with haste. Mrs. Pyre rose from her slumber and entered the library right as Mahro reached the part where Eden transformed into a werewolf-like beast; sure enough, she found the claim incredulous and returned to her sleep, commanding her little 'Jules' to "wake Mommy up in the real world already!".

Altair and Kyrie and I mostly sat at the table in silence as Mahro exchanged the tale – knowing how wary Kyrie already was of our mentor and the happenings he oft found himself embroiled in, I spent the entire discussion in a state of nervous silence, dreading an outburst from my adoptive mother at any given time as the ordeal was described. Meanwhile, Saki left to check on her clinic, wishing us farewell with a hopeful smile, and the retelling began in full.

Fortunately, as the described events spiralled further into chaos, Kyrie held her tongue, though my eyes were fixed on her hands as they shook terribly – I can't imagine I could ever maintain such composure, were children of my own ever to face mortal peril at such an age. But alas, as Mahro's tale came to a close, it was Ringo who rushed forward to claim the first word.

"Sounds like you lot had a rough go 'a things, ay? Shame about the young'un, but yer gotten through worse unscathed,

Master King Rag! The bitch'll show her face someday, fer now we'd best concentrate on me boy's graduation ter manhood!"

With this, we all turned to face Julius, who looked awfully deep in thought. As soon as we feared he had broken down and needed to be taken to Saki's clinic for repairs, he suddenly returned to the realm of the living, a pit of darkness welling in his eyes.

"You said her name was Eden, correct?" he asked, his voice more subdued than usual.

"Unless there's wax in all of our ears, then yes, that was in fact her name, *Jules!*" said Mahro.

"Dickhead."

Julius feigned indignation, but he was terrible at hiding his smirk.

"I ask because I've never contacted anybody under that name, and I've certainly not heard from anybody residing in Creviss. So how did she come to learn of our operations? I can't possibly reconcile it."

"I can't say I like any of this, especially if our darlings are getting dragged into the midst of it" Kyrie said as her fingers pattered against the table like heavy rain, "But we're lacking in concrete conclusions; mayhaps our optimal course of action is to set the matter aside for a later date, so long as despair does not invite itself upon our community? We've a development of our own to divulge, my darlings; the two of us are headed for Tenryuu after our wedding!"

Kyrie's announcement maybe shouldn't have come as a surprise, but I was amazed nonetheless; given that she had practically assimilated half of the country into the confines of her bedroom, it was an obvious honeymoon destination, but I could never have imagined the two of them being able to afford such a luxury whilst caring for me and my brother. And while I was happy for my adoptive parents getting some quality time together, that left a very pertinent question up in the air.

"Who's going to look after us?" I asked.

Ringo leaned forward on the table with a devilish grin, leaving some time for the realisation to sink in.

"Call me Grandpa and I'm throwing yer in the river."

That jesting leer of his would become ever so recognizable over the three weeks following the wedding.

Kyrie and Julius' wedding arrived just over a week after our return, and it went as peacefully as anyone could have wished for. While we were all anxious for any sign of Eden or whatever trouble she may have caused, Kyrie and Julius were finally united as husband and wife with no turmoil. Altair and I were present at the ceremony as their children, and the crowd that had gathered in a small empty field just a few minutes away from the library was composed of mostly unfamiliar faces, given that many of them were family friends or associates of Ringo. The experience felt somewhat alienating, and it was very strange to see Kyrie in a white wedding dress rather than her bewitching getup, but I could only smile in genuine joy for what felt like the first time in months as my adoptive parents swore their eternal love and fealty to one another. Mahro was unusually reserved throughout the ceremony, though it appeared to be from a deep state of nostalgia or reminiscence rather than any truly negative inference. That, or even he felt that such an occasion was more than reason enough to set aside the theatrics for a moment; once again, the inner workings of his mind were enigmatic, to put it generously.

Following the ceremony came their honeymoon; the two would be spending about a week in Shigan, the breathtaking capital of Tenryuu and a place Kyrie had oft expressed an intense desire to visit, though it was a dream that the pair of them feared to be inconceivable with their new parental responsibilities thrust upon them. While I never joined them on their trip, I'm incredibly happy Kyrie got a chance to see the part of the world she desired most, and the morale boost she displayed upon her return may well have been everlasting - I can only hope she has the will to keep smiling despite my sudden disappearance from Ford.

In the meantime, as they journeyed through the mystical land to the east, Ringo took on the task of taking care of the two of us, whilst Mahro desperately rushed around in search of information regarding Eden when he wasn't continuing our lessons. Thanks to Kyrie's amusing reluctance to lay her hands on me within more embarrassing contexts, I was by now somewhat adept at looking after my own hygiene, much to mine *and* Ringo's delight.

Ultimately, the month following our trip to Mot came and went with little drama, and there were no further developments on the Eden situation until the day before Kyrie and Julius were set to arrive, whereupon Mahro informed me that once the two of them returned, he would be joining Ringo in a trip to Creviss to investigate Eden's claimed origins - not expecting any kind of life-threatening conflict but not ruling it out entirely - and ultimately left the choice of whether or not I wished to join him up to me. Altair had already refused, having become even more reclusive after the harrowing time we had all endured in Mot, whilst I was initially uncertain; I knew pursuing Eden would be dangerous, and I was prone to making dumb mistakes much like last time. This didn't even factor in how much I wished to spend time with Kyrie and Julius once they finally returned, starved of their presence as I was after three weeks. My mind was screaming *NO!*, and any and all reason conformed to giving such an answer. Yet my soul nagged at me; my desire to see Eden brought to justice and to avert yet more tragedies like that endured by Sonia was intense. It was probably my selfish desire to prove my worth to Mahro doing the talking on that day more than anything else, but I eventually agreed to join them on the journey to Creviss, confident that no longer would I end up in his way...

...that was the plan, anyway. The reality unfolded in a dramatically different way, starting with Kyrie kicking the library's front door open so hard I'm still unsure to this day how that thing remained on its hinges. Mahro, Altair and I were sat at a table in the library, and the look of blind, world-rending hatred in her eyes as they pierced straight through our mentor told the entire story: Ringo, who followed inside shortly after, had told her of our plans as he brought her and Julius back home, and she clearly hadn't taken the news well. As Mahro answered her fuming presence with a jovial wave, she stormed up to him and slammed her hand into the table as she leaned down, breathing heavily while extremely close to his face. The infernal argument that followed is one I'll never forget.

"*Who* said you could drag my darling off on another one of your escapades and yet again place his life in peril?! In the infinitesimally small pocket of space identified as 'Mahro Katsuragi's Brain', did the option of considering how I feel about your little adventures ever *once* pop up in there?! And just *one day* after we return?! Have you *ever* had *any* degree of consideration for the wellbeing of your 'students' or do you derive a... a sadistic pleasure from putting them between yourself and harm's way?!"

Julius at last rushed into the library, silently admitting defeat and bowing out as soon as he witnessed the absolute state of his most beloved – her children, Mahro, even her own husband... none of us could prevent the verbal rampage.

"You know I won't take such an accusation lightly."

Mahro warning came sternly as he stood up and their icy glares clashed; they were each as stubborn as each other, and were equally unflinching whilst mere inches from the other's face.

"I'll concede that I was awfully hasty in putting together my next moves and should have sought your consultation. But to act like I don't have the boys' best interests just shows you don't have a bloody clue *what* you're talking about! I want this mess cleaned up as soon as possible, and if they can contribute in a meaningful way without significant danger to their wellbeing, then I'll gladly offer them the opportunity to do so."

"Your trip to Mot was solely for the purpose of procuring clothes, and it ended with Vega bearing witness to a living nightmare I would dare suggest posed more than a 'significant' danger! Do you honestly expect me to take your word that he'll be safe again when you're heading off looking for trouble?!"

"'Looking for trouble', she says!"

"Coulda sworn that was the women's domain, princess!" Ringo said with a grin.

"Shut up!"

Kyrie's boot flew towards Ringo's head – the old man barely dodged it, but it was enough to earn his very rare silence.

"Listen, Kyrie. That Eden was the spiteful type, and I just *know* trouble's going to come looking for us again; we need every advantage we can get, and your screaming and descanting is about as useful to us as a bicycle is to a fish. Do you want to enjoy raising these boys for the rest of their years, or do you want to spend the remainder of your life worrying that one day they'll turn up torn to pieces in a coffin?"

Kyrie at last stepped back, looking more disgusted than angry by now. The rest of us were stunned into complete silence, dreading how she was about to retaliate. Sure enough, she kicked Mahro in the shin with such extreme force that the entire building shivered, and even the monument to fortitude and strength himself was taken aback, gritting his teeth and wincing as Kyrie stormed towards the back of the library.

"You had more scruples when you were killing people for money, you cold-blooded bastard!"

That was her last word in the argument, and the *very* loud slamming of a door reverberated through the entire library shortly after.

This comment in particular seemed to wound Mahro far more than the kick she delivered, and he retreated back into his seat whilst scratching his neck and otherwise looking incredibly uncomfortable – whatever she was referring to was obviously the very last topic he ever wanted to be brought up in our presence. I'm sure Altair was about to ask about it when Mahro cut him off with a defeated declaration.

"Vega, please stay here with your brother. I shouldn't have even asked."

Before we could ask any more questions, Mahro stood up and walked out of the library with his hands inside his pockets. After seeing what anguish the idea had brought to the woman I very much looked up to as a mother, I was in absolutely no position to contest his new ruling, regardless of my personal desires; I knew insisting that I go along with him would only widen the rift between him and Kyrie, one that could already fit a continent within it.

We didn't see Mahro again for the rest of the day, and once I at last woke up early in the following morning, following yet another harrowing nightmare featuring the beastly Eden, Julius informed me that he had already departed alongside Ringo. Their visit to Creviss was expected to last about two weeks, accounting for the trip there and back, and Julius had been entrusted with keeping up mine and Altair's training. Kyrie spent the next few days with a wistful, guilty look in place of her overflowing energy (in addition to an awfully sore foot) and refused to elaborate further on her choice words for Mahro, going so far as to insist that she had made it up entirely - her assertion was unconvincing, but Altair and I knew from then on that pursuing the matter was pointless. Julius was nowhere near the teacher Mahro was, but credit where it's due, he devoutly stuck to Mahro's assigned schedule of four hours per week day of physical training; for as much as I accepted Kyrie as a mother by this point, Julius hadn't had nearly as much opportunity to stand in as a father figure in turn, but times like this showed he was more than cut out to accept the mantle.

It was when the first weekend in months not to feature Mahro's grand presence arrived – and indeed, the first weekend of the new year of 583 AR - that we would partake in a family activity: a visit to Ford's other half, in which we would show our faces at a small restaurant headed by a good friend of Ringo – I suppose that doesn't say much, given that Ringo appeared to have an encyclopaedic knowledge of every soul dwelling within Ford and the good graces to match. Ever since the start of our training, we had become ever more secluded from the rest of Ford, rarely leaving the library in our free time due to exhaustion or general laziness and never wandering into the village's other half other than in the wee hours of the morning during our trip to and from Mot; a chance to actually observe our humble abode in broad daylight was certainly welcomed.

Altair and I dressed in the same thick winter apparel seen in our trip to Mot – an unfortunate and very sweat-inducing choice, given that this was one of the warmer days of that particular winter season - whilst Julius shared Mahro's resistance to the cold and participated with only a thick black shirt covering his torso. Kyrie, stubbornly insisting that she attend in costume, borrowed Julius' white coat for the journey. Seeing all of Ford buried in pure white snow from atop Julius' shoulders was a delight for the eyes, but what I was unaware of at the time was that the frigid cold came to reflect the inhabitants of Ford that trekked through it; despite waving to him, old Mr. Redgrave merely gave us a miserable look back before returning to his plotted route.

"Poor geezer hasn't been the same since his missus passed." Julius said once we turned the next corner.

There were maybe only three or four others we crossed on our path, and none were so dismissive as Mr. Redgrave had been, but their greetings sounded hollow, and they oft looked at us as if there were no life or soul behind their pupils. It was when we reached the bridge joining Ford's two halves and I looked at the strangely barren river beneath it that a question which danced on the tip of my tongue for weeks finally came to fruition.

"How come we haven't gone fishing in ages?"

I found it strange that it took me so long to ask the question, given that we had not partaken in the activity since prior to the Band of the Wyvern's attack, but a dismayed deep breath from Julius and his thumb sharply pointing towards the right side of the bridge answered my question; the reason why no fish appeared to be travelling towards us was because not too far from the rapids was a series of nets spanning the entire width of the river, with the foremost one being hauled up by two weary looking gentlemen, a pittance of marine life within it.

"You can thank that lot. As much as I would love to take you boys to the river again, we lost a whole field's worth of harvest right before it was ready, as well as half the manpower you need to... you know, harvest it. They had to make up for it somewhere, and this was *apparently* the best they could come up with."

The tinge of vitriol in his voice painted my own perception of what was taking place; *Is this the best the adults of the village can do?* I thought, ignorant as I was to the true direness of Ford's circumstances – Ford *was* sending its best, but even Mahro couldn't shoot fish in an empty barrel.

The journey continued with no other disruptions, and we arrived at the front of the restaurant and were relieved by the warmth within before even setting foot inside. After barely dodging the top of the doorframe as Julius haphazardly marched onward, I was greeted by a comforting quaintness, as the restaurant was occupied by only a few others, engaging in their own subdued conversations off in the corner. The floor and walls were coated in an identical white paint, providing a stark but calming backdrop to the brown tables and chairs intermittently dispersed through the spacious building. The kitchen was occupied by two middle-aged but energetic men who greeted us upon our entry.

As Julius headed towards the counter to order meals and drinks, Kyrie escorted me and Altair to a table against the wall immediately in front of us, and she sat opposite me as Altair clambered to my right. Kyrie and Julius had been so occupied with unloading after their return journey that this was our first opportunity to engage in proper conversation for some weeks. And Kyrie was quick on the draw, unbuttoning Julius' coat and extracting from its pockets a small pile of photographs. The first atop the pile was taken from the foot of a peculiar building; it seemed to reach as high as the Skyspur, and yet was entirely man made, moulded into a spiral of white and red.

"That's the royal palace of Tenryuu, my darlings! It resides in the middle of its capital city, and we could observe its magnificence before we got off the boat!"

My brother and I were equally wowed by the unbelievable sight; a colossal tree spawned by the whims of nature was one thing, but a building of such dizzying heights was insane. How long did such a thing take to construct? How many hours of blood, sweat and tears went into the endeavour? Would I ever, across my entire lifetime, see a tenth of the money such a building would cost? I could only come up with answers of forever, a billion and never in my wildest dreams, respectively.

After our gawking came to an end, Kyrie brought the foremost photograph to the back of the pile with great dexterity and revealed yet another landmark of Tenryuu: Mount Melodias. Although the photo was taken from an incredible distance away, the mountain and its outstretched peaks stood tall against the thick snow and asserted itself amongst the geology of Tenryuu.

The next photo was of the newlyweds themselves, embracing each other on the edge of a pier as the setting sun coloured the sky in dark streaks of red. It was a mesmerising photo that I vividly recall every tiny facet of to this day, and Kyrie's everlasting smile that drew all eyes looking at the photograph was most prominent of all. Before showing us her final photograph, Kyrie turned the photo of the two around and fawned over every little aspect of it, her eyes glistening with wonder and longing – considering it would be her only trip to the country, I can't help but imagine she was staring at it with a sense of finality.

And last of all came a very strange photo: At its centre was a smiling Kyrie but rather than her usual artistic apparel, she was wearing a loose white shirt that was raised above her stomach, held by her elbows as her fingers formed into the shape of a heart above her bellybutton. Me and Altair were bewildered both by the photo itself and what in the world it purported to represent.

Our brains were just about to overheat before Julius planted his hands on my shoulders.

"I'll cut to the chase: your sister's on the way."

While Kyrie looked annoyed that he had all but eliminated the ambiguity and buildup, it took a few seconds for the revelation to register in both mine and Altair's brains.

"Our what?!" we shouted in unison.

"You'd better believe it! If my eye for pre-natal detail hasn't fogged up, you'll be holding your little sister in roughly six months!"

Yet another voice joined the chorus of rapturous excitement, and this time the two of us turned around to find Saki slowly rising upwards, as if waking from her own grave as a shambling zombie. Such a description may be inappropriate though, as she looked far livelier than any zombie that had been depicted within the library's books. I still wonder about how she avoided detection as well as how long she spent there – she must have taken a lesson or two in sneaking around from Kyrie.

Hearing the news with resounding confirmation was an extraordinary relief; after months and months of dealing with our losses and the trip to Mot spiralling beyond salvation, anything remotely resembling good news was welcomed with open arms. Mine and Altair's joy was as great as that displayed by our adoptive parents, and I caught a glimpse of one of the chefs casting a thumbs up towards Julius.

"Congratulations on the kid, but you're better off finding somewhere good to raise them; stay here and it's just another mouth to feed, another empty stomach. And we have enough of those."

The remark came from a miserable looking fellow clad in brown rags; he had skulked in a corner up until that moment, and he spewed his venom as he exited the restaurant.

Julius recoiled in disgust for a moment – as did the rest of us, truthfully, though none seemed so profoundly offended by the comment as he did - before taking a seat next to Altair.

"We can never run away. This entire village is a testament to the decades of blood, sweat and tears poured into it by Pops and plenty of others just like him. To let one hardship run us out of our home would... stain our souls with the most dizzying heights of cowardice."

We turned quiet for a moment whilst Kyrie and Saki nodded amongst themselves, though it wasn't long before Altair asked the first of many important questions.

"So what you gonna call our sister?"

"Tsubasa." Kyrie quickly and proudly announced; me and Altair looked to Julius, confused by the name, though not disliking it.

"I wanted to call her Leah. But the first rule of marriage is that Mommy *aaaalways* gets her way."

After a dramatic eyeroll, Julius was engaged in a playful scrap with Kyrie for a while after, but I was more focused on the implications of the announcement; we were not only under the care of these two, but now we were to grow up alongside a daughter entirely of their own making, treated by her as brothers. Part of me felt some small pang of jealousy that she would be inducted into the family in an... I suppose "natural" way, rather than through the harrowing course of events that led me and Altair into their care, but otherwise the mantle of Big Brother was one I was happy to accept. Already, months distant from her birth, the responsibility represented something of a rebirth to me, filling a hole that the Band of the Wyvern had bored into my heart with purpose and drive. Blood-related or not, Tsubasa was to be my sister, and my commitment to not just acting as a brother but also finding some purpose in my life started at that very moment – I was determined to protect her from the kind of life I had led.

While we spent the rest of Mahro and Ringo's time away discussing our soon-to-be sister and being wowed by Saki's detailed diagrams of Tsubasa undergoing her gestation period, the two aforementioned adventurers proved to have a strange time of their own.

Mahro and Ringo at last walked into the library unannounced a few weeks later, as the sun veered tantalizingly close to the horizon, but before they could sit down and recap their bizarre adventure, my eyes were instantly drawn to what Mahro was holding: a dog. A small, shiny-eyed puppy with a brown coat of fur, surely no older than half a year of age and panting ravenously. Slung over Ringo's shoulder was Mahro's bag, and from the moment he set foot within the building he was already hard at work laying down a mat in the library's corner and rushing to the back of the building to fill a bowl with water.

"How has life treated you in my absence, brave custodians of this physical demesne?" Mahro asked.

"We're having a sister, Master King Rag!"

Altair was quick to divulge the news whilst I sunk into an infinite abyss – a staring contest with a puppy. My mind was racing; I had no idea why Mahro was bringing a dog into our library, or how Kyrie and Julius would react to yet another new resident, or what could have possibly led to this situation in the first place, but above all, I was *excited beyond measure*! Damn the circumstances or the faecal fallout, this dog was going to stay! Nay, I would make him the mascot of our library, our village even, and this goal would be pursued to my dying breath!

"The canine's name is Maverick, buddy! Unless the resident mommy storms over, demanding we 'get this damn mutt out of her library', we can look forward to a long and healthy relationship!" Kyrie promptly stormed over.

"Get this damn mutt out of my library!"

I was stunned, given that she had never before shown such disdain for the furry friends of man, but she quickly amended her fiery condemnation with playful cackling.

"I jest, I jest! Still... I hope Master King Rag had the canine's accommodation in mind when deciding to induct him into our lodgings."

"Well, I fancy building the little mite its own cubby hole in the back should suffice. I practically put my whole house together, a dog's hidey hole is child's play!"

"I can run and fetch ya some wood from me pal by the river, he chops the stuff fer a livin' and owes me a favour or six."

Mahro approved Ringo's scheme, and the old man set off without hesitation, chuckling with childlike glee.

As Julius at last returned from his impromptu nap and took the last seat at our table, Mahro set down Maverick – who raced beneath our table with great speed – and then raised a chair from the table to my right with his foot, delicately raising his leg until it was perpendicular to his rooted right leg. Within that instant all hell broke loose, as with a wild backflip he sent the chair barrelling in Julius' direction. Were I in Julius's shoes, I would be beyond shit scared, but he barely even appeared fazed up until Mahro at last leapt into his seat, forcing its legs back to the ground just as it came inches away from producing a Julius Sandwich.

"Are you aware that we've had to replace four of those thanks to your daredevil escapades, Master King Rag, Cosmic Devastator of Chairs?" Kyrie asked.

"That title's a stunning improvement, please maintain its usage. But onto some more urgent business; I bet you're aching to know what unfolded in Creviss, eh?"

Despite his expectation, none of us were bating all that much breath in anticipation; if anything, I felt a great sense of dread considering my mind had spent the last two weeks mostly free of

Eden and the horrible course of events surrounding her. It was akin to watching helplessly as somebody lowered a blade towards a healing wound.

"I'll take that as a no, but it needs telling regardless, and so, Mahro, Teller of Tales, Cosmic Devastator of Chairs, shall... commence!

"The old man and I weren't expecting to turn up much: we had a first name we had no way to verify was in any way real and a vague location to go off of, and nothing else. So the two of us wandered in like headless chickens, bracing ourselves for disappointment. What we got... well, I'm sure many would have preferred the disappointment.

"Not even a week before our visit, the town had been struck by two murders: Maria Styrn, age 46, found in her family's home. A rather well-off lass but none of the others in her home at that time were so much as tickled, and nothing was stolen from her bedroom, just... destroyed beyond repair. The second victim was a 51-year-old named Prince Newell. But the only thing this guy was a prince of was prison, spending the rest of his remaining years in a cell for... ah, let's just say that as a parent myself, I'm not shy in saying the world's better off without the bastard.

"But here's where things get interesting: these two aren't as disconnected as they may seem. Indeed, the two were once lovers. And the modus operandi of both murders was identical: slashed to pieces, as if committed by a large, feral animal, one strong enough to claw its way through the prison walls into Mr. Newell's cell. The investigators hadn't the foggiest clue as to who could've done it, and the two of us decided we were better off not dragging the whole town into it if that could be helped.

"But there's one last piece to this puzzle: Miss Styrn was dragged away from her family to live in a village some miles away, Jort, I think they called it. They never heard from her again for fifteen years, up until she showed up at their doorstep, a frail, illiterate and barely functional teenage daughter at her side. The two had run away from Prince Nothing and with their considerable influence and resources, the family had him hunted down and tried for his crimes in Creviss, where justice was at last served and the poor little girl could get the love she had so long been deprived of. And the young lady's name? Eden."

It sounded like a bad joke, a punchline we has been strung along for well beyond the point of reason, and yet there was not a tinge of playfulness, not a hint of trickery in his voice as he delivered this information. It took us all a moment to process, and Kyrie was the first to dig the hole further.

"W-wait a minute! Her father I understand, but why go after her own mother? Was she not the one who took it upon herself to rescue Eden from her despair?!"

"If I were to squeeze the Styrn family any harder for information I would have become the new inhabitant of the late Mr. Newell's cubby hole. They haven't got a single idea, as far as they could tell the relationship between the two was fine up until the lass disappeared a few weeks before we encountered her. The family certainly didn't take our news about how her excursion ended with grace, but they agreed to keep the matter under wraps."

"So... what's your next step? Where can we go from here?" Julius asked, a bead of nervous sweat crawling down his face.

"Where *can* we go from here, Jules? We know enough about the wench to write a biography but we're not a bloody inch closer to tracking her down. All we can do is wait and hope she turns up dead in some hole."

As callous as Mahro sounded, it really was the best-case scenario; Sonia's life had been irreparably tainted by Eden's actions and at least one innocent had been killed, perhaps even more we never learned of. For her to just keel over and die was all we could hope for, but none of us were foolish enough to expect the ordeal to end in such a convenient way.

And the final, most pressing question of all came from Altair.

"Why is there a dog with you?"

Mahro looked dumbfounded, as if astonished at himself for neglecting that very important part of the story, but he was quick to explain.

"The late Miss Styrn owned a spritely canine called Layna, and as misfortune would have it, Layna produced a litter of puppies days before the lady's death. The family won't give up their mommy dearest but didn't want the burden of the pups after everything that's happened. I paid them a fair sum for the last of the litter; I couldn't stand to leave him there, unwanted and unloved. If it had a name it was known only to Miss Styrn, so I chose my own name for the rascal. Everyone, say hello to Maverick!"

The pup smiled delightfully as he was raised into the air – for once, we could at last feel as though everything would turn out alright.

Despite the dread in the months that followed, we heard nothing about Eden. Maverick would become a regular and welcomed sight around the library, often cowering under the tables but looking up at me with a pure gleam in his eyes whenever I was blessed with his presence.

Tsubasa's arrival enjoyed an extensive and prominent buildup, with a crib built in Kyrie and Julius' bedroom and the room belonging to me and Altair undergoing a radical transformation to accommodate her eventual cohabitation. Mahro's lessons continued as usual, and by March he was confident in our basic weapon handling, prompting him to introduce specialized lessons; Altair received further insight into the art of shortswords whilst my affinity for staff-like weapons would begin the long and arduous process of honing itself to perfection. Indeed, it seemed like the Eden matter had resolved itself in some way unknown to us, and by the arrival of April, we were all but free from her looming threat, ready to celebrate Tsubasa's arrival free of drama.

And then the children of Ford began to disappear.

Chapter 10: Broken Moon

I came to learn of the first incidents shortly after I woke up on the morning of April 25th. I leapt out of bed, threw my clothes on, energized myself for a productive day to come and left my sloth brother behind to seize the day. Before the door could even close behind me however, I was met by Ringo quickly ushering me back into my room. Despite my protests he refused to budge, pushing back until I was inside my room once more whilst promising answers would arrive sooner rather than later.

I spent the next hour in abject confusion, wishing only to leave that room and get some breakfast down my gullet already. Altair waking up and rushing out of the room only to get the same physical rebuttal from Ringo did nothing to help, and we spent the tail end of our isolation in a confused and peeved silence. Maverick entered our room to provide some small comfort, but his shining eyes and playful licking were no substitute for security.

Once the clock struck 10am, Mahro walked into the room at last, though he didn't appear to be in the least bit happy. His first words made it immediately apparent why.

"It seems like Eden paid us a visit."

As soon as we got over the initial shock, Mahro would elaborate on what exactly he meant: As we slept in peace, confident that life would proceed as usual for the foreseeable future, three homes had been broken into, not too far from mine and Altair's old home. From each of these houses a young child had been abducted, but most left no clue of their abductor beyond a still open window in their bedroom. Mahro took it upon himself to investigate the matter, suspecting a conventional case of child abduction or burglary gone wrong until he entered the third home, whereupon he happened upon signs of a struggle – and most importantly, shallow claw marks hastily hidden beneath a rug. This was small consolation, as she had clearly taken much better precautions in covering her tracks outside the houses; whatever trail was left was scant and in no way able to lead back to her, and not a single witness could be identified.

The ripple effect throughout the entire town was immediate and dramatic; while the event finally tipped a decent number of families to run for the hills and leave Ford behind forevermore, those who remained were emboldened and furious; the sight of armed men hawkishly observing every nook and cranny of their surroundings became eerily common, even as they engaged in menial excursions such as grocery shopping. Blazing rows would break out with increasing frequency in the streets as spurious accusations were thrown around with reckless abandon, often escalating into an all-out brawl Mahro would begrudgingly leave our side to resolve, though doing so without overtly revealing the involvement of a monster like Eden proved a great challenge. Whenever he was absent for matters such as this, Julius or Ringo would take over his permanent watch over the two of us in his stead.

And since whatever force pulls our feeble human strings apparently lacks any sense of decency, a second strike in the night of May 22nd brought the paranoia and hostility to a boiling point; this time only one child was taken, but its fallout proved to be far more significant. I woke up the following morning – once again, well before Altair - to discover Julius watching a rather loud scene from a front window of the library. As I approached in hopes of witnessing whatever had caught his interest, his hand was quick to plant itself on my head before I could poke it too far out.

"Keep your head down. This could get ugly."

Heeding his warning, I peered from the edge of the window just enough to witness the scene unfolding in front of me: The white house directly opposite our library had a small crowd gathered around its side window, which had been completely shattered. The broken window was sealed by three wooden boards. What caught both mine and Julius' interest was the ongoing argument amongst the crowd, within which Mahro acted as a mediator/human shield between a frightened young man and a crowd of roughly ten men.

"If it wasn't this fucker then *who*, exactly, took the little'un?"

"Careful mate, he's gonna summon the *foooorest monster* on you!"

"Bloody hell! Rip his fuckin' head off already!"

"I always took ya fer a freak! Sickening bastard!"

"And what's your stake in this, outsider?! His guilt couldn't be more obvious if Terryn himself told us in a dream!"

A flood of outrageous accusations were being spat at the young man behind Mahro, often overlapping and fighting for volume real estate; he looked around in wild confusion as the horde attempted to gain whatever ground they could, only to be swiftly blocked by Mahro.

"Once again, your assertion is that this scrawny fellow managed to break into this lass' room, get her through that window without so much as a scratch on his person and then hide her god knows where in the span of a few minutes! Is your brain matter a delicacy among the rats of Ford?"

Mahro finally got a word in once a gap in the flood of shouting finally emerged, though it flared up again with greater intensity the instant his lips stopped moving.

Exchanges of such a violent matter could only be sustained with words for so long; eventually, one of the brutes took a swing at Mahro, fancying himself the quickest draw of the lot, only for my mentor to effortlessly grip his arm and twist it behind his back before slamming him into the wall. As he dropped to the ground like a sack of rocks, some among the crowd all but soiled themselves and turned tail. The rest stayed for a hopeless battle against my incredible teacher, though Julius turned me away from the window and towards the back of the library before I could watch the rest of the very short-lived skirmish unfold.

After Altair and Kyrie at last woke up and the just as urgent manner known as "breakfast" was resolved, Mahro entered the library with the young man following behind him, looking behind his shoulder and out the windows with unhealthy regularity. We all formed around the library's centre table upon Mahro's suggestion to hear what exactly had unfolded.

"Uhm... thank you, Mr...?"

"Call me Mahro, and worry not, champ. Blathering idiots ending up with their faces in the wall is just life sorting itself out, I had nothing to do with it."

Mahro sat a cup of water in front of the stranger, which was quickly depleted as fuel for a lengthy sigh. Maverick made a few attempts to leap up and claim the water for his own dry tongue but swiftly gave up the hopeless endeavour with a whimper.

"Still... thanks."

"Now then, mate, can you please fill my good friends in on your situation? I've never much fancied telling people's stories in their place."

After much nail biting, the young man acquiesced.

"I suppose I can. Hello, I'm... Rydell. Ever since Rhea, June and Morgan were taken I've thought, you know, I want to do my part. If someone or... *something* is around here preying on our kids, I'll gladly give up some of my time if there's a chance I can stop anything else happening. Not like I have much to do otherwise...

"...then last night comes and... well, you've seen how that ended. The situation came at a bad time, right as I was left on my lonesome for the old boy I tagged along with to go relieve himself. Heard a faint scream, then a window smashing, and I look in the direction they came from to see this... this... this fucking *wolfman... thing!* Unless I really am losing my rag I definitely saw some... hairy, dark beast dragging her out of that room and leaping to the forest! I couldn't throw a pebble as far as this... *thing* was able to jump! Before I could even think of raising my gun it all but blended into the night!"

"And now poor little Rydell is already saddled with a guilty verdict in the eyes of the particularly retarded." said Mahro as he jumped to his feet, "I'm starting to think all Eden's any good at is making others take the fall for her own short-sighted avarice."

"That thing has a name? A...and it's a *woman?!* You sound like you know our... pet wolf monster, whatever the ungodly fuck she is!"

171

Kyrie brought her arms around both me and Altair as tensions heated amongst the men.

"To tell you the truth, it's… kind of our- my fault she's around in the first place, mate. Up until now I've thought keeping the whole matter under wraps was for the better, but all that's gotten us is an innocent young man caught in the crossfire. Trying to explain it away as werewolves after the kids start going poof… it sounds like a bad punchline." Mahro explained as he scratched his nape.

"So essentially, I'm fucked?! I'm going to spend the rest of my tenure in this dead-end shithole accused of kidnapping and kiddy loving and… whatever other charge they'll staple onto me, because you couldn't put a damn collar on your giant child abducting dog?!"

"I'll make it up to you, kid. If those old farts give you any more grief just let me know and I'll give them a talking to."

Mahro cracked his knuckles with a smile, though Rydell was not at all smiling.

"Why, thanks! My spirit can come wake you up when they break into my home and splatter my brains against the wall! Thanks for delaying my violent death by a couple minutes!"

His backhanded gratitude was the last we heard of him before he shut the library's right door behind him. Mahro crossed his arms with a short grunt, as if this kind of reaction wasn't entirely unexpected.

"The forest, eh…?" Julius mulled over the new information with a curious glint in his eyes and a half-smile across his lips. "If she's taking more kids from around here then she's got to be setting up camp somewhere nearby. He might have put us one step closer to the end of this ugly affair once and for all!"

With a newfound confidence, Julius rose from his seat and also made for the front of the library.

"My dad can pull some strings; he'll have whatever's left of the town guard combing through every forest in sight before sundown."

Julius' confidence and Ringo's subsequent action was followed by yet more weeks of silence; every inch of the forests surrounding Ford, as well as those atop the rocky cliffs that walled in much of the village, was descended upon by the energized men of Ford... only for nothing to emerge. Every acre that turned up nothing gave way to yet another with equal measures of success. Mahro and Julius seemed confident that we were approaching the end of this ugly saga, but Kyrie became horribly paranoid over the clear threat being posed to me and my brother, very rarely refusing to let us out of her sight even as her pregnancy began to take its most extreme physical toll.

The paranoia of our neighbours grew in equal proportions; by the time three weeks had passed since the most recent abduction, bickering in the streets and brawls between town guards were almost a daily occurrence – every able-bodied man in the village was sick beyond reprieve of trekking through forests day in and day out only to turn up nothing. Rydell was spared no quarter by those who held him in contempt still, and Mahro was repeatedly called to his aid by Perry, his younger sister. A rapid series of knocks at the front doors opening to a cute young lady begging our big strong mentor for help became an unfortunately regular scenario.

This would all come to a head on the night of June 19th.

Right as I threatened myself with a good night's sleep, I was jolted back to life by a harrowing plea I could hear from the distant other side of the bedroom's door.

"Mr... Mr. Katsuragi, please! Th-they dragged Ry out of our home! I don't know where he is!"

A voice unmistakably belonging to Perry rang out with such strength that her sustained screaming may well have shattered every window in the library, but Mahro must've had the ears of a god as his answer came swiftly.

"Divulge the details on the way, little lady!"

That was all I heard before the library door shut behind them.

Based on the infrequent and light footsteps behind the door, Julius had remained behind as Mahro raced off to yet another adventure. I laid my head back down on the pillow, ready to become a willing victim of sleep's heavenly allure...

Scraaaaaaaaaaaatch!

The sudden noise widened my eyes once more. My bed shared a wall with the door leading into the library, so I turned to my side, facing the wall and hoping for quiet at last – I chalked the sound up to Julius dragging a table, or anything other than an immediate threat.

Scraaaaaaaaaaaaaaaaaaaaatch!

From the second awful sound it was apparent: this was deliberate and couldn't be chalked up to something so mundane as moving a table. I feared the absolute worst, and as I turned around to confirm my fears, my brain fought against my body as it screamed to ignore whatever this was and surrender myself to sleep, where nothing could hurt me. The absolute worst is what I got once I painstakingly turned to face her.

"I've found youuuuuu~"

The shrill, raspy whisper, the towering black shadow that stood next to my bed, the ragged panting masquerading as natural breathing. Everything about this situation was entirely foreign. Its source was anything but.

"Ede-!"

I attempted to call out before her hand slammed into my mouth, pressing my head against the wall. As I clawed at the filthy, hairy hand, desperate to breathe once again, the shadow-cloaked head of this nightmarish figure bent down towards me, smiling as her maw glinted beneath the faint glimmer of light that crept though the door. Behind her, I could see a hole cleanly cut through our locked window, large enough for this monstrosity to clamber through.

"I have something to show you, Vegaaaaaaa~"

The instant her hand released from my mouth, I wasted no time in my next course of action.

"Julius! Hel-!"

My scream was cut off by her hand grasping my throat, and her mad scramble to escape began.

As she reached the window once more, she launched me through the hole and into the neighbouring wall with maddening haste, causing great pain in both my head and shoulder.

"My apologies. I continue to underestimate my own… gift."

Dazed and about ready to throw up, I was barely even back on one leg before she followed me through and grabbed me by my waist. The last things I saw before I succumbed to a concussion were the door inside my bedroom opening, the look of terror on Julius' face, and the haunting glow of the full moon.

I didn't wake up in the middle of the forest, nor did I wake up in some grand colony of great werewolves. Julius, Ringo, Mahro, all of their speculation had been shattered the moment I woke up; I was in the Basin. I had never entered this specific area of it whilst pursued by the Band of the Wyvern's beast, but its structure was a dead giveaway; a spacious dwelling with walls of dark stone, rotted and collapsed wooden tables along the room's edges long claimed by spiders, and a wooden archway marking an entrance blocked off by a mound of the same dark stone. Unlike my last unwilling expedition, the room I woke up in was lit up by a small pile of enflamed books, waste and loose clothing, whilst its stream of smoke drifted towards the blocked-up entryway. As my nose tingled with sensation and the feeling of hard stone returned to the tips of my fingers and toes, the true gravity of my situation crashed into me all at once.

Despite the fire, I was freezing cold; I had been robbed of my clothes and was sat upright against a wall. A flood of vile smells, a cocktail of rancid sweat, blood and faecal matter, it all violated my fragile nose at once, and were my stomach full I have no doubt a torrent of vomit would have joined it. I motioned for my right hand to squeeze my nose, desperate to shut out the putrid stench, only to end up screaming as a violent pain shot through my palm; I weakly looked up to it to discover my right hand had been pierced entirely through with a shard of rock, and it was so deeply embedded into the wall behind it that I immediately resigned myself to this barbaric confinement.

"Wakey-wakey, Vega~" a voice called out, and I at last looked behind the fire to discover the strangest sight yet.

Eden was seated on a crude chair, a throne of uneven stone, and surrounding her were four children. Except... they weren't normal children. As I looked closer at each of them, I came to a horrifying realisation: while not so severe or deformed as Eden herself, each of them had adopted several wolf-like features, including distorted, sharp ears, skin intertwined with raven black fur and eyes whose only colour came from the reflection of the fire. While the largest three shambled around in front of the fire, mumbling incomprehensibly as they stared at me, the last was held firmly in Eden's arms, obscuring her torso as she breastfed the distorted child. The entire scene was – to put it lightly – *fucking bewildering.* My legs hastily retracted to my chest and were flimsily held there by my left arm, in an effort to both warm myself up and conceal my body – considering I was deep underground in a cave reeking of the worst smells man can produce, looking at a monster who could easily kill me on a whim, my nudity ought to have been the least of my worries.

"Motherhood is a... beautiful thing, Vega." Eden rasped – every syllable reverberating endlessly against the walls - as she stroked the breastfeeding child's pitch-black scalp, "To receive the privilege of bringing life into the world... and then to squander it, to produce failure after repugnant failure through one's own ego and avarice... is it possible to be any less human?"

"What the... let me go..."

But contrary to her preaching, she paid my protests no heed.

"My father denied me that privilege. He took everything from me; my youthful years, my purity, and my ability to produce children. My mother, squandering the privilege bestowed upon her, allowed it to happen. She stood by and let my father taint what should have been her most sacred treasure; she let it happen for ten agonizing years. When her situation turned inconvenient, when she finally 'rescued' me, she did it to drown her own culpability beneath her false virtue; my father became the 'sole enabler' of my torture while she too was a victim, just like me. Her family welcomed her back with open arms, and I spent the next five years living the pantomime; life was 'normal', I was properly educated in human skills and customs, yet my resentment towards my mother never faded."

As the toddler finally had enough of suckling on her breast, Eden stood up and sat it down behind a fence against the wall, constructed of torn up wood and held together by inelegant strings of withering rope. Considering most of the room's hideous smells originated from behind that fence, all I could consider myself grateful for was that I could barely make out what laid behind it. As the child at last became free from her grasp, I finally witnessed Eden's even more horrifying state; the Screaming Rose had embedded itself even deeper into her chest, and its tendrils that burrowed across the entire width of her collarbone resembled thick, virulent veins. The hair that had woven itself through her body much more closely resembled fur in this state and took on a more even and symmetrical pattern throughout her body; while her arms and legs were almost completely coated in thick black, her face and much of her torso – primarily her breasts and genital region – were devoid of the fur. Her once sleek silver hair was replaced by a large mass of black, spiky clumps that reached halfway down her back.

As she placed the rest of the transformed children behind the barrier, Eden continued, "And then one day, close to a year ago if my memory fails me not, a miraculous being appeared before me, as a ball of light. An angel, a benevolent spirit, a god... I'm not sure what to call it, but it appeared before me in a dream and imparted these very words: 'When the trees wither and the ground turns to white, journey to the southern village of Ford, for a man named Mahro shall bring the reprieve you've sought for so long'"

"You're crazy!"

"That's a harsh way to phrase it, little man; has your fake mother not taught you manners?"

"What do you mean, 'fake mother'?!"

The intended anger and intimidation behind it fell somewhat flat due to my weariness, but the fury incited by her words was wholly genuine.

Eden produced a ghastly giggle as she walked towards me at last, the tapping of her clawed feet chattering with every step until she knelt down in front of me.

"You assume I haven't done my homework merely because I took upon a greater form? Greatness produces progress, not regression."

She leaned uncomfortably close to me, sniffing and stroking each and every visible inch of my body with a sickening, gleeful grin on her face; Even with no observers other than the blank eyed children gazing off into space, to say the whole ordeal felt humiliating would be a grand understatement. As much as I wished to punch or kick her, I was absolutely certain that the reaction would be immeasurably more violent. All I could do was buy myself time for some miracle to get me out of the situation.

Maybe my guardian angel will show up again, I thought.

Nay, it was all I could depend on. Given that even Mahro had no chance of finding me down here, that was my sole chance for survival.

"Of course, I haven't been spending all of my time eyeing up the prize; I'm sure you're aware that I returned home to... visit my parents. Exacting justice... there's no more tantalizing or addictive sensation in the world, Vega." Eden sat down in front of me with her legs crossed before she proceeded, "Remember the story of Luna? Even as I told and aspired to it, something never... felt right about it. I had only ever heard it passed down from my mother, and so my trip back to my hometown brought with it an opportunity for verification. A small green book hiding in the depths of the Creviss library presented me with something else entirely; contrary to my long-held understanding of the tale, the story doesn't end with Luna returning to the humans, only to find them gone and an opportunity to build something greater. No, its true conclusion is far more fascinating.

"Luna returns to her home, hoping to introduce her colony to her birth parents and live peacefully among them, only to be rejected and chased away with pitchforks and torches. Spurned by her parents, she decides to burn the village to the ground on her own, casting her last tether to humanity into the flames along with its inhabitants. She tries to rebuild in their place, only to fail miserably as everything continues to collapse around them; the werewolves are left cold and hungry by the blistering winter winds, and most perish from starvation before the rest are picked off by human hunters."

The end of her amendment to the Luna story left me perplexed; she seemed far too gleeful to find out that it truly ended in a miserable fate for the eponymous young lady, and the deep stare towards her... "children" embodied a sense of deep pride.

"So what? She dies. Why is that good?"

I knew it was a stupid idea to start poking holes in her story, but it was all I could do to stall for time, waiting desperately for Sihan-Perseli to emerge and right this wrong.

"Because I know her weakness." She quickly answered as she gazed into my eyes once more, "She wandered into that forest as an innocent maiden, ignorant to the evil, the avarice, the hatred that courses through the blood of humanity; she expected to walk back home for dinner as if her parents would ever accept her. She was similarly incognizant of her shortcomings even beyond her ascension; the destiny of our kind is to usurp humanity, to subvert and take over its foundations and infrastructure. To replace a civilization is a fool's errand. To usurp a civilization is our divine right."

Bracing me for an unthinkable proposition, Eden leaned forward once again. As she did this, the eye of the Rose in her chest began to... cry blood. A thick red rapidly emanated from the centre of its pupil and poured onto my legs. Eden rubbed two of her fingers against the warm liquid before bringing it in front of her eyes, heinously grinning as she glared at me between them.

"I respect you, Vega. No, actually, I would even be so kind as to say I *like* you. You're not yet corrupted by the worst desires of man; even when you pursued me, what I saw that night was not a vicious murderer but instead a virtuous yet mistaken little man, doing what he believed to be right. You never acted out of greed, or malice, or any of the other innate faults of man. Once fully matured, you will make for a fine general of my army."

179

My eyes widened in horror as her intent finally became clear. Desperate to avoid the fate subjected to the other children in the room, I finally acted in my own defense and smacked her hand away with what little energy I could put into the motion. My palm catching itself on her claw did more damage to me than I did to her, but the gesture at least left her confused.

"I don't understand. Look at your brothers and sisters; I've rescued them from their parents, done what nobody ever did for me. They've spent their childhoods wallowing in squalor and poverty, dealing with parents who would sooner sate their gluttony than act properly upon the privilege they were granted. I have given them something better: a future to look forward to."

I looked over to the group of children in question; their idle stumbling around and vacant stares did absolutely nothing to put me in Eden's... optimistic shoes, but I maintained my silence nonetheless.

"Do you not go to sleep every night, ashamed that the woman you call 'mother' is nothing of the sort? Do you not resent spending many of your waking hours exerting yourself, learning to fight for your own life because those calling themselves your 'parents' are simply incapable or unwilling to fight in your stead? A parent who leaves a child to fend for himself is the embodiment of neglect. If you must be saddled with a fake mother, at least come under the wing of one who shall defend you to the last."

Every single word that left her mouth was utterly insane; she expected me to abandon my parents, abandon my family, over some fanciful dream of werewolf conquest?! It didn't take long for my anger to bubble up and culminate in the final words she ever heard from me.

"You know nothing about us! Kyrie loves me! You could never be my mother! When I grow up, I want to *kill* monsters like you!"

The vitriol bubbled in my veins like a kettle in a blast furnace. The very suggestion that I would enjoy a life with this monster was so overwhelmingly insulting that had I the opportunity, I could very well have ripped the stone stake out of my palm and strangled the beast to death with my bare hands. I had known and loved Kyrie for years, well before she took on the responsibility of becoming my mother. She and Julius were unmistakably good people; taking over the role of my mother had brought upon them great sacrifice and burden, and yet they did it without complaint or hesitation. My mother's death had left me uncertain I would ever know love or kindness again; to be dragged away from Kyrie, to lose yet another mother... I would have preferred death.

And I was immensely lucky that death did not follow, as in my rage, I struck Eden in the face, as hard as my hand would allow. The monstrous woman was taken aback; she momentarily stood there in a daze, tenuously touching her face with little in the way of haste. For a moment, I foolishly assumed I had dissuaded her from the insane pursuit of inducting me into her kind. Then her hand crashed into my throat, and she brought her blood-drenched hand in front of my lips.

"You'll give me the gratitude I deserve once you're among us, Vega. All you have to do is drink the fruits of this eye once every week, and your incredible gift shall remain forever imbued."

How in the world she planned to start some... werewolf army, or whatever it was, while also supplying it entirely with this single bleeding rose is still completely unknown to me; given that she had clearly lost her grip on reality altogether, she may not have even had one at all. I had no time to contemplate this at that time, however. As her stained index finger danced around my lips, my eyes began to frantically dart around the room; if there was any time for my serpentine saviour to emerge, it was right now! And yet... nothing. Not a hiss, not a slither, not a single shimmer of gold.

Eden began to pry my lips open with her finger. It was the most awful, utterly terrible sensation in the world; her finger was coarse and stony, and I fought to hold back my tears as it felt like my bottom lip was being torn off just from the inhuman texture of it clashing with my soft skin. Yet despite that, I couldn't give in; if I gave in to the dreadful pain and opened my mouth, who knows if I would have left that cave alive? But it continued. And continued. And continued. By the time a minute of this had passed, I had all but resigned myself to a terrible fate...

...

Bark!

Until this single sound brought Eden's plan to a halt, and both of us looked towards the blocked entryway the sound originated from.

Bark! Bark! Bark!

Yet more of this sound and rapid scratching against rock soon followed. Eden leapt to her feet, assuming a violent stance and readying her claws. Yet not even this could brace her for the explosive entry that soon followed; a loud explosion soon filled our ears as a mass of dust dispersed throughout this room. From the dust, a lone figure soon emerged: Mahro.

As he entered Eden's domain and the dust died down, he took note of his surroundings with an unnerving quietness; his gaze shifted to Eden's seat, then to the deformed children, then to me, and finally to Eden herself. It was when their two gazes met once again that something fundamentally changed in his eyes; the playful, upbeat mentor defending the innocent from petty dirtbags was buried beneath an avalanche of murderous intent as he stared down this beastly woman. They embodied much of what Eden despised about humans – an unending hatred, a lust for bloodshed, a rampant desire to exact one's own version of justice, all of that and more was seeping from his hazel eyes, and he did nothing to conceal his intent. For just a moment, he looked as terrifying as the monster his gaze was locked with.

Their exchange didn't stop at a stare for long, and he raised his hands as he bolted towards her, revealing a pair of steel claws affixed to them. The choice of weapon caught Eden off guard, and so Mahro's first strike embedded his right claw into her left arm as she raised it in a futile effort to swat his hand away. He tore the blood-soaked claw out of her arm as he readied his other arm for a second strike aimed at her abdomen, this time missing but forcing the beast's back against a wall to evade his wrath.

"Katsuragi! Was imposing yourself upon this boy's life not enough?! Must you ruin everything, as always?!"

182

Eden's screeching bounced off of Mahro like a brick wall; he steadily approached her with an open stance, daring her to take the initiative.

Eden was quick to play against his gambit by launching ancient texts from a collapsed table at her feet in his direction; their frightening speed made Kyrie's reunion with Mahro look like child's play, and my mentor was forced to evade the projectiles rather than turn them against her. As his head curved around the final book – which slammed into the wall next to me, much to my shock – he was greeted by Eden launching the entire surface of the table at him; unable to dodge such a thing in time, he instead buried his claws into each half of the table, kicking it back towards her with comparatively sluggish speed to reveal the target of his scorn was now scurrying along the deceptively high ceiling. She buried her hands into the ceiling, and Mahro was just barely able to block her furious kick with both of his claws, causing him to stumble back from its impact.

Eden was quick to capitalize on this opening, leaping down and assaulting him with a flurry of swiping claws. Dodging each attack by the skin of his teeth, hyper-focused on the threat before him... I had never seen Mahro like this; every other engagement I had seen him in looked more like a way to pass the time, often walking away from a battle having exerted his wit more than his strength. The Mahro I was seeing at this time was almost the complete opposite, expressing not a single word, nor any minute sign of vulnerability. When push came to shove, it was evident why Julius was so eager for me to fall under his mentorship; even against a vile monster who could punish a single mistake with instant disembowelment or dismemberment, he never lost his cool or let her think for a moment that victory would come easily. For as frightening as his unparalleled ability was, the man himself was beyond inspiring, an avatar of the strength I desperately wished to possess even a hundredth of. Though exhausted and worn down by what Eden had done to me, I kept myself awake to watch him work his magic.

Magic is what would continue to happen; before he could be cornered against a wall, Mahro reached for his bandolier with blistering speed and interrupted Eden's flurry with three precise knives aimed at her centre mass, her throat and then her head. The first two landed deep within her while she stopped in her tracks to deflect the third and recoil from the wounds. During this momentary break in intensity, I watched Mahro open one of the small containers on his bandolier – come to think of it, it was the only one on him that remained shut when he entered – and retrieve from it a small, spiked ball with a thin wire attached to it. Before Eden could once again engage him, he swiftly grabbed two of the texts she had launched at him earlier and returned the first to sender. Once she cleaved through it and began to approach Mahro once more, he threw the second at her in a seemingly futile assault. Predictably, she slashed through this second tome, but she came to a halt soon after, looking down with great confusion at her left hand; beneath the book laid Mahro's spiked ball, and it was now clinging to the fur atop her hand.

Eden's bewilderment was punished by Mahro once again demonstrating his offensive prowess; he now rushed towards her, delivering his own storm of slashes until he pushed her back beyond the raging fire in the room's centre. As this barrier was crossed, Mahro diverted from his usual wild slashing somewhat to catch my shirt – now a blazing mass atop the fire – with his left claw and fling it towards her. As the infernal fabric enveloped Eden's left arm, Mahro rapidly changed up his tactics, barrelling towards her and shoving her as far away as possible. She clawed at his arms, cutting through his coat and leaving some grisly wounds, but Mahro wouldn't relent until she was pressed against the wall opposite me. After he swiftly retreated from the wall, a wild explosion soon emerged from her arm; my hair was sent in all sorts of directions from the magnitude, and a cloud of dust obscured where Eden had taken the brunt of this bang. I was bewildered that he had kept weapons of such excessive destructive potential against his chest, in such quantities no less, but there was no time for questions as a wild scream soon thundered through the Basin.

Eden rushed at Mahro from beneath the smoke as the latter took a moment to assess his damage, revealing that her left arm had been almost entirely removed, leaving only a sharp, bony stump above where her elbow used to be. Most of the exposed flesh on her torso was also eviscerated, and an unimaginable volume of dark red blood was pouring out of her exposed veins. Yet somehow, *somehow*, she was still gunning for Mahro. Unable to mount a proper defensive tactic in such little time, all he could do was raise his claws in the path of the incoming strike... which shattered both of them to pieces. I feared this to be the end of Mahro and braced myself for his violent death. This fear was instantly undone; before Eden could celebrate her small victory or prepare a finishing blow, he had already pulled yet another weapon from the depths of his coat: a lengthy steel baton.

Eden scowled with unbridled anger as she was pushed back yet again, with every deflection of the baton slowly chipping away at and dulling her freakishly sharp claws. Barely able to keep up now that she was lacking an arm, she sustained several strong blows across her entire body and was trembling violently, only remaining on her feet through sheer force of will. Out of options and desperate for any upper hand on the prospective victor of this clash, Eden retreated to the wall of the room opposite Mahro, flinging any loose bits and pieces lying around the room at him that she could get her hand on. Books, rocks, wooden planks, all of it flew towards him with reckless abandon, and all of it couldn't even scratch him. That being said, any ground he could gain was met with yet more retreating; the two reached an impasse as Eden approached the cage containing her "children".

An uneasy silence formed, the flicker of the flames providing the only backdrop to this stagnant standoff. An unflinching stare between the two was maintained between the heavily breathing and battered combatants, until Mahro rapidly pulled something from his coat and pointed it towards Eden. Both me and Eden were taken aback; it was the strange device used to start campfires during our trip to Mot, the one that shot lightning from its end. I assumed he had gone barking mad and for once Eden and I agreed, with the beastly woman in question bolting to the right before he could pull the trigger. A powerful bang blasted all of our ears, momentarily stunning everybody in the room. I finally looked up to discover Eden hadn't been damaged by this attack whatsoever. However... it turned out Eden wasn't his target.

"You... you *bastard!*"

The barrier guarding the abducted children had been set alight; a fire was now creeping along each plank and strand that formed this bizarre bastardization of a fence, all the while the helpless children inside could only stand and stare into space, unaware of the danger they had been put in.

Mahro didn't let the opportunity go to waste; as Eden's head turned towards the endangered children, Mahro pulled a thick, serrated machete from inside his coat as he dashed forward and plunged it into the front of her thick throat, clambering onto her back as he began to push, pull and hack away at it. Eden flailed and turned and dashed around erratically but Mahro's grip was firm, until Eden rushed backwards into a wall and sent him collapsing to the floor with a grunt. When he failed to stand up without even the slightest hesitation, I once again assumed him to be done for. To my shock, instead of finishing him off, Eden rushed over to the raging fire that had engulfed most of the barrier and began tearing it apart and battering out whatever fire dared encroach on the children, not even taking a moment to tend to or remove the blade lodged in her throat. This would prove to be her undoing, as while she was consumed with undoing the fire started by Mahro, the devious mentor in question leapt to his feet, completely invigorated and clearly having faked his distress; he put an end to Eden's life once and for all by hacking through whatever tethers remained between her head and her torso. Her head dropped to the floor with a thud, and the rest of her body collapsed backwards soon afterwards, twitching and writhing as the last of her life faded away.

Mahro obviously never intended to let the kids die just to defeat Eden; he hastily pulled yet another small item from an outside pocket of his coat and threw it beneath the centre of the fence, releasing a transient gas that defused whatever fires still raged on it. Just as the danger threatened to pass, the eye of the Screaming Rose embedded into Eden's chest had one more surprise left; it began to pulsate and release a red glow while the eye itself blackened, and Mahro could be seen reaching for his chest in pain and seizing up with identical timing. It took him a few seconds to connect the dots, and by then the pulsating and glowing began to intensify, demanding that he remove it or suffer the same fate it would soon succumb to now that its host's heart was dying. He couldn't hide how mortifying a development this was; he wanted to be rid of this monstrous item for good, and yet it demanded he continue its wretched existence. Resigning himself to the Rose's servitude, he knelt down and ripped the deeply embedded Rose from her chest in one swift, tough motion. Eden's body twitched one last time whilst the tendrils of the Rose retracted and whipped Mahro's stern face, assuming its base form a few seconds later and bringing a bloody end to the life of Eden Styrn.

After removing the spike from my hand, Mahro and Ringo brought me through the windings tunnels of the Basin with Maverick following behind, and I at last saw the surface after what felt like an eternity. A large crowd that appeared before me as a colossal blur had gathered at the entrance of the Basin, placing lanterns in a large circle to illuminate the area; I had no idea what the time was, as my watch had unfortunately joined the rest of my apparel in the fire, but a hint of brightness on the horizon suggested that daybreak was soon approaching. Mahro gently placed me against a mat on the floor before returning to the Basin with Ringo, whereupon Saki tended to the grievous wound in my palm, horrified by my injury but relieved to the point of tears that I was alive.

The crowd remained in a state of perpetual, incoherent murmuring until Ringo and Mahro finally arrived, with two of the transformed children being brought out by each. Whilst they placed the children on the ground next to me, panic and wild confusion followed as the people of Ford deliberated on what the hell had happened to them, as well as from which families they had been taken. From what I could hear, two of them – Rhea and Morgan - were identified by their parents before a particularly galling suggestion was posed by an unknown man.

"Whatever they are, they're... *monsters,* like that thing! I know we've suffered enough, but all we can do is put the little'uns out of their misery! Before they can bring us to further ruin yet!"

The bickering and shouting went into overdrive; while most were violently opposed to such a hasty conclusion, a small contingent of the crowd sided with this fatal option. Eventually one among said contingent stalked towards the four of them with a break-action shotgun in hand, only to be blocked by Mahro.

"Out of the way, outsider! Ever since you've set foot here everything's gone to shit! The least you can do is let me send the little ones to the heavens!" demanded the wielder – a man sounding middle-aged and wearing some kind of overalls, as far as I could tell.

"I know the tragedy that was your birth and the life you've subsequently led is irreversible, but what makes you so sure this... change in them isn't? For a man bemoaning tragedy, you're awfully hasty to take on more of it needlessly."

Mahro was entirely unflinching, as was his trigger-happy target of derision. This was when I recalled what Eden had told me: *All you have to do is drink the fruits of this eye once every week or so, and your incredible gift shall remain forever imbued.*

I attempted to sit myself up as the two of them continued to bicker, desperate to impart this information, only to collapse onto my back yet again. Saki gripped my hand in an attempt to comfort me.

"Vega, please lie down. This'll tide over and we'll take you back to the clini-"

"I have to tell them something..." I faintly murmured, though Saki heard me well enough to lean down to my ear, upon which I delivered my message: "Eden... she said they needed to drink her... blood, once a week."

Saki looked terribly dumbfounded; my explanation was cursory to the point of absurdity, given that any energy I spent shortened my wait time for the Fainting Express, but she was more than able to extrapolate my intent.

188

"If you'll pardon my interruption, Eden, this... monster, told him that the children needed a dosage of her blood each week to sustain such a form."

Clever girl.

Of course, this did nothing to deter the shotgun-toting man.

"So what? You expect honesty from a fucking child kidnapper? It was a failsafe in case she kicked the bucket so that these... these things, they could take over in her place! The mercy and inactivity of Ford and its people has only brought us ruin; the time for decisive action is now!"

From the crowd emerged equally loud shouts of anger and agreement, though nobody on either side of the debate dared approach the... 'pragmatic' speaker. After a moment of smugly soaking in the praise, the cocky bastard chose, against all common sense, to point his shotgun to Mahro's head.

"Step aside, let me end this all peacefully, and you can walk away. Keep being an arse... and you'll join them."

I didn't need my vision to work all too well to tell that my mentor had the situation under control somehow; a cocky, gun-toting idiot was nothing compared to Eden.

"If you're waving your big stick around, you might want to check it's loaded first." Mahro kindly informed him as he leaned down, as if taunting the shotgun itself with his eye's proximity to its barrels.

"What the... o-of course I loaded it, you thick-headed cunt!"

The click that followed afterwards suggested he wasn't all too confident in the answer.

The inspection was instantly interrupted by the shotgun barrelling into the man's face thanks to a nasty shove at its exit point, sending him to the floor with a bleeding nose. Most of the crowd dispersed in a panic at the first sign of violence, flocking to the forest path as if Mahro were turning the gun on them himself. To those who remained, my mentor made our next course of action clear.

"We're going to keep these little ones at the clinic and wait to see if their deformations at last revert. Any objections, nurse?"

"None at all." Saki answered with great relief.

The next week of recovery in Saki's clinic was both well-needed and harrowingly familiar; if I had ended up here twice in the span of a year, who knew how much I would need Saki to pull me away from death's doorstep over my entire lifespan. When I first woke up there, I discovered that my right hand's palm had been covered up and tightly secured with a silky cloth. Foolishly touching it led me to discover that some kind of liquid or cream was pressing against my hand – according to Saki, it was to help my palm reconstitute itself properly after Eden had pierced through it, though it did nothing to undermine the torturous pain I caused myself by touching the stove. On the bed to my left I could hear Rydell muttering in his sleep, occasionally twisting and turning violently as his murmuring intensified. The curtain between us kept me from seeing the extent of his injuries, and I think I was better off for that.

The deformed children, on the other hand, seemed to fare better. By the third day, they already began to show signs of improvement, slowly but surely regaining their ability to speak. Come day four, the physical deformities painstakingly began to undo themselves, and at last all four of them could be identified by their parents. By the end of the week I spent within that clinic, they had returned mostly to normal, and were at last returned to their families. Once I was discharged myself, with my right hand to stay firmly wrapped up until a point of Saki's discretion, I walked out to find a tired Mahro slumped against the wall, whistling a tune from his homeland – it sounded slow and sombre, not at all befitting the man under normal circumstances but somewhat relieving at such a time. As I leaned over to pat him on the shoulder, he suddenly sprang back to life and stood up straight.

"Hey, buddy. Little Sis is waiting back home."

He dropped this bombshell on me so casually that at first I thought it was a joke – it wouldn't be the first time he had messed with my little brain in such a way, but this certainly wasn't the time for such jeering, and even he was cognizant of the proper time and place for jesting.

"Really?" I asked.

"She was born three days ago. I'm sure she's eager to see you."

Too deep in elation and nervousness to properly answer, I quietly followed behind him as he set off towards the library. Walking back home to greet a new member of the family, after all of the carnage had finally subsided... it was a tantalizing, almost overwhelming sensation.

"Though I hate to be downer, it won't all be good news for you; after your birthday, I'm heading off for a few months to see my family. I didn't want to leave you lot on your own until Eden was dealt with, but looks like we don't have to worry about her any more. I have the utmost confidence you'll keep everyone you love safe while I'm gone."

"Aww..."

Though disappointed, I at least found some small relief in the fact that his absence wouldn't be permanent.

"But um... thank you for everything." I answered.

Between his lessons and rescuing me from Eden, I felt as though not even the word 'everything' could truly articulate the extent of my gratitude, but it was all I could say.

"*Hah,* you make it sound so final, Vega! If anything it's *you* who needs my thanks; there's nothing I resent more than wasted effort, and you and your brother have proven to be very capable young men in your own right. You very well ought to be proud of yourself."

I took his praise to heart, finally allowing me to smile for the first time since Eden had encroached on our home; while my involvement may have been minimal, my actions had played a role in Eden's defeat. Out of the entire ordeal, that was only true comfort I could take from it.

The rest of the journey continued with few words exchanged thereafter. The anticipation that built with every step became more and more suffocating, up until I finally opened the door to Kyrie and Julius' room and laid my eyes on Tsubasa for the first time. Both Kyrie and Tsubasa were fast asleep whilst Julius lightly leaned against his newborn daughter's crib, beckoning me to remain quiet as I approached. Within the crib laid a beautiful baby girl dressed in pink and white and lying as still as a stone, save for the rising and deflation of her chest. Her scalp was lightly populated by strains of blonde hair, and her skin was fair and devoid of imperfections. Now that she was here, in the real world, rather than a distant hope, I could say for certain that I would endure everything inflicted unto me by Eden again if my adorable sister was waiting for me at the end of it.

"She has my eyes." Julius commented with a smirk - his own eyes were a powerful blue, and I didn't yet need to see them in my sister to know they were a perfect fit.

"Now that the worst is behind us, we can finally live like… well, a normal family." He continued as he placed a firm hand on my shoulder, "I hope we're good enough for the three of you."

I maintained my silence and my gaze on Tsubasa, but knew in my heart that I wished for the same; I'd had this feeling before, that the worst calamities to afflict us had come and gone only to be let down later. And yet, this time it felt different, as if we had gone through hell and at last returned to normality; it would take something remarkably horrifying to undo our victories.

Chapter 11:
Consumed by Time

Much to our relief, this peace would be mostly maintained for the next decade, at least in our personal lives. Mahro would take a few months' leave to visit his family every year or so, each time returning with a new coat delicately hand-crafted by his wife, Minami. Along with a new coat came a new family photo he would enthusiastically wave around before even saying "hello". Whilst taking his leave, Mahro would once again loan Julius the weapon he had used during the Band of the Wyvern's attack, hoping against hope it would never need to be used. Fortunately we avoided major incidents, though the same could not be said for all others in the little village of Ford.

Mrs. Pyre returned to military service shortly after Tsubasa's birth, and was henceforth seen very rarely. She may have been better off for it though; as Tsubasa slowly grew up and both me and Altair began to devote whatever time we could to being in her company, the village of Ford continued its rapid decay.

Each year, more and more of its inhabitants would run for the hills, unable to bear the sordid, bloody history of their once idyllic home. Rydell and his family were among the first to leave following the Eden incident, though he at last offered Mahro his most sincere thanks for his efforts before taking off. I don't know where he ended up, but I can only hope he's better off for it. With less inhabitants came less of the bickering and shouting that came to define the streets of Ford, at the cost of the village becoming ever more uninhabited and ghostly. Abandoned homes and factories were reclaimed by nature, housing more wildly overgrown plants than people. By the time I turned 11 years old, the once lively population in excess of 400 prior to my mother's death had been reduced to a measly 190.

As I blossomed into my teenage years, Mahro and Julius at last allowed me to delve into the specifics behind the Screaming Roses, and their effect on the world: whilst the people of Ford migrated, so too did tales of this strange, rose-shaped object that could imbue supernatural and horrifying abilities into those who answered its call. Before long, a well-hidden secret exploded into a gold rush, as more and more fools sought an easy ticket to solve their life's problems. While the rate at which they were found barely increased and there were very rarely incidents involving them, entire industries revolving around the pursuit of the Screaming Roses sprang up practically overnight, though the battered town of Ford was having none of it, profusely turning away those who would intrude on its people purely in pursuit of ambiguous power. Whoever was lucky enough to stumble upon a small box buried beneath the earth, containing the most desired artifact in the world, was essentially set for life, provided they could hold onto their lives until after money and monstrosities exchanged hands.

Then the most significant loss of all struck; as a six year old Tsubasa sat in my lap, reading a book about butterflies in the front of the library, Julius arrived with a bitter announcement: Saki had unceremoniously disappeared, leaving the clinic under a very perturbed Julius' jurisdiction. According to a note she had left behind, her entire clan, the Shrouded Anemones, had been exterminated by an unknown assailant, save for a handful of its members. Hearing that her younger brother Koga was among the living, she hastily took off for Tenryuu, not even sparing a moment to wish us a formal farewell. After all of the good she had done for me, and how much I had come to depend on her, for Saki to sever her ties to Ford in such a fashion was painful; I spent the next few years resenting her somewhat, wanting her to at least have come to say goodbye, but the wound eventually faded. In the end, I hope she found happiness with her brother. The only memento I had of her to speak of were the last replacement fingers she had grafted onto my hand shortly before my 12th birthday; Julius was now entirely saddled with that responsibility, and while he absolutely tried his best, he still lacked the finesse and craftsmanship of our respected nurse. Every subsequent replacement brought its own set of challenges.

Beyond the village of Ford, things were hardly any better; tensions between Ennui and Morosus were reaching an unfortunate boiling point by the time I turned 15, with the powder keg of conflict waiting to be set alight by any slight infraction. And the infraction setting the keg off would be anything but slight; according to official records, the Emperor of Morosus - the preposterously named Yaorimal Quazimyres (alternatively titled Fat Bastard by Mahro) – sent an undercover group to abduct the 12-year-old daughter of a Morosus general, demanding the schematics to Morosus' mass-produced battleships be delivered in person by the general, beneath the notice of the army he served. Determined to save his daughter, the general took the schematics to the Emperor, hoping for the safe release of his daughter. Instead, after handing over the schematics, he was immediately executed, and his daughter was kept as an unwilling spouse of the Fat Bastard.

Once this harrowing event at last came to light, war was immediately declared by Morosus, desperate to take the offensive before Ennui could adapt their technology to subvert their most prevalent warships. Around this same time, efforts to recruit any willing and able-bodied young men extended to every corner of Morosus, including the decayed village of Ford. Barely a week had passed since the dawn of the war before the recruitment posters littering Ford's walls far outnumbered the number of able-bodied men in the village, though the number willing to take up the mantle for their country could in turn be counted on one hand; general sentiment among the people of Ford was that we had been left to die by our oh-so-benevolent governing bodies following the Band of the Wyvern's attack, and the lack of support in the wake of Eden's actions did nothing to quell this distaste. I was too uneducated in the workings of our government to offer any conclusive opinion on the matter, but the general sentiment was not one I vehemently disagreed with, either. While I had no interest in becoming what Mahro called a "dog of the military", committed as I was to digging my feet in and remaining in Ford... Altair had other plans.

Perhaps it was not so much the announcement itself that caused us so much distress but more his manner of revealing it.

"After I turn 16, I'm getting the hell out of here. I think I'd fit in better with the military."

He chose to disclose this, of course, at breakfast. In front of me, Tsubasa, our parents and Mahro. He had grown somewhat distant from Tsubasa ever since Saki left but he was cruelly unflinching as she begged him to stay and started tearing up when he wouldn't budge whatsoever. I can count myself lucky that Mahro took it upon himself to spend the following hours arguing furiously with my brother, for never before or since have I been so tempted to send Altair's teeth flying from his mouth. Instead, I took Tsubasa outside to play with Maverick, who was less energetic now that the years were catching up to him but remained extraordinarily merry in our presence nonetheless. It was then that I swore I would never leave her side, after she inevitably asked if I would follow in Altair's footsteps. I suppose the worst part of ending up in Tenryuu is that I broke that promise, though I obviously had no choice in the matter. But a broken promise is a broken promise, and the only thing more improper to break is a young lady's heart.

The last conversation I had with Altair has been stuck in my head ever since; on the day of his departure, we woke up early in the day for a short spar; both of our combat skills had grown exponentially under Mahro's tutelage, and our last clash proved to be a little more intense than usual, in no small part due to my animosity over his departure. That being said, we were jovial and friendly once again by its end. After he bid a still bitter Mahro and our family farewell, I joined my brother for a stroll through Ford as he made way to the front gate. It started with a stilted, awkward silence until I produced a question I was somewhat nervous to ask.

"Are you sure about this?" I asked my brother, expecting an immediate 'yes'.

He was not quite so swift as expected, but after some brief introspection, his end result was not all too different.

"Well, I wouldn't have come this far if I weren't, right?"

"Still, you didn't have to be so... dickish about it."

"I know, I know, Mahro gave me a mouthful over that. You'll be fine looking after Tsubasa, right?"

"That's not the point. You know how much this is hurting her. Couldn't you at least stay a bit longer?"

No matter how much I implored him to stay, he met me with the same vacant look in his eyes he had carried for some months up to that point. *Don't you dare pity yourself as you bring harm to all of us*, I thought, though my tongue had more sense than my brain.

"My bed's already made, brother. The least I can do is go lie in it."

His answer, for the first time, carried some small tinge of regret or hesitation – despite this, I chose not to bore into it in the hopes of making him stay, given that his ties with the rest of the family and our mentor were already shaky.

"So… why did you choose to go?" I asked as we approached the bridge in Ford's centre.

Bringing himself to a halt above the river dividing Ford's two halves, my brother merely gestured towards the vast array of abandoned buildings scattered along every corner of the village; factories whose walls displayed more weeds and plants than metal or bricks, houses fallen into such disrepair that even the most daring of devils would call them a safety hazard, and a shrinking population almost entirely apathetic to the decay of our beloved home, trapped here only by their inability or hesitance to pursue greener pastures. By this time the population had decreased further yet to about 140 people, few of whom looked particularly excited to be neighbours.

"Look at this; our industry is stagnant, our culture is dead and buried, the only history anybody can attribute to this place is tragedy and bloodshed. The books will tell a history of shame and misery, while all of the good we try to do won't even be a footnote. I hate to say it, but the only path left to tread for Ford leads to a dead end; Kyrie and Julius can cling onto that glorified bookshelf they call a home all they want, but I'll have no part in it so long as their obstinance drives a stake through my ambitions." He spoke with a reserved annoyance as he intermittently glanced at a dilapidated house on a distant hill – our old home.

Were I any less emotionally mature, I would have probably clocked him in the face for speaking ill of our adoptive parents, but I instead chose to dig into the root of the issue.

"Is this about Mom?"

...in truth, I found it hard to call the late Stephanie Vadere my mother, since Kyrie had well and truly excelled in taking up the mantle, but to call her anything else under these circumstances felt strange and disrespectful.

"It isn't *just* about Mom, Vega. Every time I see that godforsaken house out of the corner of my eye, I remember her death like it was yesterday. I'm never going to live that down, and I may very well take that atrocity with me to the grave. But I could live with that. I would gladly let the nightmares haunt me to their hearts' content if I knew anything good was waiting at the end of it. And aside from Tsubasa, I just... don't think there is. The village of Ford will continue to decline until all that's left a pile of ash where prosperity used to be."

"And by running away, are you not contributing to its downfall?"

"You've got it upside down, Vega; I want the best for all of us, and I don't think we'll find the best by squandering our potential in a place like this. Take this as a lesson: all of you are better off leaving this place in the dust. Spend the rest of your life digging this grave and you'll inevitably fall in."

A grave, eh?, I pondered, *Turning your back on a place like Ford and wandering into a battlefield, to avoid graves? Ridiculous.*

I began to turn away, both to leave Altair to his own devices and to stop him from seeing the frustration in my face.

"I never took you for a philosopher, military dog. Go on then, find your own paradise in whatever mire of blood and bodies you're tossed into. Let me know what adventures a man on a leash can get up to, and where they take you. Let me know how it all ends, big brother."

He said nothing in response, but I could hear that it took him a while to depart at last.

Do I wish I had been more careful with my words and actions? Of course I do. I would have loved nothing more than for

Altair to have remained alongside me and Tsubasa for the rest of our youthful years, and the thought that I could have changed the outcome of that conversation tortures me to this day. But as he further articulated the pitiful state of Ford after almost 10 years of degradation, I felt a great sense of... defeat. The kind of defeat I hadn't felt since Eden had dragged me out of my home and put me on the doorstep of becoming a beast, just like her. Except this time, Mahro's efforts hadn't been able to sway his mind; on my own or with the help of my mentor, I was helpless to stop Altair from running away and wished for nothing more than to be rid of that ugly sensation, even if it meant turning my back on him.

I didn't hear from him again until a letter arrived via Cladio about six months later, wherein he joyfully described that he had been accepted into the Morosus military and was assigned to guard the border between Morosus and Ennui for the foreseeable future. A nice, cushy position distant from the raging wars enveloping the seas while giving him the escape from home he had so desperately yearned for. We tried our best to feign our excitement, but even Tsubasa found herself hard pressed to approve of what her big brother had done. Nevertheless, all we could do was wish the best for Altair and wish for his eventual safe return.

Chapter 12: Seeing Red

Two days after Tsubasa's 8th birthday (that being June 24th 591 AR), I sluggishly forced myself out of bed not expecting much of note. My 16th birthday was soon to follow, and yet I couldn't find myself all too excited about it; once I turned 16, I was expected to take up some kind of occupation within the village of Ford, and yet I had great trouble coming up with anything that could compliment my skills or experience. I had been very well taught in how to beat up ne'er-do-wells and fend for myself, but I was awfully ignorant in the ways of agriculture or craftsmanship, both being areas of expertise Ford was desperately lacking. Wanting to help restore Ford to its former glory however I could, if only to spite Altair, I was leaning towards the idea of learning to become a blacksmith, but I had largely resigned the idea to later consideration. In the short time left I had to be a kid, I was going to make the best of it.

Taking care not to wake up Tsubasa, who lay down in her bed on the other side of the room, I walked over to the mirror facing our front door. My hair had grown medium-long and shaggy, settling into a deep black like my mentor. I had gone to sleep in a white tank top and grey shorts – no doubt a strange choice for anyone to sleep in during the worst summer had to offer. I don't wish to make excuses, but I never took comfort in sleeping without at least one layer of clothes on both my top and bottom halves ever since the Eden incident wrapped itself up. Spending any prolonged amount of time without a shirt on sent a horrible chill up my spine, far too reminiscent of the sensation I endured while stuck in that cave.

Now wasn't the time to contemplate my strange, unwanted quirks, though. Standing in front of the mirror, I came to one very strong, very undeniable conclusion: I looked pretty good! As quiet as I could, I began to pull off all sorts of action poses, the sort Mahro was rarely seen abstaining from, and fending off hordes of invisible assailants with my incredible technique and composure. I was simply unstoppab-

"Vega, you got a moment?"

A voice blasted me out of my bubble from behind, shattering my fun and causing me to turn sharply in embarrassment.

In the room's doorframe was Mahro, in his most fascinating coat yet: covered in mostly black, and yet decorated on its back with a crimson flaming bird and a blood red tiger, complimenting each other and forming a near perfect circle, the bird's many tails ending up as the only protrusions. It was a wonderful visual, but not a wonderful time to compliment his fashion – I had done so enough by this point.

"You ever heard of knocking, gramps?!"

"Look, I… haven't the time for theatrics right now. Can you come with me for a moment?"

His request came with a strange quietness; it's easy to assume he was just being considerate of Tsubasa, but there was obviously something else bothering him.

Before we even had any breakfast, we were walking towards Ford's front gate. Mahro's hands rarely left his pockets, an offputting sight if only because his hands were oft flailing and reaching for any curio his gaze met or manufactured. Our usual chatter – including but not limited to speculating on what trouble Altair was getting himself into and Mahro teasing me over what girls I allegedly had a fancy for – was alive and well, which served to make the disparity in his body gestures even more bizarre; whatever was on his mind wasn't all too awful, but this may well be the only time I've ever seen him act so… nervous. I would soon come to learn that this was for a *very* good reason.

Our destination, as he informed me once we left the boundaries of Ford, was a port a mile or so away from my home. We emerged from a lengthy forest path to find a run-down and mostly deserted end point; the sparse and decayed white paint enveloping the three buildings making up the port indicated that it was by no

201

means a prosperous one, and only one small vessel lay in wait. The pungent, briny stench of the sea was overpowering, and the landmass stapled onto this small part of it was hardly any better for wear, littered with trash and disrepair. Mahro already knew of our destination, leading me towards the largest of the three buildings: a two-story establishment roughly the size of our home, with two iron doors on opposite sides marking the only entrances and exits. The only window was a sorry, smashed up little thing on the second floor, covered up by wooden boards that themselves were barely clinging onto life. The building would by no means have looked out of place within the industrial district of Ford.

"State your business."

Wondering where the voice came from, I was stunned to see a stern pair of brown eyes glaring at me from behind the rusty metal grille of the front door.

"Long time no see, Boss! Are the rats still keeping you company in there?" said Mahro as he walked in front of the door, bending down to meet the building's custodian at eye level.

"I'm telling you mate, I *wish* it were just the fuckin' rats here today. You owe me a new door."

After this 'Boss' fellow at last unlocked the door, we quietly walked through a short series of corridors until we came face to face with a battered wooden door containing a large hole in its centre, as though a small bomb had gone off right next to it. It looked like it was barely kept upright by the locks securing the door's top and bottom perimeter. I was still in the dark as to why exactly Mahro had brought me here or what his own intent even was, and so I could only dread whoever was behind that door.

"I never thought a girly's foot could cause damage like that, but I suppose you still have a lot to learn after 60 years on this godforsaken rock we call Morosus..."

A girl's foot did this?!, I thought in abject terror.

Kyrie could commit great violence to our surroundings when she was angry, but never to the extent that she could kick a hole clean through a thick wooden door, even at her most tempestuous! Who in the world were we dealing with?!

"I'm... sorry for the trouble."

Mahro apologising for anything is a scenario I could never have imagined, but I suppose you still have a lot to learn after 15 years on the godforsaken rock we call Morosus.

"If I cover her travel fee, can we sweep this whole thing under the rug and let her leave with us? I'll even pay for the door if you demand it."

"We're supposed to bugger stowaways off to Creviss and let them be dealt with properly, but... I tell you what, you've been good to me, Katsuragi. Pass me 40 Sera for the travel, 60 for the door and another 20 for drinking money and it's all under the rug; as far as I'm concerned, the door will have spontaneously, uh... fallen apart, you know?"

Before his words could even finish reaching my ears, my mentor procured 120 Sera from his wallet and all but forced the sum into Boss' hand.

It was at this point that my confusion overwhelmed my patience. Wanting to know what the hell was going on, I stepped forward to ask Mahro about the situation when a voice rang out from within the room.

"Now can I leave, you money grubbing slug?!"

The voice was high-pitched, no doubt belonging to a young woman, but its demands struck my eardrums with the violence befitting that which was inflicted on the door. Indeed, I may even have seen the door's hinges creak in agony. Not wanting to waste any more time or risk any more broken doors or limbs, Mahro ushered me inside. Lying on her back, with her head hanging off the edge of the miniscule steel slate embedded into the wall and supposing itself to be a bed, was Mahro's eldest daughter, Matra.

Even as she lay upside down, I had no doubts as to her identity from the moment I saw her; her features matched those seen in his latest photograph perfectly. Her eyes were verbatim Mahro's hazel own, her pristine legs that now ran against the wall were concealed by a cloudy white skirt and thigh high stockings of matching colour, and beneath the scarlet tank top and silver-white cardigan that enveloped much of her torso, she was as well-endowed as her mother (my apologies for my deviant eyes, Master

King Rag). She offered her father a cutesy little wave, though Mahro failed to reciprocate.

"Oy trouble, shut your flaps or I'll make him give me another 20 for booze!" Boss snapped back, prompting Matra to stand up, enraged.

"I bet you'll spend all of it on drinks anyway! What's a measly 20 going to last you, five minutes?!"

"At this rate you haven't got five minutes before I throw you to the boys in Creviss, your dad's pleading be damned."

The two were now standing face to face, and the anger from both was utterly radiant, threatening to burn the entire building down with its potency. It was at this point I noticed Matra was taller than me; Mahro had mentioned she was older than me by roughly eight months but given that I towered above many girls my senior who remained in Ford, a lady of such stature was a shock, even if the difference was hardly noteworthy. Mahro's blood must be something real powerful.

"I bet you couldn't last five minutes pleasing your wife you chubby old sa-!"

"*Matra!*"

Mahro bellowing turned all of our heads, mine most of all – I had never heard him raise his voice with such fury, and my ear being directly next to him did no favours for me.

"He's been kind enough to let you off for your... your world-rending stupidity; don't push your luck!"

Matra at last quit her protesting and slinked back onto the bed with her eyes gazing towards the ground. Boss whispered something in Mahro's ear as he left us to our own devices and shut the door behind him, though he made sure not to lock it.

"So, what's the story, little one? Why did I wake up to a letter telling me you've been stowing away on a passenger ship? I've told you time and time and time again that a young lady such as yourself shouldn't travel by your lonesome. Not even Melodias can anticipate what putrid types lie in wait out there; anything could have happened to you!"

While his stare was unflinching, Matra couldn't bring herself to meet his eyes, wallowing in her shame as she tried to formulate a response; I decided against interjecting, not wanting to risk stoking my mentor's fury or making the situation worse.

"I'm... sorry." she finally mumbled as she closed her eyes.

"I didn't ask you for an apology. Tell me why the hell you're here or I'm dragging you to Creviss myself."

"Ah! I uh... well, I... got into an argument with Mom, and so I, I snuck out. Tenryuu is... um, thanks to the war, they're... suspending all travel in and out of the country in July, starting from uh... let's see, was it the 9th...?"

"*They're what?!* First I've bloody heard of it! And why did you think it was a good idea to come all the way over here with nothing other than the clothes on your back, knowing you may well not be able to return?! I would like to think I raised you better than that, Matra!"

Given that Ford could barely even be identified as a village by this point, I wasn't at all surprised that the news was utterly foreign to us, but this was no time to be all smart-aleck about it.

"I'm sorry! I'm sorry. I'd just... rather be with you than Mom."

As she bowed her head and closed her eyes, I couldn't help but find her strangely cute, but the look in Mahro's eyes made it exceedingly clear that it was taking everything in his power not to slap her straight across the face.

"Did you not once consider your sister? How is she going to deal with her beloved big sis leaving her behind for however long this pisstake war lasts? And what about your mother? You would really abandon her due to some stupid disagreement over... hang on, what did you disagree over with such intensity that you would sneak onto what was for all intents and purposes a one way trip to Morosus?!"

Matra took a while to answer, but eventually she at last looked up at the two of us with tears in her eyes as she answered between heavy breaths, "It wasn't so much a disagreement, she... I lent her a book of mine, and after a few months I... asked if she still had it. She insisted she gave it back, and when... when I pointed out she still had it, it just... got worse from there. I said something along the lines of 'you wish I wasn't born'... and she said yes."

"I tell you, you really are your mother's daughter..." said Mahro with an annoyed huff.

As she rubbed her eyes against the sleeve of her cardigan, Mahro was deep in thought, tapping his nose with his finger as he contemplated his next course of action. After an uncomfortable amount of time spent looking at the two of them, he at last provided me with an instruction.

"Escort my daughter back to Ford if you would. I'll be back later, just... got to make some arrangements."

And with that, Mahro sluggishly departed, scratching the back of his head up until he was out of sight.

For the first half of our return journey, not a word was exchanged between me and Matra; I didn't want to risk offending or hurting her further after the volatile reunion with her father. It's not as though I was entirely inexperienced in matters pertaining to the opposite sex, but my own mentor's daughter was here, in the flesh, and nearly as bombastic as the man whose almighty blood flowed through her veins. As far as I could tell, I was treading turbulent waters; upsetting Matra risked causing strain in my relationship with Mahro, but was saying nothing leaving just as bad an impression? I debated these grand matters with myself as my eyes ran over her body; despite her light clothing, she was sweating hard enough to fill an ocean, and was quick to raise her arm to block any brief rays of sunlight that cracked through the leaf-laden trees. As we travelled this lonely, quiet road, I was able to make further observations about her; when not strewn against the floor of a cell, her hair was complimentary to the rest of her appealing exterior – its colour matched her tank top, covering her head in a sea of red, and the bulk of it just about grazed her shoulders while her thick bangs came to a stop just above her eyes. If this were anybody else, I would have been quick to compliment her looks... but again, this was my mentor's daughter. All I could do was silently watch until she at last sparked a conversation.

"I take it you're... Vega, then?" she asked, her eyes at last meeting my own after five minutes of abject silence.

206

Her eyes were still ever so slightly red, but the gleeful smile on her face suggested she was in much better spirits.

"...yes. Master King Rag talks about me back home, then?"

"Master... who?"

"Your dad. Altair called him that once and it... just stuck."

She snorted and brought our journey to a halt after I explained the origin of this laughable moniker.

"It may be needless, but I suppose I should introduce myself then. Matra King Rag!"

With her name given, she brought her hands together and completed her introductory bow. Once our eyes met again, I returned the gesture.

"Round here, a... handshake, that usually suffices."

Before the sentence could even finish I wished that I could turn back time at that very instant, concerned that I had shown a degree of callous rudeness to an esteemed guest. Offense was taken not, however, and she answered the call by grasping my left hand with both of her own and shaking it vigorously – her hands were far softer than my own but I could determine that they too were not unused to physical stress.

"Oh, is that the one with the fake fingers...?" she asked once she released her tight grasp.

"Hey, they're as real as the rest of them to me!"

My answer was facetious but hasty – I was unsure if she would read between the lines and pick up on it, but her small chuckle suggested I was in the clear.

By now I found myself able to loosen up, but I was uncertain what sort of conversation I could initiate; I didn't want to ask about her home, given the emotional turbulence she was no doubt still confronting in her mind, and yet I had very little to discuss otherwise.

"Are you... alright?" I asked in lieu of anything even approaching specificity.

"How could I *not* be alright?" she answered with a wide grin, "Dad saved me from getting thrown in some dingy jail and I get to see where he's spending all his time nowadays!"

She certainly was an optimistic one. And for some reason I took it upon myself to drown Matra's flames of curiosity.

"It's nothing special. A ghost town would have more life in it."

"It can't be *that* bad! There's plenty in Tenryuu that's recovered from worse if what Dad told me is true." She argued, and I wasn't in much of a position to contest.

"*Heh*, I'm beginning to sound like Altair."

"Where is your brother, anyway? Since you were there, I was hoping he'd be not too far behind..."

While awaiting an answer, she raced ahead of me, walking backwards with her hands behind her back as she leaned forward, peering into my soul with great curiosity.

"Aw... was I not good enough?" I asked.

She answered by glaring at me with her lips in a pout.

"I jest, I jest. Anyway, Altair just... fucked off the moment he turned 16. He's sitting on some wall on the other side of the country because our humble little abode with more empty buildings than people just couldn't sate him."

Matra raised an eyebrow at my harsh language – given that she was eight months my senior, I wasn't expecting such a reaction.

"If you used such vocabulary around Mother you would come to know the taste of soap before you could start praying to Melodias."

"I never took you for the prudish type, Miss Doorsmasher."

"Hey, I never said *I* gave a shit!"

I'll admit, she forced a laugh out of me; by now I was reasonably sure her company would be more than welcome among our lot.

By now the front gate of Ford was visible, and already I could see the two guards stationed inside the left half of the fortified wall surrounding the gate gazing at my companion with confusion; any outsider voluntarily entering the ghastly, decrepit village of Ford was normally met with confusion and tireless scrutiny, and I can only guess that my presence was what saved Matra from a laundry list of questioning – at least courtesy of them.

"Who is this 'Melodias' anyway? Your dad keeps bringing her up but he's never explained it for love nor money."

My answer didn't come quickly - Matra spent a few seconds soaking in the sight of my mostly abandoned home, appearing genuinely enthralled by the sight of plant-infested and empty buildings as far as the eye could see.

"What a beautiful place... ah, right, sorry. Melodias is... um, a bit of background would help, come to think of it."

She came to a stop in front of the clinic, formerly owned by Saki but now run by Julius in her permanent absence. She didn't seem to have any reason to stop here in particular, but she let out a sigh of relief as her posterior rested against the semi-circular stone patio at its entrance. Not wanting to stare down at her for the next stage in our conversation, I followed suit, sitting down about a metre away from her and imitating the way in which she crossed her legs. I ought to thank Julius for hanging some fresh lilies in front of the clinic that morning; the sweet scent did a lot to drown out the bitterness under which she had wallowed.

"My country has two prominent religions, each following their own philosophy, deities, all that boring stuff. The first and most prevalent is the Eisha. I don't care enough to know much about their workings or doctrines, but the gist I got from Mom is that they preach all about 'forgiveness' and 'embracing your fellow man' as their core tenets. They don't follow or worship any god, instead believing that spiritual power manifests from unity and... look, from what I can tell, it essentially boils down to the power of friendship. It wouldn't be out of place in *Chronicles of the Cosmic Queens*." she said, finishing with a dismissive sneer.

I had not a single idea what her last comment was referring to, but I abstained from asking as I wanted her to finish the religious talk without detours keeping us there from dusk til dawn.

"The second, and the one followed by Mom, is the religion of Raisha. I guess I'm *technically* a follower given I was inducted as a child... but I would have better luck remembering what I had for breakfast on this day ten years ago than recalling the last time I so much as graced one of their texts with the tip of my nail!"

She paused for air as she playfully wriggled her toes around – for some unfathomable reason, she had made the entire journey here in a pair of beige sandals that left more of her feet exposed to the elements than not. Was she tempting the god of splinters?

"The Raisha is more or less a mirror image of the Eisha – it inspires its followers to seek improvement of the self. And unlike the Eisha, they do in fact follow a god – Melodias."

Immediately, something didn't sit right with me.

"The religion promoting self-improvement is the one that follows a god?"

"*Hahaha,* I made the same observation once. Mom gave me that 'you're right but I'll never admit it so shut up' look and I didn't fancy a mouthful of soap, so I dropped it." Matra answered with a nostalgic smile – I'm not sure I would recall being threatened by my own mother with such... joy.

Nevertheless, while she had provided me answers as to who this Melodias was, that opened up a rabbit hole of my own pondering – strictly speaking, I wasn't religious, and had never pursued the topic in my own time. Best I could summon was hearing rare mentions of a 'Tarryn' among others in the village, often in the context of praying to him or cursing another in his name, but nothing beyond that. Ford had no designated place of worship even before the Band of the Wyvern's attack.

That being said, I couldn't deny my own experiences either; what I had witnessed during said attack – acts of teleportation and apparent clairvoyance at the hands of Sihan-Perseli – didn't mesh with our current understanding of the world. Such things were written off as impossible or at least never observed in any of the texts in Kyrie's library. And further questions were yet raised by the Screaming Roses; who in the world could have created them, other than an immensely powerful but possibly malevolent being beyond our imagination? The thought that anything so strong and yet possessing such malintent could be watching my every move sent a chill down my spine.

"So, what god are you wishing for extra birthday presents from, Vega?"

As she leaned towards me, the sensation of her warm breath momentarily derailed my train of thought, and I was tempted to divulge the event involving my guardian and the seemingly self-evident proof of divinity. And yet, I couldn't bring myself to speak, for obvious reasons. For more or less my entire life up to that point I had been fighting for some kind of workaround to communicate what really happened on that day I ran into the Basin, and it's all been fruitless. It was pointless to try and tell it to Matra.

"I uh... believe in what I can see. Nothing more, nothing less."

Matra raised an eyebrow, but I considered an easy way out of the topic superior to an utterly futile endeavour.

"Well, Mr. All Seeing Eyes, are you content in just seeing these?"

She pulled a small bag out from inside her cardigan – within said bag were a selection of rectangular sweets in distinct shades of red and orange.

"My tongue begs to differ, thank you very much."

I withdrew the reddest of the bunch, throwing it into my mouth without hesitation. The sweet set of teeth I had spent the past eight years cultivating finally backfired on me as at the end of a sweet, grape-like taste came an earth-rending scorch upon my tongue, and my mouth flew open to unleash a deluge of flame.

Matra, of course, was delighted by my much-deserved bewilderment and self-battery against my tongue as I fought against the fire I thought was reducing it to ashes. She keeled backwards in uproarious laughter as I slowly realised I was not in fact burning to death.

"Every time!"

"*What the hell?!* I like my tongue, thank you very much!"

"This is how we taunt our friends back at home. Did Dad not bring such a tradition along with him?"

"I know he has a flair for the dramatic, but your dad isn't a teenage girl, Matra." a voice rang out among the vacant streets of Ford.

As if he had suddenly materialised, there to our right stood Julius; he was dressed in his all-white uniform and no doubt on his way to the clinic, only to be blocked by two deviants. The two of us shot straight up.

"I have... *no* idea what you're doing here, but I'm glad to see you're well. How's Myra?"

"Oh, um... she's fine."

Matra quickly glanced at me, her eyes detailing with crystal clarity that my silence on the matter of her stowing away was urgently required. Julius was no idiot – eight years of raising me and Altair made him remarkably perceptive as to when we were lying or beating around the bush, and this intuition extended to Matra. But she herself was just as perceptive, and attempted to ward off his suspicions.

"Myra ended up as part of Mr. Entari's routine and everyone seems to like her. She also got herself a seat in the makeup and costuming department!"

"Glad to hear it! How's your mother?"

Matra drew a blank as she stared at him – Julius smirked, having snapped up his prey.

"You got into another argument with her, right?"

"*Hmph*! And what would give you that impression?" she asked as her arms joined her legs in the art of crossing.

"Not an impression so much as precedent; last I visited Dias, little five-year-old you disappeared for three hours only to turn up inside a box at that temple. Something about Mommy Dearest being too rough with your hair, if my memory fails me not?"

"Why would you remember something like that?! Is five-year-old me the object of your desires?!"

"Of course not! You know I... I like them younger than that!"

His extremely incriminating answer arrived with the dramatic gestures oft employed by Mahro, and yet he had not the stature or velvety, enchanting voice to pull such a heinous reply off to comedic effect. All Matra and I could do was stare blankly as we internally debated what was worse: the joke itself or his choice to shout such a thing in the middle of the street.

The journey to the library was filled with Matra taking in the sights of Ford, with Julius insisting and reaffirming that he was joking as we walked away; we of course knew it to be the case, but watching the man who was ostensibly my father beg us not to get him in trouble with Kyrie was an amusing instance I didn't want to put an end to.

...am I evil?

Putting aside my dubious morality, the first sight to greet our eyes once the library's doors opened was Tsubasa sitting alone at the central table, dressed in a dark blue dress and with her blonde hair tied into pigtails by red, flower-like bobbles. She was deeply invested into reading the cards of a board game she was playing with an absent Kyrie, but before long she looked up towards us at last and ran up to me in glee. After her arms coiled around my waist and I gently stroked her hair, she looked up to Matra with an uncharacteristic disdain in her eyes and took a step behind me.

"...only I can marry him!"

I didn't even need to look at Matra to feel a powerful, murderous intent piercing through my skull.

"You got wax in your ears? I told you, brothers can't marry their sisters! A-and I'm not going to marry her! I only just met her!"

Tsubasa at last stopped using me as a human shield and walked in front of my impromptu companion.

"...what's your name?"

"I'm uh... you know that weird guy who keeps beating up your big brother? Well... I'm his daughter! Name's Matra!"

As she extended her hands towards Tsubasa for a handshake, my sister retreated back to my rear, tugging on my shirt.

"Run, big bro! She's here to beat you up too!"

"Yes, and then we're going to tickle him to death!" Matra said as she chaotically thrashed her fingers around.

"Stranger, thou would dare encroach upon this demesne for the singular purpose of terrorising the youthful? Have thee any shame, or is such malevolence how thy divinity remains sustained?"

Kyrie at last made her entrance into the disastrous scene, showing up in her seat and with her legs crossed atop the table without a sound – her age was slowly beginning to show, given that she would go on to turn 30 that very year, but it had not at all been a deficit to her uncanny ability to materialise mid-conversation.

More notable, however, was the change in her outfit – as far as I could tell from her incessant fangirl speak, newly introduced powers for her idol Tsubasa Euriclytes Pandemonia had resulted in a costume change for the witch in question, replacing the plain blue in her costume with a popping purple. Alongside this fictional metamorphosis came a physical one, as Kyrie's former bedroom – now serving more or less as a museum to the object of her admiration – was completely overhauled to reflect this change. Over the next year, an unfathomable number of Cladio could be seen hauling exotic physical goods through the skies, to no displeasure of yours truly. The crown jewel of these deliveries was, of course, an amended costume for the scarily dedicated Kyrie. If Kyrie were inclined that way, I imagine she would have sooner married the witch than Julius.

"You would stand before me in such garish colours, Witch of the Underworld? Do all the people of Pecronia conduct themselves with such ill grace or are you the blight among the blighted?"

As Matra shot back, the distance between the women closed, and both Tsubasa and I knew this was about to get ugly and utterly, *utterly* incomprehensible.

"To tarnish my proud Pecronian origin is to tarnish thy soul; hath thee any regard for our esteemed history? Know thee not of the Fifty Year Conquest of Kalamar? Aware not, are ye, of our role in averting the Third Astral Calamity of the Holy Kingdom of Mycia? Thou Noremians should know thy place; thy existence is hardly a footnote compared to our own."

Matra snorted and crossed her arms, apparently having extracted meaning from all that drivel.

"The only footnote I see is your very existence, Defiled Witch of Imperishable Miasma! Your accomplishments, esteemed as they may be, pale in comparison to your humiliating usurpation in the 945th year of the 12th cycle! Did your people take such pride in licking the pungent filth and muck off of Noremian boots? Is it celebrated in your history books? A dog is more shameful in defeat than a Pecronian!"

"Victory is found not in the past, but in the present before us! Let us engage in personal warfare, vile defiler of my boundaries, and atone for your infractions against my people as you stormed South Avengard, and I'll wipe off that ugly grin you displayed as you snuffed out the lives of all those innocents!"

"Innocents?! *Peh!* The only legitimate Pecronian is a *dead* Pecronian? I shall do you the dignity of uniting you with your ancestors in the Immortal Transient Vortex of Souls, where you shall be free of entertain the perished with anecdotes of your woeful, cursed existence!"

BANG!

"Lady Melodias, *what* have we done to deserve the curse that is the female sex's ability to speak?!"

Mahro dramatically fell to his knees after kicking the door wide open, angrily shaking his fist to the skies all the while.

"It's a bit of fun between us girls, Mahro! The only fun you derive is from giving my darling Vega a beating!"

Kyrie pulled a surprised Matra into her grasp, delighted by her new verbal playmate. The mention of my name hardly roused me whatsoever; I was still trying to process what a 'Pecronian' was or what kind of idiot would name a place 'Avengard'.

"Truth be told, Kyrie, it's usually the other way around; he can hold his own something fierce."

In a rare display, Mahro was giving me an earnest, straightforward compliment… not that I was cognizant enough to register it for a few seconds afterwards.

Once 9pm struck and Tsubasa at last went to sleep, the rest of us were gathered around to hear what Mahro had to say regarding the Matra situation. Ringo had been summoned by Julius, but obligations elsewhere in Ford meant the contents of the discussion would need to be relayed to him at a later date. The good news came first; Julius and Kyrie had given their blessing for his daughter to stay with us until the two of them returned to Tenryuu together, and Matra took this especially well; upon the suggestion that she take up what was once Altair's bed, I was hesitant at first, getting goosebumps at the idea of sharing a room with a girl I barely knew even if she was Mahro's daughter, but I ultimately acquiesced, having no real ground to stand on other than subjective awkwardness.

The bad news was that their return would be indefinite; according to Matra, the ban on travel in and out of Tenryuu was expected to be enforced until the end of Morosus and Ennui's ugly little scrap. Tenryuu initially remained indifferent to the ongoing war until a royal vessel of Ennui sank a large passenger ship of the former nation, sentencing most onboard to their untimely deaths and spurring the country to act against Ennui with immediate effect. Mahro didn't see eye to eye with his home country's judgement; as far as he was concerned, such a move was about repurposing Tenryuu's passenger vessels into weapons of war, in an effort to make up for their pitiful naval prowess. Either way, he had no power to override the ruling, and so he and Matra were scheduled to depart on July 6th, the day after my 16th birthday and the latest they could possibly leave.

I barely spoke a word for the duration of the meeting; Mahro had become such an integral part of my everyday life that the thought of him leaving for a prolonged period, perhaps forever, was a sudden and uncomfortable weight on my shoulders. Disappearing for a few months to visit his family was one thing, but years without his presence was orders of magnitude more severe. If anything, I looked up to him as much as I did my own parents, and for the inner workings of our mad world to suddenly rip away that connection through circumstances entirely beyond our control felt... cruel. I couldn't begrudge him for choosing to leave, mind you. The only thing he loved more than a chaotic brawl was his kin.

I retreated to my bed as soon as the meeting wrapped up, consumed by these thoughts. Just before I at last drifted off to sleep, I could faintly hear Matra enter the room at last, mumbling to herself about the tightness of Kyrie's loaned pyjamas.

Chapter 13:
A Lively Graveyard

I woke up the day after Matra arrived to find Tsubasa had also clambered atop Altair's former bed in the middle of the night, and the two girls were lightly clinging onto each other as they slept. I found the sight unfathomably cute, but I had a much greater concern: wearing my shirt in bed amidst the aggressive summer heat made me wake up with a dreadful amount of sweat both crawling down my skin and embedding its eternal stench within it, and so my first order of business was bathing. Purifying the filth from my mortal vessel, as Mahro would so eloquently put it. Our bath was the only place in which I could find any comfort while unclothed, and so my ventures into it were much enjoyed, if prolonged to the annoyance of the other inhabitants. It was five minutes into this particular venture, as the room filled with steam and I closed my eyes, that a voice shocked me out of this deep comfort.

"*Huh?* First they tell me you have baths *in* your houses, and now you're telling me they're *this* small?!"

The bewildered female voice stunned me for a moment, and I scrambled to conceal my nether region even though I was both submerged in bubble-laden water and enshrouded by clouds of steam.

Indeed, the intrusion came from our newest guest, Matra. She stood by my side in Kyrie's pyjamas, with her fingers gripping the shirt, no doubt itching to remove it and submerge herself into this pleasurable domain.

"Wh-what the hell are you *doing?!*" I asked.

"Huh? It's a bath, silly."

More objectionable qualities of this encounter would arrive yet, as a yawning Mahro would slowly emerge from the mist behind her.

"Ah, my apologies, Vega. She asked where the bath is located, and I forgot the uh… one person limit you strange Morosus folk employ."

"So there really aren't any hot springs here? How do the people of this country *live?!*"

By now my head had half submerged beneath the bath, waiting with bated breath for this odious exchange to be over. I'm almost certain Mahro just entered to draw out the torture. And it worked.

"From what I can tell, it comes from being a bit more uppity over the skin on our bones, little one. Even bathing amongst family is something of a taboo, and for as odd as you may find it, that's what the world of Morosus bathing revolves around, much as my world revolves around you and your sister."

"Ah, smother me more, daddy!" Matra yelled as she threw her arms around her father.

I was certainly ready to start smothering. With a pillow.

"What *is* this, 'Peep on Vega in the Bath Day'?! Shoo, begone, away with you!"

Finally, the two of them scurried out of the bathroom without a word further, and I was left to my own devices once again. I could already tell the next ten days were going to be… different.

After Matra's turn in the bath, Mahro compelled the two of us to join him behind the library before breakfast. She raced off ahead of me, and by the time I reached my destination, she was aggressively stroking Maverick as the old boy lazed around, poking out his tongue with sanguine euphoria. As she stood up, Mahro squatted and reached inside his worn equipment bag.

"You have my appreciation for joining me, fellow travellers of mortality! With the two of you present, I wish to entertain a prospect most fascinating."

From the bag he produced a wooden staff - with a round, blunt end and a leather grip in its centre - and threw it in my direction. A pair of wooden batons soon followed, only they were aimed towards Matra, and we each stylishly claimed our weapons from the air before we could even realise what scheme he was concocting.

"Now, Matra, baby, I... can't let you shoot my student in the face. Do you object to this arrangement, or shall I crown him with an apple?"

It took a few seconds for the pair of us to realise he was setting us up for a mock fight; her confused frown turned into an excited smile as she shook her head, and her assault soon followed. I stood firm with the staff pointed towards her as she approached in a zigzag, not expecting much of consequence considering how much more time Mahro had spent training me than being with his own children. Such expectation was quickly put to bed as she sent the baton in her left hand flying towards my head; I quickly whacked it away with the staff, but this provided her an ever so slight opening to approach me from my left and trip me up with her remaining weapon. Not wanting to end up with yet another mouthful of dry dirt, I dug the thin end of the staff into the ground and fumbled around it as I regained my footing, ending up face to face with a fully rearmed Matra.

"I'm glad to see you haven't been slacking in my absence, Matra. My esteemed student, will you permit such humiliation to stand?"

Mahro produced an apple from the endless depths of his bag, and he began gnawing away at it with his front teeth as the battle's standstill persisted.

Insulted by his allegation and having been hoist by my own hesitancy, I began advancing on Matra, rapidly spinning the staff around my body in an effort to ward off a counterattack as well as misdirect her gaze.

My first real strike was aimed at her leg – she struck a cutesy pose as her right leg raised, barely avoiding the attack. Maintaining my composure, I aimed my next swing at her stomach – the ease with which she twirled around this particular attack and left me looking the fool was even greater. It was just as our eyes met once more that her right leg felt the brunt of my staff, and she was sent tumbling to the ground with a comical yell. After spinning the staff yet more for dramatic flair, I stood at her feet and pointed it towards her face, rewarding myself with a smug grin.

Such smugness wouldn't last long; Matra bashed my foot with the back of her own, and the follow-up kick to my shin sent me crashing down – on top of her, ending the opening bout in a draw. My head unfortunately crashed into her stomach, rather than a foot above that, but the three of us laughed the matter off as Matra and I returned to our feet, ready to duel for hours to come. The first of our many clashes set the tone going ahead, and after our clothes were thoroughly stained in dirt and our legs and arms were bruised and barely able to cling onto our weapons any longer, I claimed the upper hand slightly more often than not but came to greatly respect her strength and intuition regardless. From the admiring glint in her eyes, the respect was clearly mutual.

Throughout her stay, we tried a couple times to initiate Matra into the Cult of Kyrie's Game - of which I am titled Grand Lord of Obstinance by my adoptive mother due to my tendency to turn every match against me into an endurance test, not faltering but not taking the offense all that much either. Every one of these attempts ended with Matra giving up in the span of five minutes, swearing that she would never touch it again. Unlike Julius who was prone to these sorts of antics in the right mood, her fourth declaration of abstinence proved to be final.

On the other hand, she was more receptive to a board game oft enjoyed by me and Tsubasa; whenever afforded some free time, the three of us could be commonly seen sitting at the centre of the library playing *Conquest of the Forbidden Isles*. The game purported to accurately reflect the nascent days of civilization, before the names Morosus, Tenryuu, Ennui or Vana were twinkles in their founders' eyes, and the global search for the mythical Gates of Heaven that drove so much of their advancement. Despite the historical premise, its art was largely composed of cute-looking women, having been purchased by Kyrie shortly after Tsubasa's birth – it appealed to the aesthetic proclivities of all among this short-lived fellowship, but it cast more than a little doubt as to its self-proclaimed authenticity.

The rules were simple on a surface level – at the start of the game, four cross-shaped tiles would be placed down, two containing an island and the other two containing only water. Players could choose their starting location in a clockwise rotation, establishing their formative empire of two soldiers and a ship wherever they pleased. Starting in water made you an esteemed member of the Water Nomads, while instead opting for land saw you entering the fray as the indomitable Kingdom of Stone. Each player drew from a deck of cards respective to their faction until six were distributed among members of the Kingdom of Stone and the Water Nomads, and each rotation of the game added one more cross-shaped piece to the board, with three of the remaining ten containing an island ripe for conquest. The cards – each bearing an illustration of a fictional female commander and describing her abilities - allowed their holder to perform actions such as relocating their faction to an adjacent piece or attacking enemies, and even if one were to switch from the Kingdom of Stone to the Water Nomads or vice versa, they could continue using the cards of their initial faction until the end of that turn. Any players belonging to the same faction were ostensibly teammates, but the game's ultimate goal would crown only one victor; to truly conquer the Forbidden Isles, one had to enter the Gates of Heaven.

The Gates of Heaven would emerge when all four pieces of it were excavated from different islands by the players, and it arrived as its own board piece which was placed down by the player who discovered the last of its four components. To top off the chaos, all players were at last allowed to attack those of the same side. This would trigger an avalanche of everybody rushing towards the Gates of Heaven, but victory was not so simple as merely getting there; one was forced to maintain their presence before it for three turns before they were allowed passage. This final trial was the ultimate test of each player's military prowess, and victory was incredibly hard fought regardless of how many stood in defense of their prize.

Our first game got rather violent towards its end; Julius returned from the clinic to find three raging animals racing towards a gate. I was first there, having placed the Gates of Heaven directly next to me much to the great annoyance of Tsubasa and Matra. The two girls raced towards me, each agreeing on a ceasefire with the other, but my third turn was soon approaching. Crossing my arms with exacerbated smugness, I watched as they were reduced to merely one card between them, held by my little sister.

"*Gahahahaaaaa!* How can you possibly win, little girl?! I stand before the golden ticket to divinity! Such a right... is not yours to claim!"

I was simply unstoppable – I took endless glee in boasting to the eight-year-old, and I knew deep in my heart that turning this game against me was impossible.

Much to my bewilderment, however, she grinned back at me as she revealed the final ace up her sleeve.

"Meridian Tryst! Choose one adjacent enemy to fight and draft any others, ally or foe, into your assault! For all your talk of 'rights', you're about to look super wrong!"

Tsubasa slammed the card into the table, almost knocking our units out of the war before it could even start – my sister never received any combat training from Mahro, under the impression that Julius and I were more than capable of serving as the family's protectors, but his enduring presence over the prior eight years had certainly left its mark on her in other ways.

I was so caught up in how proud I was of her powerful delivery that my feigned, exaggerated reaction – falling backwards in my chair while I cursed these damn women – was delayed by a second or two, though this did nothing to nullify their cheering. I got back up to face defeat like a man and watched as the last of my forces were surely eviscerated, whilst Tsubasa moved her army into my spot in the battle's aftermath. Having lost all of my forces, my next turn started with a single unit being placed in my starting tile, but by then all hope was lost; Tsubasa and Matra's army each numbered significantly higher and building an empire to combat them would take the entire game. Matra spent the next three turns hunting me down like a rabid dog, choosing to lick the boots of

222

Cosmic Empress Tsubasa rather than face inevitable destruction, until the latter entered the Gates of Heaven at last.

"You enjoy getting beaten up by girls, then?" Julius asked me, amidst all of the cheering and dancing from the victor, her willing footstool and a suddenly present Kyrie.

"If we count our sparring, we currently sit at 15-12 in my favour."

It was Tsubasa's victory if I were to be pedantic, but the two were willing collaborators – I'm not so uncharitable as to rob a victory from Matra.

"Some victories are worth more than others, Vega. What use is there in claiming each of your enemy's toes if they lop off your head?"

"I'm sure you would prefer to keep a lady's toes over her head, gramps."

"...little shit." said Julius, smirking as he lightly punched my shoulder.

After this bombastic victory, Matra and Tsubasa got along as if they were long-distant sisters; in a place so desolate as Ford, I was just relieved to see she had made a friend other than her own brother, even if this relationship was never destined for longevity. I suppose her ignorance of how abruptly this union's end would come only widened the growing pit in my stomach, but I wasn't about to let my own reservations and dread interfere with their happiness.

What concerned me far more was the prospect that these may have been the last days I would ever spend with Mahro. He promised we would meet again once this war wrapped itself up, but I could tell from the vacant look buried within his nonchalant demeanour that this was a promise he had no guarantee of keeping; it's not that he wished to torment me, not at all, rather that wars between our nations are not well-renowned for their brevity. The previous major war – sparked by Tenryuu's ultimately doomed conquest against my home country, Morosus – dragged on for a painstaking *17 years*, ending around the time Ringo reached adolescence. And according to the old man himself, both countries took decades to recover, with every family fighting tooth and nail to put food on the table. Even if this newest clash proved to be much shorter-lived – and there was little hope for this, given Ennui's much-reviled obstinance and sheer military might – the fallout would take an unconscionable amount of time to progress beyond. Simply put, these being my last days under Mahro's tutelage or companionship was a strong possibility, and it was an ugly, demoralizing sensation I failed to rid myself of, even as I answered his confident glances with hollow smiles.

I suppose Matra's greatest contribution during her stay was setting me on the right path; she invited me and Tsubasa to join her in the forests of Ford, under the premise of sightseeing but turning out to be more or less for collecting a memento or two of her stay. Having recently been privy to tales of Eden thanks to Morgan, one of the young girls who had herself fallen victim to the vile were-woman, Tsubasa was still wary of what laid behind the trees and gently refused, leaving me to escort our lady friend through the spooky darkness. I wasn't all too used to the sight of the forest at summer's peak; instead of a thick layer of snow caked in a flurry of footprints, the earth was muddy or otherwise solid and dull. The single brown path that led us through the forest was enveloped by dead leaves from a spring long past, and we saw an uncomfortable number of small animals' decayed carcasses along the way. The air was completely stagnant, not too dissimilar to the less eventful tunnels within the Basin.

But none of this seemed to deter Matra whatsoever.

Indeed, despite my dire assessment, there were some niceties buried beneath the ruin; even Ford was blessed with the occasional patch of vibrant flowers within the forest once summer made its debut, and this year was no exception, bestowing us with rich reds and hypnotic purples.

We initially exchanged very little in the way of words; our interaction was relegated to Matra asking what on earth this strange flora or fauna she was pointing to was, followed by a brief identification and description from yours truly. It was only while she was dancing her finger around a small, brown critter with golden wings on her palm that we at last got the ball rolling. The creature, and I suppose Matra herself, made for a pleasant contrast from these dismal surroundings.

"That's what we call a Charming Asparitas; its scientific name is too painstakingly long to recall off the top of my head, but I know that they spend roughly 15 hours a day sleeping and tend to rest inside trees rich with sap. Not the most common of the lot but they make for a great aid in tapping if you catch a glimpse of one entering." I explained, feeling at least a small amount of pride that my voluminous book smarts were paying off in the art of (hopefully) impressing girls.

"...I like the wings!"

Or maybe not.

"So what's your job around here, Vega? Master of Bugs?"

"Oh, no, no, no! I just picked up a few things here and there, I'm not terribly fond of them, or most animals that aren't our old boy Maverick. Truth be told, I don't have a job yet, or much of an ambition to pursue in the first place. I'm supposed to find one once I turn 16, but I... have no idea what to do with myself."

Matra paused for a moment, releasing the Charming Asparitas from her hand and watching it fly into a nearby tree. My words sifted through her mind as the two of us sat atop a decrepit log, and the smug grin on her face suggested it was her turn to feel self-important and proud.

"Last time he came home, Dad told me something that I think you would do well to hear too. 'Seize thy destiny from the thrashing maw of that which has passed!', or something along those lines!" she said, pulling off all sorts of ridiculous gestures as she imitated her inimitable father.

"Can you translate that from Mahrotongue, pretty please?"

"The day we make Mahrotongue the one true language is the day civilization leaps forward! Not by inches, but bounds!" she declared with a boisterous laugh as she puffed out her voluminous chest, "I *think* what he was trying to say was-"

"That's a vote of confidence for your pops, I see."

"Zip it!" Matra yelled as she yanked the back of my hair – it was a graceless reminder that a haircut was well overdue, "Anyway,

I suppose it comes down to this: What you do in the future should be... let's see... influenced by your past? Guided by it? The proper word eludes me, but you understand what I'm getting at, don't you? Ah, sometimes I wish I had taken up translating Dad's every spoken word into a proper human tongue. An industry of endless demand, lying there, untapped!"

"Tell me about it. Give me a text written in Mahrotongue and my grandchildren will still be deciphering it in my stead before I croak." I answered somewhat flippantly – Matra pushed herself up against me, wrapping her arm around my own.

"Your grandchildren? I suppose you have your eye on a lucky lady to make your not-grand children with? I'm sure the competition is stiff~" she asked with an enchanting grin, using her words as a crowbar as she attempted to pry open my heart.

Her warm breath, her soft bosom pressing against my left arm, that devilish glint in her eye as she silently awaited an answer... it was all too overpowering. It felt as though I was dancing on a knife's edge, just one more look into her eyes away from saying something very stupid and fumbling the relationship I had spent the better part of a decade building up with Mahro, the man I idolized most. It took several moments of racking my brain before I finally grasped an out from the jaws of embarrassment.

"I thought we were talking about jobs?"

Blunt indifference probably wasn't the ideal course, but it seemed that she had gotten what she wanted, as her grip loosened at last and she sat upright once again with a grin.

"What *are* your options, anyway? I can understand if you don't want to leave Tsutsu behind, but-"

"*What kind of nickname is Tsutsu?*"

"*Hmph!* You should be quite honoured! She shares an honorary moniker with one of the prior queens of Tenryuu! Queen Tsutsu Bangaichi, esteemed daughter and final heir of the Bangaichi lineage!"

"A queen, eh? I suppose you could've picked... *worse* names..." I sighed in relief, "...dare I ask what legacy she left behind?"

"Happy to oblige! Queen Tsutsu Bangaichi declared war on Vana for reasons still unknown, sent the captives she didn't have executed to work as slaves in the Pegasus Isles, enjoyed bathing in the blood of young boys and she *maaaaay* or may not have deflowered dozens of them! She was eventually hung via her entrails by her own royal guard at the age of 23!" Matra explained, her disposition remaining horribly cheerful the entire time.

"*Never call her Tsutsu again!*"

Cue more pouting from Matra – though it's not like she would go on to heed my warning anyway.

"More to the point, I'll never leave Tsuts- *Tsubasa* behind! I gave Altair so much shit for doing the same he could have turned all the empty land in Ford into a farm. I suppose I would like to give blacksmithing a try, but all I'm good at is swinging sticks around; I can't say I would be able to make anything worth swinging."

"But you know how they feel, right? You know the properties of a good weapon, you understand whether or not something is well made, don't you? It's true you don't know the steps, but surely all those years of getting clobbered by Dad has taught you how to tell your end result worked out?" she answered, looking at me as if this was common sense.

But her answer *was* surprisingly insightful – as much as I wanted to rebuke her accusation of my getting pummelled by her old man, I was caught up in the undeniable truth of her words. In truth, I started to feel embarrassed, realising I had talked myself out of an obvious career path for months.

"I suppose you make a good point..."

"I only ever make good points, and don't you forget it!" the ever-so-proud Matra declared as she crossed her arms.

"I suppose I'll ask Ringo to put a word in to Lyn for me, then. If nothing else, I could at least dodge conscription if it comes for Ford – not that there's many left here to conscript in the first place."

Although I sounded as though I was just settling for the closest olive branch I could desperately grasp, I was actually a little excited by the matter, finally having made up my mind for the first time in years and content that I could at least make something of my life. I looked back to Matra, expecting a confident, reassuring gesture to push me forward.

Instead, her eyes had gone blank and she was seemingly frozen in place by some horrible revelation. After some light poking at her shoulder, she at last snapped back to reality.

"I didn't tell my boss I was leaving!" She yelled, almost sending me flying off the log with the force of her voice, "Ugh, Loren is going to kill me, strip me of my job and then kill me again!"

It appeared this Chief Loren wouldn't need to do the deed himself, as the despair-filled Matra leaned back on the log until her hair was mingling with the weeds and roots littering the ground; for that moment, she had resigned herself to becoming a plant, free of human tribulation. It took some vigorous motivation and pulling of her arms from yours truly to set us on our journey back to my home, with Matra never having taken a memento from the forest after all.

I woke up on my 16th birthday to find a veritable army waiting outside my door. Mahro, Kyrie, Julius, Tsubasa, Matra and even old Ringo himself turned up for my grand waking entrance, and the library's main hall erupted with overlapping shouts of "Happy Birthday!" the instant I set foot beyond my bedroom. After an avalanche of embraces and further celebration, I was pushed backwards onto my bed by Tsubasa and Matra, with each girl locking one of my arms in place.

"You have to wait here, bro! We have to bring presents!" said Tsubasa.

"*Awwww*, but I want breakfast..." I whimpered, feigning resistance against their grip.

"One brings their fasting to a conclusion hundreds of times each year, but each tick of the mortal clock arrives merely once! You would do well to cherish your youth while you possess it yet, Vega!"

Mahro was last to remain at the door as the rest scurried elsewhere - the girls released their grip after he raised his hands towards them, and before I could get my head straight, his arm was around my shoulder.

"Let us hope this is not the last tick taken in my company, dear friend."

Tsubasa produced a cute, confused grunt as my mentor stood up again, having picked up on Mahro's sounds but not the substance of his words, and I wasn't about to cast rain on her parade by sating her curiosity; this was the last day we would get to spend with our new friend, possibly for as long as we lived.

Soon enough, Kyrie, Julius and Ringo returned, each carrying a box or two of varying sizes. The first I opened, upon Kyrie's insistence, was a decently large wooden container from the woman herself, within which was a vast mass of blue fabric. Unfolding it revealed a vibrant blue cloak, adorned with a white fur-coated collar.

"Oh... thank you!"

I was genuinely grateful for the gift but also somewhat confused by the timing; the middle of summer hardly seemed like the best time to bestow such a thick, sweat-inducing item of clothing upon me.

Then again, just as every year must bring a birthday, it must also bring a winter season, I told myself - its utility was destined to remain in circular motion.

Endless cheers of "Put it on, put it on, put it on!" came from both Kyrie and Matra before I could even finish looking it over, and they fawned without end once I at last complied. Regardless, once I stood before my mirror, I took quite a liking to how it looked – its borderline regal look wasn't complimented well by my dull, crease-ridden shirt or stark black underwear but I could easily see it as the cherry atop a desirable outfit. Before long I was standing before the mirror with pride, not as Vega Pyre, but as Vega, King of the Universe.

"See, it fits like a glove!" Kyrie yelled as she brought her arm around Matra's neck.

"You're right... he really *does* look like Galactic Commissioner Starsenal!" Matra said, bringing her hand to her mouth in awe.

"Are you going bloody daft or is this more of your... *woman rubbish?*" Mahro ever so elegantly asked, receiving a symphony of hissing from the girls as a reward.

"Got yer answer, pup!"

Ringo was no slouch in making his own fun - he seemed to be enjoying this more than anybody else, in fact.

"Are you going to open the rest now?"

Surprisingly, it was Tsubasa who took it upon herself to set the morning back on its proper track.

I was hasty in uncovering the rest of this small hoard, wanting to fill my painfully vacant stomach. In addition to the cloak from Kyrie, I received a pair of black boots from Ringo, a handmade wooden carving of a dog from Tsubasa, and an encyclopaedia on all things plant-related from Julius (which was derided for 'being boring' by all others present save for Tsubasa and Matra, but I was more than pleased with it).

The last of them came from Mahro and Matra, as the former produced a small box from one of his wide exterior pockets. Inside was a flexible white armband adorned with a red tortoise. Apparently, the two of them had managed to sneak off to Mot and back completely under my nose just to procure this, and I can personally attest to the fact that such a journey was conventionally not too short – they could have borrowed transport from someone else within or just outside Ford, but I suspect the both of them were too prideful to depend on such means.

"The tortoise is a wonderful, wise old beast we could stand to extract much knowledge from! Tenacity, fortitude, longevity; any quality that contributes to a long and victorious life, you will certainly find it within its supreme shell!" Mahro spoke endlessly as I tried the armband on, finding it to fit extraordinarily well.

The pattern itself was hardly all that captivating, but I was moved by its meaning. I'm not sure if a promise of eventual reunion was what such a gift implied, but that's how I chose to read into it.

A small party was held that evening to commemorate my coming of age, in the front garden of Ringo's home. I dressed myself in a sharp white dress shirt with a black collar and cuffs in addition to deep blue trousers, taking my newly received armband to complete the look. Julius took it upon himself to escort me there about half an hour after everybody else had departed, and our lengthy, quiet stroll along the river was much welcomed after the fairly chaotic two weeks that preceded it. Once we arrived, I laid my eyes on Ringo's home for the first time in many years; it was by no means egregiously large, much like the higher-class homes found within Mot, but it certainly stood out among the otherwise quaint, modest dwellings typical of Ford. The fact it had a front garden at all was remarkable - said garden stretched as wide as most other houses within the village, and for the occasion its lot of short, freshly-cut grass laid beneath an array of chairs and folding tables draped in white cloth, seating faces both fresh and familiar.

My arrival sparked an avalanche of applause from everybody present. Seeing so many gathered together in one place, especially in a desolate village like Ford, was a strange sensation, but rapturous celebration from no less than 40 people was something I wouldn't take for granted any time soon. I was all but carried into a seat, sharing a table with Kyrie, Julius and Tsubasa. Ringo went off to chat with a handful of his own elderly-looking compatriots while Mahro and Matra shared a small table near the front gate. I couldn't help but feel ever so slighted that the two of them were sat at the perimeter of the garden while I was placed at the centre stage, considering this was the last night I would be spending with the two of them for a completely unknown amount of time. But Mahro's never been one for making goodbyes more painful.

The festivities began almost immediately upon my entrance; a makeshift stage was constructed in front of Ringo's front door where the old man and his pals would take turns singing all sorts of jolly, old-fashioned tunes, with a team of their fellows playing along on tattered drums and trumpets that surely hadn't seen much of the light of day for the past decade. It was amusingly slipshod but watching Ringo sweat himself onto death's doorstep from the mere act of slapping some drums made up for it in ways the spectacle of a real show could never replicate.

Not even ten minutes passed before Matra showed up at our table with her chair in tow, painstakingly forcing a wedge between me and Tsubasa that could still barely fit her at the forefront along with us. Mahro remained by his lonesome, often staring towards us or scribbling something down in a notebook whenever I did glance towards him.

"*Soooooo*, Tsutsu, how do you feel about your big bro being a cranky old man now?" Matra asked as she clutched my sister in dramatic fashion, casting a devious smirk at me.

"He's always been a cranky old man!" my sister answered.

"*Hmph!* I'm not old!" I yelled as I crossed my arms.

"If this dashing young man's an old'un, what in the flippin' heck does tha' make me then?! A fossil?!" Ringo asked, staring into the contents of his glass.

"At least fossils end up in history books; there isn't one old enough to find you in, pops." Julius answered, receiving a stomp on his foot as a reward.

"Fetch us some liquor, bell boy, before you too become history!"

Ringo dragged his little man out of the chair and launched him towards the large table stacked with drinks both alcoholic and non-alcoholic.

"What's a... bell boy?" Tsubasa asked with a curious frown.

I was surprised to find a word she couldn't yet ascribe a definition to given her demonstrable (and perhaps hereditary) acumen, but it's worth remembering that to the best of my knowledge Tsubasa has never actually left Ford, where no hotel or temporary guest housing of any sort has ever been established.

"Well, little'un, a bell boy is a... yer know, *boy*, who runs around and does everything fer ya! When yer Vega's age, yer'll be my... ooh, what was it, *fifth* bell boy...?" Ringo said, intermittently derailed by drunken hiccupping.

Safe to say, Tsubasa was having none of it, though her anger would prove to be amusingly displaced.

"I... I'm not even a boy, you pervy old man!"

"*Pervy?!* Where yer getting' such verbiage from, lass? Spit it out or yer'll only have the 'l' left!"

"She called you that!" the little deviant shouted, her finger pointed squarely at a stunned Matra's face.

"Hey, you! What happened to our sacred oath to 'never squeal on friends for real'??!!"

"...oh, sorry!" Tsubasa apologised with a bow before her finger instead snapped towards my face, "He called you that!"

Ringo laughed off this fresh new spurious allegation, though he quickly tempered his enjoyment and brought his arms back to the table as he delivered some news to me.

"Speaking of jobs, kid, I put in a word with Lyndra fer ya. She's coming tonight but runnin' late, so try not ter get shitfaced before she shows up, hear me?"

"No bad words, pervy old man!" Tsubasa shouted, prompting an angry, shaking fist from the pervy old man.

Julius finally returned with a thin platter in one hand full of drinks – glass bottles of whiskey for the adults (myself newly inducted among them) and blackcurrant juice for Tsubasa. Before Julius could even do the honour of handing out drinks, Ringo snatched one of the glasses from the platter and necked it in one gulp, to my astonishment. Following a prolonged belch, he at last came up with a witty retort to the eight-year-old.

"Y-yer a... bad word..."

Once all of the beverages were passed around, everyone got to drinking, Tsubasa most enthusiastic among them. While everybody else gulped down their drinks in such a manner that suggested they had wandered a desert for ten years with not a drop to drink, I glared at the bottle for a while, apprehensive about my first tango with such vices, until Matra leaned towards me with a gleeful, dreamy smile.

"I'm so *jealous* that Kyrie lets you drink this the moment you turn into a man..."

The stench in her breath and the wear in her lively voice suggested that her enjoyment in no way matched her tolerance for the activity.

"I've been an adult for... eh, however long now, yet my mom still won't let me buy the stuff, let alone drink it at home! Loren lets me take a sip or two while I'm off duty, but still... anyway, you should get right to it!"

With the friendly pressure mounting, I at last brought the bottle to my mouth, taking care to avoid my bottom lip, and slowly raised it, anticipating a fairly strong taste for my first time. True to the legends, this first encounter with the world of alcohol was a stark punch to the gut, and I took a moment to recuperate before taking another swing at it, this time having developed some small modicum of tolerance against this stark but strangely pleasant drink.

"How's your first tantalizing taste of adulthood, then?" Matra asked, just about managing to meet my eyes as she adopted her signature grin.

"My first taste of adulthood was... 16 years ago. I've never been a boy!"

I started to fluster from the instant regret of saying such a monumentally stupid thing, but the girls laughed nonetheless, maybe even more so at my self-embarrassment.

"When I'm 16, I'm going to drink a whole bottle! In one go!"

Her declaration of drunkenness made, Tsubasa crossed her arms and puffed out her chest – the manner in which she did so was unsurprisingly similar to our mutual friend, who looked awfully smug about her blatant influence.

"And not a millisecond before that age barrier is surpassed, young lady! I would prefer my precious offspring abstain from such vehement vices, but thou art of adolescence, Vega; I shall not attempt to halt thee."

Kyrie sounded somewhat disappointed that I was so quick to grasp the neck of a bottle – considering she was indulging in the very same activity, I could handwave it as a jab at herself more than anything.

"Adolescent or not, he's a boy. Perk an ear for him even when you're old and frail, lest he become as bad as the old boy over there."

A new, gruff voice rang out to my right, sounding as though it belonged to a middle-aged woman. Sure enough, there stood a stranger behind Ringo, one I had caught passing glimpses of during my life in Ford but never actually talked to. She had arrived at this momentous celebration in grey, rugged clothing covered by a dust-stained white apron, and her eyes carried an air of intensiveness, sizing up my worth even at an occasion that called only for carefree celebration.

"*I'm* the bad one?! Bloody hell Lyndra, ever heard 'a dressin' fer the occasion, ya scruffy wammal?! Or is that yer only set 'a garb?!" Ringo shouted.

"You know my schedule's tight; if you want me in fancy dress so bad why don't you rip these off yourself?" Lyndra asked with a dry smile, leaning down to further taunt the old man.

"Couldn't pay me all the money in the world to!"

Of course, the only things Ringo would kiss that night were the necks of many, many bottles.

"Vega, I'm more than happy to give you a shake. Come to my workshop two days from now, 9 in the morning. You ought to enjoy yourself for the night, and you don't want to try using the bellows drunk, believe me."

The unflinching stare into my eyes told me everything about her; there was an iron-clad conviction behind them, one that had been forged by years and years of practice. The idea that a woman of such discipline and experience was so much as giving me the time of day humbled me greatly.

"Tha-that's great! Hope I don't disappoint you."

"Don't work yourself up about it, you could set half of this ghost town aflame and you still wouldn't crack the top ten disappointments that week." Lyndra glumly answered before she settled down at a table nearing the stage.

The rest of the night was pleasant; as the sun at last become one with the horizon, a series of blue Tenkite lights atop the front garden's fence all turned on. Upon questioning, a very inebriated Ringo gave Tsubasa a history lesson on what Tenkite actually is: a bright blue mineral found in vast quantities well beneath sea level, applied in an unconscionable number of ways. It can be used to create batteries, processed into energy for contraptions - such as the long fallen into disrepair platform leading to the formerly occupied homes within the natural walls of Ford – or used as an explosive alternative to gunpowder, just to name a few examples among his list. Its name was derived from Tenryuu, given that it was originally thought to be found exclusively within the boundaries of said country, and this enabled its dreams of conquest up until deposits were discovered within Morosus and Vana too, enabling the beleaguered nations to put up a fight and end the war at last.

The real highlight arrived courtesy of my sister, starting with a strange declaration directed at Ringo.

"Grandad, I'm a dragon!"

"Yer a what?" the bewildered old man asked, cleaning out his ears with his pinky fingers.

"I'm a dragon! Watch!"

With our attention drawn, she revealed in her palm a familiar orange sweet – I couldn't help but grin, knowing what she was about to inflict upon the old man. She all but threw the sweet into her mouth, and after a moment of chewing, she unleashed a violent torrent of flame from her mouth, scaring the soul out of the old man and singing the fringe of his grey hair.

"Even with their confectionaries those... dragon shaggin' *bastards* are still tryin' ter off poor little me!" he screamed as he leapt back to his feet, pointing his finger towards Tsubasa and Matra like a knife.

After the chortling and angry condemnation died down, I momentarily left the bustling table in peace, choosing to take a seat near Mahro's table and sit opposite the man himself. There was only a single half-empty glass of clear liquid at his table; not a surprise, given that despite his theatrics giving off an air of drunken foolhardiness, I rarely ever saw him consuming alcohol. He didn't even seem to notice me at first as he stared towards the forest opposite Ringo's house, his eyes consumed by the vast shadow that had once hidden all sorts of horrors. Tucking my chair in at last alerted him to my presence, and for the first and last time in those two weeks, he met me with a genuine smile.

"You look like you're enjoying yourself, my friend."

"Of course; it's nice to see so many people here *without* somebody starting a fight."

"That's good. Cherish times like this, for I dread they're soon to become scarce." Mahro advised, his smile gradually souring, "Not to sound like I doubt your abilities, but... I'm glad you're here and not with Altair. The thought of you too getting dragged off to war and suffering some terrible fate... it keeps me up at night, I confess."

"You got cold feet about heading home, old man?"

"*Hah!* I just don't want these past nine years by your side to have gone to waste, that's all..."

My apologies, my esteemed mentor, but a plague rat salesman would have been more convincing.

"Just try not to cry into your pillow every night while we're apart – you're a big boy, Master King Rag! I believe in you!"

I suppose it was a cocktail of drunkenness and bitterness over his departure that led me to see him off in such a way, and I wish our last conversation had been more respectful on my part. Nevertheless, he rolled with the punches.

"Thank you. I'll try my best." He bluntly answered, staring into the forest for several seconds more before he looked towards me once again, "You're real lucky, you know that?"

"I'm *what?*"

What he was saying was completely unconscionable to me - between my mother's death and witnessing the slow degradation of Ford and its community, not to mention the entire incident with Eden, I imagined myself to be the exact opposite.

"You're lucky, and you're in your right mind not to take it for granted. You were barely standing on your own two legs before life sent catastrophe after catastrophe your hapless way, circumstances that for all intents and purposes should've left you... dead, I suppose. And yet you've always had someone at your back, someone to hold your hand as you tread the darkest of man's hearts." His eyes struggled to meet with my own, but he continued nonetheless after a brief drink, "Tragedies are hardly abnormal; every day, there's another little Vega or Altair enduring something horrible, watching his life completely uproot before his eyes and powerless to stop it. How many of those have a safety net, I wonder? Were the same thing to happen right here, right now, would anybody in Ford be willing to do what Kyrie and Julius did for you, knowing that only a blood-stained history and a cascade of uphill battles await? I don't know if I could."

His talking seemed endless and meandering; I could only sit in silence, wondering if he was building up to any kind of conclusion or just rambling about whatever entered his mind. I can't even imagine what could have incited such an exchange – the man was coy about discussing both his own personal life and that of others, and our talking outside of training pertained to virtually anything else. Considering this was possibly our final talk, perhaps he was releasing that which he wished he had told me in the years prior?

"It's not to say I regret my lot in life; I have Minami waiting back home and two beautiful daughters I get to grow old with. I couldn't have asked for better, and I would go through all of it again, knowing what kind of life awaits me at the end of that dreary tunnel. I suppose in a way, I was as lucky as you; among our lot, only Minami was truly by my side up until I met Ringo, and I somehow didn't end up with my head on a pike before the old man set me on the straight and narrow. It's just... I don't know, I just wonder how things would have turned out if I enjoyed the kind of upbringing you did. Logic dictates I should have by all means ended up in a better place, and yet knowing my circumstances to be as they are, I wouldn't change a thing. Tragedy is what united us, is it not?"

"And why should that be the only thing that unites us? You and me, old man, we're like... like glass and whiskey, you see? I can scarcely imagine life without you." I spoke more and more brazenly, still in some degree of disbelief that this may actually be our last conversation.

"I suppose I would be the whiskey in this... thought-provoking union? I don't break so easily as glass."

Mahro grinned like a child who had gotten away with sneaking sweets from the kitchen, and it took a moment for me to identify the meaning in his words.

"Well... well, neither do I!"

"Well if you're not the glass, does that make us both whiskey?"

"I guess so, but if both are whiskey, who or what is the glass?" I asked.

"Ford?"

"...Ford it is, then."

Our line of philosophical pondering ended with a mutual grunt of amusement – his depressive disposition couldn't entirely do away with the Mahro I knew and very much loved.

After the end of this ponderous pisstake, Mahro slumped back into his chair with a heavy sigh, no doubt weighed down in thought.

"You... mentioned Ringo 'setting you on the straight and narrow' which I, quite frankly, find extremely hard to believe." I asked, quickly glancing at the old man before I continued – his torture had escalated to Tsubasa, Matra *and* Kyrie breathing fire at him, "Whatever did happen between the two of you? Sounds like a story I'd love to hear."

Mahro turned silent for a moment; I could tell he wanted to say *something,* but the exact words were eluding him.

"I-I think that story is best saved for when we next meet. It's a tale I believe you could learn from and that I should have disclosed much sooner, but it's by no means pleasant – let's not invite the demons of my past into a toast to your future."

With his piece stated, he took one last gulp from his glass, and spent a while solemnly gazing at the stars.

"Me and Matra... we have to leave early in the morning. I would love to hang around for just one morning more, but it can't be done."

I could feel my heart sinking as he told me this, as if he had torn it out with his own hand and cast it out to the sea. While processing what he said, I looked in the direction of where I originally sat to find Tsubasa and Matra dancing in front of the stage as Ringo began to unleash his inner (in)famous musician once again. Contemplating Tsubasa's no doubt unamused reaction only attached further weights to that sinking feeling – for all of the grievous physical harm I had endured before her age, I knew the emotional toll on a girl her age could be just as crushing.

"It's about time we headed off now, come to think of it; I can't drag my little one out of her hangover if I'm also tired."

Leaving no time for me to protest, he stood up with a chuckle. I too stood up in a hurry, wanting to say something before he disappeared for what I could only assume to be a decade, at the very least. Despite this, every attempt to summon the proper words produced nothing but a lump in my throat, and I was left completely unable to express myself, struggling beneath the pressure that this long-dreaded day had wrought upon me. I suppose my worry was needless, as Mahro approached me and brought his arms around my back, bracing it with the firmness and stability I found myself sorely lacking at this time.

"This isn't the end of anything, my friend; next I'm here, I have the utmost confidence you'll have helped make Ford a place worth living in once more." He murmured into my ear as he delivered a powerful pat to my back – none of this was flattery, for every syllable sounded as sincere as he had ever been. "We'll meet again."

I sat back down once more, looking to the stars as Mahro had done so just moments ago. In my quiet contemplation, I tried to imagine a life where Mahro was gone potentially for good, only to draw a blank – his antics had become so integral not just to my growing up, but to my everyday life that I simply couldn't conceive of what life was like before he introduced himself into it.

My pondering was cut abruptly short by a soft, damp sensation on my cheek. Stunned by the sudden stimulation, I quickly turned down to discover Matra right next to me, standing back up straight – she had kissed me on the cheek, and while I was caught terribly off guard by such an action, she looked as confident as ever, crossing her arms as she grinned in such a way to suggest that she enjoyed my confused stumbling far more than she ought to have.

"I'll try and send a message when we're home, alright? It's been fun!"

After one last display of that enchanting, sultry smile, she walked away with Mahro, waving her hand at me until the two were out of sight once again, possibly forever as far as I was aware.

If I had known our reunion was to take place a little under 18 months later, albeit under much more contentious circumstances, would I have been so anxious and troubled during that conversation? I suppose it matters not, but it leaves me to wonder just what other surprises life is ready to throw at my hapless head; I doubt the events leading to my arrival in Tenryuu are the end of it.

Chapter 14:
Avian Rhapsody

Mahro and Matra's departure left all of us in a dour mood for an awfully long time, nor did a letter ever arrive; it was not so much the absence of the former, given that excursions of around 3 months to visit his family were a regular occurrence, rather the painful dread that my 16th birthday was the last time we would ever get to see each other again, now that all-out war was not so much on our doorstep as it had invited itself in for dinner. Even on the normally docile wall bordering the No Man's Land, as Altair called it, my brother was seeing an awful lot of real world experience, according to his letters. Each and every one of said letters provided immense relief, if only for the fact that they confirmed he continued to draw breath as of sending it.

Tsubasa, of course, didn't take Matra's departure well; upon waking up the morning after my birthday and discovering our fiery-haired friend was gone, possibly for good, she stormed back to our bedroom in a fit of shouting and crying, refusing to leave for any reason other than dinner. Her temperament cooled with time of course, but she carried an air of having been wronged for the rest of the month, at the very least. I did a better job of concealing my disappointment, no doubt thanks to my relative maturity, but those same feelings were undeniably present beneath the surface.

Unbeknownst to Kyrie, I had requested Lyndra to make some... *alterations* to the cloak she had graciously gifted to me once I had spent a few months under her tutelage – now attached to the left side of its interior were scabbards containing two knives, one short and serrated and the other more resembling a machete, though its blade was duller than one as it was intended only for menial labour and dealing with whatever foolhardy, weapon-waving drunks and robbers I may have come across in my few travels. On the right side were a few other pockets she had sewn in, mostly for miscellanea – a small blue lighter lent from (and never returned to) Mahro, a handful of old shopping lists, a pen with which to write said lists and a thin shard of flint made up the entirety of their contents much of the time.

All in all, life... went on. Mahro's absence was a huge personal loss, but for the first time since the Band of the Wyvern's march of terror and Eden's subsequent string of abductions, Ford had finally settled somewhat. Settled in a state of disrepair perhaps, but it was the first glimpse of long-awaited stability. The population had reduced to a little under 120 citizens, and at least before my unexpected departure from Ford, any who would mean harm or had used their personal tragedies to enact their wrath on those around them had either tempered their fury or moved on to greener pastures. My 16th birthday was the first prominent reminder that maybe, just maybe, a future for Ford was in the cards after all.

I'm not sure if it's still December, but I distinctly remember my last day in Ford being on November 27th, the year after Mahro and Matra's departure. The date sticks out to me because it just so happened to be the birthday of my late mother, and it would have been her 42nd had she not been robbed of her life a decade prior. By now it's difficult to remember all that much about her, having spent more of my life with Kyrie Pyre as a mother than Stephanie Vadere, but I know that the wound remained fresh; after my six-hour shift at Lyndra's blacksmithing workshop – the elegantly named Bombastic Steel – I planned to visit my old, abandoned house, if only to reflect on how far I had come since I last called such a place my home.

As midday approached, I joined my family for lunch; much to my delight, I learned that later that day, Mrs. Pyre was returning from active duty to spend the next month in our company, and I didn't fancy squandering what little time she had with us given that it was the first we had seen of her in nearly five years. If I had known that would be the last time I saw Kyrie, Julius and Tsubasa before I ended up in Tenryuu, I would have most certainly tried to say something worth remembering me by. Instead, I gave Tsubasa the most soothing hug I could muster as I wished the rest of them well, a sequence that preceded any other workday.

Bombastic Steel was certainly... perhaps not all *that* bombastic, but it stood out among Ford, for sure. Being one of the only active workshops left in Ford with any kind of chimney, it was by no means difficult to identify among the mass of much larger factories that had long been reclaimed by roots, completely untended to for the better part of ten years. In comparison, Lyndra had made certain to put me on clean-up duty whenever her precious little workshop threatened to see its black metallic walls share a similar fate; not to suggest this was all I did under her tutelage, however, as she was indeed a great teacher in her respective art.

"Afternoon, Big Lad."

Lyndra's voice was as rough and dry as ever as I stumbled into her cramped domain – I guess that wasn't the case for Lyndra herself, given that I was noticeably taller than the lady in question.

"Afternoon, Lyn."

I hung my blue cloak up on the corner of the door leading to the break room – Ford was certainly chilly by the time November came with all of its incumbent frost, but one step into Bombastic Steel brought upon me a swift reminder of summer's own perils.

And perilous is what this workshop's interior was; in addition to being cramped, the walls were all constructed of a black metal, in much the same way as its exterior. Our single source of light came from a dim, flickering Tenkite lantern that sat on Lyndra's desk at the back end of the room – the hearth also provided its own source of light, but it was used more scarcely than one would expect in an establishment whose only output is weapons of warfare. When I first started, such a place felt awfully suffocating, and I found myself tripping on bits and bobs hiding within the dark more than I care to admit, though by my second November within these walls I had come to enjoy it somewhat. It was by no means a second home, but it provided a commendable facsimile of summer's virtues once we were knee deep in snow, and we enjoyed some well-needed peace and quiet even when the heat within matched the heat without.

"Looks like your brother can talk his way into more than just women's undergarments; an addendum to our contract came through, the Border Boys are requesting armaments and whatnot for some fresh meat arriving in a few months. You know the drill." Lyndra said as she tossed me a heavy red binder.

The binder possessed on its cover an official crest of Morosus, that being the head of a pitch black wolf. It was uncomfortably reminiscent of that... thing... which had pursued me through the Basin in my youth, but I had seen such an icon enough times to overcome such discomfort.

"I'm on it. Plan to chip in before your lungs *give* in?" I asked with a smirk as Lyndra produced a crude ebony pipe from a purse on her desk.

"I don't need lungs to kick your ass." Lyn answered as she lit the end of the pipe aflame, grinning at her own devilish retort.

As the stone-laden hearth roared to life once again, I unceremoniously used its light to read the contents of the binder:

"To Lyndra Cressida, representing the establishment Bombastic Steel,

At the request of L-Sgt.(standing for Land Sargeant, a decently respected rank among Morosus commoners) *Altair Pyre, we humbly implore you to provide the desired objects, as listed beneath this body of text. A military courier will be sent to receive the goods at a point no earlier than the end of the upcoming January, and payment will be provided in due time, proportionate to the quantity of usable goods as well as their quality.*

The items sought include:
- *A minimum of eighty steel daggers, seven inches in length from the tip of the hilt to the point of the blade, with accompanying scabbards.*

- *A minimum of twenty crossbows that can withstand at least eight test firings at maximum draw without a noticeable decrease to accuracy or usability.*
- *A minimum of forty wrist-mounted bucklers, surpassing 50cm in diameter but not exceeding 55cm.*

We once again thank and commend both you and your establishment for your contributions to the war effort.

Signed,

L-Cpt (Land Captain) Judeau Stoake."

Only the front page was of relevance; the rest were simply old documents left inside by Lyndra.

"I see, I see. Taking credit for all my hard work again, you old hag?" I said as I threw the binder to a flimsy steel table beside the hearth.

"Put your back into it, Big Lad!"

Moved by her enthusiasm (and my need for a paycheck), I got to work with haste.

Not to suggest that this working relationship was as one-sided as this exchange may have presented it to be; once she finished smoking after what felt like hours, she at last joined me before the hearth to assist me in heating up the steel we would go on to use for the first of the daggers. The steel was kept in great abundance within a warehouse at the back of the building that matched the dreary working space we more often found ourselves in, alongside heaps and heaps of other necessities including wood, leather and Lyndra's tobacco (a necessity according to Lyndra alone).

Barring the last of those, which was contained to a small box atop a dusty metal shelf, each material was segregated into its own little department. The steel was arranged in large, thin sheets of ascending size, with a small pile of scrap for discontinued but salvageable projects at its feet. Three large, pyramid-shaped stacks of chopped up wood lay in the centre of the room, while to their right were many racks covered in brown Ateria leather both dried and drying; I had made some tidy money on the side via hunting trips with Julius as of late, so I have no doubt the skin belonging to a few of my own catches was also represented within this warehouse.

It's worth noting that Ateria leather has an unusual quality, contributing to its use in whatever armour left the confines of the workshop: while entirely vulnerable to piercing projectiles (and thus making a crossbow or hunting bow the ideal tool for taking an Ateria down), it afforded full mobility to its wearer while remaining remarkably effective at reducing the efficacy of blunt damage, and was even known to stop small calibre gunshots all by its lonesome on occasion, albeit not consistently. While it didn't entirely eliminate the need for steel plating beneath any armour it was grafted onto, its strength afforded us more wiggle room to shave off dead weight, and this small advantage made Ateria a prized target for hunting within Morosus now that war had kicked off – that these creatures resided exclusively within our nook of the country made it all the more fortunate. It was an ambition of mine to leverage our abundance of Ateria to reinstate Ford as a worthy participant in Morosus' economy; my brother scoring a few contracts for us was just the start of a long but rewarding road, in my mind.

It was for this reason that I gravitated towards working with apparel rather than arms so the bucket list consisting exclusively of weapons was a mild disappointment, but I suppose I had become used to it by now; every day, as I hammered away at each slab of metal that would soon become a functional armament, my mind would begin to drift as the task became more and more mindless. Every strike of metal would bring to mind my lessons under my mad but well-liked mentor, and the loud clang would fill my ears that so desperately wished to be filled with his wisdom and wisecracking once again. I suppose it would be unfair to call my reminiscence that of 'better days', given that it was only after his departure that Ford, if not beginning to recover, had at least overcome the worst of its economic and communal freefall. That being said, I couldn't help but feel that hole in my heart a whole 16 months after he had left, the wound perhaps staying forever fresh had I not washed up on his doorstep. My lot in life was comfortable, but it felt hollow without the man whose approval I desired most there to watch me flourish. I was firm in my conviction to help Ford back on its feet, but it was tough to reconcile that he may well not have lived to see its rebirth; he was 44 years of age when he departed, and knowing the war could have gone on for decades... the odds of Mahro visiting Ford again were grim.

By nightfall, we had begun work on five of the requested daggers and were set to finish them off and continue down the list the next day - now that I mention it, I hope my sudden disappearance hasn't put too much strain on old Lyn, provided the village of Ford wasn't razed to the ground by my assailants.

Now here is where the problems began; as I wished the smoking Lyndra farewell and threw on my blue cloak for the journey to my old home, I instantly had a grisly sensation jolt up my spine. A sensible man might think it to be from the cold, but it was... something else. I had this dreadful feeling that I was being watched; that every rustle of bushes and cawing of the black birds that perched atop the abandoned factories was an omen of trouble to come. Unable to put my finger on anything concrete besides vague unease, I marched on towards the Vadere household at last, scanning every nook and cranny as I made the arduous trek up that hill. There were a scant few villagers of Ford out in the chilly winds, often sitting in front of their homes smoking much as Lyndra was certainly doing at that moment, though none seemed at all fit to save me from the trouble that was soon to encroach me.

Strolling past the library, I exchanged a glance with the much-beloved Maverick; he had become lame and lethargic by this point, and his fur had started to lose some of its brown colour and fill in the void with a humble grey, but he still had the vigour needed to shower the grass outside my window with urine. I didn't fancy smelling whatever flowers grew there. Still, I took the time to stroke his head, contemplating what snack I would bring the old boy from our kitchen for doing his business *outside* the library that time. A biscuit, perhaps? Maybe even a bone? Whatever I settled on, I don't remember.

"Evening, Vega. My, time has made you a very handsome young man indeed!"

I looked up to discover Mrs. Pyre leaning out of the window nearest to me – she too was becoming frail as she aged, her time in the military no doubt contributing to that, and was very nearly fit for retirement from her tumultuous career.

"Good evening, Mrs. Pyre. I'll be back soon. You'll have to tell me all about what you've gotten up to now that this whole war thing has lit a fire under our arses!" I said, stroking Maverick as I patched over my sensation of discomfort.

"I've many stories, young man! Would you like a drink ready for your return?"

"Coffee should do me well, Mrs. Pyre."

"Coffee it is then. See you soon!"

And that would prove to be the last I saw of anybody in my family – what a shame that her favour went to waste.

As I stood before my old home, my only company being the crescent moon and the dim stars in the sky, a lot of familiar sensations began to flow into me as I came the closest I had been to this house in ten years. I could vividly remember the metallic sound of my mother unsealing lock after lock before the bright morning sky was allowed within her domain once more, followed by the rush of footsteps produced by me and my brother as we bolted off to find out what strange escapade Kyrie was up to that day.

At the risk of sounding ungrateful for everything she and Julius had done for me, the one downside of eventually living with Kyrie herself was lacking the anticipation inherent to the journey there; the walk down this hill afforded an opportunity to consider what the rest of the day may bring, while life with Kyrie and Julius brought us just one door away from the beginning of that day's chaos. Nevertheless, as I gazed at the shattered windows, the decayed and rotting wooden steps leading up to the front door and the walls coated in more filthy moss and weeds than clear blue, I remained glad that we were allowed to stay anywhere else at all, and at Kyrie's home no less.

Getting into the building at all proved to be tempestuous; the wind began to accelerate as I took my first step, and the first of the four wooden steps shattered beneath my foot. Luckily the rest held up better. The door took itself some force to open once more, its internal locking mechanism having rusted well before my arrival, but a shoulder bash or two got me inside, freeing me from the noisy, violent winds but subjecting me to a veritable avalanche of cobwebs within, only outnumbered by the arachnid carcasses that lay within. The small lighter lent to me by Mahro cleared the webs from my path, and I at last happened upon our old dinner table, covered in abandoned plates and cutlery – if any food had remained on these plates as of the day the Band of the Wyvern attacked, it had long been claimed by the critters that scurried in the shadows.

Ignoring the stale stench of long-outdated food that emanated from every cupboard, I took a seat at the dinner table, using the lighter to bring a half-used wax candle at its centre to life before Mahro's unintended gift returned to my pocket. It was time to lay back in my seat, and I intended to contemplate on just how far I had come since I had last set foot in that house, wondering just what my mother would have thought of my strange and eventful life that followed.

It was only then that I noticed the outline of a figure in the corner of the room, in front of the door to mine and Altair's former bedroom. Its body shape was distinctly human, certainly that of a well-built man, and yet his face... it appeared *bird-like* – a beak protruded from where his mouth should have been, and his hawkish eyes shone with a crimson red beneath the candle's flame.

As soon as our eyes met, his assault began; he broke into a sprint, grasping an empty glass jar from the kitchen to its left and launching it at my head as I leapt to my feet, snapping off the back of the chair next to me to use as a shield from the incoming projectile. As it shattered against my makeshift defenses and embedded tiny but painful shards into my right hand, I heard the stranger approach from my right, grasping a white cloth in its hand. In the time it took to reach for my mouth, I unleashed the longer of my two knives from my cloak and sent it soaring upwards, cutting into the stranger's forearm but stopping at the bone – this was enough to send his aim way off course, and the cloth landed on the floor behind me with a wet thud after the arm's grip went slack.

Not wanting to take any chances, I shoved the stranger against the kitchen counter and delivered several blows to his head with a frying pan – hardly an ideal weapon, but it was the closest solid object in the vicinity; I would have gladly resorted to anything so long as it stood a chance of subduing my assailant, and subdue the trusty frying pan did. The stranger laid motionless on the floor, and it was at this point I noticed something incredibly offputting: his beak had shattered, and beneath it the mouth was stitched shut with bloody wounds covering each lip.

Disgusted by what I had witnessed, I returned my knife to its rightful place and rushed to the front door of the house to seek help. From Julius, Lyndra, even our neighbours, anybody would have sufficed. Anybody except what greeted me outside the door: no less than ten strangers cloaked in all-encompassing black, adorned with the same bird-like mask and blazing eyes that belonged to the one laying still inside my old home. Before I could even begin to question the absurdity of my circumstances, I reached for my knife once more in a frenzy, more than ready to kill them all now that I knew this was an orchestrated assault rather than the whim of some anonymous idiot.

"You better have dug ten graves, you bastards! Who wants to die first?!" I screamed as I raised my knife, in an attempt to both intimidate my imposing attackers and alert anybody who happened to be nearby.

But not only was my own former home abandoned, all others near it had been long vacated also - the chances of anybody living in Ford actually having heard me are slim.

My screams were also ineffective as a deterrent; as soon as I finished, they all began to advance, and the following fight was… one-sided. The first two to approach were caught in a single swing, recoiling as I left a cut in their reaching arms – despite my threat, I was hesitant to actually put an end to a human life, even in a situation as dire as this; I imagined the burden would weigh on me too heavily to bear, but this restraint may have ultimately been to my detriment. From behind the first two came an attacker wielding a thick baton made of an unidentifiable metal. Unlike Matra, this next opponent was not at all tricksy or clever in his approach, instead choosing to launch an attack straight at my head. I barely recovered from my first swing to bring my knife back up in time, and it shattered into pieces with a colossal bang as the two weapons collided at great speed.

With a small shard of steel left protruding from the knife's hilt, I threw it with hideous velocity at the baton-wielding stranger's face as he jumped back with a brief glance towards his companions, and it managed to bury itself as deep as it could into his right arm. As I took a moment to recover from such a powerful throw, I could only be discouraged by the fact that he didn't even scream; I have no doubt their mouths had been stitched shut in the same manner as my initial assailant, but it certainly didn't feel good to see my attack produce not a single sound other than the distant tearing of fabric and flesh.

As he knelt to the ground, I rushed over and tore the baton from his hands, sending him to the ground with a violent swing just in time to face yet more attackers from my rear - batons were by no means my forte, but any weapon with decent reach was just fine by me, and I didn't fancy losing *both* of my knives that night, assuming I emerged with my life. The first among the next attacking wave sprung forward, dodging my swift swing aimed at his head and punching me in the gut. It hurt like a bitch for sure, but I have no doubt the hardy hilt of the baton crashing into his skull immediately after was far more agonizing. Three of his buddies approached me as he slumped to the floor, two remaining barehanded whilst the third brandished a thin, spindly spear that forked into two sharp ends – that being said, each end was coated in a strange, yellow-orange gleam that seemed strangely familiar to me.

After bashing one attacker's teeth in with the baton and disabling another with a strike to the knee and then chin, I was immediately reminded of what this was via two sharp sensations in my hip – it was the same substance Julius had used to incapacitate my... I suppose "real father", before he tore the Screaming Rose from his heart.

Instantly my vision began to blur, my legs were rendered no more stable than a pencil thin tower of jelly, and my strikes against the one who had landed this blow against me became all but ineffective; it took repeated, exhausting battering to his head to at last bring him down, and as he crumbled to the ground I soon followed. The last thing I saw before I lost this fight once and for all was one of the still standing attackers squatting down and covering my mouth with a white cloth.

It was as this cloth and the hand behind it clamped down on my bottom lip that an image painfully burst into my mind – as if repeating history, I could vividly see Eden, kneeling before me in that cave, trying to convert me into one of her own as she tried to pry my mouth open.

Come now... why bother resisting?

Her voice rang out in my eardrums, and I could only sit there silently, my eyes and mouth seizing up as I waited for the torment to stop. Whatever was in that cloth would soon acquiesce, as it rendered me unconscious moments later.

Chapter 15:
An Unexpected Voyage

Much to my dismay, this was no nightmare brought on by thoughts of my mother, of my old home and life before the Band of the Wyvern's attack. The reality of my situation became instantly apparent when I woke up to abject blackness, my vision completely obscured by a dark piece of cloth. From what I was slowly able to discern by wiggling about, I was tied down to a chair at both my wrists and ankles. There was also a faint, nauseating sensation underneath it all, as if I was slowly rocking back and forth. The crashing of waves against the creaking walls made it quickly apparent that I was inside a ship. My first instinct upon becoming cognizant of my whereabouts was intense panic – I feverishly fought to escape the bindings, all the while racked with questions. How long had I been captive here? Where in the world was I? And most horrifying of all, *what* had become of Ford after my abduction? I still have no idea if they simply left with me in tow after subduing me or decided to raze Ford to the ground for good measure; despite their far smaller numbers than the Band of the Wyvern, there were likely fewer yet living in Ford who could even put up a solid fight against them.

Questions could only continue to mount as my fight against the restraints proved to be utterly futile. Who exactly had taken me, and for what purpose? At the time I hadn't the faintest clue I could use to ascribe motive or identification, and I still have all but thin air to go off of; my chance encounter with a Band of the Wyvern member upon my arrival in Dias took a hammer to my entire ten years of mental fortitude built up after their alleged destruction, and I find it hard to believe such a meeting was just a coincidence. But were these truly the comrades of Pat? If so, then why would he not be among them? And why would he be waiting in what was clearly not their eventual destination?

I was left little time to ponder on questions I couldn't answer, as the sound of slow, heavy footsteps and creaking wood steadily grew in volume as my hearing returned to its fullest capacity. Before long, a door immediately in front of me opened, and the footsteps came to an end right as it slammed shut behind whoever had entered.

"You piece of shit! Who the hell are you?! Where am I?!" I demanded, not at all sure what to expect.

Sure enough, I would not get any answers; a small metallic clang reminiscent of a hammer striking a blade – though far more diminished in volume – was the last I heard before I was grabbed beneath the chin by a hand enveloped in leather. My head was forcefully raised, and my dry, dehydrated mouth was wedged open by a steel spoon, forcing me to consume whatever "cuisine" laid atop it. Compliments were the last thing I would be giving the chef; it tasted like raw Ateria meat that had been grinded into paste and heated exclusively by a lighter for some 20 seconds. All I wanted to do was throw it back up, perish, even, if this was all my captors had in store for me. And yet, my head was forcibly held up, made to swallow this putrid, barely edible food, until all of it had made its way into my body.

Much to my extreme distaste, this *was* all they had in store; I had no way of tracking the time whatsoever, and I stopped counting how many times my stomach was subjected to this torture somewhere around the 15th serving. In every instance, not one word was spoken by my captor/s, and by following in the path of the first meal, they were meticulous in providing me no opportunity to retaliate or strike back. Any venom I spewed at them, any insult I threw at their face, it all apparently bounced off of them like a ball against a brick wall.

Trying to sleep fared little better; it seemed that at all hours of the day, strong footsteps were likely to be patrolling around the halls laying beyond my door, along with an intermittent violent rumbling coming from somewhere close by, presumably an engine of the ship or some other facility within. Drifting between dreary dreams and the pitch blackness where daylight should have been began to blur my distinction of dreams and reality somewhat; seeing my home of Ford in my dreams and imagining the very same buried within the black veil covering my eyes became functionally identical.

Yet even my dreams were burdened with great helplessness; they all involved me, in some form or another, being held back or only able to watch the horrors within. I saw Ford burning to the ground anew, razed by some shadowy, unknown force that brought only the destruction of all I loved. I watched Tsubasa cry out my name, desperately searching for me within the vast blackness even as I stood metres away from her, watching with pained eyes as she too became absorbed by darkness. I saw the library I had spent a decade treating as my home being reduced to ashes, becoming yet another indistinguishable flame in the bright, orange mass of Ford. Whenever the footsteps weren't there to deprive me of my slumber, the images that haunted my every dream and waking moment did a more than commendable job.

But then one night, I woke from my slumber to discover the ship had apparently come to a halt, no longer rocking back and forth – it was short-lived, certainly not feeling much longer than whatever I had come to understand as being an hour, but it left me intrigued nonetheless. Having spent possibly weeks in a delusional state of drifting between dreams and the real world on a whim, anything to latch onto beyond miserable forecasts of life back home were welcome. Where had they stopped? For what purpose? It certainly wasn't their final destination, given that the ship stuttered and roared to life soon after. But then what kind of place would host a ship carrying human cargo, in a time of widespread war no less? Vana has stayed uninvolved in the wartime proceedings – my first assumption was that I had been taken to said country, but turning up on the doorstep of Dias Village, which rested on all but the other side of the world, very soon after this put that theory to bed.

Such questions were ultimately futile; just hours later, or so I can only guess, the footsteps approached once more. And these were not the footsteps of one person, as I had been conditioned to dread. I must have counted about three of them before I was suddenly shook to full awareness by my chair lifting tumultuously above the ground, by at least a few inches. Minutes of orderly carrying through the halls followed; either the voiceless grunts escorting me and my chair were extremely deft at navigating in perfect synchronicity with one another or the halls were so spacious as to make error near impossible, but we at last arrived in a room with a rather cold chill to it. My nose had long forgotten the scent of real food, and so it proved to be an absurd shock to the senses to smell… *anything* good! Freshly cooked chicken and bread pulled fresh from the oven were most prominent among the smells, and the steam of boiled potatoes grazed against my face.

For a moment, I began to think some elaborate prank had been played against me, and this was just more of Mahro's trickery taken to its extreme. As my mouth curved upwards and my head raised, my blindfold was quickly and roughly torn off, only to blind me with an intense light. My first exposure to real light in weeks left me as vulnerable as a newborn, but after several seconds of trying to force my eyes open, I at last began to make out shapes once more: in front of me was a mostly empty table, covered in a bland grey cloth but stretching as far as I was able to see. Before me laid three trays and a vacant porcelain plate, the former containing the food I had previously identified along with small bottles of spices and salt dispersed before it.

"Welcome… to our feast, brother."

The dry, raspy voice rang out opposite me as the restraints around my arms and feet were loosened, and colour fully returned to my eyes, at last allowing me to fill in the visual blanks: the table stretched as wide as a house, and filling every seat between me and this mystery speaker were more of the bird-faced attackers I had been beaten down by some time ago, though none of them were there to eat as their places at the table were barren. More of them stood to my rear, the two foremost among them each holding a forked rod tinged in yellow. The floor was coated in a rugged red carpet, and behind the army of bird-faced, black-clad men laid pristine wooden walls, untainted by so much as a speck of dust, let alone any kind of paintings or possessions. My first instinct was blind fury; I barely even had the fortitude to speak, and yet were my soul to allow it, I felt as though I could spring up from my seat and choke the life out of everybody in that room. The guards at my rear were all that kept me subdued, for the time being.

"The end of this journey is... approaching, brother..." the voice continued – it most certainly didn't belong to Altair, so I can only wonder why in the world he would refer to me as such.

Finally laying my eyes on the origin of the voice only produced a cavalcade of further queries: the speaker was a rather frail, diminutive man slumped against the back of a wheelchair, looking much the same as the one Sonia had used last I saw her in my travels to Mot. And Sonia was the *only* person I knew who was wheelchair-bound, which made his apparent familiarity with me all the more confounding. His hair was covered by a black hood, but I could make out small tufts of white hair beneath the veil. The stranger's face was further obscured by a jagged, uneven mask covering the surroundings of his eyes and reflecting the candle at the table's centre with a metallic gleam. And his smile... I can't quite put my finger on it, but it caused me a profound discomfort, as if it were trying to forcefully bore happiness into my raging soul.

Most troubling of all was what he wore around him: Kyrie's cloak. The instant my eyes laid upon them, I may well have leapt out of my seat, dashed across the table and buried my fist deep within his head just to reclaim the last fragment of my adoptive mother I could possibly hold onto at a time like this, were I not cognizant of just how quickly such a scheme would be shut down by the men standing behind me.

"Give that back! *I'll fucking kill you!*" I screamed in bewilderment, interested only in letting him know just how much I hated his guts if his immediate death wasn't an option.

After this demand, he began to mumble under his breath as he covered his mouth with my cloak – I was too far to hear what he was saying, but I could tell his voice had taken on a strange, newfound intensity. Before long, he properly addressed me.

"Brother... please calm down. I assure you... whatever transgression you have deemed me guilty of can... be resolved." the stranger calmly answered, "But first, I believe a... proper meal is in

order, don't you agree? Our... *ahem,* cooking, has not been to your...
liking, if I understand correctly?"

All I could do was slump back in the chair and wriggle some
life back into my hands and feet as I peered at every corner of the
room, awaiting an opportunity or a weakness to act upon.

"Tell your chefs to go fuck themselves." I said bluntly, "Who
the hell *are* you?"

Yet more mumbling ensued, leaving me to wonder what in
the world was wrong with him until he returned to the realm of the
sane.

"Oh... Brother, all will be explained in... due time. Please, let
your stomach do the... the talking."

His words certainly struck a chord with my stomach, which
began to rumble with the magnitude of an earthquake as my eyes
withdrew to the food in front of me.

"Some arrangement you have here... bulking me up, just so I
can wring your neck easier? I'm almost grateful, you stupid son of a
bitch!"

With not an ounce of gratitude, I grasped a roll of bread like
a starving beast and all but shoved it into my mouth – I couldn't be
less concerned about checking whether or not it was poisoned, or
had nails inside, or possessed any other sort of vile trick. My only
objective was to erase the taste of grim paste that had become my
sole connection to the outside world for no less than a few weeks.

"*Stupid son of a bitch, he says! About me!*" he snarled next,
this time loud enough for me to hear.

His next few words remained inaudible, up until he snapped
back to the façade of friendliness.

"Our vessel must be... strong, and healthy!" said the
stranger, weakly cooking up whatever enthusiasm he could muster.

My being called a 'vessel' set off an immediate alarm in my
head; this was no convoluted gesture of kindness or treat, as one
could maybe, if weakly, argue for by this point. Indeed, this
diminutive bastard had some kind of... *purpose* for me. At once, I
threw the leg of chicken I was halfway through onto the porcelain
plate and stood up. I could hear some feet shuffling closer behind

me, but they were mostly drowned out by the thumping anger in my head.

"I don't care *what* you have in store for me! I'm *nobody's*... vessel, or slave, or what have you!" I shouted as I began to flip over the trays containing the food, spewing their contents all over the table and floor, "You could make me the 'vessel' for the god of sunshine, rainbows and... *flying puppies* and I wouldn't give a shit! I'm *me*! I have people who need me! I have a place to call home! I wouldn't trade *any* of that for your 'vessel' *bullshit!*"

Beyond infuriated, I slammed both of my fists into the table as I sat back down – if I was going to throw his plans back in his face, I was damn well going to make sure he wouldn't forget.

"A place to call... home..." the stranger mused – his unnerving calmness when he didn't retract into my cloak was eerily reminiscent of Eden and her unflinching commitment to turning me into one of her kind. "That must be nice. Maybe that's where all of this... anger, this... scorn, where it all comes from? But no... you haven't *had* a real home in... ten years, have you?"

The nausea in my stomach grew close to rupturing – he was obviously referring to the death of my birth mother and my subsequent relocation to Kyrie's home. But it's not as though these were circumstances worth sharing around the world, akin to an epic tale of a noble mentor taking down a scheming beast beneath the depths of the earth. Was this person also from Ford? Surely not; I had never, in my many years of living there, encountered such a person, wheelchair-bound or not. But if not, then why did he know so intimately of my circumstances? How long had his gaze been locked onto my every footstep? It was far too chilling to think about. And think about it I wouldn't need to.

Shortly after the stranger finished speaking, the boat produced a violent creaking noise and began sharply tilting to the right. While I clutched onto the bottom of the table, which was thankfully rooted to the ground, legions of the bird-faced men began tumbling out of their seats – backwards if they sat to my right, forwards and over the table if they sat to my left. The sound of colliding with the rightmost wall and those beak masks shattering became abundant, as did plates and porcelain flying onto their hapless heads. Before the boat's tilt began to correct, to my far right laid a dark mass of birdmen, many of them wounded by either their tumble or the objects flying onto them.

This was my chance.

Without even hesitating for a moment, I leapt from my seat and gunned for the stranger the instant the ship corrected to a traversable angle. The look on his face was priceless upon realising what peril he was in, and he took off as fast as his wheelchair could carry him. I almost caught him by the fur-coated collar of my cloak up until I heard the sound of a blade cutting through wind, and I pulled my left hand back just in time to not be disarmed, in a rather literal sense. Despite the ship beginning to tilt in the opposite direction, albeit not so violently as the first time, five of the birdmen had found their footing and were rushing at me, the only weapon among them having been thrown in a futile attempt to send the rest of my left hand to where three of its fingers had long gone.

Assured I could catch up to Snarl Boy, I stood facing the incoming crowd, ready to put up whatever fight I could manage. By all means, I should have been rendered completely weak and defenceless after an eternity of inactivity and horrific sustenance, and yet I remained powered by a single thought.

If I don't get off this ship, I am going to die.

This was the kind of urgency I hadn't felt ever since Eden's putrid fingers danced around my lips – Mahro wasn't here to save me, but I at last had the capacity to save myself. The first attack swung and resoundingly missed; as his arm flew over my head, I grasped his waist with both arms and launched him into his peers after a single rotation. It wasn't especially forceful but combined with the uneven terrain we found ourselves on, all but one of them tumbled over either from being hit by their flying friend or from their attempt to dodge him.

The last stopped in his tracks behind his collapsed friends, slowly drawing a short sword from the sheath at his hip. At this final opponent's torso there was a small golden badge, no doubt signifying a commendable rank among his peers – though there was nothing for *me* to commend about him. Stepping over his disabled friends, he calmly walked forward with the sword pointed towards my face, up until he was only a few metres away.

At this point, his approach became rapid, but I was quick to see through such a trick; stepping to the side, I grasped his sword-wielding arm with my right hand and swept at his feet with my right leg, sending him tumbling to the floor. Maintaining my iron grip on his hand left his arm twisting and the rest of him suspended just above the floor up until he released the sword from his grasp, at which point I threw his arm to the ground and clambered after the weapon for myself.

As soon as my grip wrapped around its hilt, the back of my leg was struck by his foot, and while I maintained my footing, his hand grabbing onto the back of my shirt forcibly twisted me around. Knowing that one slipup or moment of hesitation would be the end of me, I steeled myself for what I had to do; Mahro had always been apprehensive about the topic of death, declaring it to be ugly even when necessary, and despite the harsh life I had borne witness to up until that point, I had always taken his lessons to heart: life is precious, and there is no such thing as an unsalvageable soul.

Which is why – despite the objective need for it, considering my death was the alternative – I couldn't help but feel as though I had disappointed him the instant I ran the sword through my attacker's neck. I closed my eyes as he fell dead to the ground, contemplating the magnitude of what I had just done. Whose son did I just kill? What would Kyrie and Tsubasa think if they learned I had blood on my hands, even if I could justify it? Would this irrevocably alter our relationship and their view of me?

All of these questions burned in my mind, and yet, after just a moment of consideration...

...I... didn't feel much...

The bitter ugliness of it left a bad taste in my mouth, but little else. The fallout I dreaded was long distant. My confusion, my anger, my indignation at Snarl Boy... wondering about a man I knew nothing about and who would have gladly killed or subdued me had I not retaliated seemed like folly. I ran my blade through this man with apprehension, expecting to crumble in self-doubt and regret, yet came away from it with a strange kind of confidence: I had the will and the strength to defend my own life from those who would harm me, even without Mahro watching my back. And Snarl Boy was next and last on my list.

Pulling the bloodstained blade from the final attacker, I charged out of the room as the ship continued swaying unevenly, intent on finding Snarl Boy and putting an end to his snarling once and for all. Fortunately, I had emerged just in time to witness him turning to the right at the very end of the hallway to my left. I furiously gave chase, keeping a vigilant eye out for any ambushes. Only one came, right before the point at which I was to turn; one of the grunts emerged from a room to my right with a knife at the ready, holding it with both hands in front of him. He must have been taken aback by my sheer speed, however, as he recoiled upon seeing I was just a few metres from him. Wasting no time, I swung for his neck as I dashed past, burying the blade halfway through his neck and staining my hand in thick blood. I had no time to dig it out or cut through the other half, so I abandoned my weapon to continue giving chase, hearing a hard thud against the floor as I turned the corner.

The final door leading to the ship's exterior remained opened and was swaying about with great force as both the heavy winds and the swaying ship left it in the crossfire of an eternal war between natural forces. Undeterred, I maintained my speed and dashed through it right before it momentarily slammed shut again.

What I found was vast darkness and downpour; as the sounds of waves crashing against the boat, the pattering of rain above my hapless head and the creaking of the vessel itself became significantly louder, I looked around to find I was stuck in the middle of a vast sea, in the dead of night no less. I could vaguely make out the shapes of a few landmasses in the distance but couldn't distinguish a single detail of them. I knew I was on a ship, but I was still left utterly speechless to see just where I had ended up. My daze was only momentary, as my priority soon shifted to locating Snarl Boy again.

Sure enough, a strange, uneven whistle soon alerted me to his location, and I rushed along the edge of the boat as the swaying started to intensify once more, which forced me to lean against the single iron railing to my right just to stay onboard when the tides got particularly tumultuous. I would have never forgiven myself for falling overboard when my prey was so tantalizingly close.

Reaching the forecastle deck of this monstrous vessel, I saw what seemed to be the last flicker of a golden light some indeterminate distance away, disappearing for good the moment I blinked. It seemed strangely familiar at the time, but it's only now that I can recall where I had seen it before: the Basin. Sihan-Perseli had had more of an influence in my escape than I could have realised at the time – I suppose I should thank her when she shows up in another ten years.

This light was not all that I found there; Snarl Boy was sat in his wheelchair, looking ahead. As if... anticipating something. My rapid footsteps soon alerted him to my location, and he quickly turned around, facing me with a look of horror.

"They couldn't stop him! Worthless... insolent wretches!" he snarled, rubbing his putrid face all over my cloak's insides yet again.

"No, Mother, that means there's... hope. She is watchi-"

Snarl Boy's regular talking was cut off by my hand grasping his throat, and I shoved him against the railing in front of us while kicking away his wheelchair for good measure – it fell into the depths of the ship's sidewalk, clanging and bashing the entire way.

"What the *hell* is wrong with you?! Where are we?!"

My demands made, I loosened my grip on his throat to allow an answer to force itself out – I had no plans to let him leave with his life, but any clue I could extract would have been a bonus.

The moment after I asked these questions, a loud, bird-like shriek rang out. Having not actually seen a bird in weeks and in a state of incredible delusion, I looked behind us, expecting more of the bird-faced men to approach. This allowed Snarl Boy to shove me back with surprising might, and I barely managed to stay on my feet, bewildered that this frail bastard had such strength yet to spare. But he knew he couldn't beat me in a straight fight- he clambered over the railing to his apparent death, right as I realised something dreadful: we were on a collision course with a giant mass of rocks protruding from the sea.

It was as I turned to my right, hoping to somehow run and escape my imminent demise, that a bird swooped into view from my left, flying well beneath my eye level before rising in front of me with a laughing Snarl Boy clutched in its talons, my cloak fluttering violently against the winds as he made his bizarre escape.

Bereft of options and unwilling to let him escape with his life *or* my cloak, I bolted to the edge of the ship with every ounce of speed I could procure from the depths of my battered body, leaping onto and springing off of the railing to his great surprise. My hands clutched the back of the cloak right as the ship barrelled into the rocks – my ears were filled with the painful sound of wood and steel grinding and gnarling against stone. The ship's engines erupted like a volcano as they too collided with the rocks, transforming the entire right side of the ship into a blazing inferno as it buried itself against the protruding spires.

It was only as the fire began to spread and the sounds began to wane ever so slightly that a new, quieter sound became more apparent: choking and gurgling. Snarl Boy was clutching at the rope that united the neckline of my cloak, and my entire body weight dragging it down can't have made undoing it an easy feat. Regardless, right as the last sign of life appeared to be draining from his face and I at last looked away, confident that even if I were to inevitably fall to my death, he would come with me… it came undone.

The cloak remained in my hands as I tumbled back to the ground, unable to see where I would land. For all intents and purposes, I was either landing on solid ground or in violent, hazardous waters – neither had an optimistic survival rate. My anger, my fury, my unending urge to snuff out his life… all of it faded away in an instant. All I could do was gaze at the stars; if I couldn't die surrounded by my loved ones, with Tsubasa's hand clutching my own… dying while gazing upon *something* beautiful could at least be a small consolation. But the beauty of the cosmos couldn't overpower the single thought I was prepared to die with.

If only I were stronger. If only I were like Mahro…

With regret consuming my thoughts and the wind pushing against me with more and more intensity by the second, I closed my eyes, ready to accept this wasteful end to my life.

...needless to say, I landed in the water.

My entire back crashing into the tempestuous surface was bad enough, but my right leg was far worse off, having landed on an unfortunately positioned broken chunk of wood with a sharp edge, rendering me barely even able to move. Despite this, I was forced awake from the daze induced by my acceptance of my incoming death, and I fought against all of the pain racking my body as I desperately swam upwards, not knowing if I was swimming to the shore or back into catastrophe. It took a few minutes of arduous, painful swimming, but the moment my hand crashed into soft sand, I could finally relax, assured that if I would not survive the night, my body would at least be found.

Crawling as far as my dimming consciousness would allow, I could only smile, happy that my family wouldn't be forever left in the dark, not knowing that my corpse was lost at sea. Tsubasa could say that... her brother died doing his best...

"So that's how you wound up on my doorstep, my friend?" Mahro asks rhetorically – having heard my retelling of what had happened since his departure, he looks... troubled.

Of course, I myself am equally confounded – though Sihan-Perseli once again intervened, I didn't even attempt to factor in her part in this tale as I told it to Mahro; I could already feel a strange tingle in my throat as I explained what happened on that boat, and so I beat around the bush in regards to what specifically happened, leaving out her involvement in directing me here and the strange golden light in front of the ship that was no doubt her doing. That being said, I'm a better liar than in my youth, so none of it struck Mahro or his daughters as particularly strange or discrepant.

It's been maybe an hour or so since I woke up in his house, and in that time the three of them have each taken an elegant wooden seat from the other side of the room to sit by my side. It's not just Mahro expressing great dismay – Matra looks utterly lost for words, and her eyes haven't met my own again for the entire duration of my retelling, whilst Myra has been looking around the room an awful lot, looking more confused than anything.

"Above all else, I'm just... glad you're alive. Looks like Saki's teachings helped you out in the long run, eh?" he continues, trying to smile.

There's a glimmer of the joyous mentor I spent almost a decade at the side of, but I don't blame him for being overwhelmed by the sheer absurdity of our circumstances.

"I don't even know where I would begin untangling such a mess. You're so... strong!" says Myra with an admiring glint in her eye – her voice is far softer and warmer than her sister's, though no less resplendent with energy.

"Thanks." I answer, though I feel her admiration is undeserved – a moment later, my eyes drift from the younger sister to the older sister.

Matra has an awfully sour look on her face and is still facing the wall above me rather than... me. That look really doesn't befit her. Up to me to force out a smile...

"Bet you're glad you didn't have to wait *that* long to see me, then?"

"Is this a joke?" she snaps back, still refusing to meet my eyes – it doesn't even appear to be directed at me, but rather the circumstances themselves. "All my atoning, all my solitude... and then a reminder of my sins washes up right before me. Perhaps cruelty does fall under Melodias' definition of 'love'..."

There follows a heavy, thick silence in the room, save for Mahro's deep exhale as he buries his face in his hand. Myra is first to break the lengthy silence.

"S-Sis, it's not *his* faul-"

"Did I *say* it was his fault?" Matra bites back between gritted teeth.

It's hard to believe, but there's a definitive tone of menace in her voice as she stares her sister down, forcing the diminutive Myra to shrink back and hold her tongue. To say she's different from the warm and loving big sister figure Tsubasa had come to know and love would be akin to describing Eden as a 'nuisance'.

"I'm going to my room. Don't disturb me."

And thus, the punchline emerges - she finally meets my gaze, only to deliver a command that demands distance.

The forceful shutting of the door behind her causes me to jump up a little, but I'm otherwise relieved that the tension has subsided – as much as I want to catch up with her, something about my arrival has clearly bothered her. I suppose the best source of answers is my own mentor, who is staring at me apprehensively.

"So... what's the matter with her?" I ask, not expecting much of consequence.

Julius had of course informed me that she had a habit of exaggerating how hard done to she truly was, her three-hour disappearance as a child remaining the prime example. Surely, she was just on the receiving end of one bad day and would have her spunk back after a good night's sleep... right?

"I dreaded you would ask... and yet, it wouldn't be right to keep you in the dark." Mahro dourly answers.

...shit.

"My baby girl... I'm sure you already know most of this, but she'd had a scrap with her mother and my wife, Minami. Typical stuff. Tsubasa's had her moaning matches with Kyrie, Myra had her fair share, it's just part and parcel of raising a young lady. But this one apparently turned quite egregious; the pair of them exchanged words I would rather not repeat or hope to hear leave the mouths of women, and it ended with Matra running away, hoping to stay in Morosus with me after travel to and from this country was effectively banned.

"You've met Matra's boss Loren by now, right? Well, he was in the cave beneath Mount Melodias, following up on a violent incident that had taken place some days before, and was expecting my little girl to join him later that day. When Matra left, Minami didn't take it all too seriously at first. She and Myra figured she would be back in a matter of hours, or had prematurely joined Loren in his work. And as far as I'm aware, both were in the dark as to the upcoming travel ban, as Matra had only learned about it from Loren.

'Then a number of hours had passed, and neither hide nor hair of my baby girl showed up. Minami threw on a pair of sandals and ordered Myra to stay in the house as a storm began brewing. She travelled up that bridge and towards the mountain, making her way behind the temple to find herself in the cave. Loren was present, but there was no sign of Matra. In a panic, Minami explained to him that she had disappeared without a trace earlier that day, and Loren agreed to help find her, having painstakingly wrapped up his investigation by his lonesome.

"And then they left the mountain's depths, only to find the storm and rain had gotten exceedingly violent; lanterns and other little knick-knacks were flying off of walls they had spent years lying dormant against, trees surrounding the village began to uproot and topple, and the waters of the river below their feet raged endlessly, thrashing ever to and fro. It's like the gods of the winds and rain had been saving up all of their grotesque power for *this* particular moment.

"Loren insisted they wait for the storm to die down before traversing the bridge again, fearing for Minami's safety. She refused to heed his warning, forcing herself to travel along it and drowning out his shouting with the winds. And then… a loose poster from elsewhere in Dias was carried around by the winds and ended up crashing into her face. She stumbled and fell, into the river. She knew how to swim, of course, but… her foot was caught beneath some thick rocks at the bed of the river. She tried her best, bless her soul, but… she eventually drowned."

Mahro's head retracts into his hands the instant his retelling concludes, and I can only share Myra's look of abject misery as the reason for Matra's behaviour becomes crystal clear – her guilt must be devouring her from the inside.

"I'm sorry to hear that, Master Katsuragi. I truly mean it."

"You need not worry about me, my friend." He answers, bringing his face back up at last with a frown, "It's Matra you have to watch out for; over a year later, she remains awfully downtrodden about the whole ordeal. As much as I would love to see some life in her again... I can't force it to happen. She needs the space to confront this herself, even if it takes a lifetime. Can I ask that you afford her the same respect?"

...I'm conflicted. It would be brazen of me to think I can wrap up Matra's inner turmoil with a neat bow overnight, and yet I don't want to just give up on her, as it sounds like Mahro has done. Then again, if even *he* can't solve this, what chance in the world do *I* stand? I'm a diluted facsimile of the man; anything I could do about it, he could do infinitely better. Besides, can I afford to involve myself in her struggle when I have to... to...

"Wait a minute! How am I going to get home?!" I cry out suddenly, scaring the skin off of Myra but not making my mentor flinch one bit.

"Not happening anytime soon, I'm afraid – there's no legal way out of the country." he starkly answers, as if my question were as certain to come as the night.

"Well... can we not get word to them? I'm fairly sure Cladio can be hired to send mail an-"

"No can do. Country's at a deficit of the pups, so they're being used solely to send word to family in the military. Anything beyond that isn't considered 'essential' enough to send, I'm afraid. It's why we couldn't let you know about what happened until you arrived – if our gracious leaders had their heads any further up their arses, one swift kick would quickly decapitate them."

"You've got to be fucking kidding me..."

With my avenue for return seemingly closed off, my head slinks back into the pillow – I'm looking at an awfully grim future, where my family may well spend the next decade believing me to be dead, or to have abandoned them without a trace. Will they even recognize me by the time we next meet? Will Tsubasa have long departed, following her own pursuits in adolescence after all hope of my return is lost? Are they even *alive*?

...I can't accept this.

Fighting Mahro and Myra's vociferous protests, I force myself to stand up, and I stumble towards my cloak that is currently suspended from a hanger against the door. If even Mahro can't or won't help me return home, then it's up to me; Tenryuu's obstinate laws, Snarl Boy and his companions, the sheer time investment needed to walk all the way from one end of the world to the other, none of them can deter me from forcing my way home, come hell or high water. But right as one of my metallic fingers grazes its soft fur collar, I collapse to the ground, tremoring and barely able to move any further.

"If you're going to run face first into some Tenryuu dog's sword, at least rest up first." says Mahro, a tinge of bitterness seeping into his voice. "I have no objection to you staying under my wing for as long as is necessary. I take it you have no qualms with our provision of hospitality, my little chicken?"

"Of course not!"

Myra seems to have already accepted me, smiling at me as she hoists me from the ground and carries me back to the bed – much like her sister, she's deceptively strong, and handles my entire body weight with relative ease.

"I know your heart must ache, Vega – I felt much the same when Big Sis disappeared. But hold on to that hope! You'll see your family again one day, I promise you!"

She spouts her platitudes with such earnest enthusiasm and with such a radiant glint in the hazel eyes so graciously bestowed upon her by Mahro that I feel guilty not a single smile or sign of agreement can be forced out of me; I'm not even sure if they continue living at this moment, so how can I possibly work myself into a state of excitement at the prospect of seeing them again?

"That being said, a problem of equal importance yet of far greater obfuscation presents itself; where has this 'Snarl Boy' gotten himself off to, and what else does he have up his sleeve?"

Mahro's query strikes like a bolt of lightning – in my worry about returning to Morosus and the safety of my family, I barely even factored in the magnitude of the further dangers that now bar my path. First Snarl Boy, who had the resources and manpower to abduct me and ferry me across forbidden waters with a decently large ship, and then Pat showing his foul, Wyvern-branded mug at the worst possible time, as if done with deliberation. If the two are working in cahoots, that only raises infinitely more questions. Why was Pat in Dias, at the exact moment of my unanticipated arrival there thanks to my failed abduction? One could simply chalk it up to coincidence, or a grand conspiracy running throughout the back of it all, coiling around all of our necks like a snake. I have a feeling it's the latter, though not with Snarl Boy or Pat at the helm.

"Don't vex yourself needlessly, my friend. Get the rest you need. I'll call in a few favours from some old friends and look into the matter in your stead. Myra, you can keep the house for a few days, yes?" Mahro asks of his spritely daughter, who nods with emboldened energy. "I knew you were up for it. I'll leave a list before I head off, pertaining to some... *precautions*."

The strained tone with which that last word eeks out of his windpipe is no doubt eyebrow-raising, but all I can do now is place my trust in Mahro once again – the pain of perhaps never watching Tsubasa grow to adolescence or not being by Maverick's side at his final moment is unbearable, but curling up into a ball and crying isn't going to help whatsoever. I'm lucky to even be alive, and I can't afford to carelessly waste this last chance thrown at me by life.

"Let's leave our man to it then, my little chicken. Good night."

Mahro heavily dims the lantern hanging from the centre of the ceiling before closing the door behind himself and his daughter.

Of course, sleep does not come quickly to me. The darkness of the room is all too reminiscent of the darkness that profaned my eyes even during my waking hours as I was held prisoner on that ship, and sleep carries its own perils. Nothing about my situation is going to unravel quickly, I dread, least of all the conspiracy surrounding Snarl Boy.

Chapter 16:
A Wolf in Dragon's Scales

"Hehehe!"

Myra rummages through her light red handbag, her back facing me the whole time as she concocts some hare-brained scheme in her dome.

It's been roughly a week since my arrival in Dias, all of which I've spent recovering inside my mentor's home. Mahro himself hasn't returned yet, but Myra has been a fine host in his stead; despite my lack of knowledge or experience with Tenryuu cuisine, she's proven to be very adept at understanding my culinary tastes, and my shoulders and back have become so familiar with the pressing of her soft hands that I almost don't want to get up and start walking around again, lest the necessity for that walk out with me.

That being said, the manner in which she's cooking up something devious is all too reminiscent of her older sister when she too was of this age – Myra told me she turned 16 on May 8th of the current year, making Matra the older of the two by 18 months (though hopefully the Myra of 18 months from now won't follow in her sister's... dourness). Her enthusiasm was endearing at first, but now the sheer amount of time she's spent digging inside her bag and giggling is beginning to concern me; I can't begin to imagine what could possibly be so amusing about the contents of a woman's handbag to... well, a woman. After much fumbling around in her handbag, she at last produces a rectangular box, similar in size to some of the heavier books among Kyrie's collection.

With a stylish twirl on her heel, she at last unveils her intentions.

"Ready for a makeover, mister?"

"...excuse me?"

As I sit up on the edge of the bed, the dread begins to set in; perhaps absentmindedly saying yes to the requests of even your friends can backfire, given that Myra looks ready to set me up for a job as a clown. I'll stick with Lyn's verbal abuse, thanks.

"Well, to cut a long story short, Dad wants me to touch your face up a bit to look more... Tenryuu...y? We'll work on the word later! Ever since we got wrapped up in this stupid war thing, the country's been hard on 'detecting spieeees!', so if you catch the attention of the wrong rotund bureaucrat taking a stroll through our humble abode, you may well end up getting dragged to Shigan under the guise of 'being suspected of spying!'. Just a little touch up should help you avoid the displeasure of dealing with them, right?"

That's an... unconventional plan, and one I ever would have expected to come from Mahro, though I can't help but sigh in relief that my nose won't be big, soft and red anytime soon.

"...y-yeah, sure."

My consent sets Myra off like a fuse; in an instant, she's standing in front of me while opening the box to reveal an array of brushes and... actually, I can only name the brushes. The rest remain firmly within the realm of womanhood.

"Now then, please keep your head still as I mould you into one of our own, hehehe!" she instructs as she leans forward with a thin black tool resembling a pencil.

As she repeatedly grazes my eyebrows in an upward motion, I take the opportunity to give Myra a proper observation, now that I'm somewhat in my right mind again; her clothes are the same as those she wore upon our first meeting, accentuating that her frame is slightly slimmer than that of her beloved older sister, and not quite so voluptuous, though her chest wobbles with the same vigour as she shuffles around between strokes, sizing up her next adjustment in the manner a bird would stare down its prey. It doesn't take long to detect that Myra's perfume is shared with her sister – it's hardly significant, but I take some pleasure in knowing the two share at least some small common ground. Though given our scant familiarity, I sincerely hope she isn't interpreting my smile as one of erotic pleasure.

274

"I take it you like those clothes, then?" I ask, casting my eyes towards her navel with a little strain as she laughs boisterously.

"How could I not? Such a fine, lascivious sight sets the crowd on fire, and the costume treats my skin well, like the arms of a tender lover!" she says with a smile.

"You wear this before a *crowd?*" I ask.

"Mm hm! Every Tuesday, Wednesday, Saturday and Sunday, in fact! Mr. Entari's most glamourous right hand needs the most glamourous attire, after all!"

"He has more than one right hand?"

It takes her a few seconds to comprehend my comedic ingenuity, but it lands well enough.

"*Ha!* You wouldn't be the slightest bit out of place among our band."

"I think I've had enough of 'Bands' for one lifetime."

With the first stage out of the way, Myra lays down the tool and begins rubbing a black powder into my eyebrows, copying with her thumb the motions her brush had taken.

The conversation turns dead once more. The warmth of her hands is comforting, but the only sign of life to emerge from me for a while is a painstakingly slow bead of cold sweat crawling down to my right eyebrow. Myra's free thumb thankfully relieves me of that torture.

But just being in her presence is... perplexing. She embodies the exact cheer of the younger Matra I once knew, as if completely unperturbed by the tragedy she had not only been affected by but had all but witnessed.

Aren't you bothered by what happened to your mother?

For a moment, I entertain the remarkably stupid idea of asking such a thing, but the sentence sputters out by the second word; if a woman who was barely as acquainted with me as a stranger posed such a question, I would very much think it indecent.

"Aren't I...?" Myra asks as she leans forward with a smirk, her blood red hair tickling the front of my shoulders.

Of course, the problem is I said enough of it for the fish to clamp down on the hook. And the look on her face suggests she very much wants the question finished.

"Aren't you… cold?"

Ugh… the conversation may be salvaged, but the hair on my back bristles from the mere mention of the biting temperature.

"I'm positively freezing!" she unexpectedly answers as she begins tending to my other eyebrow, "But you can't let a spot of grim weather rule your life, you know?"

It sounds like she's simultaneously talking from experience yet trying to avoid discussing her experiences. Not that I'm a stranger to being evasive, but it's understandably mystifying now that I'm the one being strung along. Nevertheless, I would only make us both feel worse by prying, so I suppose I'll ignore the elephant in the room entirely.

"That's a refreshing outlook to take; most are swift to falter at the first whiff of trouble. A little more inspiration would do the world many favours." I say with a small smile, "Still, I suppose the strength to overcome such times isn't innate to we humans, or hard times would be as distant a memory as the straw huts we once called homes."

"You can say that again." Myra says as her eyes drift upwards – I'm not sure if she's rolling her eyes in annoyance over the idea or making a point of looking towards Matra's bedroom.

The transformation is at last complete, and Myra presents before my face a rectangular mirror. I look… distinct, I guess would be the word? My sparse eyebrows are now as dense as Ringo, and through what must no doubt be witchcraft, Myra has somehow managed to make my face look noticeably more stiff, similar to Mahro in many ways; I'm not even going to begin theorizing how she's pulled off such a seamless disguise. The only part of my head that looks familiar is my hair, and Myra has even taken the time to sort out the scraggly black mass it's spent the better part of a month as; I'm not entirely fond of my hair being brushed downwards on each side, and it's beginning to reach just above the height of my jaw in its present state, but in terms of our actual goal it gets the job done.

"Appreciate my handiwork? Have my years of theatre experience not borne fruit on this day?" Myra asks, joining in on my giggling.

"I could use a haircut..." I answer facetiously, "But you've done a great job. I can hardly even recognize myself."

"Aw, thank you! Now that'll be 50 Sera!"

"You would demand payment from the beaten and robbed?!"

"If I'm in the mood for it!" she answers with a wink.

"Considering your efficacy in extortion and aptitude for disguising, I'm beginning to think you would make a killing in the assassination market." I say in jest, though the wide grin on her face suggests she may be seriously pondering the idea.

Of course, she never actually demands payment, and she even assists me in some brief exercises to sort my body back into a stiff but functional state. On Master Katsuragi's instructions, she provides me with some of his old clothes, a tidy set consisting of a black shirt and baggy green trousers with a brown belt to tighten them around my comparatively thin waist. I'll admit it's ever so slightly exciting to be conducting my affairs in clothes used by the man I look up to most; not that I wish to let my face show it. I bid Myra farewell as I throw on my cloak and set out with a clear goal in mind: sending word to my family.

Having thought the matter over extensively while laying idle these many prior days and nights, I've come up with something of a scheme: if the use of Cladio is reserved for sending messages to those within the military under the reasoning of "necessity", then surely the same could apply to Tenryuu's military allies? I'm not aware of the specifics surrounding their wartime alliance, but even on opposite sides of our enemy, are we not a united front?

...

...if I may be entirely honest with myself, I'm not expecting much success from this angle, but it's the best shot I have. For my family's sake, I have to try, if only to save them from stewing in uncertainty.

I step out of Mahro's front door to find myself on a raised wooden patio, the fence surrounding the door adorned with hanging flowerpots that now carry more snow than flora, complimenting the white sheet of snow that envelops the entire village of Dias. The only place to escape such a fate is the river immediately in front of Mahro's house, crashing and flowing unperturbed - Mahro never told me if his wife's body was ever recovered, so I would... rather not think much more about it. The river runs beneath that fateful rope bridge before disappearing into a dark cavern at the foot of the mountain.

Descending the steps of the patio, I turn around to get a good look at the Katsuragi home: in contrast to many of the more humble, cramped dwellings found in Dias Village, the home of my mentor is a staggering two stories tall, its very active chimney peaking ever so slightly below my own home's greatest heights. The overall shape is symmetrical, as is the distribution of black, red and white rectangles painted onto its walls. Each of the windows bears a flowerbed beneath them, though they share the same fate as their more adventurous brethren hanging from the fence. There's something awfully idyllic about such a home; much like the worn down, tattered but still beloved library I've called home these past ten or so years, it stands as something of a microcosm of the corner of the world surrounding it. Then again, even I can faintly remember a time when the library's outside was far better tended to – I could never forgive myself should such a fate befall this gracious dwelling.

At last divorcing my gaze from what I suppose will be my temporary home, I finally start walking towards the village – behind Mahro's isolated home is a large rock wall, with the rest of Dias lying above it. The only path back is a small dirt offshoot that trails up the hill to my left and enters Dias close to the rope bridge underneath the great mountain's shadow. The riverbank by my side is largely barren, save for two moderately sized trees, devoid of leaves but shielding the earth beneath them from the worst of winter's fury. Now that I'm so close to it, the mountain really is imposing; from any great distance it's hardly fascinating, but at its feet, I have a great feeling of danger just from looking at it – each of its peaks are abundant with loose rocks I'm certain any strong wind could send barrelling into the river, and the one path up to the central summit looks long abandoned, with many a toppled tree barring the course of those daring enough to scale the landmark.

As I approach the body of the village, I at last catch a glance of the eldest of Mahro's daughters, steadily walking across the rope bridge, alone and with her hands cautiously gripping both sides. I have no doubt the location evokes some painful thoughts for her; I decide to wait at the foot of Loren's office, conveniently situated right next to the dirt path. As Matra approaches the end of the rope bridge, I can't help but feel ever so slightly nervous; aside from our initial reunion, she hasn't once visited me during my unexpected stay. Part of me expects it to be due to business or some other factor beyond my knowledge, but the possibility that she's deliberately avoiding me is… well, it's uncomfortable, but now may be the chance to confront that.

She at last sets foot on earth once again, and our eyes soon meet. Those eyes were once filled with a distinct energy and enthusiasm, unmatched by any living thing in the entirety of Ford save for Tsubasa. They offered the most pleasant sight that village had seen in years, and now she stands before me, offering the same kind of contrast but for an entirely different reason.

Her eyes look completely dead.

The mesmerising hazel tint of her iris, the glint of the morning sun bordering her pupils, on the surface it's all present and accounted for… but there's *nothing* behind them. As she comes ever closer, I can only come away with the impression that she's looking through me rather than at me, and the bitter frown on her bright lips is doing nothing to assuage my nerves.

Standing directly in front of me, she doesn't even seem to react to my presence whatsoever, nor the stellar work done unto my face by her own flesh and blood. I gulp and shift my eyes towards the bridge, completely lost as for what I should or even *can* say.

"You're up and about once again, then." She says with hardly any emotion, sounding almost disappointed that I dare walk the same ground as her.

"Either that or... your eyes are playing tricks on you."

"There are no words to describe how intensely I wish that were the truth." Matra says as she stares towards the ground to her right, "It's been ill omen after ill omen, and then *you* show up? Did my ancestors spit in the face of Lady Melodias? I cannot possibly fathom what we've done to deserve this."

...

I'm speechless. I'm having a hard time convincing myself this is actually Matra and not some impeccable facsimile of the woman who provided the sullen populace of Ford with such great company last year. Her stature which once served as the fuel for much amusement at my expense now only serves to block out the sun's grace, and she cannot even bring herself to look into my eyes again. I'm not sure what I expected, but I certainly didn't set myself up for such a drastic shift in her personality – there's practically nothing remaining that once distinguished her.

"I'm sorry to impose on you and your family. If there's anything I can do to make it up to you, say the word."

As unmanly as it may be, I all but prostrate myself before her, wanting desperately to see her smile or at least wipe that hideous frown off of her face. But the frown is unbudging, as are her crossed arms.

"I have not attributed blame to you, and yet you're so quick to offer the back of your head to my heel, desperate to take upon blame where there was none. Were you not trained by my father, I would never believe you could untangle your way out of your own hair, let alone an abduction."

Her remark is disarming, and she forces out every word with odious contempt – I never thought I would say this, but talking to Matra has become *infuriating*.

"You're an awful liar, Matra; your words don't blame me, but everything else about you does."

To the surprise of nobody, fighting fire with fire only earns a hawkish, unflinching stare directly into my eyes and an enraged pout.

"I'll only demand from you what I demand from Myra and my dad: solitude. Don't force your nose into my affairs. I will speak with you if and when I deem it necessary. Am I clear?" she asks, refusing to even blink as she awaits an answer.

...now I see why Mahro gave up. When you know the person she was in the past, it's hard not to latch onto it, and try to drag it kicking and screaming back into the present. I wanted to believe that I could bring back with words the parts of her soul that fate itself has taken a hammer to. But... it pains me to acknowledge this... trying to talk sense into her is a hopeless endeavour; prolonging this is just going to eat away at my mind. There's already plenty of vermin trying to feast on that.

"I don't like it one bit, but I'll do as you wish."

She's still not smiling, but her frown at least seems less intense, and she ascends towards Loren's office with one last reply.

"Thank you."

The door decisively slams shut behind her, along with any hope that the vibrant young lady hiding beneath that husk can be restored.

I couldn't stop thinking about Matra's drastic change in disposition as I asked for directions towards and eventually fumbled my way into my destination: the delivery office situated close to the village's centre. I drew a few curious looks on the way, more likely from my clumsy, uneven walking than my actual appearance, but the unwanted attention was making me a mite nauseous. Now that I'm inside the office, I can relax at last. There's a distinctly pleasant aura in every nook and cranny of the building, with its interior walls lavished in a dark, sensual red. Candelabras hang with authority from the ceiling, purging the darkness from every corner of this space. A row of empty seats stacked upon one another lie to my right, though it appears their disuse has not led to neglect for their condition.

"Morning, stranger. You got yourself a face but it ain't at all familiar. What trouble you causin'?"

I've been in here for ten seconds, and already the abrasive-sounding young lady behind the counter is jeering at my expense, surely feeling all high and mighty looking down at this stranger from behind the glass screen. Her comically stuffy uniform – an odious green shirt and overalls – only makes her cockiness more irritating.

"Cut the attitude. I'm just visiting family." I hastily answer.

She looks unconvinced, but I can't say it's entirely inaccurate; Mahro has played as much a role in raising me as either of my parents. I hope more than anything that that feeling is mutual.

"Well then, state your business, big guy. If it's anything other than sending word to your dad or brother or whoever in the family's off being a real man, you may as well turn your behind around and escort yourself back through that door." She says with a grimace, no doubt expecting a quick exit – her harshness is oddly unbefitting of her age, sounding more applicable to someone like Lyndra.

"Oh, I'm here to contact family in the war." I answer.

"Whoa, you're actually giving me something to do?!"

In a bewildered fit, she fetches a stack of documents from beneath the counter, revealing sheets written in Tentongue but full of empty boxes, bearing headings asking my name, destination and other essentials.

"Apologies for my earlier conduct. Please, let me fill it in for you. First up, name?"

"Vega Pyre."

My name instantly provokes a queer look – I can tell she's thinking *what kind of name is that?!*

"Uh… and where are you staying at the moment?"

"At the home of Mahro Katsuragi."

Mahro's name raises an eyebrow, though it seems to be more of a welcome surprise than cause for alarm.

"Next up, recipient?"

"Altair Pyre."

"Mm hm. Destination?"

"Uh... well, he's stationed at the border of... Morosus, so-"

"*Are you for real?!*" she suddenly shouts, knocking the wind out of my sails with her volume, "Listen well, twigdick: we're only authorised to send Cladio *within Tenryuu!* Are you blind and deaf or did you earnestly think you could pull one over on me?! You're either extremely brazen or extremely stupid!"

Ah... this is how it is, then. It was foolish of me to expect anything else, and I'm just about ready to scurry out of the door, never to be seen again within the premises. But her scorching, high-pitched condemnation is interrupted by a rapturous laugh, followed by a hand slamming into my back and scaring the living daylights out of me. I would recognize that hand even through a foot of butter: it's Mahro.

"He's brazen alright; he gets it from me!"

The instant she lays eyes on him, the young lady stiffens and stands straight up, looking paralyzed by fear.

"M-M-M-Mister Katsuragi..."

"I told you, kid: Mahro's fine, I'm barely a mister!" he says with a childish grin.

"How long have you been there?" I ask quietly.

"Hmm... well, I entered right as you mentioned you're 'visiting family'. Quite frankly, I'm beyond flattered that you regard my daughters and I with such a calibre of respect and admiration! Truly brings a tear to my eye!" he answers as he rubs his right eyelid with his knuckles.

"You're a convenient excuse, old man."

For as much as what he's saying is true, it's not an aspect of our relationship I wish to wave around in the open. The disrespect with which I handwaved it eats away at me a little, but he laughs it off as always.

"Little Miss Meryl, if you could just do my good friend here this one favour, I'll make it worth your while."

Mahro is quick to back up his words – before any agreement is made, he passes a paper note through the slit in the glass barrier, worth 200 Sera.

There's a golden glint in Meryl's eyes as she mulls over the morality of her choice... for all but half a second. The note vanishes into her pockets, and after a brief look around the entire room, she speaks once more.

"If anybody asks, clumsy little me just... happened to let one of our prized Cladio slip, and it flew off somewhere to the west. Got it?"

Mahro and I enthusiastically nod in agreement, and she beckons me forth to fill in the rest of the sheet, giggling in anticipation the whole time. Once this is done, I can at last write down a message for Altair, and after a moment of consideration, I transcribe what I deem necessary onto the blank page:

> "Altair,
> It's Vega. I'm writing this with haste so forgive me if I miss anything important. Long story short, a group of men dressed up like birds abducted me when I went to visit our old home. Their leader was some raspy kid on a wheelchair with a strange mask over his eyes that kept calling me 'brother'. I was held prisoner on a ship for roughly a month until I managed to escape through a combination of my captors' stupidity and a collision at Tenryuu's coastline. I've ended up at Mahro's home village and I'm staying with the old man for the foreseeable future given that I have no real means of getting back home. If you can, send back word on how our family is doing - it will do me unimaginable good to know they're well. And please tell them I love them."

Now that I've actually described the course of events in text, it sounds... batshit insane - I have a dreadful feeling it'll end up being discarded as some kind of sick prank, weaving fantastical tales while assuming the guise of Altair's missing brother, burrowing deeper into my family's emotional wounds. But if there is a way I could ascribe any kind of authenticity to it, it's not coming to me; all I can do is hope my big brother can pull his weight and bring my family some peace of mind – something I have no certainty he will live up to, given his continued distance from us. Disgruntled, I hastily throw the folded up message into an envelope and hand it to Meryl, who speeds off into the back of the building.

As we leave the building at last and begin making our way back to his home, I finally strike up a conversation with Mahro, if only to distract myself from the reality that my family learning of what became of me has been left solely in my brother's hands.

"I didn't realise you were back."

I keep my volume to a necessary low, given that the streets of Dias are scarcely populated at this moment and there is no crowd to drown out our conversation.

"*Hah!* I only just returned, my friend! I just so happened to catch you wandering into that little old office with zero plans and I'm sure even less expectations!"

That's not fair, Master King Rag. I had... *a* plan. Not a good one, but I digress.

"That's enough about my affairs. You seem pleased about something. Do you bring good news?" I ask, suppressing my desperation.

"Not so much *good* news, but news nonetheless. I dragged a pal along to check out the ship you arrived here in. The military's taken notice by now and they're conducting an in-depth search and salvage, but before they stuck their nose in we verified your story, and we took with us the scant few documents lying around that may end up with a bunch of dogs sniffing up and down our door otherwise." he answers, tempering his grin as he pats a small bag slung around his shoulder.

"Documents?"

"You can take a look when we're back. Nothing world-rending from my quick scan of its contents, but you may as well sate your curiosity."

"Right then..."

I return my hands to my pockets, lost in thought about the day's events. Matra's sour disposition was sure to ruin my day but Mahro's sudden return is a relief, and not just for his saving throw in the mailing office.

"I take it you ran into my darling, eh?" Mahro cuts to the chase, disrupting my chain of thought, "That dour tint in your eye says yes. Whatever she's said to you, don't beat yourself up over it; I know I wasn't myself for a while when my own father figure passed away, bless his noble soul."

All of a sudden, I can distinctly recall some of the last words I heard from Mahro before he left Morosus for good: *I think that story is best saved for when we next meet.*

"I suppose it's time you kept your promise, Master King Rag." I say, closely examining how he reacts.

He remains dumbfounded for a moment; for once, I fear I may have actually spoken well out of turn, and I look away in shame, hoping he didn't hear me. But my aim eventually becomes clear, and his answer is bogged down by an uncharacteristic sigh.

"Ahh... his death is only tangentially related to *those* proceedings, but it's related nonetheless. Join me for drinks one of these nights, my friend. I would prefer not to disclose such happenings while either of us is sober."

Myra was delighted to see Mahro has returned – I thought she was running with her arms outstretched to throw them around me, and I can't lie, I was ever so slightly jealous to see that affection given exclusively to Mahro. Not that he's at all undeserving of whatever admiration he gets. Regardless, I have a more important matter at hand: In my hands rest these "documents" Mahro tells me pertain to yours truly. I'm not expecting much, given that there are only four sheets within the pile – the rest of the day will presumably be uneventful, proceeding as if these were immaterial while I focus mostly on restoring my physical condition. Now that I've settled down next to my bed, it's about time I got this over with so that I may move on to more productive ventures.

The first page is mostly barren, even with much of the bottom half having sustained intense damage from the ship's fires, and the forcefully dried off paper inflicts an undesirable sensation upon my fingers – for once, the fingers of flesh and artifice both are shivering in unison. It lists my known locations and activities, but the depth with which it describes my ongoings is unsettling; it covers a standard daily routine for me in a list of simplistic bullet points, down to my walk to and from Bombastic Steel and my more recent hunting trips with Julius. Such an abduction was obviously pre-meditated, but the degree of pre-meditation is only becoming clear to me as my eyes scan the document; my hunting trips with Julius were often dotted about a month apart, yet listed within are at least four separate sightings of us on such excursions. I dread to imagine just how long we've been under their watch, and nausea swells in my stomach.

The second page is a lot more intact, though I fear it's not better off for it; the entire surface area of the page is taken up by a stunningly detailed black and white illustration, purporting to depict who I can only assume to be... *me*. The proportions of my face are slightly off, my hair is drawn with an exaggerated thickness and diminished length, and my nose is slightly larger than the real deal, but otherwise it captures me scarily well. If I have to take a guess, it's as if an insanely talented artist was given the task of recreating my image without ever having seen me, and so based their craft on another's recollection. Snarl Boy didn't strike me as the artistically literate type, nor did his entourage of birdmen – so who could be behind this?

Putting aside the questions for now, I turn to the third page to find an assessment of potential risks – it's specifically noted that my cloak is to be removed with urgency whenever the opportunity presents itself, given that I keep a few weapons and tools concealed within. My stomach is in excruciating knots; I take great care not to produce items from my cloak in public spaces, and certainly not in front of Kyrie or at home. Indeed, the only occasion I can recall doing so is during my excursions with Julius. Other notes on the page state that my combat aptitude is undetermined, and so I should be approached while isolated and with great caution. If I can take any small relief from reading this page, it's clear these secret observations only began *after* Mahro's departure; any viewing of our lessons would have revealed my abilities very swiftly.

The final page is now before my eyes, and...

...

"Humanitas".

The actual contents become white noise to me, as throughout the page, I'm referred to exclusively by that name. I can feel the blood vessels in my eyes pulsating as I relive the events of

12 years ago. The sick, visceral feeling in my gut is evaporating, and in its place a murky, nascent fury is dwelling. The black beast pursuing me through the Basin, whimpering and attempting to call me by that name with its dying breath. My biological father and his followers referring to me as the very same Humanitas. I have in my hands proof that Snarl Boy is linked in some way to the long thought to be annihilated Band of the Wyvern, the very same Band of the Wyvern that this Pat fellow bears the very brand of. This should be a victory, a stepping stone to solving this ordeal once and for all... and yet, I can only feel an intense, pounding rage throughout my entire body. The thumping of my brain demands I lash out, and as I scrunch the sheet up in my hands, I can only think of one productive outcome to any of this.

"Where are you going?"

I can only faintly hear Myra's question beneath the fog clouding my brain, and I can't waste time answering it - I throw my cloak on once more and storm out of the front door, obsessed only with reaching Loren's office. I don't even know if Pat is still confined within its walls, but I won't get an answer to that question by standing around with my thumb up my ass.

I race up the stairs to his office once again, not even bothering to knock before making myself a guest of the red-laden world within. Loren is nowhere to be seen but Matra is sat on a chair to my left, her crossbow neatly placed on the seat next to her as she looks up from a thick book, her face displaying abject shock. After our momentary shared look, I set my sights on a door immediately in front of me – it's the only one here aside from the entrance, so surely the smug bastard is lying behind i-

"*Wait a second! What in the world are you doing?!*" Matra screams as she tugs at my arm, which I'm quick to roughly pull from her grasp.

"Me and Pat just need a little *solitude.* Let me pass."

As much shallow joy as throwing her words back at her brings me, my vitriol only emboldens her further, and she hastily blocks off my path with her arms outstretched, bearing an expression of great offense.

"Nobody can just storm in here and have tea time with inmates as they please! You need Loren's blessing and supervision! Did you lose a bunch of head meat in that crash?!"

Once again, I spend any amount of time in this new Matra's presence and I already can feel a blood vessel in my head pounding near to the point of bursting.

"If need be, I will force you out of my way. I need answers. *Move.*" I coldly order her compliance, but she's not budging, "What good will it do you to play the loyal lapdog in Loren's absence? All you're doing is making it harder."

My abrasive request is met with a sharp slap across the face, almost knocking me off of my feet with its sheer force. As I straighten myself once again I look back at her to see a scowl of frustration tearing across her face as she shakes some feeling back into her hand – regret is beginning to mingle with my intense rage, but the need for answers comes first.

"Step aside. I'm not warning you again." I ask as I ball my fist – never in a million years would I ever strike one of Mahro's daughters, but I dread that a desperate bluff such as this may be all I have left in my argumentative arsenal.

Before it can bear fruit or cease to do so, the door behind me flies open; Mahro rushes in, followed by a ragged Loren.

"Myra told me something seemed to upset yo- why is half your face red? What the *hell* is going on?!" Mahro asks as his glance sharply swaps between the two of us.

Great, just... great... I may well have straightened the stake against my chest and given Matra the hammer. But no matter what, I need answers.

"I read the documents you handed me! The guy wasting away in there had something to do with me ending up on that ship, I know this for a fact! I know it might not turn up anything useful, but I *need* to speak to him!"

"You seem fit to speak only with your fists, young man." Loren says as he approaches me with his arms crossed, "I'll overlook your intrusion given your... undesirable circumstances, but make your talk quick. Matra, go in with him, make sure he doesn't strangle the bastard to death."

289

She doesn't look pleased at all about the arrangement; she's already taken one of her batons into her right hand and looks primed and ready to knock me into next month, but Loren's orders are thankfully staying her hand. I offer Loren my thanks as we enter the back of the office, and the discussion between the two men at my rear fades out as the door shuts behind us. What it pertains to, I've no idea, but if Loren is chewing my mentor out for letting this happen...

...then, my apologies, Master Katsuragi.

Having come to my senses over the past few minutes, I'm reluctant to even look at Matra as she guides me to Pat; the heavy breathing indicates I've put her in something of a foul mood. There's not all that much noteworthy about this part of Loren's office; it's a thin grey corridor, constructed of a stone interior beneath the wooden shell visible to the outside world. The walls and floor feel rough and disquieting, and they remain as barren and devoid of life as the colour that envelops them.

As soon as we turn the corner, Matra turns on her foot and stands before me once again.

"You have an awful lot of nerve, you know that?! Causing trouble for us the moment you're back on your feet. How in the world were you raised?! You have no respect for us or our customs whatsoever."

"You? Talking about respect?" I answer with a bemused chuckle.

"Silence yourself before I shove you in the cell next to him and sentence the key to a lifetime of rusting beneath the river!"

"A lover's quarrel on the way to visit your dear old pal, eh? Do I *really* mean that little to ya?!"

Hearing that contemptible voice, Matra and I pick up the pace to find the musty old bastard wasting away within these walls. Indeed, Pat is seated within the cell furthest across the room, stuck in his reeking clothes and looking hardly worse for wear than when we first met. A big, stupid grin adorns his very punchable face.

"I'm not quite sure *what* you mean to me yet, 'old pal'. If anything, that's what I'm here to find out." I say to him, holding back my urge to spit at this contemptible mess of a human being.

Matra unlocks the cell and escorts me inside, gripping her baton with such intensity that a cold shiver runs down my spine, fearing what will become of me if I end up as its target.

"Don't let your lady friend spook ya, uh... Hum...ilitas, was it? God, the old geezer came up with some real retarded names..."

Pat slowly drifts off into a world of his own as I'm left dumbfounded, unsure which of my many questions to produce first.

"My name has only ever been and only ever will be Vega, but apparently, your loathsome ilk referred to me as 'Humanitas', if tha-"

"Right, right! Humanitaaaaaas! How's things been? Been doing some exploring? Got any action with your lady friend here while I been wasting away?"

He poses the last question while making an awfully vulgar gesture with his hands – I'm not even going to dignify his crudeness with a reaction.

"Funny you mention exploring, I just so happened to be taken for a voyage by an unfavourable lot – some kid in a wheelchair ordering around a clan of bird-faced men in black. They too called me 'Humanitas'." I say, watching closely for how he reacts.

"Curious, that! What a... lucky coincidence, meeting two people who've been hands on with your dirty laundry, in the span of a week no less!" Pat answers, as spry and energetic as ever.

"I don't think luck has a damn thing to do with it. The ship stopped just a few hours before I escaped. Certainly along the coast of Tenryuu. Considering where we found your sorry hide, I'm having a hard time believing you were uninvolved in all of this."

"Do I strike you as the dishonest type, Vargo? We all went our separate ways after our pops went and got himself killed by- by a-a teenager, of all things! Fancy- fancy that! Dumb bastard spends decades preparing... whatever, and it's all undone by some kid! If nothing else he knew how to grasp defeat from victory's maw! If I were in his shoes I'd be glad I'm dead! Could never live with the humiliation! *Bwahahahahahaaaa!!!*"

As Pat positively laughs his arse off, I'm struggling to register any of what he's saying as the truth – if his word is true and my father was in fact also Pat's own, that would make us... brothers? I'm ready to dismiss it as an utter fabrication, the ravings of a madman facing a life of confinement and trying to plant the seeds of his insanity in my mind before he spends the rest of his mortal days staring at bars... but Snarl Boy himself also called me 'Brother'. I dismissed it as some strange quirk or formality, but... was his word literal?

It's times like this I sorely wish Saki were around; she's always had a knack for sniffing out mistruth, and I would love nothing more at this moment than for Pat's web to be set alight.

"You're suggesting the two of us are brothers?" I ask in desperation.

More than anything, I'm hoping he'll clarify in such a manner as to stop my family tree from tangling itself beyond repair... but the savage smile suggests that he's about to do no such thing.

"Only half-brothers, Vinga; the old man had... three wives, I think? Your mummy ran off with the three of you. From there the house of cards came tumbling down..." he says, at last sounding somewhat bitter and furrowing his brow as he looks at me.

...oh dear. This complicates the matter far worse than I could have imagined, assuming his word to be true (and for as loathsome as the bastard is, his story is consistent with what Snarl Boy said and he's given off no obvious tells of lying). If Pat is just one outcome of my father's other wives... how many more long-lost half-siblings are out there? How many of them are collaborators in Snarl Boy's scheme?

But there's something far more concerning about what he just said: *the three of you*. I've *only* ever had Altair as a brother, and Tsubasa was not only born well after the Band of the Wyvern incident, but to different parents entirely. For the first time since my initial abduction, I feel utterly lost, bereft of any idea of what to make of this information and the uncomfortable position I find myself in.

"I... I only ever had one brother. What the hell do you mean 'three of us'?!" I ask, unable to stop the rage from seeping into my questions.

For the first time in the entire conversation, it's Pat's turn to look genuinely shocked by what I just said.

"Hm? Last I heard, your sweet old mummy ran off with you and both your brothers. Their given names elude me, but that was definitely the story we heard."

I... *what?!*

Is he delirious, hallucinating people who never were, or is this some elaborate prank at my expense, a covert collaboration with Snarl Boy to wear me down mentally as their greater schemes unravel in the background? All of this strange, contradictory information with such conviction...

I refuse to accept it.

I have one brother.

His name is Altair.

He is the only brother I've ever had and ever will need.

Even if this scumbag is my half-brother, as odious a concept as that is, I would sooner have the earth open up beneath my feet and swallow me whole than accept him as family.

"I suggest we leave – there's already much to process. We'll regale what transpired to Dad and-"

Matra is cut off as I rush towards Pat, grasping him by the collar.

"I don't give a shit about any of your fantastical delusions! Are you working with the kid in the wheelchair, yes or no?!" I scream in his face, burying my urge to slap the stink right off of him.

"*Bwahahahahahaa! Aaaaahahahahaaaa!!!* I couldn't organize a bread sandwich! What makes you think he'd want a fool like me wrapped up in all this?" he says before continuing to laugh gutturally.

Matra's hand forces me away from Pat once more, and she quickly drags me out of the room, though I do nothing to resist – it sounds like Pat really had nothing to do with the abduction scheme after all. The scraping of the key as it locks his cell once more only adds to how horribly unnerving this information truly is; two ghosts of my past came to haunt me, and for entirely disparate reasons. I can't reconcile it whatsoever. I would ordinarily wager that it's the machinations of Sihan-Perseli, but... *what* would she gain from this? Why would she intentionally put me in harm's way, in two different instances no less, if protection is her aim? I dread the only answers I'm going to get now would come from her but... well, I'm sure I don't need to articulate the problem with trying to do that.

"There we go, did that make you feel better? Are you satisfied?" Matra asks in a mocking tone as she stands with her arms crossed.

"Quite the contrary; what I've learned here disquiets me greatly, and yet it has left me with no clue on how to pursue the matter further. I'm utterly lost." I answer.

At last, she loosens up ever so slightly, taking charge of the return journey with a miniscule spring in her step.

"I'm sure Dad will figure something out. I wouldn't lose all hope just yet." She says as we approach the door back into the office.

As inspiring as it is to hear Matra talking in a positive light for once, I eagerly wish she could practice what she preaches.

Chapter 17:
Subterranean Sophistry

Mahro was quite stunned by what I had learned from Pat – he had never investigated my family history all too thoroughly, but agreed that Pat's story lined up with my own. However he too all but threw his arms in the air and couldn't come up with a concrete plan to deal with the more troublesome branches of my family tree, beyond waiting to hear word back from Altair, which itself seemed like only a faint possibility.

Which leads me to where Mahro, Myra and I have ended up the following day: behind the temple standing before the rope bridge, there's an extensive cave running through Mount Melodias, slowly spiralling beneath the earth. The smoothed out walls of the cave's expansive main corridor are tinted with an ephemeral blue light, and there are a scarce few segments of the cave guarded by locked wooden doors, each laden with signs indicating a variety of natural hazards. The path we tread is also free of imperfections, and the radiant sheen of the blue lanterns is prominent most in our path, serving as a handy pathfinder through our environment.

Dias never struck me as a particularly industrious village, especially in comparison to a place like Mot, but Mahro has talked at some length about how instrumental the bountiful minerals within Mount Melodias were in the days when Tenryuu aspired to military conquest, and such success ultimately led to the village's formal foundation and expansion beneath the mountain. Nowadays, as he says, it's aimed far more at cultural output than industrial, but there's a definite air of pride as he elaborates on the distant past of his treasured home. I ought to take offense, given that I hail from one of the nations his own sought to conquer, but even if he weren't the man I look up to most in this world, such events are so distant to me that they feel more like a fantastical work of fiction the older men in my life enjoy roleplaying to the tune of than recent history.

Myra has clung to my arm for the entirety of our visit – it's not all too dark inside here, thanks to the aforementioned blue lights, but there's still the odd unilluminated corner here and there that could justifiably cause her concern. As for myself, I welcome the change in scenery; the air is still cold and bitter, perhaps moreso than the outside world, but seeing the world in a colour other than cloudy white for the first time since my arrival has been a welcome change. It's been hard to take my mind off of yesterday's events, but this goes some way to providing sorely needed relief. And of course, Myra's body pushing against me has done more than enough to keep me warm and pacified – though I suspect I would feel the same regardless of our environment.

But after several minutes of nothing out of the ordinary, my eyes are drawn by a curious sight – within an open room still illuminated in blue but noticeably darker, I see a familiar figure resting on her knees: Matra. She seems to be staring into the ground for no apparent reason, and the sparsely populated but thick pile of texts at her side is not currently in use. Out of sheer confusion, I'm almost sidetracked from our actual purpose and set forward to talk to her, up until Myra's hand presses her hand against my chest.

"Don't interrupt her." she softly whispers, "It's hard to do *anything* that doesn't upset her, but this is a line we're better off not crossing."

I'm confused, but I'm really not in the mood for another shouting match; Matra's given me nothing but ugly looks ever since the incident at Loren's. Little time passes before considerable distance is put between us.

"What *is* she doing, anyway?" I ask, "I thought she was out doing work for the Chief…"

Before she begins, Myra breathes out as though she had been holding it in for a week.

"If she's not with Chief Loren or locked away in her bedroom, this is where you'll find her, inert as a statue, maybe mumbling to herself that she is failing to gain from the thing she has repeatedly attempted and failed to gain from…"

"You're beginning to sound like her now." I say with a tone bordering on callousness.

Mahro's head turns with a raised eyebrow and Myra looks ready to protest, but she eventually drops her hand.

"You're right. My apologies if you're uncomfortable around me…"

"I'm anything but, believe me! Your presence brings me great comfort, and I wish for it to stay that way. I just wish… ah, nevermind, what were you about to say?"

"About Matra… did she ever tell you that our mother followed the way of Raisha?" she asks.

I'm left astounded for a moment, racking my brain for where exactly I have heard mention of it before. As I'm looking around, I take notice of an elaborate blacksmithing site to our right – under the watchful eye of an elderly gentleman, its hearth roars with a radiant green and the tools surrounding it look a thousand times as polished and functional as the barely held together deathtraps littering Lyndra's lot. I would love to see the look on her face, but I doubt the old girl would even want to set foot outside of Ford for any reason.

Myra begins to detail the everlasting standoff between the Eisha and Raisha, assuming my memories to be absent of the relevant information, but once I look away from the blacksmith, the information suddenly clicks.

"Ah, that's it! Your sister mentioned it back at my home, and went over the gist of the two sides and their quarrels. Something about aspiring to improve the self, correct?"

My knowledge impresses my would-be teacher, and she nods in approval – her smile warms my heart in a way that only Tsubasa's can match.

"Looks like you've retained that fairly well!" she says.

"*Hmph!* Kyrie always told me I was a quick learner…"

"Back on topic, I never took much notice of what teachings Mom actually followed, beyond the daily lessons about discipline and always aspiring for better – I found them horribly annoying as a little girl, and I've never felt right for only seeing the wisdom in her words after her passing. But one thing I did take note of was her belief in an afterlife, and humans' ability to interface with it; she very strongly believed that through enough meditation and honing of the mind, we can interact in some way with the deceased under the right conditions. I'm unsure about talking or communicating directly to them, but she claimed more than once to have felt the spirits of our grandparents throughout the last few years."

...suddenly, it makes sense. I don't even need to ask, and yet my ever so intrusive curiosity demands I verify it.

"So Matra's trying to... reach out to your mother?"

"More or less." Myra glumly answers, "I think it's a hopeless endeavour myself, and it's only causing us greater pain. But what do I know? I'm just a 'proprietor of party tricks', whatever it is she called me..."

"I for one appreciate your tricks; last thing I want right now is a party." I say without thinking – now she's blushing as she looks up to me.

"You two done waffling about the one who isn't here to defend herself?" Mahro asks – he's clearly joking, but in retrospect it does feel a bit disrespectful to his eldest child, as well as a woman I still consider a friend, despite our mounting grievances.

But that doesn't particularly matter now, for my mentor now stands before a thick wooden door at the bottom of the spiralling subterranean network, with a cloud of steam seeping through its perimeter. As Myra and I approach the door, the heat coming from behind it feels egregious, certainly in contrast to the cold we've spent the better part of half an hour wading through. I can already feel the sweat tumbling down my forehead as we at last catch up.

"What the- what in the world is behind this door? Are you dipping your toes into cannibalism, old man?" I ask, much to Mahro's amusement.

"What, don't they have underground hot springs concealed beneath mountains in little old Morosus?"

"Underground what now?"

"You've spent the better part of an entire month either inert or working your body to death, with harrowingly little inbetween.

298

You need to refresh yourself, and I'm not just saying this because you reek."

Annoyed by the accusation, I take a brief sniff in the direction of my armpit and... oh dear, he has a point.

"Great idea, instead of being eaten by flies I can burn to death well beneath the surface of the world."

While I feign indignance at the idea, I do little to stifle my grin.

"That's the spirit! Onwards, my miasmic compatriot!"

The matter settled, Mahro at last opens the door, encouraging Myra and I to follow in his stead.

Behind the door is an avalanche of steam, obscuring all but a few metres in front of me. A rotund receptionist wearing a white headband immediately to my right insists that I take off my shoes and leave them next to the entrance alongside no less than five strangers' own, and the moment I comply my feet are taken aback by the rough, heated wood. The sloshing of water beneath suggests that the only barrier between me and a boiling cauldron is this very floor. The receptionist speaks no further, returning his nose to a book I cannot discern the contents of, much like the box labelled 'Lost and Found' in bold black, and we pass by four thin wooden doors as we walk past, all but one of which proclaim themselves to be occupied according to a thin stone slab embedded in the door.

Sure enough, Mahro locks the door behind us, uniting our room with its neighbours in its occupancy. I can't hear a thing from said neighbouring rooms; either they're awfully quiet, or these walls carved from stone are doing a perfect job at suppressing their sound. The steam is still thick and obfuscating, but the room we find ourselves in is small enough for me to make out the majority of it; it looks largely the same as the main corridor, but there are four small cubicles each obscured by a red curtain, two to our left and two to our right.

"We'll take these two, you hop in whatever identical red curtain tickles your fancy. Just head in when you're ready, don't concern yourself with waiting for us." Mahro says before he disappears behind a red veil, soon imitated by Myra.

Taking the cubicle closest to me, I take a deep breath before I remove the shirt lent to me; sure enough, I can barely even take it off before a cold shiver races along my spine, even as I'm immersed within sweltering geothermal heat. It recurs with faltering intensity as I take to removing the clothes at my lower half.

Now that I put some real thought into it, this is far from the first time I've trekked beneath the earth; the Basin was no doubt extensive, though now that I've witnessed what Tenryuu's subsurface has to offer, I somewhat wish it weren't so dilapidated and hollow. Would it have altered my fate at the hands of Eden? Could she ever sustain herself and her delusional aspirations of conquest in a place such as this?

If anything, I think the Basin's desolation was what made it a prime target for Eden to settle down there. Were she to make anywhere else her territory, it's improbable Mahro could have ever come to my aid. Maybe some things are better off left broken?

...or maybe Mahro is onto something by bringing me here; I need to take my mind off of these kinds of things. Worrying myself to death over long-resolved events and even the present won't do anybody any good, least of all me. As the cold shivering at last dies down, I place the clothes against a pair of hangers inside the cubicle and take a white towel from the opposite wall, using it to obscure my nether region as I step out. It's thankfully empty, since Mahro and Myra are still inside their cubicles. Heeding his advice, I step into the spring itself to be met with a breathtaking sight.

For what is ostensibly just a big bath, there's an undeniable beauty to it. From every inch, transient steam rises in perpetuity as the water bubbles and bursts with a satisfying pop, replenishing its own supply as quickly as it fades into nothingness. There is a ring of earthen black stone surrounding the pool of water, with its only release coming from a closed filter integrated into the wooden platform I find myself stood atop. On the wall surrounding the entrance are two Tenkite lanterns, one on each side, and they tint the sea of steam with a comforting blue warmth.

After soaking in the sights and neatly placing the towel against the floor, I at last descend down the steps, apprehensively dipping my toes into the water as I brace myself for some burns.

Surprisingly, the water is not nearly as hot as it looks, and the rest of my legs soon find themselves submerged, followed by everything else beneath my chest level. The further I submerge, the more I am treated to a pleasant sound of heat racing to burn away the dreadful cold embedded in my skin. Feeling mentally content for the first time since I was dragged out of Ford, I set my head against the edge of the spring, closing my eyes as I immerse myself within the warmth of this chamber...

"*Whooooooooooooo!*"

A high pitched yell shatters the pleasant silence, and I look up to find Myra *leaping off of the platform*; she too is stark naked - her body concealed only by the thick steam and not through any effort of her own - and she lands in the centre of the spring with a thunderous splash that sends water flying into my face, though I thankfully cover my eyes before they end up scalded.

But more importantly... *what is she doing here?!* Before I can stammer out a question regarding why I am sharing a bath with a woman, and the daughter of my mentor no less, said mentor pipes up with a hearty laugh.

"*Hah*, Julius had that same look of awe on his face when we first dragged him here! You're more like him than you are cognizant of!"

Mahro stands atop the platform yet; he's *thankfully* far more enshrouded than either Myra or I at this moment, and he calmly descends into the body of water before I can be embedded with a sight that would haunt my every sleeping moment.

"I... I still can't quite get over the concept of communal bathing... especially alongside the fairer sex."

Then again, I find the concept strange even among those of the same sex.

"Imagine how *I* felt when I first visited Ringo's home! *Baths for one?! What absurdity has befallen my eyes?!*" Mahro says with a nostalgic grin.

"I couldn't believe it when Dad told me! Apparently your custom goes so far as to lock the rest of the world out? Taking that whole room up for yourself... how greedy!"

Her own piece said, Myra sinks low enough into the water to conceal most of her neck. At the risk of sounding lascivious, I can't make out her feminine figure beneath the water, so I suppose I can rest easier knowing my own body will enjoy the same concealment.

"Hmm... when *did* you first visit Morosus, Master King Rag?" I ask, having at last settled down.

"I was there for business once or twice before, but my first time actually staying round the old guy's lodgings was... the year before Matra was born, I think? Would've been 25 or 26, I believe."

"I see... what was Kyrie like at the time?"

"I'm not the best judge of that; I wasn't awfully kind to her when we first met, and I may or may not have put a damper on her twelfth birthday. I have no doubt my own behaviour tainted my memories of those times. I'm sure she was more well-behaved than I gave her credit for. One thing I can tell you hasn't changed is her verbosity! *Hah*, I didn't even know what an 'esotericist' was until the pint-sized dictionary told me in blistering detail, offended that I shared not her lexicon!"

How old *was* Kyrie when we first met? She would have probably been around Myra's age if I recall correctly. Considering how little she herself has truly changed in the lifetime I've spent alongside her, I can't help but laugh at the mental image of a younger-looking Kyrie running around, spouting the same bewildering nomenclature found exclusively in the stygian depths of a thesaurus.

"Maybe some things are better off static after all." I answer, smiling at my mental image.

"That's the spirit, my friend. There's a silver lining to everything short of the end of the world itself." says Mahro.

"And I'm sure many would contest even *that*." Myra adds.

The room returns to silence for the time being, and I gradually feel my body welcoming the warmth further yet – before long, I begin to dread having to emerge into the biting cold once more, but it's not worth tainting the moment thinking of what's yet to come. Even my dented, battered metal fingers are free of the bitter tinge of steel that ordinarily taints the touch of water.

Mahro is first to break the silence at long last.

"So, my friend, how did the job with that old lady work out?"

"She would have you know she's a spritely 51... but either way, it worked out rather well if I say so myself. Altair's worked his way up the chain of command somewhat, so he got us a contract or two to make their weapons and a few other miscellanea." I answer.

Mahro looks slightly disappointed that I got roped into indirectly helping the military regardless, but he shrugs the sour expression off.

"Work's work, my friend. You're in a much better place than I was at your age, as a matter of fact. Or... *were* in a much better place, at least."

"Now that Lyndra's on my mind, maybe I *am* better off hiding here forever – whether I was kidnapped or frolicked off of my own free will, she's going to wail me into next week for disappearing like that." I say, provoking some subdued laughs from the three of us.

"Whatever happens, please don't worry that you're putting a burden on us. She may not show it, but my eldest is glad to see you alive and... I'm not sure about 'well', but... let's stick with 'functional'. And it looks like Myra here's taken a liking to you, so all's well, eh?"

Mahro's reassurance is followed up on by Myra nodding profusely – I dread to ever let my mentor learn so, but I've taken a liking to her myself; to see it reciprocated warms my heart.

"...thank you. If the gods demand I be torn from my family, then I couldn't have been delivered to a better doorstep."

As I deliver my most sincere thanks, I feel strangely happy – I would of course prefer not to be torn away from my family, especially a Tsubasa still in her youth, but every word I just espoused was entirely genuine. Were I able to shift the world to my whims, I would no doubt manufacture conditions under which we could all co-exist within the same sphere, but life simply doesn't work out with such convenience.

Once our stay comes to an end, Myra and Mahro are first to depart from the spring. I follow about half a minute after, closing the door as a loud draining sound begins to swell. The clothes lent to me by Mahro are hung up on a drying line within the room, and the otherworldly steam has done a good job releasing whatever foul body odours previously crept within them. We leave our used towels in a basket next to the stoic receptionist and the moment the entrance flies open, the cold strikes back with aggressive, unrelenting force. I can barely even withstand the contrast, but a strong pull on my arm from the entirely unaffected Myra allows me to confront nature's violence.

A few minutes into our return journey, we come across the blacksmithing site once more; it's now unoccupied and securely locked up, and the emerald fire within has died down, but I'm still impressed by the prowess of such tools. I'd love to see what comes out of such handiwork...

"Ah, right, you'll need some kind of armament on you just in case someone tries to carry you off into the night again, won't you?" Mahro says.

As much as I would like to take up his offer, the weapons on display are not at all cheap: a standard sword costs upwards of 80 Sera, a far cry from the 50 or so that Lyndra would charge for such an item. A staff ranges from lows of 60 to outrageous highs of 500 for the more extravagant pieces, albeit ones looking more fitting on a wall than in one's hands. Grateful but not wanting to burden him any further, I begin to reject the offer.

"I still have the knife in my cloak, that should suffice-"

"It already failed you once, didn't it? Not even the two of them could save you at the time, am I correct?"

Ugh... he's *too* sharp. I can't help but faintly nod, resigning myself to whatever plan he offers.

"I already told you, don't be afraid that you're putting a burden on the lot of us. I'm happy to cover for you anything south of 300 Sera, so don't get your undergarments twisted by varmints."

I finally acquiesce with a reluctant sigh, and Mahro chuckles in victory.

"And if you really feel the need to repay me for it, then there *is* something Loren and I could use some help with; at the end of the path coiling around our jolly old mountain's central peak, there's a run down building where we used to keep Cladio before we made the... *unfortunate* discovery that their shaggy little coats don't protect them from the cold all too well. We're thinking we could renovate it into something useful, but don't have much of a clue what to do with it. Could you take Myra up after her show wraps up one of these days and sort the place out a little? Just a little cleaning up and reporting on how the place is holding up should do it. Loren can provide more of the specifics."

Myra's eyes light up at the idea, and even if I weren't being subtly pushed into it, I would jubilantly agree nonetheless – after so many years of Mahro pulling me away from death's door, any minute chance to scratch his back is one I'll take without hesitation.

It's been a little over a week since I agreed to traverse the mountain path, but despite his prior promise of expanding on his past exploits, such an opportunity has yet to arise. The man himself isn't often given to alcoholic beverages; Myra and I have shared a couple drinks as the sky tinted with red, while he's mostly been content to watch from the other side of the room or gaze into the stars outside his window.

However, this morning I've found myself in a peculiar location: a small, sparsely populated theatre not far from the centre of Dias – I can still see the glistening fountain at its heart with crystal clarity through the thick alleyway to my right. There must be fifteen others present at most, the majority of them both female and around Myra's age. Her recently re-applied makeup has done a fantastic job at warding off unwanted attention, though it begs the question of how long we're going to keep this act up.

As the muttering continues, I'm shook out of my skin by a tap on my shoulder, and the hairs on my neck bristle as a soft but uncomfortably close voice enters my ear.

"You a friend of the redheads? You ain't a familiar face here, I know that for sure."

Her dialect seems ever so slightly unusual, and I turn around to discover a young lady with boyish brunette hair, settling her feet against the seat to my left and leaning back without a care in the world. Her clothes look remarkably similar to Matra's own;

the only noteworthy differences are that her shirt is short-sleeved and white, and its neck hole reaches further down her upper torso, whilst her feet are covered not in black boots, but red trainers akin to what young boys would wear for running around in a muddy field – they hardly signal professionalism, but they're not unpleasant in their own right. On the seat next to her is a short-barreled breech-loading rifle, though its sling is still kept firmly around her arm.

"My being here is a long, dreadful story, but yes, I class them as friends. I take it you're more familiar with them than with I?" I ask as I turn around in my seat to face her.

There's no point trying to be shady about my outsider status, and she doesn't sound antagonistic, at least for now.

"Yup, up until a year ago it was just me and Milkbag under Loren's wing. Made it real fun for me when she ran off to Daddy in a huff; I'd never worked so hard in my life!" she says boastfully.

"*Milkbag?*"

Where in the world did Matra earn a moniker like that? Was it just given out of spite by the burdened co-worker to my rear? I dread to think what names I'll end up ascribing to h-

"Why is it only the girls that get it?" she says, interrupting my train of thought, "Where do you think milk comes from, exactly?"

She looks at me like I'm completely retarded as she... cups her breasts and begins flailing them around with as much reckless abandon as her overalls will allow – I can't help but burst out laughing at the ridiculous sight and its apparent defiance of all established physics, and she quickly drops the act as eyes start to turn.

"Little uncouth for a title, isn't it? She isn't a walking chest with a pair of pretty eyes, after all." I say, trying to sound virtuous but struggling to hide my amusement.

"You're right; she's just a walking chest." She says with a devilish snicker, "She used to call me a 'raging lesbian' but ever since her... *reinvention*, it's back to just calling me Yuna. That's my name, by the way. Don't forget me!"

"Well, Yuna, you don't seem like a 'raging lesbian' whatsoever. You look like a very *calm* lesbian." I answer with a smirk.

It isn't long before the sole of her foot crashes into my own – I'm quick to retaliate, and the two of us jolt to our feet, ready to take this encounter to its greatest extreme.

"You're a fast one, stranger!" she says, dancing betwixt the chairs – I'm quick to mimic her rhythmic movements.

"Thank you. You're not the first lady to tell me that!"

...she is, but I'm not about to let her know that.

"Will I get to be the first lady to kick your ass?!"

"Not in a million years!"

As if on the cue of a pin drop, we rush towards each other, raring to stomp on the other's foot. A discordant cacophony of tapping and stomping fills the air as we draw a dismal but bemused crowd. With each swift attack and miss, Yuna just as quickly retracts her foot as I try to make a counterattack. She's insanely fast, surpassing Matra and possibly even Mahro, and the sheer amount of pressure she's placing on me in the most ridiculous scrap I've ever taken on in my life... it's *unreal*.

"Wow! I do anything like this with Milkbag and she folds in seconds! Honour me with your name, pretty boy!" she says during a brief respite.

"Vega Pyre, missy!" I answer with a cocky grin, "and I would prefer you call me anything other than pret-!"

I can't even finish my sentence before she leaps at me like a rabid dog, shooting her leg through the air and landing on the spot where my foot used to be with such force as to crack the stone beneath it. As our wild dance of destruction lingers on, the crowd slowly begins to cheer and yell, commentating on the clash and reacting in waves to every near miss. It's by no means a real fight, but demonstrating my aptitude before an audience... there's a strange sense of pride I gain from it. For her part, Yuna looks like she's never had this much fun in her entire life. Never let it be said that I can't please a lady.

As the intensity of the cheering reaches its climax, I decide on the kill shot – her left foot lands first whenever she jolts backwards, and I make it my mission to catch it with my right as she recovers from leaping backwards. I dial up my aggression, taking us across the rows of chairs that ought not to be stood on, until my opportunity presents itself.

As she jumps back down to my level, I rush forward, ready to clamp down on her foot.

She's taken aback by my rush.

She stands there.

Firm.

This is it!

STOMP!

...

...

My right foot indeed clamps down on her own, but there's one small problem.

Her right foot too is clamping down on my left.

The duel is a draw.

The reaction of the crowd is mixed, some expressing relief, others a middling disappointment, but one stands out above it all.

"Fine footwork, young master Pyre."

The appraisal comes from a short, stubby old man standing atop the stage – there are maybe three hairs left on his head, the walking stick in his hands looks almost as old as *he* is, and the black suit he stands before us in looks better fitting for a funeral than for such a presentation.

"Thank you, sir. I was trained by the best."

"*Hmph!* Come on Entari, you know my old man coulda whooped that crusty old Katsuragi any day!" Yuna says with a dramatic huff.

Entari... Mr. Entari? Ah, so this is Myra's boss...

"I can tell you've some experience to back up that talent. How's about an interview?" Mr. Entari asks of me.

I can't help but laugh – I'm finally getting a workout, after sifting through hell and with no small amount of blood on my hands, and now this harmless old guy offers me a job doing party tricks.

"I appreciate the offer, but I'll pass. I'm just passing by." I answer, trying to let him down easy.

"As we all are, I suppose. You should at least take pleasure in the fleeting, for man oft only unveils its significance well after he needed it. If you cannot stay long, then I hope you enjoy this transient tale of ours."

Long after Yuna and I return to our seats, the entire audience is abuzz with discussions pertaining to the pandemonium we just incited, but the two of us are much too exerted to speak with substance. Right as it threatens to become overbearing or irritating, the sound of a deep horn pervades our eardrums, signalling the show's beginning.

The black curtains in front of us swiftly open, and the crowd falls dead silent. Drums rapidly beat as the stage is shrouded in darkness, and they die down right as the background lights up in radiant blue to reveal Mr. Entari dressed in a colossal suit resembling an extremely fat but regal man, gorging himself on a variety of unsavoury and unhealthy foods held in his hands as he sits atop a throne. After his hands are emptied, he bellows and wails as his stubby arms fail to reach even his own knees. The sound of incessantly beating drums arises.

"My foooooood! Where is my fooooooood?!"

His cries trigger the arrival of Myra from stage right and a similarly dressed woman with long black hair from stage left, both bearing a tray full of what he enjoyed most.

"Emperor Quazimyres, I offer the kingdom's finest! I humbly ask that you accept this offering!"

Myra is first to speak among the two, though her gentleness is met only with fervent snatching and gluttony, not a word of thanks having transpired.

"This is not up to snuff! Begone, tramp!"

Emperor Quazimyres drops the now emptied tray on Myra's head, who comically collapses after a delay of stone stillness.

Her companion is next to receive judgement, and the great Emperor initially seems content – until the trumpets dramatically swell and he coughs and wheezes for several moments, producing from his mouth a thin black hair. The disgust scrawled across his face is palpable.

"What is *this* I see?!" he bellows with such tempestuous force that the woman before him can barely stand, "Callous whores and putrid bores, the lot of ye! Replace this sack of filth with a lass who can do her job!"

With this, Emperor Quazimyres dramatically raises the tray as high as his stubby arms can reach before throwing it down onto the second attendant's head, who drops "dead" to the ground as the drums mount in intensity. Myra feigns a look of utter horror before being escorted to the right exit of the stage by the Emperor's guards, alongside her compatriot's cadaver. The stage dies down for a moment, and the crowd mutters amongst itself, bewildered by this shocking turn of events and wondering if the real Emperor is as despicable in the flesh as he is in fiction. I'm not entirely sure what to make of it myself, but if any of what I heard back home was even remotely approaching the truth, then I ought to share in their disgust.

"Woah... it looks so real!" Yuna says from behind.

"I take it you've never seen someone perish before your eyes, despite your profession? To me it looks about as real as one of those comics my mother reads, about space witches or... what have you."

"Woah, sorry 'bout that, tough guy." Yuna says, feigning intimidation as she raises her hands.

After some shuffling around within the now darkened space, the back of the stage gradually lights up with the blue of the night sky, soon followed by a despairing Myra. She weakly stumbles forward, her hands clasped together at her heaving chest, before falling to her knees at the foot of a fake tree that reaches thrice as tall as Mahro himself.

"O, despaired am I! The Emperor and his boundless, unremittent gluttony has left me in despair! He has taken the soul of our people, the pride of our once great colony of Numena, and now he has taken my sister! How much more must I endure before I can be afforded the same swift end?"

Myra wails incessantly as she throws around all sorts of dramatic gestures – she's really putting her heart and soul into it, however farcical the whole production may come off as at times.

It's at this point that a silver-enveloped knight, riding a mighty, gold-plated... *steed* (an obvious contraption on wheels covered by a flimsy sheet, with a rather dopey-looking horse painted on its side) enters the scene. After much extravagant looking around and posturing, he at last dismounts the fantastic beast and kneels before Myra.

"Fine lady!" the high-pitched man shouts, much to the disdain of my ears, "What is thy quarrel with thy wonderful world? In every shadow, there lies a spark of hope, a glimmer of light! Within us all lies the power to harness this light, and forge a better path for the good of the world! Willst thou join me and my esteemed army in defeating thy piggish monarch?"

As if struck by personality-altering lightning, Myra hops to her feet triumphantly, striking a heroic pose as she nods furiously.

"In the name of my sister, I shall bring a swift end to his cruelty! No more shall I slumber in shadow; only with courage and bravery can I bring an end to the foul demon!"

Ordinarily I would be mumbling about how such a character shift makes no sense, but mentioning her sister like that... I can't help but think about Tsubasa again.

I'm obviously not dead, but it's impossible to ignore the parallels between the fiction before me and the shoes she must undoubtedly find herself in. Assuming my family yet lives, how *has* Tsubasa taken my disappearance? I certainly hope she hasn't taken her frustration out on our parents, but at 10 years old, how else could she really harness such anger? Journey across the world to find me with nary hide nor hair to uncover my location? Even if she were twice that age, Kyrie and Julius would never allow it; two of their children have abruptly left their lives, so to allow their third to slip between their fingers would be unthinkable.

Looking at Myra, as she scurries around preparing for the next scene, I'm feeling a strange sensation. I would hesitate to call it jealousy, but... what else could it really be? We've both been cruelly robbed of our mothers far too early in our lives, but at least she can be surrounded by the rest of her family as they grieve and move forward, whereas at the height of my contentment, and after thinking the worst was behind me, I'm thrust into the middle of nowhere, and even the man I admire most can only provide aid in extremely limited capacity.

The thought that I might miss many of my sister's greatest achievements, her birthdays, the opportunity to watch her grow into a stunning young woman... it pains me. It pains me far more than any sword, than any spear, than any words. Envying the daughter of my strongest, most fortuitous guardian in such a pitiful way just disgusts me further yet. If he were to know of it, no look of scorn from beneath his furrowed brow would be able to do it justice, no matter how intense.

"Chin up, dopey! The grand finale's here!" Yuna says as her hand slams into my shoulder, forcing me back into reality.

Apparently a grand battle ensued as my all too existential thinking clouded my eyes; the stage is caked with those feigning death and an army's worth of fake armaments littering their "corpses". Myra stands before Emperor Quazimyres, with a giant hammer as tall as she herself grasped in her hands and a burning look of determination in her eye.

"You little wretch! I saved you from poverty and destitution, and this is how you repay me!"

The rotund royal can only screech and wriggle his head around in a fury as an inevitable death approaches.

"*Saved* us? You took away our freedoms, our futures, and you declare yourself a saviour?!" Myra says as she readies the hammer – in motion, it's obvious it's not genuine, instead forming its head out of some soft material, "We are all the masters of our own destinies! Let this one death curb millions more!"

And with her final declaration, Myra brings the hammer forth in a violent downward motion, leaping into the air as its head crashes into the Emperor's own. As she releases her grip and the hammer falls, his head is replaced by an exaggerated fountain of red pouring from his 'neck'. Taking care not to become showered in the fake blood, Myra joins her fellow actors in celebration of this great deed. The high-pitched knight takes it upon himself to see us off as all actors present line up and face the audience.

"The great land of Numena, as well as all those swallowed under Ennui's stygian veil, can be reinstated once more! Let her people know freedom once more, and let the sun rise with the gleam it has ill displayed in the many years under this tyrant's reign! And thus, our tale comes to an end, but that of our brave heroes fighting the menace of Ennui does not! Farewell!"

A few claps emerge from the audience, most vociferous among them being from Yuna. As she jeers and cheers in delight, I can't help but smile as my eyes meet Myra's – you certainly don't see anything like this in Ford.

Chapter 18:
A Shadow in the Blue Sky

"What did you think, eh?!" Myra excitedly asks as she approaches Yuna and I.

The warmth of the blacksmith's hearth has been much-welcomed at this time of year, and so we've stood by and made small talk behind its walls as we waited for her to wrap the production up.

"I've never seen a military recruitment drive so... exciting. Bit on the nose though." I answer with a grin.

"Try saying something that *ain't* backhanded, genius!" Yuna says as she sticks her tongue out at me.

With a heavy sigh, I acquiesce.

"Myra... your acting is genuinely something amazing. I really, really believed that you were trapped in the most desperate of situations, doing whatever you needed to claw your way out of it, and I was pleased to see a happy ending waiting for you."

While somewhat exaggerated, the praise is genuine, and Myra looks very pleased by my appraisal.

"Next month we're changing up the show again. I can't give away any production secrets, but can I assume you'll be first in that line?" she asks me with an adorable shyness.

"He'll be second in line, as a matter of fact; if only one could enter, I would fight tooth and claw to be in that seat!" Yuna answers in my place.

"And here I thought *I* was her biggest fan..." I say mockingly, to which Yuna sneers.

"Guess it's time I left the two of you to your own devices; I've gotta look after Mom, and you've gotta... I dunno, snog in the corner somewhere. See ya!"

Yuna races off before I can protest her erotic assumption – Myra seems more amused by it if her stifled giggling is any indication.

The two of us at last enter the blacksmithing shop – if it has a name, it certainly wasn't anywhere to be found outside. There's very little to describe about it; opposite the aforementioned workstation is a wall of armaments, with their prices crudely scrawled onto small scraps of paper beneath them. The only other things of note are a door on the opposite end – presumably leading to a bedroom – and a picture of an elderly lady on the wall, to the left of the workstation. Myra's clearly not used to the stuffiness of the smoke, but I certainly had it far worse under Lyndra's domain – on the whole, the shop seems like a very admirable place to perform one's craft in. After looking over only a few of the wares on offer, a voice stewing in gruffness and sounding in desperate need of a cleared throat rings out.

"I don't know who you are, or what you're doing here, but you got the look of a fellow craftsman in you. Would you be happy to give this old man a name to work with?"

I look to my right to discover an elderly man sitting in front of the blazing emerald fires, facing me as he removes his headband and throws it to a table at his side, allowing his mass of grey locks to envelop much of his hardened face. Beneath the sullen and droopy expression, I can tell he looks at least a little excited to see someone enter his lonely abode.

"Vega Pyre, sir, and your assessment is certainly astute; as a matter of fact, I do practice smithing as a trade, though I'm still more or less a student of the art."

The old man grunts with pride.

"I told you, never doubt me eyes, Yuria." The elderly blacksmith says as he glances at the photo upon the wall, "But, young man, 'sir' never fit me; it makes me feel old, *eheheh!* It'd do my weary heart good to be called Helbez once more. Don't hesitate to get a feel of my work, young man. I hope it lives up to your expectations."

He swiftly returns to working before the emerald blaze – I can't imagine being so trusting as to turn my back to strangers, but perhaps age makes one a better judge of character? For Helbez's own sake, I desperately hope this is the case. After watching him hum and hammer away for a few moments, reverberating a sturdy clanging throughout the entire room, I at last turn my attention to the wall of weapons as Myra wanders around the shop, taking an interest in one of the few corners of Dias she hasn't yet investigated.

Each column neatly organizes every weapon in horizontal fashion, and from left to right, the general sizes of the weapons go from larger to smaller; spears are located to my left, while daggers and short swords remain distantly to my right. I can say with some confidence there's more weapons here than one would need to arm all of Dias Village.

"Out of curiosity, Mr. Helbez, why are there... so *many* weapons here? My master and I make them more or less to order, but surely there's more here than all of Dias could fill their homes with. Is the cost not incalculable?" I ask.

As if he's heard the question a thousand times before, he chuckles and turns his head towards me, his striking hand unabated.

"Oh, my days of worrying about keeping the lights on are long behind me, mate. Me missus took care of that, rest her gentle heart. I persist for the sake of the craft. Whenever my ticket to the puffy clouds is redeemed, I hope there's a great anvil up there for me to spend all eternity striking at..."

"Come on, you're still vibrant and young! No old man could be *this* productive!" Myra says – how I *wish* some of her enthusiasm could rub off on Matra.

As I take one of the longest spears into my hands, the seemingly egregious pricing is justified to me just from the quality of its hilt – a veritable masterpiece of design, pieced together with the finest wood one could buy and stainless steel rings reinforcing it every foot or so, and yet not at all uncommon amongst all the armaments present. Smooth and seamless, in a jarring contrast to the rough, coarse material Lyndra and I would painstakingly shave down best we could, and yet would maintain imperfections aplenty by their end.

"Myra, would you kindly stand back for a moment?"

She's in a world of her own, gawking at some lengthy axes to my right, though she is quick to snap out of her daze and acquiesce. After a few decent swings, I can confidently declare the weapon feels as good in motion as it does in stasis, though its heavy metal blade is a bit much for my liking.

"Like 'em on the lighter side, ay?" Helbez asks, apparently having been watching my little display.

"I'm not sure I would say 'light', but certainly a grade or two below *this*."

I return the heavy spear to its rightful place, adorned by its price tag of 150 Sera – now I'm beginning to wonder why the price is so *low*.

"Aye, then per'aps we can go for something more… 'you'?" Helbez asks, much to my confusion, as he lifts a stack of metallic molds from beneath a desk and plants them atop it, straining its weary wooden supports.

"Ah, I would rather not impose on whatever you prefer worki-"

"Don't fret, mate. I always believed a warrior should have some hand in bringing his armaments to life."

As Myra and I close in on him, the eyes of the young lady at my side begin glistening at the prospect.

"I'm not exactly a warrior…" I say under my breath as I scratch my head and look to the side.

My brooding is interrupted by the pommel of a sword clonking off of my head and tumbling to the floor.

"Pedantry never got we anywhere, young man. We're all fighting some battle of our own, and battles are fought by warriors."

With Myra watching from the sidelines like a kitten enchanted by a fish that remains ever out of reach, Helbez and I have spent a few hours discussing every facet of my ideal armament. First we settled on using a thick, dark type of wood found exclusively in the thick inner woods at the heart of Tenryuu, from trees the old man claims have absorbed the bodies and souls of those wandering and lost. The concept of hauling a cursed weapon at my side is awe-inspiring but no doubt begging for bad omens; I can only hope I am not in fact going to be taking the spirits of the lost and damned upon my back.

Out of the molds that are present, I decided – after much contemplation and inner turmoil – to select a rather unique head for the nascent armament: its blade bears at its top a supremely flat edge, straight as an arrow and sharp enough to cut one in motion, whilst serving as a clean contrast to what lies underneath, that being a curved edge that drops off like a waterfall before levelling out once more, bringing the blade to its completion with a firm, straight line to its side of origin. Its purpose is to deter more than to draw blood, and I can certainly make an argument for its intimidation factor given that it's awash with sharp edges, and yet I see a peaceful serenity in its form, buried beneath the first impression of bloodlust.

"A glaive it is then. It'll take me 'til the end of the day to get this piece done. I assume you're in no rush, young man?" Helbez asks once our designs are finalized, to which I nod affirmingly.

"I have good reason to believe the two of us will be occupied until the sun is a distant memory." I answer, my affectation for Kyrie's more... creative descriptions bubbling to the surface after having immersed myself in the craft.

"*Hah*, well, even behind closed doors, you're best tempering chaos, lad, 'specially with the fairer sex." says Helbez – it takes me a while to understand where he's coming from, but by the time I see Myra's tumultuous smirk, it kicks in.

"It's nothing so wild as whatever you're thinking, Helbez. More importantly, you'll accept the 250 Sera charge we agreed on once I return to collect it, correct?" I ask as Myra and I approach the door.

"You bet it. Even if you get eaten by some... albino, tree-hoppin' bear up there, you can take the magical carriage to the heavens knowin' I ain't robbed you of the entrance fee, son." Helbez answers with a grim laugh.

"Your kindness warms my heart." I answer.

I'm more or less ready to leave, but as my hand closes around the handle to the outside world, I come to a dead stop. My eyes are struggling to part themselves from the world of wonderful weaponry they've immersed themselves in. What I stand within is a veritable museum to the craft I'm pursuing in the hopes of restoring Ford to greatness once again. To walk away without learning anything from the man behind them would be foolish. But there's a lump in my throat – whilst the old man seems to enjoy the scant company he receives, our conversations scarcely delved into the specifics behind his work. I want to hear him elaborate on how he goes about his business, but I'm not confident I'll get the answer I would like.

...but I have to try.

I've sworn up and down that within my lifetime, Ford will see prosper once again. For as improbable as it seems, to not seek advice from a living legend when I share the same room as him... it would be madness.

"Mr. Helbez..." I say after a heavy breath, "After I collect the final product, could we... sit down and discuss the craft? I'm eager to learn from you."

For the first time since we entered, Helbez's body turns so that he can look me in the eye, a look of bewilderment scrawled across it.

"And what would you need that for?" he asks, "It's not that I wish to impede a promising upstart, but I would... I would prefer my secrets die with me."

Whatever his reasons for secrecy, I'll refrain from prying... but Lyn would never let me hear the end of it if I was deterred from such a wellspring of wisdom by the first rejection.

"I believe it would be an unfortunate waste of talent to bring your skills to the grave with you. But my motives aren't entirely altruistic; I hail from the small village of Ford, and it has seen tragedy after tragedy ill befitting its stature in the world. With each passing day, more of its people depart, never to be seen again. Much of it is abandoned, stripped bare of life altogether. And I... I can't stand the sight of it, knowing what sort of prosperity it once enjoyed. It's a long shot, but if there's any chance my work in the field of blacksmithing could reclaim at least some of its former glory, then I want to learn from the best. I want to return to my home a wiser man than when I was ripped away from it."

A thick silence consumes the entire room. Helbez's stare remains firmly fixed on my face, his eyes not closing even for a second. Certain of yet another flat rejection, my hand begins to reach for the handle once again. Until he at last speaks.

"We can... have a chat or two in the coming days. Don't go expectin' the world, but Yuria wouldn't forgive me for turnin' ya down outright."

So... there's hope. It's murky, but I might be able to learn a thing or two from the finest craftsman living. My nerves are too racked to smile, but I've never been so grateful in all my life.

"Thank you, Helbez." I say as Myra and I depart at last – the old man returns to his tireless craft, the clanging returning as if it had never left.

The harsh clash between the bubbling, brothy depths of Mount Melodias and the frigid surface immediately above the grand underground expanse has done me absolutely no good – despite it being about as cold as this time of year usually gets and wearing the same amount of clothes loaned to me by Mahro as any other day, my fingers have endured such great pain that they feel almost entirely numb now that our ascent is nearing its conclusion. Myra appears nonchalant and utterly unperturbed despite enduring the same contrast, having added only a thin leather coat - also an old item of Mahro's – to her person. I sincerely have to wonder how her toes have never required amputation if *this* is how she always reacts to such conditions. But after getting anything at all out of Helbez... my soul feels refreshed with an endless, excited warmth. Something so measly as the weather can't snuff that out.

Myra comes to an abrupt stop against the edge of the mountain path, and gestures for me to join her in a spot of sightseeing. We stand hundreds of metres above Dias Village; it's a breathtaking sight, and not just because of the intense cold. I can only faintly recall a fleeting feeling of freedom such as this at one other time in my life: the Skyspur. Except there are no longer any colossal tree branches in my way – what I see before me is miles upon miles of Tenryuu's vast lands, obstructed only by the veil of thick, blindingly white snow that dominates as far as the eye can see. The sun at our heads distinguishes distant natural monuments, and I can even make out a vast desert and multiple human settlements from a distance barely comprehensible. The people of Dias are barely measurable from such a vantage point, and those of its neighbors are utterly indistinguishable from the blanket of angelic white that clouds their homes.

"Your home is beautiful." I say to Myra, "Indeed, this is the kind of beauty I wish I could find more of in my own home country."

"What can I say? Beautiful homes create beautiful people!" Myra says with a gleeful grin.

"I can't agree more."

A devilish smirk forms as my eyes lock on to her mostly barren legs – once she finally realises what I'm up to, her subsequent pout of disapproval incites a chuckle from yours truly.

"I don't just mean looks, you know!"

"Yeah, yeah, princess. Let's go wrap this mess up already. I hate the cold."

Brushing aside the matter of my crumbling moral compass, I continue along the predestined path. Myra stammers in an attempt to argue with me, but ultimately rushes back to my side without having formulated a coherent word.

The site at the top of the mountain path is a travesty. Even as the barren husk once filled with Cladio lies buried beneath a mass of snow, I can tell just from a glance that its state of disrepair is so advanced, even Kyrie could never attribute a word of strong enough severity to describe it. Not a single plank of rotting wood or misshapen stone that composes what would once have been called a building is free of defect, and most of it is entirely unsalvageable. As I precariously tread closer, I can without a doubt identify what was formerly a wasp nest lying in a desolate corner of the room, though it's no doubt fallen victim to the passage of time as it too is barely distinguishable from the husk we now find ourselves inspecting the interior of. A counter where greetings once took place, bent and misshapen large metal cages that housed our flying comrades, a metal safe in the wall that has rusted completely shut... I'm standing in the epicentre of a dead, barren relic of the past.

"Wow! Never seen something like... this!" Myra says.

"You seem awfully happy."

"But isn't it romantic? A place once taken by us humans, for our own ends, and now reclaimed by the nature it once arrogantly trampled atop. It's an awe-inspiring sight!"

As I pick up a plank that hasn't felt human contact in a number of years somewhere in the double digits, and it snaps in two mere seconds after I raise it from the snow-coated ground, my answer comes sharply.

"I'm truly in awe."

"This building may be rotten but so is your heart..." Myra says under her breath.

My stern glare lets her know that yes, I *did* hear that. She fumbles around with her hands as she tries to correct our course.

"Anyway, let's get to it! The day is still young!"

Surprisingly, the day is indeed still young; given the position of the cloud-cloaked sun, I can reasonably guess it to be around midday. I thought I had spent far longer discussing with Helbez, but apparently it wasn't so time-consuming as I had expected. With a strange contentment, I turn to Myra and answer her excitement with a nod.

"Let's get to it."

The rest of the day progresses blindingly fast. We've little more than the clothes on our back and our bare hands for dealing with this mess, but we've made some remarkable progress; our first order of business was clearing out all of the rubble, debris and material relics of the building's former self. In desperate need of relief from the biting cold, I set alight the small mountain of rotting wood, ancient texts and once-organic matter that had come and gone a few metres from the entrance to the building. It was little relief as we continued to rummage through the abandoned husk, but the occasional break from the toil to warm my hands up was a welcome addition.

At some point, Myra became fascinated by what could possibly be behind this rusted safe in the wall; it appeared barely large enough to contain even my hand, but in her own words, *sometimes the smallest possessions are one's greatest treasures*. If she weren't a performer by trade I would have mistaken her for a philosopher.

Once it refused to budge even after an old key had been located beneath a rickety floorboard and unlocked it, I whipped out my knife and took to the arduous task of prying it open. Around 5 minutes of painstaking effort produced nothing, and I was on the cusp of giving up as I could tell that my only remaining defensive tool was bound to warp and bend at any moment. I ruthlessly tried one last time, expecting nothing to come of it, only for the safe to pop open effortlessly and send me tumbling onto my arse.

Myra rushed past helpless little me to get her hands on its contents, barely avoiding a nasty cut to her leg as my knife-wielding hand lay idle against the ground.

"You're as reckless as your father, you know that?!"

I rose to my feet, but she was already far too entranced by what she had found to care or possibly even hear me.

And so, here we sit now: as darkness slowly encroaches, we've hauled an old but still stable desk to treat as a bench in front of our makeshift bonfire. As the stars begin to emerge in the abyssal black of the sky and lights both blue and red roar to life in the little village of Dias below us, Myra is still consumed by what she found within the safe: a pocket-sized book containing important business notes pertaining to the building's prior operation, as well as a series of faded photographs in its last few pages. A middle-aged, olive-skinned male appears in the vast majority of them, sometimes accompanied by a young girl we can assume to be his daughter, but both Myra and I are unable to discern his identity.

"Maybe Loren is best for questions like these; his watchful eye has kept its gaze on our home since I was a little girl, so I'm sure he'll at least point us in the right direction."

Myra's head tilts as she gazes deeper into the final photograph of the book, containing a forward-facing shot of the former inhabitant.

"Is it of such importance? Whoever was here before us must not have cared enough to take it with him; why would he be pleased to see it turn up now?" I ask, raising my voice to combat the crackling of the flames.

"How do we know it was left here by choice? Maybe he was... chased out by a pack of wolves?!"

"Well, he's had some fifteen years to come and get it again. It's not like the wolves started living here, as far as we can tell." I answer, to which Myra settles down and sets the book aside.

...

...

...

The conversation has come to an uncomfortable halt.

Myra's eyes are fixated on the vibrant flames as the contrast between the blazing monument and the stygian sky becomes ever starker. While the dark obscures much of her face, the light of the flames highlights her bright lips and the hazel tint that often envelops her pupils appear golden and radiant. This really is the least of my concerns given my circumstances, but it bears mentioning: Mahro's daughters are every bit as beautiful as the man himself is incredible. My eyes can't help but be drawn to her lips as she nods and hums to herself. Were I willing to give up my old life altogether and start over in Dias, I may well have leaned over and kissed her on the cheek by now, resigning myself to whatever battering from Mahro would follow... but I can't.

With a heavy sigh, I lean forward to bask my face in the warmth of the flames.

"What's bugging you, Vega?" Myra asks as she shuffles to my side.

"I... hm..."

I can't even begin to articulate my thoughts with any degree of cohesion.

My continued silence incites Myra to shuffle ever closer, and her hand slowly shifts across my leg; I assume she's trying to comfort me, but the sensation against my leg feels alien and intrusive – not that I have the heart to tell such an innocent young lady such a thing.

"Is it your family?"

"That's one part of it. Your dad tells me it's impossible, that it can never happen so long as war continues to rage on the waters, but I still can't accept that." I say, pausing to look at Myra's face before I continue – she appears attentive and sincere in hearing out my problems, which gives me the strength to continue, "I would never expect him to give up his life here for my sake, not at all. But the Mahro I knew, the one I grew up with and looked up to, would never have been so… quick, to cast away all hope. After I've heard whatever Helbez is willing to disclose, I want to return home as soon as the circumstances permit, laws of the land be damned, but you and your family have done so much for me during these times of strife that to take off, it… it would tear my soul in two; you've shown me nothing but kindness and hospitality, and to repay that by bumbling off without a clue, all while people I've never known or met are on my tail for reasons I couldn't hope to discern… it would be an utter waste should I end up writhing in a ditch."

My piece now stated, I lean back and close my eyes, unsure how Myra will react – I've never felt right uttering a word that could in any way be inferred as a degradation of Mahro's character, but to deny that I don't at all see eye to eye with his opinion on the matter of my returning home would be entirely unhelpful in its own way.

"I don't think he would mind."

Myra at last speaks after sitting further back on our makeshift seat and wrapping her arms around her slender legs.

"Even after what happened to Mom, my dad has always held firm in the idea that we decide our own destinies, even if it results in self-destruction. Both of us want to see my sister back to her old self, to look at us like family rather than strangers if only for a moment. But you can see for yourself what all my attempts to sway her have done."

"…destiny, eh?"

The word itself strikes a chord with me; there's clearly some purpose to me ending up here, given Sihan-Perseli's presence and clear involvement in my escape - perhaps even my initial abduction. But I know nothing of the destiny she holds in store for me. Is it one I want any part of? The concept of a distant puppet master manipulating my course is a hard and terrifying one to comprehend, and impossible to treat as an unconditional positive.

"Then again, if this 'destiny' stuff is all predetermined, then why would it bring you all the way here? I would like to think that the gods' machinations have some purpose behind them to justify such a dramatic change to your life, but... what could it be?" Myra asks.

It's a question with no clear answer; there are far too many conflicting variables to isolate any one of them as the reason for why I'm in Dias and not Ford. Pat is connected to my past. Mahro is the man I look up to most. Helbez might be the key to Ford's future, should he be willing to part with his knowledge.

But at the end of the day, my goal is to restore my home and its glory; whatever trials and tribulations are thrown at me, no matter how odious, I hope I can walk away from them all and return to my family as a stronger, wiser man. Perhaps the specifics of my situation aren't so important to the whims of fate as is the effect it'll all have on me.

"Either way, my family is all the way on the other side of the world, and our home is decaying even as we sit here. I can't possibly imagine what I've done to *deserve* such hardship, so it must be some sort of trial. If I can return home having overcome such horrible circumstances, perhaps Ford stands a chance after all."

"That's great!" says Myra, "So... are you going to leave, after all?"

There's a glimmer of sadness beneath her question, but she bravely maintains her smile.

"Not immediately. I'll speak with Helbez as much as he'll allow, and see if the groggy bastard cowering in Loren's office will reveal anything more that pertains to my family history. Then once I feel my debt to your father is repaid..."

These last words won't come easily, but it's a promise I have to make – for my family's sake as much as my own.

"...once that's all over with... I'm leaving."

Despite my conviction, I'm expecting some kind of stunned silence from Myra, but she instead reaches for my hands, raising them to roughly the same height as her chest.

"If that's your destiny, then it's your choice to pursue it! But while you're here, if there's anything at all I can do to help, don't hesitate to ask." she says unflinchingly.

"Anything, eh?"

Our eyes meet once again and remain locked. Even as her back faces the raging flames the golden glint in her eyes lingers evermore – if eyes truly are a window to the soul, then Myra's soul must be a treasury to rival the wealthiest capitals of the world. I'm paralyzed, unsure of how to return her gesture. I doubt she would be opposed to a frie-

SCREEEEEEEEEEEEECH!!!

...I've heard that before.

Oh no.

A chill is running laps up and down my spine as I race to recall its origin – it was certainly nothing good. Perhaps it was sometime in Ford, maybe while at Mot? Or...

...

The ship.

I turn around to see the moon – and a *colossal bird-like creature* intermittently blotting out its light with one of its abyssal wings. From here I can't possibly hope to gauge its true size, but considering the volume of its screech, and the fact it can almost entirely obscure the moon with just a wing...

"Myra! Quick!"

In a sheer panic, I take her by the arm and race back inside the abandoned building.

We retreat to beside the entrance door, breathing lightly through our noses as we await any activity. There's nothing for a few moments, but I have no time to dwell on why or how they're here. Myra wriggles in discomfort as she presses against me, but it can't really be helped; that bird can only mean trouble.

The coast seems to be clear; the flapping of wings directly above us is heard in passing, and once its sound becomes a memory at last we take this as our cue to leave the building... until two people land feet-first with a colossal crash in front of our fire and send us fleeing inside once again. Myra seems unusually composed as she presses her back against the wall on the opposing end of the door. The lack of any footsteps indicates they're not actively searching for us, so I take a peek out of the entrance to discover... *bird-faced, black-clad men.*

As the two of them stand in place, apparently mystified by the origin of this flame, I rush out against Myra's quiet protests and send my fist crashing into the birdman to my right as he turns to face me. His body is sent flying into the flaming pile, and while he writhes around in the flames, he utters not a single sound. As this happens, I turn to face the second, and—he's already flying towards me, with a yellow-tipped knife aimed at my stomach! I desperately block its path with my right hand, and the pain is instant and immense. What burrows deeper than the knife is the memory it drags kicking and screaming to the surface; this is the same spot Eden had pierced through when she abducted me ten years ago. My eyes cloud in the same horrifying darkness as that day, my body shivers as my mind registers the freezing, bitter air beneath the Basin. The wound had never perfectly healed, but this...

This really isn't helping!

Before long, the paralysis begins to affect my arm; I can barely even keep it from drooping down to my side. I take a swing at my attacker with my left arm – his beak opens up, and clasps my arm within it, biting down with violent force.

Is... is it really going to end like this? I can already hear the screams coming from Dias, reaching deaf ears in the drab deadness of night...

...did I cause this?

Is the price for my temporary sanctuary inevitably the lives of innocents?

I – I...

"Sorry, Vega!" Myra shouts as she rushes out of the front entrance, a thin plank of stiff wood wielded in her hands like a hammer.

Before I can object or beg her to save her own skin, she sends the makeshift weapon crashing into my attacker's forehead, sending a jolt of pain through my arm as his beak's grip is forcibly removed but also releasing his grip on his knife. Myra doesn't relent; whilst the attacker is stumbling backwards, she jumps towards what was just moments ago out seats and launches herself towards the dazed assailant, coiling her legs around his neck and sending him careening to the floor that she lands on with great elegance.

As she maintains her hold on his throat and he writhes futilely, I sigh in confused relief – she never struck me as one who could hold her own, but it beats having to escort a helpless little girl around. I knew first-hand that Mahro had trained Matra well, so to assume the opposite for Myra was foolish on my part. As my right arm goes slack at my side, unable to move despite my greatest efforts, I reach for the back of the knife embedded within it with my free arm—

"Watch out!" Myra shouts as she points behind me.

Within an instant the knife is out of my palm and based only on the sound of rapid, beating footsteps at my rear, I send it flying towards the head of the infernal birdman desperately stumbling towards me – the force sends him flying back to the ground, dead. The flames that continue to engulf him crackle and twist wildly as the wind accelerates.

"We need to get back down there!" I say to my now standing companion as I point towards her home that lies under siege.

"Not until we deal with *that!*" she answers as she swiftly tears a thin layer of black fabric from her fatally choked target's coat, taking to wrapping it around my bleeding hand with unnerving swiftness.

Each backward and forward jolt of my hand comes with a small pang of pain, but by the time she's done the wound is far better off, if only for the lack of winter's fangs biting down on it.

"Thank you. How foolish of me to think your dad wouldn't teach you a thing or two." I say once Myra has wrapped up – I ought to pay Mahro far more due diligence.

After Myra rips the saber from the still burning birdman's waist, the two of us begin sprinting down the mountain path in unison. Our prior trail through the snow lends us an easy descent, mostly unencumbered by the dense snow that envelops much of the path, though my poorly functioning right arm throws off my sense of balance and I stumble forward more than a few times, barely maintaining my footing for the duration of the run.

"Are these the very same birdmen that dragged you out of your home?" Myra hurriedly asks as we race along the path.

I nod with an unamused grunt.

"I found it suspect they would send so many to capture one man. But considering all of my captors died on that vessel and I remain pursued yet... there's something larger at play. So long as I remain here, you and your family aren't saf-"

"Let's save that for later!"

Myra refuses to so much as entertain the idea of attributing blame to me. I only wish her admiration were deserved.

By the time we reach the bottom of the mountain path, I finally regain most of the function of my right arm, and I'm going to need it; what happened to Ford those ten years ago... it's back with a vengeance – screams come from every direction, with the sounds of glass shattering and doors enduring a battering intermittently joining the chorus of torment. I have no Basin to retreat to, no wing to hide under until the scary monsters are dealt with...

Myra and I have no option but to carve our own path through.

Chapter 19:
Running Fire

One can't take a single step into Dias Village without encountering chaos of some form; the blue lights lining every street and crevice punctuates battle after one-sided battle, as the bird-faced invaders lay siege to what was a sanctuary just ten minutes ago. In an otherwise utterly unremarkable little corner of the world, men who thought they could live the rest of their lives out in peace are wearily taking up arms, pushing back against this monstrous threat until their last breaths. I only need to hear the screams and clashes and blows of combat to know that they greatly outnumber the amount that surrounded me on the ship.

We remain unassailed long enough to run into the centre of Dias Village; the statue standing proudly atop the fountain at the heart of this small park remains cloaked in shadow as the violence rages on and the vivacious azure lights begin to flicker and die out in the distance, one after the other.

"Where should we go?" I ask Myra as we come to a stop in front of the fountain – given that it's *her* home under siege this time, I feel deferring to her guidance is more than warranted.

"I-I don't know! They're after you, aren't they? Why don't you remain hidden while we-"

"I'm not cowering in the corner while you solve my problems for me! I'm asking you, Myra Katsuragi of Dias Village, what is the best course of action we can take to keep your home safe?"

Her idea firmly denied, she falls into silence as she directs her gaze towards the grand mountain we had scaled just hours ago.

"We live close to the caves – Dad and my sister should both be in the area. Whatever happens, we'll be stronger together."

"That's a plan. Let's go."

The strategy meeting comes to an end and the two of us begin racing through the streets, our destination firmly in our minds.

There's a distinctly urgent feeling that runs through the marrow of my bones. I don't have any more second chances. I know that if I hesitate or stall for even a moment, that could bring incalculable cost to either myself or those amongst Dias. Mahro's greatest lesson during the course of my training is proving very appropriate for the time and place: *Indecision is death.* And the time for indecision has long passed.

It only takes a few steps into Dias' market district before our first clash with trouble looms over us – beneath a blue light that hangs from a towering post, a bird-faced man is holding a saber to a kneeling middle-aged man's neck as his partner in crime rustles around inside the man's establishment – a... stall for old and ceremonial weapons? He's taking all of the stall's contents, placing loose items in glass cages found beneath the counter, and throwing them into a large brown bag. I come to a screeching halt, my mind overcome by the sheer absurdity of what I'm witnessing; as far as I'm aware their only real intent is to take me to some unknown place, so why are they taking this detour for some dinky old weapons? Valuable, perhaps, but of no use to a force already this well armed and organised.

Myra too is momentarily stunned, and the two of us can only watch in bewilderment until we're at last noticed.

The hostage taker is quick to throw the stall's owner to the ground and kick him in the stomach before turning his blade on us, and the thief carefully sets the heavy bag to the ground before leaping over the counter. Before I can even register what he's doing, he swipes a small pouch from the counter as he scrambles over and launches it towards Myra with a powerful overarm throw – she gracefully dodges the projectile, and is more than prepared when the hostage taker charges towards her. In what is clearly intended as a decisive, killing blow, he raises his saber to plunge into the frail little lady, only to slowly crumple to the ground once she runs her own across his body, fatally lacerating his stomach.

Of course, this is no time for me to stand idly – as Myra's assault takes place, I begin my own, barrelling towards the thief as I draw my knife. I aim for his head with a sideward slash and the bird-faced bastard grasps its blade with his mouth, as had been done to my arm earlier. Only there's one significant difference: My arm remains entirely free, and I put it to great use by crashing it into the thief's head, sending him into the counter with a spiral and denting the metallic storefront, presumably along with a few of his bones. His neck soon comes to a rest against its edge, and so I introduce the back of my foot to his head, resulting in a gruesome crunch as his head goes entirely limp. A rather callous end by my standards, but I consider it far more callous to lay waste to entire villages in pursuit of one man – a peaceful end is one they don't deserve.

Our first brawl does not go unnoticed – yet more of them emerge from nearby stalls, no less than four this time. Three of them are rushing towards us unarmed as a larger, more imposing figure walks slowly towards us, a great club wielded in his hands. With no time to waste, I snatch my knife from the dead man's beak. Now that I'm back in action, it's about time I prove that all of Mahro's training wasn't completely devoid of worth.

The frontrunner rushes towards me with his fist raised – as it comes flying towards me, I dart to the side and grasp his arm. He's soon spinning with the speed of a ballerina and none of her grace, until I leap up and send him crashing to the ground with the full brunt of my foot, shattering his beak in the process.

Myra's free hand presses against my back as she sends herself soaring into the air. I stand upright just in time to watch her plunge the sabre into the top of the second birdman's head and subsequently launch herself onto the head of the third. His confusion and wild swinging towards her as she more or less dances atop his head grants me the opportunity to lunge forward and cleanly pierce his throat with my knife, allowing her to leap back to the ground – he doesn't even so much as gurgle or reach for his lethal wound as he collapses to the ground... up until a thunderous thud erupts and his body is sent flying into me courtesy of the big guy's bludgeon. Blood and viscera erupt from the fatal wound and momentarily blind me as the cadaver pins me to the floor like a tactless stalker.

I wipe my eyes just in time to watch the big guy raise his weapon towards Myra, who ducks and weaves past the first few strikes as I struggle to shove the body off. Sure enough it's off me in a few seconds, but a panicked shout from Myra directs my eyes towards her before I can stand; she's collapsed onto her stomach, with a miserable looking contusion against the back of her leg. I scramble to tackle him to the ground as his bludgeon is raised far above his head, but the eruption of gunfire from the way we came forces me to stand down; a torrent of blood bursts out of his neck, and the weapon tumbles to the ground behind him as his hands and fingers spasm uncontrollably. Otherwise, he barely even appears to register the hit, and darts straight towards the newest combatant: Yuna.

She's stood some fifty metres away, which gives her ample time to pull off a few more shots – her second attack pierces the raging bull's chest, and a spent metallic casing ejects from the side of her rifle. Without a hint of hesitation, her hand flies into a pouch at her waist to produce another bullet, and it enters the armament with the same blinding speed. One effortless pull of the trigger later, her third shot rings out through the streets of Dias, this time striking the hulking mass in his head. He stumbles backwards for a moment, seemingly ready to advance forward forevermore... but ultimately caves in to his wounds, going limp and joining his underlings in the underworld.

As the colossal figure crashes into the ground, Myra and I let out a sigh of relief as great as our final opponent was massive. I waste no time in helping Myra back to her feet – her arms and back have worked up a nasty sweat and she still looks a bit shaken by her close brush with death. As her current custodian, I could never forgive myself or expect Mahro's own were she to die for my sake.

"If you're unfit to carry on, then by all means find somewhere to-"

Right as I begin to offer Myra a way out of the conflict, Yuna's hearty laugh cuts me off.

"She ain't Milkbag, but she's more tenacious than she looks, buddy. She'll walk it off." The rifle-toting tomboy says with a sly wink.

"There's no time for walking, Yuyu – we need to find my dad and sister as fast as we can. Would you join us?" Myra asks.

"I kinda have to, don't I? What *would* you do without me?" she answers, glaring at the freshly perforated giant she just toppled.

The three of us race through the rest of Dias Village, getting into violent but short-lived skirmishes along the way. Leaving a trail of bodies in our wake, we at last arrive at the foot of the bridge leading up to the mountain. We don't have the time to stop and objectively assess the damage, but from the corners of my eyes, I can tell that much of Dias has already been utterly ransacked – every nook and cranny of this street that could conceivably contain any kind of valuable is overturned and shattered. Doors are battered inwards, often off of their hinges entirely, and Yuna's shot more than a few dead as they walked out of a family home or business, leaving them to weakly crumple atop a sack of their ill-gotten gains. Most others within the village who have chosen to fight back lie dead in the streets, their wounds too grisly and numerous to document. What a terrible fate I've wrought upon these people...

It's as we rush past the entrance to Loren's strangely unscathed office (I can only assume he's holding down the fort inside) that another familiar face finally emerges – Mahro!

He rushes forth from the dirt path leading to his home, battering back one of the bird-faced underlings that is barely managing to avoid or deflect his strikes as he runs backwards. In Mahro's hands is a weapon far more unwieldy than any I've seen in my 17 years of life – its handle is crudely constructed of cheap metal and twine, much like all of the weapons wielded by our invaders, but its jagged blade of uneven sharpness reaches more than half as tall as Mahro himself. I've never been trained in the use of such weapons, but Mahro swings it with nearly as much efficiency and grace as what he does in fact specialise in. Eventually the underling is chased into a wall, and that wall is no doubt the last thing he ever sees – as his head turns around in a panic, Mahro's blade crashes into his torso and cleaves cleanly through it as the scraping screech of steel on bone fills our ears, sending the enemy's entire upper half soaring upwards into the air and showering both Mahro and his surroundings with a vibrant red.

"Looks like they didn't put *all* their eggs on a ship-shaped basket, Vega! You leave for one moment on my behalf, and it starts raining the bastards! Can't take my eye off you, can I?" my mentor says as he looks disdainfully at his weapon – the impact has removed at least 30cm of blade from the top, and what remains has been bent beyond repair.

"Nice moves, Pops! Where'd you learn to use a beauty like that?!" Yuna asks, her eyes still gleaming after Mahro's impressive display.

"I picked up a few techniques from an old friend. More importantly... where's Matra?"

Mahro leans to his right as he waits for Yuna to answer, burying the broken blade into the slumped lower half of the bisected birdman.

It takes a few moments to register, but a light bulb goes off in Yuna's head.

"Ah, she said she was going to her usual meditation site. Ya know, the one near Helbe-"

Before she can even finish, all of the blood drains from Mahro's face, and he rushes off across the rope bridge in a hurry.

"They're in there in droves! I'm coming, baby girl!"

A horrified look is shared between me and my two remaining companions – wordlessly, we agree to follow in his steps, and Myra is first to rush across the bridge, followed by myself and then Yuna.

It's as my foot touches earth once more that a familiar sound rings out yet again.

SCREEEEEEEEEEEECH!

The three of us look up to witness the giant black bird flying from behind the rightmost mountain peak, and approaching the village at incredible speed. Once it's flying roughly ten metres above the ground, human-shaped figures leap down towards Dias Village, presumably landing on their feet as mine and Myra's first assailants had done. Yuna doesn't even hesitate to bear arms and keep her rifle trained on the beast – she's no doubt waiting for an opportunity to fell the avian nightmare without its corpse crashing onto some hapless innocent's head.

Once she sees her opportunity, she finally takes a shot – Myra and I are ready to cheer on her great accomplishment. Except the beast's death is not what we get – instead, in the blink of an eye, it *separates itself into two beings*. The schism formed between the two causes a few birdmen to prematurely fall and crash into buildings head-first, but all three of us stand in horror, wondering if we aren't just stuck in some demented madman's fantasy.

Who in the *world* is after me, and just what do they have at their disposal?! Domesticated birds are one thing, but birds that can tear themselves apart and reconstitute... it's gruesome. It sounds like a bad joke.

While one of the birds stays its course and continues dropping off grunts around Dias, the second immediately darts towards us. The three of us begin running towards the entrance of the cave, hoping to escape its wrath, but the darkness of the night makes its true speed deceptive; in an instant, it's upon us.

At first it seems as though the bird itself is trying to divebomb us, giving up its life to exterminate these three pests who dared divide it from its other half, but as its mouth opens for another awful screech, it separates into *hundreds* of smaller black birds! The swarm of vengeful birds clouds our view long enough for the few birdmen that remained on its back to make their landing, and by the time they disperse and fly away, slowly reconstituting themselves a few birds at a time into a greater form, three average-sized birdmen, one holding a yellow-tipped rod, the second wielding a flimsy sabre and the third barehanded, stand between us and the mouth of the cave.

"That one first."

I issue the command to Yuna as my finger darts towards the rod-wielding birdman – at the same time, the three of them begin their simultaneous assault, my main target acting as the forerunner.

Yuna is in the dark as to his significance but complies, slamming another round into her weapon. The rod wielder looks at her warily, aware of his place on our hit list. This leaves him open to my knife, which I send flying towards his chest. He just barely reacts in time to block my attack, sending my knife flying behind the three of them with a loud twang, but I don't think anybody could block a good shot from Yuna; after a colossal bang, his role in this fight ends with a whimper. His companions don't even so much as acknowledge him as he tumbles onto his side, blood spewing from his head.

While Yuna and Myra deal with the barehanded combatant, the one that stands in *my* path is yet another sabre bearer – since their directive is to take me alive, I can safely assume he'll be going for non-lethal wounds, more than likely to my legs. Baiting a kick aimed at his own leg, I pull it back just in time for his attack to arrive, resulting in his sabre burying its blade multiple inches into the dirt. Incorporating Mahro's flair for turning his opponents' weapons into opportunities, I stomp on the sabre as hard as possible, snapping the cheap metal blade in two, and then shove his head down onto the protruding broken blade as he stumbles forward.

Even though it was my plan, I'm still surprised by how flimsy his weapon proved to be - come to think of it, even the glorified wall decorations they were earlier plundering would make more effective armaments. Are they tearing up my mentor's home to arm themselves better, even though I'm also present and hair-raisingly close to their clutches? It's bizarre but... it seems they have ambitions beyond tormenting me for the rest of my days.

I stand up, expecting Myra and Yuna to have wrapped up their end of the fight, only to see Myra flying towards me. I dart to the side as she hits the ground, rolling around momentarily before she shuffles back to her feet, dirtied, bruised and panting heavily. Wondering what on earth could have sent her this way, I look in the direction she came from to find Yuna struggling to hold her own against the last of the three; their hands are interlocked, at some kind of physical stalemate, and her treasured rifle lies snapped in two at the ground. Apparently there are *some* among their ranks

338

who know what to do with their hands beyond flailing them about like an idiot, but that's not to our benefit whatsoever.

More troubling, however, is that he's backing Yuna up against the end of the cliff, and the thrashing river is waiting for her to fall down with its arms lovingly open. Before long, the birdman proves the stronger of the two, and Yuna slowly loses her footing and uncomfortably shuffles backwards. Without even thinking or taking the time to retrieve my knife, I rush forward, aiming my fist at his temple. Before I can make any kind of contact, his vacant glare snaps towards me and his foot swiftly rises to kick me in the shin. While the pain is awful and I can't help but crumple to the ground, his momentary lack of footing gives Yuna the opportunity she has long sought, and she pushes forward with all of her might to topple the hardy combatant. Resting atop him with her knees pinning down his arms, she proceeds to ruthlessly batter the upper half of his head with her fists, pounding and pounding and pounding until the face underneath the mask is mushy and every one of her knuckles are either a raw red or bleeding outright.

How fortunate I am to never have incurred her wrath.

Her retribution enacted, she scrambles towards her busted armament, stroking its barrel as her eyes comb over the damage.

"Shithead! To treat my darling with such brutality…"

"Will you accompany us inside?" I ask of her as Myra and I are raring to go.

"I'm dead weight without something to shoot… I'll run back to Loren real quick, see if he's got anything to spare. I'll catch up, alright?"

Yuna excuses herself once I quickly nod – one less pair of arms for the ensuing fight is certainly a detriment, but standing around bemoaning our loss won't do us any favours.

Me and Myra enter the cave to discover a long trail of corpses – from the wounds, their ends came through all sorts of means: claws, throwing knives, large blunt objects… and I only know one man who would keep all of these disparate tools on hand, every minute of every day. Sure enough, half a minute of running brings us to Mahro, who stands alone amidst an array of the dead, all clad in black and beaks.

In his hands are two savage looking claws, pointed towards the flood. They're certainly not the same ones destroyed by Eden; the metal claws carry a stark white tint, appearing almost luminescent even against the backdrop of azure light, and its wooden grip would be not at all out of place among Helbez's goods. Blood descends from each tip of the tools of death in a rhythmic pattern, slowly forming small, grim pools at my mentor's feet. Mahro himself looks ragged – he's borderline hyperventilating, and he definitely didn't come out of the slaughter entirely free of damage, sustaining shallow but numerous wounds across his body.

"Dad!"

Myra rushes towards him, getting to him just in time to prop him up as he threatens to collapse.

"What—what god did we piss in the face of to deserve this...?" he says to himself.

It's difficult to watch Mahro be so devoid of his usual confidence and tenacity. I doubt he'll even be able to walk to Matra like this, let alone carve through whatever's in his way.

"Sorry old man, we got tangled up in a mess of our own."

As I speak, Myra hastily dresses some of the wounds to Mahro's legs and arms, using some loose pink fabric from her own costume as bandages. It's not great but her actual technique is fine; I would assume that whatever of Saki's teachings rubbed off on my mentor got passed down to her.

"I'm still standing, my friend; you need not mourn when I'm only one foot in the grave." My mentor answers with a grim chuckle, "Though I must ask, can you please make your way to Matra without me, for the time being? I simply cannot persist like this; I need a moment to recuperate, and I'll be no use as a pincushion."

Walking over to one of the freshly made corpses, I tear a spear of decent length from a dead birdman's stiff hands – it's a handy weapon in an environment like this even disregarding my own preferences.

"Leave it to me."

340

Mahro weakly smiles before I take off, leaving Myra to tend to him as I descend further into Mount Melodias. The odds aren't in my favour, but I would scorn myself forevermore were I to falter when trusted with Matra's safety.

There's an eerie silence for much of the journey – what few establishments reside within the mountain are already thoroughly cleaned out, their occupants either dead on the ground or not present at all. The blue lanterns scattered intermittently through the tunnels guide my path, though a few of them are cracked and flickering. I begin to wonder if Mahro had truly put an end to all of the mountain's invaders... until I reach the final stretch. Even from around the last turn, I can hear it: a discordant, uneven pattering of what sounds like tens of feet, filling the air with the sound of painstakingly slow but heavy ascension.

Once I finally stand atop the straightforward descent that houses the entry to both Matra's location and Helbez's workshop, I'm met by a harrowing sight: no less than fifteen of our invaders are making their ascent, all carrying sacks full of familiar weapons – *Helbez's weapons.*

Is... is the old man dead?!

Our enemies surely possess some capacity for cruelty, but they... they can't have...!

The boiling rage begins to take hold as my presence is finally noticed; thud after thud reverberates from the walls as their plunder is set aside in place of armaments, many of which are stolen from Helbez. A few of the sacks roll feebly down the hill whilst others stand firm, but either way, a veritable army of birdmen, now equipped with weapons from this age and not three long past, are charging directly at me. All that can stop this grievous misuse of the man's life work is me.

None of them are leaving here alive.

The higher ground I stand at is a huge advantage – the first to reach me is a diminutive looking birdman, holding a short rod with a steel ball attached via a chain. It's reminiscent of Mahro's rope-bound weapon somewhat, though it looks far more manageable to counteract. He begins charging up for an attack, and it's unclear where he's actually aiming, but before he can make good on his threat of a clobbering, I launch the side of the spear at the left half of his head and send him twirling around in a daze – the weapon in his hand twists and turns in the air before crashing into the wall at my left.

Seizing the opportunity, I ram shoulder-first into his centre mass and send him tumbling to the ground, coming to a stop against the sack he was hauling just moments ago. As soon as a few of his companions begin to encroach, my foot comes crashing into the back of his head and he's sent tumbling and flailing into two of his companions along with his ill-gotten gains. I would prefer Helbez's work remain intact, but if it finds use even in its destruction, then I suppose its purpose is more or less being served.

Those further down at least have the wit to move out of the way, but their ranks are noticeably more chaotic and disorganised now. At last putting my preferred weapon to use, I deliver a strike to the chest and then neck of a birdman swinging around one of Helbez's shortswords. The weapon drops to the ground, but with a quick flick of my foot, it flies through the air once more, reflecting the mesmerising blue light around us in every which way. As soon as its hilt faces me, I take it by my left hand and cut cleanly through the neck of the next combatant, who attempts miserably to flank me with a knife.

His head has yet to even hit the ground before my spear is jerked away from my grasp and its blunt end comes crashing into my stomach; an unarmed opponent has emerged, and he wastes no time snapping the spear in half through his brute force. In an instant, the end of the spear is turned against me, but I fight through the pain in my gut to deftly step aside before it plunges into that same place. Indeed, breaking the spear turns out to be his final mistake, as the broken hilt that remains in my right hand is soon forced through his throat.

Releasing the hilt and allowing the newest failure's corpse to roll down the path, I reaffirm my grip on the shortsword as I turn to face what remains; it appears the next four are approaching cautiously, choosing to co-ordinate their attacks so as to catch me off guard *eventually*. After a slow and intense staredown, all of them suddenly make their move: the two outer birdmen rush to my left and right with one of Helbez's spears in each of their hands, and the two remaining in front of me charge straight at me with curved knives from the same creator. I'm confident I can take all of them in close combat… up until the two at my front take what appear to be attempts to bait me into punishing a premature attack and turn them into rapid backhand throws, one aimed at my stomach and one at my right leg. I react just in time to avoid a deep wound to my gut, but the second knife grazes the edge of my thigh and tears through the thin trousers, leaving a wound that begins lightly bleeding.

Worse yet, the spearmen make their move as I recoil from the pain – I barely manage to avoid their unified vertical strikes by dropping to the floor. Fortunately, their swings come to a swift stop as the heads of their weapons crash into the floor, inches from my arms. I release my grip on the shortsword and reach for the farther ends of the two spears' hilts, mustering whatever force I can to raise them up and then jerk them in the directions they're facing; the two birdmen refuse to give up their grips on the weapons, and ultimately run each other through with the spears, flailing around helplessly as they spend the rest of their short lives utterly inseparable.

I don't even have the time to celebrate my quick thinking before I can feel a violent tug on my legs; before my brain can catch up, I'm being swung through the air by the two now weaponless birdmen, each holding a leg, and their grip soon releases. My plummet feels deathly long, and once I finally hit the ground, the downward slant sends me rolling and barrelling further and further. Each impact with the ground deals a significant blow; by its end, my arms are flailing and feel as though they barely work, and my legs are so beyond racked with pain they could snap right off without me even realising. I only come to a stop at the feet of yet another birdman, who is soon joined by another at each side of him.

As the one standing immediately above me readies a familiar white cloth, I try to raise my legs, hoping to roll back and send him on his own downward spiral with the full brunt of both. A quick stomp to my right leg puts an end to that plan, and I scream wildly, barely able to stand the torment. The birdman holding the cloth begins to kneel down, and soon takes up most of my vision.

So... is this how it ends?

Dias has laid down many lives just to keep me safe, Helbez may have been sent to the grave along with his vast knowledge, and I can't so much as hold up my end of the bargain by staying out of their hands for even a moment? Sure, Mahro could come later and sort everything out singlehandedly. But as the hand draws ever closer to my mouth, I'm consumed more and more by the dread that the next time I wake, it'll be in the presence of Snarl Boy again, with Dias long at our backs.

This village has given up so much to protect me... why can I not protect myself when it counts...?

...

BANG!

The instant all hope seems lost, that joyous sound rings out against the craggy halls beneath Mount Melodias, and the birdman standing above me drops to the floor dead, the cloth still gripped tightly in his hand. As my remaining adversaries turn to face what must no doubt be Yuna, the sound of a door first being bashed multiple times and then flying open soon follows, and after a subdued sound of something tearing through flesh, one in front of me falls next – a bolt lies embedded in his forehead.

The rest of the fight takes place outside of my vision, but its outcome is decisive; after half a minute of their insurmountable barrage, I'm finally approached by both Yuna and Matra. Yuna's gotten her hands on a longer looking firearm – certainly not one she seems too fond of, though it's been more than serviceable thus far – but she looks otherwise no worse for wear.

On the other hand, Matra looks completely exhausted – her arms are covered in blood-soaked bandages, and their effectiveness is no doubt downplayed by the vast sweat running across every inch of not just her arms but also her forehead. I would offer my sympathies but... well, I doubt I'll get much warmth in return.

"Thanks, girls." I say as the two of them raise me to my feet – Yuna keeps her arm around my back as I find my footing once again, "Loren felt generous, I take it?"

344

"Haven't seen hide nor hair of him." Yuna answers, "He probably headed elsewhere in the village. I just snagged this baby from underneath his desk, I'm sure he won't mind!"

"Putting your hands all over what isn't yours, Yuna? Even as the world changes around you, you're as static as ever."

There goes Matra, running her mouth just to piss people off.

Releasing me to stand on my own two feet, Yuna begins leading the three of us towards Helbez's workshop with a huff.

"We have bigger fish to fry at the moment, Milkbag. If you want to put me on trial after the f-"

"Stop calling me that!"

"This is what I mean!" Yuna shouts as she comes to a dead stop, blocking Matra's path, "Your brain is filled with worthless shit, and your priorities are even worse!"

"Ladies! You'll have to slap this out later; we haven't quite cleaned out all of the filth."

As I kick a forked spear up from the ground and into my hands, my warning to the two of them directs their eyes to what my own are fixed upon: an imposing black-clad figure emerging from Helbez's shop.

With a height that necessitates ducking beneath the door's frame, his stature alone is enough to send tremors of terror through anybody standing before him. His boots cause the mountain itself to quake with every step towards us, and the beak attached to his face, which has remained identical on each and every combatant we've downed yet, is filled with jagged yet perfectly interlocking teeth, giving the appearance of a sadistic smile as he glares at the three of us. Most intimidating of all is the weapon he wields; it initially appears to be a normal scythe, albeit as crudely constructed as the rest of his legion's armaments, until my attention is drawn by the other edge of the scythe scraping against the floor, affixed with its own blade identical to the one above.

From behind him… nothing. No striking of Helbez's hammer. No brilliant emerald flames or the crackling thereof. Not so much as a whisper of life within his domain.

"Did you kill him?!" I scream, expecting some sort of head gesture to confirm my fear.

"Irrelevant. Your life is the only one of consequence."

He's... *speaking?!*

"Companions of Humanit-"

"*Shut up!* What right have you to decide the 'consequence' of people's lives?! You've sentenced many good men to their deaths in pursuit of me! And I don't fancy putting their sacrifices to waste!"

My declaration made, I prepare myself for battle, gripping the weapon crafted by Helbez tightly in both of my hands and pointing it squarely towards his face – I have no doubt this bastard has slain the old man, and with him my greatest opportunity to restore Ford to greatness.

Yuna walks wordlessly to my side, loading one of her crude looking bullets into her rifle's chamber. Matra maintains her distance, twirling a rigid bolt betwixt her fingers before seamlessly planting it within her weapon's groove.

"It appears your companions will not back down. What a shame; I would have granted them swift and painless dea-"

The imposing figure's monologuing is hastily cut off – a bolt rips through the air and subsequently through the birdman's forehead, sending him recoiling backwards.

I smile in sadistic glee as he begins to tumble backwards – until he regains his footing and leans forward, his growling and gnarling resonating through the entire cavern.

Confused but determined to snuff out this final flame of destruction, I begin to charge forward with the spear aimed at his downturned head. It's as each end of the weapon is only inches away from his face that I come to a dead stop; with a harrowing screech that reverberates through the entire cavern and most certainly some distance beyond it, his entire upper body flies backwards, with his arms contorting in all sorts of grotesque manners.

The most concerning development is the *red pulse from his chest*; the memory of witnessing Eden's transformation is firmly burned into my mind, and my eyes turn bloodshot as the pulsing grows more and more intense. The radius of the pulses grow along with their intensity – the impenetrable natural walls of the cavern begin to rapidly decay around him. A thick rain of dust envelops the birdman like a shower of murky rain as the very flesh in his arms begins to burst out of his black leather vambraces, rapidly expanding and mutating into giant growths resting behind his arms. Each crawling vein and contorting muscle is accompanied by a symphony of sickening, bloody sounds that could unsettle even the deaf.

It's as the remains of the mangled vambraces begin to crawl up his arms and twist and weave themselves into raven black facsimiles of feathers that the look in my companions' faces turn from confused to utterly mortified. The two of them can only stand there and lower their weapons in shock as his transformation continues; the completion of his misshapen wings born of mutilation incites further changes to his now exposed arms. They appear to be of an olive-tinted complexion, but the bulbous veins sprouting and intensifying in colour across his arms and his fingernails contorting into talons as his grip on the scythe remains firm do more than enough to classify what stands before us as *utterly* inhuman.

"H-h-how can something like this even exist?!" Yuna shouts as she aims her rifle at the still contorting birdman, panicking at the monstrous sight.

"I learned in my youth that ignorance is blissful. I'm sorry I couldn't preserve yours. But we can end this nightmare, right here." I say in an effort to reassure Yuna.

She's more or less forced to regain composure once the imposing figure at last rises to his feet, bearing garish and gory black wings. The red pulsating has come to an end, and he spreads his newly gained wings as far as this claustrophobic cavern will allow with a rapturous cackle.

"Congratulations, you were granted wings in the last place you would want them. Let's get this ordeal over wi-"

The *instant* I blink, my eyes open to find the ecstatic birdman flying towards us, aiming to pin me down with the handle of his weapon.

Yuna's swift intervention is all that stops my throat from likely being crushed by the impact – as I spin to a stop next to her, our enemy lands with grace a few metres away from us.

"You have been blessed with good companions, Humanitas. Upon my word as Nihos, warrior of the Gora people, I regret that I cannot send you to the black gates with them." the birdman says with unsettling sincerity.

Despite being acutely aware of the threat he's making, Yuna and Matra look as energized and aware as ever.

"You two, can you try and keep his head in place, somehow? I may be asking a bit much, but I could end this fight with one well placed shot, should a lack of a head end this monster's life." Matra asks in a low tone as we and Nihos slowly circle around each other, anticipating one another's next move.

"We'll try, Milkbag." Yuna answers, and I provide no contest – that being said, I don't anticipate an easy resolution.

As soon as our backs face the slope leading back up to the surface, Matra hastily begins her ascent.

"Running for help won't save you." Nihos declares as he flies towards us.

Under the assumption that his attack is aimed at us, I stand in front of Yuna, prepared to take him on under the knowledge that he won't allow me to leave as a corpse. His scythe is raised in an apparent attempt to attack us, but it's as I thrust forward that he suddenly raises himself into the air, diverting his course towards the fleeing Matra. Much to his displeasure, one of the ends of my weapon buries itself into his left leg, but as the torrent of blood emerges from the wound tearing through his leg, the weapon is jerked out of my hands and I'm sent spiraling to the ground. Nihos weakly attempts to continue flying upwards until he too comes crashing to the ground, leaving a trail of dust and blood as he slides some way upwards and snapping his weapon cleanly in half. I can't help but smile with some small satisfaction as I bring myself to my feet.

"Hah! All that buildup for nothing!" Yuna says as she races upwards, aiming her rifle squarely at our grounded opponent.

But in the blink of an eye, Nihos leaps into the air from his downed position, rotating with blinding rapidity until he slows down just enough to send one of the halves of his weapon flying towards Yuna, its blade rotating so fast as to appear circular. My rifle-toting friend attempts to evade it, but isn't quick enough to prevent the improvised projectile from tearing into the flesh of her left shoulder and leaving its other end, having torn out a distressing amount of it.

Yuna's agonising screams reverberate through every wall of the cavern as many around her are stained by her blood, and she collapses backwards as her right hand limply holds onto her weapon, raising her upper body just barely enough to gaze upon her attacker.

Desperate to save her life, I scramble for the hilt of one of Helbez's sabres that lies idle within one of the many dispersed bundles littering the slope, and race upwards as Nihos ascends into the air, filling the tunnel with a sickening screech before he flies swiftly downwards, hovering maybe half a metre above the ground. The blade of his remaining scythe is aimed squarely at Yuna's neck, but she's not taking the attack lying down – she plants her head against the floor and shoots her feet upwards, crashing her feet into the incoming weapon and sending him wildly off course. He ends up flying awfully close to me, and with a swift slash my sabre tears through most of his left arm and wing, sending the severed mass to the uneven ground where it tumbles, writhes and ultimately dies.

Nihos lands not so gracefully, kicking up an even greater torrent of dust as he grinds against the slope to an eventual stop. I take the opportunity to help Yuna to her feet, in spite of the pain caused by her grievous injury. It takes a lot of wincing and groaning, but before long she's back on her own two feet.

"*Watch out!*" Yuna cries out.

Indeed, the instant she's up, so too is our adversary, who is charging at us with his intact wing raised as some kind of shield.

Yuna slowly raises her gun in an attempt to shoot the rampaging birdman in his tracks, but she's not fast enough to stop him from barrelling into us like a pissed off bull, and he smacks me into a wall with his mutilated arm as his wing outstretches.

My vision is hazy and my ears are ringing, but I can just about tell how this next stage is playing out: Yuna's gun flew out of her hand during the impact, but that isn't stopping her from leaping to her feet as he glares at me and throwing a punch any sane man would consider futile. His head turns just in time to open his beak and clamp down on her wrist with his malformed, jagged teeth. In a bizarre twist however, Yuna slams her right hand down on the top of his beak, burying his teeth even deeper into her arm and unleashing an ungodly deluge of blood from her left wrist.

As my vision slowly becomes clearer, I finally see why she would do such a thing – Matra is waiting some distance above us, lying on her stomach as her crossbow has become unrecognizable; it now stays rooted to the ground via a bipod, and its flight groove has somehow been extended to such a length that I cannot begin to fathom what devilish construction would be required to create a weapon of such flexibility. What scares me far more is what lies within the flight groove – a thick, gnarly looking bolt more fitting for a *ballista* than a hand-wielded armament, and yet her weapon is able to house such a monstrosity.

The look on both of their faces says it all: Yuna is pleading with Matra to take the chance and shoot, regardless of the damage done to her, but she hasn't the strength to issue the decisive command verbally. Meanwhile, Matra looks paralyzed by indecision, betraying a lack of confidence in the plan she herself has formulated. Nihos' head still writhing around yet, tugging and tearing at Yuna's arm by the second, must no doubt make her shot ever the more perilous... so it's up to me to make the shot a sure one.

Resigning myself to whatever may become of Yuna, I force myself to my feet once again, sabre in hand, and rush behind him as fast as my legs can take me. He tries to turn his head to look at me, and his right wing begins to flail as he attempts to stop me, but his flailing does nothing to halt me as I bury the saber into the back of his head, right up until its hilt and his head are bonded.

"MATRA! DO IT!"

The final order has been issued. I maintain a firm grasp on the hilt, stopping any movement of his head to the best of my ability while I wait for Matra to act upon my command.

And with a deep breath... she pulls the trigger. Within an instant, the titanic bolt buries itself in the side of Nihos' head and tears it off of his neck, with all of Yuna's arm up to her elbow joining its graceless descent.

The battle is over, but I don't have even a second to sigh in relief: Yuna's fallen to her knees and is already crying profusely, a sight I never thought I would bear witness to and one that makes me all the more guilty, knowing it happened in my defense. I try my best to help her up, but I myself can barely even stand. Before I can even dream of helping Yuna, Matra races over to us, leaving her weapon on the ground. With a deep breath, she raises Yuna into her arms and quickly turns towards the cave's exit.

"Are you coming?" she hurriedly asks.

"Just give me a few minutes." I answer.

Matra looks confused but doesn't stick around to argue.

Indeed, there are two matters badly weighing down my mind, ones I cannot return to the surface world without accounting for.

The first is Nihos – I approach his headless corpse and tear open the thick, grisly fabric concealing his upper chest… to discover *nothing*.

There is no Rose.

There's not even a hole where one used to be.

There's absolutely nothing.

I can't even begin to wonder what the ramifications of this are – the effects of a Screaming Rose without the artifact itself? It's preposterous, and yet I have proof of it right in front of me.

But it's no use wondering about it now; I have to check on Helbez. I hurry towards his shop with haste, feeling Nihos' dead eyes boring into my back and sending me on my way with an intense dread.

The air is thick and gloomy as I push open the door to Helbez's workshop – the once prideful walls full of his life's work are now either barren or broken, and the entire room is shrouded in darkness. I'm just about ready to leave, not wanting to find the old man's corpse gracelessly tossed against the ground, until a dry cough emerges from his usual spot.

My hopes raised, I swiftly walk across the shop, hoping to find him miraculously alive and well. But as I lean forward and can at last make out his diminutive shape amongst shadow... he's alive, but not at all well.

Even within this dreary darkness, I can make out several thick bruises against the left side of his face. A small line of blood is trickling from his ear, and he can't even open his eyes as he stares down at his legs. In his legs is the culmination of our united efforts; even on death's door, he's committed to bringing the weapon to completion, using whatever energy he has left to wrap a few centimetres beneath the bottom of its blade in a thick black twine.

"Here's... here's..."

The old man begins to mumble weakly as his head raises to where his deceased wife's picture has long rested – unbeknownst to him, it's now fallen to the ground, and its glass is shattered beyond repair.

"Ah, what was I going to say...?"

I leave the old man to his own devices as I watch him work; it's hard to ignore that he is on a short mortal leash, but leaving him to his own pleasures will do him more good than a futile rush to the mouth of the cavern in his final moments.

"There's ah... something that... worries me dreadfully, my beloved. Now that the reaper's... coming for my neck... will I get to see you after all? I've... made thousands of fine pieces such as this, but... they aren't to bring more life... they're for taking it. How many... how many have fallen to my works? What debt do I owe... to the gods? How many young men's years were cut short... thanks to me?

"And yet... here I am, sealing one last deal before I... pop off this mortal coil, eh? So this young man can... keep what's most precious to him. ...what an awful contradiction, ay? If I give up my life's work, that's life I'm... not protecting. But in the present... my life's work *is* present, and it's... no doubt been used for both great and ill. ...aww, Yuria... whatever will the gods think of me? It's as if... no matter my life's course, they'll... disapprove. Do you think of them as... hard to please?"

As he stares at the wall, his hands finally stop moving, having concluded their motions, and he turns on his seat to place it against the table – against the faint blue light coming from outside, its blade glimmers proudly, and the light slips in between the subtle grooves of its lengthy handle.

"That's it for me... I can feel it in my bones... he'll be here eventually, no doubt about it. Hope my old bones don't... rot too fast."

Helbez slowly collapses backwards off of his seat – I finally intervene, propping up his back with my arms before he crashes into the ground. The old man groans as his right arm reaches weakly upwards – his eyes are completely closed, and he appears entirely unaware of my presence.

"What's this...? Angels... why waste your time on a mumbling old sack? Let me... crawl my own way... there..."

And with his last words spoken, Helbez's body goes limp, and his last gurgling breath fights its way out of his mouth. I wish I could have said something to ease his quarrels, but after a life of loudly striking metal, I suppose silence is the greatest parting gift I could offer.

Chapter 20: Of Ill Temperament

I reunite at last with Mahro and the girls at the mouth of the cavern, with Helbez's final masterpiece held in my hand and his final words haunting my mind – what I want more than anything is to put this to use in such a manner the old man would approve of.

The scene isn't pretty – to the right of the cavern's exit, Mahro and Myra are tending to Yuna's bloody stump to the best of their ability, but the hotshot herself has long passed out from blood loss, her very light breathing remaining the only sign of life. Matra instead lies with her back against the inside of the cavern's wall several metres away, in a slumber of her own.

"I take it the old man's a goner?" Mahro asks – I nod in confirmation, and he releases an ugly sigh of discontent, "I figured as much. I feel as though I never appropriately thanked him for everything he's done for the lot of us, but you can't buy a ticket to the heavens with gratitude."

Not that it's a contest, nor do I wish to make one out of misery... but the old blacksmith's death is especially taxing on my mind. Even if I was separated from my family, I at least had an opportunity in the village of Dias to hone my craft, with the finest craftsman I've ever met at the helm. A man whose every word and motion in the realm of weaponsmithing conveyed decades of wisdom and conquered hardships. The fact that he met such an end, indirectly by my hand...

Why am I here? Why am I in Dias?

I thought I had found some purpose in my arrival at Dias, but now it's gone. I should have left at the earliest possibility. How many masters of their craft and promising upstarts have met their end because of my selfishness?

"But it seems our trouble is coming to an end; those... avian bastards are scurrying off to the village entrance. Maybe they're making their getaway now that their pockets are sufficiently lined with *our* hard work."

Mahro's bitterness incites a feeling of intense guilt in the pit of my stomach – I remained safe in the end, albeit with a few nasty bruises and wounds to show for it, but they still brought his home to ruin in their pursuit. I open my mouth to express my sincere remorse until he suddenly cuts me off.

"Can you check in with Loren for me? I caught a glimpse of him rushing back into his cave, which I suppose marks the end of his role in all this..."

"R-right. I'll do that." I say before taking off, leaving Yuna and the Katsuragi family I have so incessantly blighted to lick their wounds.

Taking no time to knock, I burst into Loren's office.

"Oi, Chief! How did it turn out in the—the—"

I can't even finish my sentence once my eyes finally meet Loren's, for they lay cold and lifeless, splayed across his desk along with the rest of him. There's a deep, grisly laceration in the side of his neck, and his hands lie dormant near a wide, emptied drawer inside his desk. As his blood continues to seep down his chest, beyond the initial shock of what I walked in on, I realise one very important thing: whoever did this must still be near. And since the door leading to Pat's cell is busted off of its hinges, I have a very good idea who the culprit is.

Lacking the time to so much as close Loren's eyes, I rush out of the building, scanning the ground and nearby surroundings for any clue as to Pat's whereabouts. Sure enough, to my left lays a thin trail of blood. Who it belongs to I cannot say, but before the trail dries up, it points me toward the next left turn in the road. It's uncharted territory for me yet, but I'm not letting that bastard get away with this.

I sprint through the thin alley the road leads into and emerge into a wide street, which serves as an extension of the market district; the entire scene is a graveyard of commerce, as

355

each and every institution present is so utterly pilfered and ruined that their original purpose is indecipherable. A thin line of grass runs through the centre of the stone-laden street, and an uncomfortable amount of it is stained by the blood of lifeless innocents.

The street is empty of the bird-faced burglars, save for a few a considerable distance away who are retreating with their ill-gotten gains, stopping at nothing and trampling over those they slew to reach their destination.

And among them... Pat.

Pacing lackadaisically among them without a care in the world, no less, with a jagged and bloodied knife gripped in his right hand. Not that it needed confirmation, but I have my proof that the bastard killed Loren.

"Stop! *Stop right there! Pat, you bastard!*"

I don't know if he registers what I say, but he rushes on with no intent of stopping or even affording me the time of day.

As I begin charging down the street, I raise my weapon in his direction, more than determined to run the piece of shit through. His demeanour in casual conversation was already infuriating enough to make me want to rip his face off; murdering a trusted friend of my mentor and his family more than justifies making good on that desire.

But I make no more than ten steps towards my goal before a hand emerges from a green and white-striped tent, and it clamps down hard on the end of its haft. The force is enough to keep the glaive in place as I barrel forward yet, sending its other end straight into my gut and forcing me to one knee. To my surprise, the hand releases the haft, though its blade falls to the floor whilst I lock eyes with the owner of said hand as he casually strolls out of the tent.

Standing before me is a slender young man; he appears to be maybe a few years my senior, but his face lacks the distinct hardiness and weariness of a man like Mahro. His hair is jet black and tied into a thin ponytail that sways against the raging winds, but it's otherwise elegantly slicked back, contrasted by the radiant blue lights around us seeping into its grooves and nooks. Beneath a spotless, blood red jacket as thin as it is outlandish to find in a warzone, he wears a grey shirt, and his hands remain firmly in the pockets of his formal black trousers, themselves secured by a brown belt.

The most harrowing detail however reveals itself once he finally turns to fully face me - tattooed onto the right side of his face is a distinctive character, one I'm all too familiar with: "Wyvern."

"*Who the hell are you?!*"

I take up my weapon once again as I demand an answer, taking two steps back as I keep its end pointed towards his throat.

The threat is brushed off by the stranger with a casual laugh, and his voice proves to be as cocky and haughty as his exterior implies.

"*Oh, hohohoh*, Humanitas! Didn't your *mother* teach you any manners?"

...

In an instant, my mind is racing with so many questions that it physically hurts. I can't even begin to articulate one before the seeds of another begin to sprout, only for the rabbit hole to burrow ever deeper and deeper with each second that passes. All I can concretely think of is that since he knows my former identity, and what became of my mother... he's with them, without a doubt.

Gripping onto whatever willpower I have left in order not to execute him on the spot, I make my demand loud and clear.

"I don't care who you are or what role you have to play in all this. You're coming with me, and you're going to answer *all* of my questions, or your head's ending up on this like a stuck pig. Am I cl-"

"Why so *violent*, Humanitas? I believe there's a misunderstanding here; *you* are coming with *us*. As your half-brother, I can attest to the fact that our family reunions are *wicked!*"

"Half-brother! Ridiculous! I refuse to entertain the notion! You're a lowlife thug, you're gutter scum not deserving of the spit on our tongues, and you'll do exactly what I say if you want to keep using that mouth you love so much!"

The only way I can answer is with blinding rage as my weapon draws ever closer to his throat – I don't want to accept it, but something deep in my gut is telling me that his words are in fact the truth; his hair colour matching my own and the fact that Pat himself verified my heritage is indeed playing a part in this whole catastrophe are more than enough to provide weight to his words.

Surprisingly, his guard lowers and he throws his hands up, with a small diamond resting in between his middle and ring finger on his left hand – given that the tent he walked out of contains precious gems yet to be pilfered, I must have happened upon him at an *unfortunate* time.

"Alright, little man, if you insist. I'll 'spill the beans', as it were."

His eyes close as he offers his surrender, though his strange smirk leaves me reluctant to lower my weapon and move in closer to restrain him.

"That being said..." he continues with a sly grin, "Do me this last kindness: allow poor little Temperantia a peaceful final meal, would you?"

Before I can approve of his strange request, his left hand raises above his head, and the diamond drops seamlessly into his throat. It only takes a second before his struggle begins; I move my glaive out of the way as he collapses forward, grunting and producing all sorts of violent sounds from his throat as he painfully struggles to swallow the priceless gem.

"You stupid bastard! If you wished for death that badly, I would have gladly offered it to you, and with a brevity you ill deserve!"

My taunt comes from a place of both bewilderment and triumph – if the dumb bastard wants to take his life in such a boneheaded manner, he can be my guest; I'll simply beat all of my answers out of Pat once I get my hands around his neck and—

My train of thought is cut off by the sound of Temperantia actually *swallowing* the diamond – he keels forward with both of his hands on the floor, a thin trickle of blood oozing from his mouth. I bring my weapon to my side and hold it with one arm, confident that he's won this battle for me.

"And you can't even kill yourself right, can you? I'm almost impressed, but surviving this just means I get to beat some ans-"

As I speak, I at last blink for a second to visually process what just occurred... and that's when he strikes. I'm initially alerted by the squelching sound of… *regurgitation*, an instantaneous one no less.

And it's as my eyes open that the diamond *crashes into my left eye*. With such velocity that my grip is forcibly released as I keel over, trying to place pressure on my eye after the saliva-coated gem falls to the ground and blood begins to leak from my eye. My pulsating eye is soon cloaked in a murky red, exacerbating the extreme pain with a complete and utter inability to see out of it. My right eye too is regularly spasming and blurring, as if aching to share in the torment of its counterpart.

"Carrie, you can come out now. You'll be safe, I promise." Temperantia says to an unseen figure – my right eye can just *barely* make out that he's speaking to somebody inside the tent.

Timid footsteps soon follow, but the pain brings my eyes back to the ground as the blood starts to seep from between my hands and onto the stony ground, filling in the thin seams left by its engravings.

"Take this, and remember what Big Brother Humilitas told you, alright? Humanitas is ailed by an evil demon – it wants to get in the way of the Angel and stop her no matter what. Humanitas isn't himself. You can help him, but it's going to hurt him. And that's alright; sometimes we have to hurt the people we love to turn them back to the light. Give him a *good whack*, and the demon will sleep. We'll bring him to Humilitas and he can expel the demon once and for all. Do you think you're strong enough to do it? For me?"

"Y-yes…"

I-is that a… *little girl?* It's hard to imagine one accompanying such a vile man into an area actively under attack, but I've certainly observed stranger happenings. Still, judging from her voice, she must be of around the same age as Tsubasa.

All of these questions soon become moot – the last thing my right eye sees in between its spasms is the blurry image of a young girl dressed in white, contrasted by her blonde pigtails and thin, red-framed glasses, before the wooden club in her hands swiftly smashes into my face.

Chapter 21:
A World in Stasis

Dias.

My home.

Its attackers may be departing into the romantic night, but their actions will no doubt send shockwaves through all who live in it.

I've always seen a little bit of myself in Kyrie's boys; their drive and determination was always spectacular, for varying reasons, mind.

I thought that moulding them down a better path than my own, putting their strengths to use for the forces of good, would somehow cleanse my own soul of its wrongs.

And yet, I now stand in the exact shoes they wore a decade ago; I'm bearing witness to what is no doubt the start of an agonizing decay.

Bereft of hope and assets, the people of Dias will start to leave, looking for greener pastures, until the very heart of this place has eroded.

It was this chaos, this seemingly inevitable destruction that would be left in my wake, that turned me away from my original path to begin with.

I gave up my clan, my brothers and sisters in the Shangra, to preserve what innocence I had left, only for it to inevitably spiral out of control yet again.

I wonder what Gillian would have said at a time like this.

"Peh! Tough luck, ain't it? You and violent ends are like peas in a pod, my friend. Betcha wouldn't 'a sold us out if you knew what misery waited at its end!"

...yeah, something like that.

It's not as though I haven't lived a good life until now; Minami was loyal to the bitter end, she left me two beautiful little girls, and my efforts to right my soul's wrongs have put me in some of the best company I could ask for.

As much as I dislike grandiose shows of affection, it does make me dour that I can never express to the likes of Julius, Saki and especially Ringo just how much they mean to me, even if they themselves don't recognize it.

And it goes without saying that Vega stands prominently among them; I wouldn't offer my wing to just anybody.

He's wrapped up in blaming himself for what happened today; for all of his aspirational qualities, he is by no means a good liar.

That being said, lying is not at all an aspirational quality of your average man... but the lives we lead are far from average.

If there's a word for the opposite of a poker face, that young man is the dictionary definition of it, for his face is a perfect mirror into his soul.

None of this would have happened were it not for me.

On an objective level, it's not *inaccurate*, but I find it ill-fitting to ascribe culpability when the only alternate he had was a nasty death.

Waterlogged corpses... I've seen one too many of those for a lifetime or three.

To see not just a student but a trusted friend end up in such a way would wound me in ways I can't even imagine.

...

...

Back when Ringo proposed the deal at the end of a sword, I was sure I would come to regret it; I spent my youth among the Shangra Clan, treating them as comrades.

To turn against them for mine and Minami's sake didn't sit right with me, and it didn't for years.

The thought of people I considered friends burning to death beneath that old wharf plagued my every thought for years to follow, waking or otherwise.

But I also don't doubt that staying that course would have seen me in a shallow grave, having lived a short, insignificant life; if it weren't a botched job as was the case with Ringo, only with a much less merciful recipient, it was only a matter of time before someone else turned coat and roasted me alive with the lot of them.

So, I'm at least grateful that for as bad as Vega's situation is, his grave is far from dug as of yet.

Speaking of whom... it's been a while since Myra spotted him sprinting out of Loren's office in a frenzy.

It can't be good news, so I sent my little chicken after him, just to keep an eye on if anything happens to him.

And if the frantic creaking of the rope bridge is any indication, one or both of them is on their way back.

I'm hoping it's the latter.

"Dad! Dad!"

She turns the corner of the temple, alone.

"Where is he?" I ask as I return to my feet – it only takes one look at her face to tell something went awry.

"I saw... a little girl, she bashed him in the head, then some strange man picked him up and carried him towards the village entrance!"

"Keep an eye on your sister and Yuna. If Yuna starts acting up, do your best to keep her stable."

And with no further words, I take off on yet another rescue mission.

But... knocked into next week by a little girl? Vega, my friend, you are far more trusting of them than I.

Of my many brushes with death over the years, little girls and those devilish puppy eyes of theirs are responsible for no less than half of them.

Gillian probably took up at least three quarters of what remains.

As I bolt through the street where Vega was last seen, I realise that the sensation seeping up my spine is all too familiar; as if fighting against the gods of time itself, I've had to drop everything

362

in a blind pursuit, utterly unprepared beyond what rests within my coat.

Eden – something of a footnote in the tumultuous life I've led, but no doubt the most harrowing life experience that young man has encountered yet.

Indeed, no matter his efforts to hide it, the rare times in which the subject was approached within the halls of his home, he'd offer a convenient excuse to leave the room and hastily shuffle out of the scene.

Not out of some sense of misery, or sorrow. More... discomfort.

He'll have to get used to it, I'm afraid – whatever course of action he takes after this, life won't be made easy.

I don't blame him for what happened one bit, but certain sects of Dias are a superstitious lot; a stranger walks into our paradise one day, only for hell to descend upon it the next?

He'll never hear the end of it.

In some ways, I feel as though he would be better off trying to make his way home.

CLANK!

I'm brought to a stop by that sudden metallic sound.

What lies under my foot is what Vega carried in his hand only moments ago – Helbez's last work.

That impeccable haft... the artistry of what is ostensibly an instrument of death...

...

My feet take off once more, telling me not to concern myself with trivialities in a scenario like this.

But the conclusion is inescapable.

I was deluding myself this whole time.

Certainly, the prospect of taking him under my wing brought some small shred of excitement to this bitter old soul, but in the end, a part of me couldn't deny the inevitable.

He's carving his way back home, no matter what, whether I consciously help or not.

...

363

The girls and I need to have a talk once this is all wrapped up.

My attachment to Dias, the only true home I've ever had, can't override what I know now to be the sensible option.

But for my girls to uproot their entire lives over what any sane being would consider a foolish quest... I expect it'll take some convincing.

Well, maybe not so for Myra.

The two have become fast friends, and all she really has tying her down beyond her other friends is her work with Mr. Entari, though I doubt the village of Dias will have no time for theatrics when it comes to cleaning this mess up.

Matra, however, is much further from the realm of certainty.

Their relationship has turned noticeably bitter, and I wouldn't be surprised if she used her efforts to contact Minami's spirit as an anchor with which to avoid the tumultuous journey in our path.

Were it any other person I would accuse them on the spot of callously using death as a shield from their calling.

But Matra... she hasn't been right since that day we returned.

She entered Loren's office with a grimace after he broke the bad news to me first, expecting a rough slap on the wrist.

She exited Loren's office in tears.

My baby girl's always been a hardy young lady; this is the only time I ever saw her so much as shed a tear since she was small enough to rest upon my one arm.

Ever since then... hardly anything.

She took Minami's textbooks and spent most of her days henceforth locked in what used to be her mother's room, conversing only to pass the time needed to reach the front door.

Dragging her along on a journey with Vega, especially after their rocky reunion, surely can't do her much good.

Either way, I'll leave it to my girls to decide.

In the end, those matters are left for after his rescue.

For now I stand some fifty metres away from the village entrance.

After scaling up to the roof of the building standing opposite our entrance arch, I pull the battered spyglass from my pocket.

With that shakily grafted heart on its side, two letters S intertwining within.

Gillian's final gift - with mine and Minami's amendment, it now stands as a reminder of both my greatest loss and the only man I ever truly feared.

Before I can fully lose myself to sentiment or disdain, I bring it to my right eye.

Within the large dirt patch outside of Dias, three colossal birds are hovering around 10 metres above the ground, with large, tightly knit nets gripped in their talons.

The wind force of their wings perturbs my hair, as well as the many blue lanterns hanging atop the entrance arch.

I'm in disbelief... they must each be the size of my house three times over.

A vast hoard of Dias' goods is entrapped within each net, and the bird-faced men are ascending to their mounts upon steps formed of many smaller black birds.

Hmm... these fellows sure have some odd creatures on hand - maybe they should have started a circus instead of... *this*.

Six of the birdmen remain, and they're equally distributed between the two birds to the left and right.

Pat is being escorted onto the back of the rightmost bird, playing his mouth to what I guess are his saviours.

Seems like they're in no position to smack him one, though.

And atop the centre bird... *it's Vega!*

His eye looks to be in terrible shape, and I can't even discern if he's conscious, but I can bless my lucky stars that I have a chance yet.

More curiously, sitting to his side is a blonde and bespectacled little girl, adorned in a red-frilled white dress and scribbling away in a dense book resting in her lap.

This must have been the little girl mentioned by my very own – she's cute as a button and has that undeniably innocent charm to her... which makes her the *deadliest* sort of little girl.

At the head of that very same bird is a black-haired young man with a ponytail – he looks awfully similar to Vega, not just in hair colour but in his face, too.

I suppose that Pat bastard wasn't yanking our leg after all; maybe this whole event was the most convoluted family reunion in recent history.

Tenryuu has certainly been host to many of them as dynasties have come and gone, but none this... petty.

The black-haired young man walks over to who is presumably his little sister, exchanging words and a ruffling of her hair before he returns to the creature's head.

Quite the dynamic duo... just where would these two young'uns fit in the hierarchy of a presumably decades old order long thought to be decimated?

The Band of the Wyvern, ascendant from the ashes... I'm just glad Julius isn't here to see this.

While he remained sympathetic to the two boys, he also somewhat rode the high of having cut off the wyvern's head and lighting up its carcass for years following their assault.

To see that corpse risen and rejuvenated... it would be a horrible blow to his ego.

"We're set! Gara, let us make haste for Arcadia!" the young man says.

"*Caw!* Roger that, bossman!"

The...

Hang on!

The *bird* is talking?!

Its voice is eerily similar to how I imagined a bird's tongue to sound in my head – shrill, abrasive and unpleasant to the ears – but I can't afford to wallow in the shock.

It's taking flight, along with its brethren.

Now I really need to move!

I feel the tiling of the roof rumble as I leap back to the earth.

I roll forward and preserve my momentum right as the earth threatens to turn me into a bloody splatter.

My every rapid step kicks up dust, though not as much as each earth-rending flap of the black birds' wings.

They finally begin their return journey right as I pass through the entrance arch.

Their bodies are still some fifteen metres above the ground, but the sacks of burgled goods are slothful yet, just barely beginning their ascent.

It's right as the centre bird's net starts to gain significant height that my fingers barely manage to claw onto its net.

Before I know it, I'm uncomfortably high in the air.

20 metres.

30 metres.

50 metres.

The sky is too dark yet to discern my height beyond that – all I know is that one mistake is the barrier between me and an early grave.

Not that I'm at all unfamiliar with dodging *those*.

"*Caw!* Bossman, something's wrigglin' round down there!"

"As big bags of loose shit tend to do, Gara! Pay no heed to it!"

What an astute pair – the exchange comes right as I clamber my way into the net itself.

Golden trophies, weapons and articles of historical import concealed in glass cases, dense books rich with not just the culture of Dias but the engineering that makes it tick in the present day.

If it had value, these bastards have pilfered it.

I should—

...

No.

However improbable, I don't want to be responsible for a whale's weight of goods raining on some poor sap's head during his night-time stroll.

We can always make more books, craft more weapons, restore what once was.

You can't restore a life.

And I've far too much innocent blood on my hands for five lifetimes, let alone this one.

It takes a moment for my mind to adjust to such a harrowing height, but before long I'm gripping at the flying beast's thick fur, pulling my way up to its back.

Only now do I notice that the two birds to my side are diverting on their own courses.

Pat and I momentarily lock eyes.

His shit eating grin is the last I see of him before he disappears into the veil of night.

As if cursed by the bastard himself, the wind pressure is beginning to intensify.

Thunder and lightning rips through the stygian air, and the building rain is making my ascent a slippery, difficult one.

After a few close calls however, I finally force myself to the top of the beast.

My eyes meet with the little girl next to Vega some seconds before hers meet mine.

She's concealing that drawing pad between her legs now, clutching onto it as though it carries as much value as the hostage next to her.

Though the instant she sees me, her sedentariness is thrown to the wind.

In a hurry, she leaps to her feet, screaming.

"Tom! Tom! Someone's climbing up Gara!"

"I told you somethin' felt funny, dickhead!" a shrill reply follows.

As their exchange plays out, I take to freeing Vega from his hasty restraints.

A short blade in my coat makes quick work of the shoddy ropes binding his arms and legs, and I begin to get my hopes up as he fights his way to his feet...

Only to crumple atop the beast's back once again.

He's obviously disoriented, and that grisly wound encroaching on his eye can't be doing any favours.

"I'll... I'll... kill the..."

"Conserve your strength, my friend; we've yet to touch down." I say as I rest my palm on his back.

"There's a misunderstanding here, Mahro Katsuragi."

The young man's voice rings out against the thunderous rhythm of the rain; his shadowy silhouette gradually gains definition as he approaches from the darkness, smirking as he toys around with a curious button-eyed doll betwixt his fingers.

"You won't be *touching* down from this flight, Katsuragi. Indeed, your end will not be so graceful."

Returning the doll to his pocket, he comes to a stop at the midpoint of the bird's spine, holding a pair of knives in such an odd manner that their hilts run into his long sleeves.

The little girl sits near the head of the bird, timidly watching our exchange as she hides behind her drawing pad.

But his threat is nothing more than a bluff.

He's putting up a front of confidence, but it's clear he knows not just of my name but also my acumen in the art of combat; his eyes are darting all over the place, and his breathing is noticeably too rapid for such apparent composure.

"Tom, was it? You've done your homework for sure. Order this bird to touch down immediately and I'll spare your life."

Not that I particularly *wish* to spare his life, but I would rather play the intimidation card before diving headfirst into the murder.

"That name is reserved for my friends, Mister Katsuragi! And last I checked, heh, we're *not* all that chummy now, are we?"

He doubles down on his stance, and his breathing becomes noticeably unhinged – he could come at me any second now, but no amount of surprise will help him.

"When you return to the earth as a bloody splatter, tell the man at the black gates who sent you! Tell the man at the black gates that your life was snuffed out by Temperantia! Now, *die!*"

What a strange name... its familial connection to 'Humanitas' is evident, but it's an arduous task for the tongue – Tom will suffice.

But with his drivel delivered, his assault immediately follows.

With no care for approach or tactics, he darts straight towards me for the two seconds it takes to close the distance.

369

His swings are as wild and chaotic as the storm we're barrelling through, and I easily dance around them, reversing our positions without so much as a papercut.

The uneven ground and unfortunate climate aren't making this easy, though.

Tom no doubt lacks my real world experience, but he's accustomed to rushing around with such turbulence.

If there's an equivalent of 'sea legs' for clashing atop colossal talking birds, that's the one quality this young man brings to this brawl.

Though it *does* call into question when and how he would obtain such experience; either he's fought under such circumstances before, or he specifically trained atop his pet mid-flight to prepare himself.

Neither are favourable for me.

Nonetheless, he repeats the same strategy once I myself approach the midpoint of our carrier – I can end this with one swift motion, provided I reach for his neck.

That's the plan, until one of the knives suddenly flies towards me following a backhanded motion of his left hand.

Through the raging rainstorm, I'm barely able to notice it in time to catch its blade with my bare hand, mere centimetres from my eye.

Every evil bastard has his favourite body part to target, I've noticed.

And my new friend seems to have a scary affinity for eyes.

Ignoring the bleeding in my hand, I notice that a thin chain is running from the knife to his wrist and roughly tug at the weapon.

Tom yells out and stumbles towards me, but the lashing out of his right hand's knife in all sorts of directions forces me to back off once more.

Inexperienced kids playing around with experimental weaponry – the only combination more calamitous is my mouth and Kyrie's cooking.

He reminds me of an awful lot of a young lad who joined the ranks of my former clan, shortly before my... *departure.*

370

Calling himself Shadow, he fancied himself as some kind of ninja, and had a tendency to break a thing or two in his path to showing off to the few girlies among our group.

Not like Gillian would've let him get it wet anyway.

Still, Tom has enough of a grasp on his toys to retract them back into his hands once his attack fails to land further hits on me.

And no prizes for guessing what comes next: yet another straightforward assault.

This time his little toys see some more use; he leaps and spins around wildly as the full reach of his knives is let loose to tear through the rain itself.

I manoeuvre around the lot of it effortlessly, but he's proving difficult to approach.

If anything, the fact he's not letting a scratch land on his mount despite the mad flailing shows an unprecedented steadiness and precision I ought not to underestimate.

But with his landing, I have an opportunity to strike.

Time for an old favourite.

The "Black Morning Sun", named by its reclusive and unfortunately deceased creator Helbez.

A dramatic name for a weapon so simple as a rope and a steel ball; anybody could tell it came from me.

Ideally I want to subdue the bastard, but this should do if I find the need to send him on a one way flight instead.

As our eyes lock, I begin bending and contorting the flexible weapon around my arms and waist.

He's understandably wary, which gives me a chance to take the offensive.

Faking him out until he reacts to a near miss by ducking, I sweep the back of the beast and send him tumbling atop its blackened feathers.

Repeating the movement from the opposite end of its swing, Tom raises his legs in an attempt to leap over the steel ball and back to his feet – all too many an inexperienced opponent place an unhealthy emphasis on rushing back to their feet, and Tom is no exception.

As the steel ball eviscerates every drop of furious rain in its path, I raise its trajectory in such a manner that the rope constricts around his rising leg, sending the steel ball crashing into his ankle with a loud impact.

Now I've got him.

I begin to swing around in such a manner that an athlete would, distorting his confused screams in all sorts of inhuman ways as he feels the full fury of nature's wrath, hundreds if not thousands of metres in the air.

I end the motion swinging him above me from behind, sending the haughty Tom crashing into the neck of his own pet, metres from his horrified little companion.

"CUAAAAAAAAGHH!"

…shit!

The very ground I stand on is as tempestuous and uneven as that surrounding an erupting volcano, as this Gara birdie is flailing about all on its own now, no doubt driven to action by my blow to not only my enemy but his mount.

Before long, as I can barely hold my own against this unholy union between the battering rain and my terrain, Tom's knife comes crashing down close to his ankle, and the detached steel ball is unceremoniously kicked aside, rolling off of the bird and tumbling back to the distant ground below.

What a dismal end for a treasured companion…

It wasn't for nothing though; as Tom returns to his feet and the bird begins to settle down, his legs creak and bend as if he can barely support his own weight.

And yet he continues gunning for me, flailing weakly as he closes the distance.

One quick and precise blow to the face sends him on his back.

Before he can try anything else, I clamp down on Tom's chest with my left boot – his body seizes up and he can do nothing to retaliate.

"You don't have to die this night. Order the bird to land back at Dias and surrender yourself to us."

My demand is clear and direct – any sign of refusal or retaliation is license to bring a swift end to his short life.

"A-A-Ack...!"

The defeated mumbling is all that escapes his mouth – I've done this enough times to know I'm not applying enough force to prevent any coherent words from escaping.

"The gods of time are impatient, Tom! Issue the order! *Now*!"

The mumbling comes to an end, and with the deepest breath he can afford, I anticipate he's finally going to play nice.

But what leaves his mouth is a swift yet distinct whistle.

The bird begins convulsing once more, this time of its own volition.

I'm forced backwards by the aggressive motion, to which Tom hastily crawls away, in the direction of the little girl.

"That's a fun party trick, T-"

"M-Mahro!!"

A distinct plea for help rips through the battering rain, and Tom's devilish grin is directed well behind me.

I turn to find the bird's rear shaking with an aggression far exceeding the rest of its body, and Vega is barely clinging on to the side of the beast.

Between the convulsion of our vessel and the rain-coated fur giving hardly a decent surface to cling on, even I would barely be able to last beyond a few seconds.

Paying no regard to Tom, I sprint towards my dear friend, sliding forward on my stomach so as to extend my hand to him.

But right as our fingers are on the cusp of intertwining – he slips and falls, screaming into the abyssal night.

And I swiftly follow.

Tom and I can settle this score another day.

This feeling, it's...

Exhilarating.

Falling through the sky at its most violent.

Harassed in all directions by the endless rain.

The feeling of a knife at your back, or of hands wrapping around your throat...

It can't even begin to compare.

Falling into the complete unknown, not knowing if what awaits me some immeasurable distance below is hard ground or water deep enough to stand any chance of survival.

I feel... alive.

Which is a strange thing to say as I potentially fall to my death.

But it's the honest truth.

The adrenaline, the thought that my very consciousness is dancing elegantly along a knife's edge.

It's the first time I've felt alive since I learned of Minami's passing.

And I haven't felt *this* alive since our days with the Shangra Clan.

Wherever he's ended up, Gillian must be having a very hearty laugh as he watches this old fool wax poetic in his head as he has either minutes or seconds to live.

"Bwahahahaha! Why bother thinking about these things at all, my friend? You'll make for a pretty blood splatter on the ground either way. Best enjoy the fall!"

...yeah, something like that.

I hope it's warm enough for you in Hell, *my friend*.

That being said, if I don't do something about this situation swiftly, I'll soon join him in there.

Led by the ever so faint sound of Vega's screaming, I narrow my eyes, trying to comb out his shape within the dark night.

I see a reflection of the moon within a lake – if we're lucky, we're not far from Lake Sheine.

It's about an hour's walk from Dias in peak condition, which neither of us is in by any means, but that bridge is best crossed once we approach it.

The glint of the moon allows me to at last make out Vega's shape in front of me.

I've never had to navigate through the air personally, but I heard some advice from one among my old clan whose name unfortunately eludes me.

Shape oneself like a bullet, and you'll rip through the air.

My arms snap to my side and I direct myself in Vega's direction.

I'm quickly gaining on him, and before I can crash into him, I pull an old friend from a deep pocket within my coat.

A small, visually unimpressive device of great power, one I swiped from Gillian shortly before my final contract under the Shangra – and the encounter that changed my life forever hence.

I point it to the ground immediately below me and tug on the trigger.

A cataclysmic sound erupts while I'm helpless to cover my violated eardrums, and a bolt of lightning bursts out of its end, briefly setting alight a small grove of trees far below and illuminating the world around us for less than an instant.

But that tiny window is all I need to sum up our situation.

By my best estimate we're about 30 seconds from impact.

We're somewhere along the edge of Lake Sheine, but we'll need to head closer to its centre to not smash our legs to bloody stumps.

The wind is providing an ever so slight push towards our destination, but that alone won't suffice.

Then I'm left with one option – it's a near-certain death or certain death.

Before I collide with Vega, I pull off my coat – Minami's last present to me.

I hold my much-used coat by its sleeves in my left hand as we at last reunite in the air, keeping my grip on the young man with the breadth of my right arm.

"M-Mahro?! What the hell?! I thought they wanted me alive! It can't end like this!" he screams, understandably bewildered.

"I've a trick up my sleeves yet, my friend."

Well, not so much *up* my sleeves as it does directly involve them – keeping Vega in place with my legs, I tie the sleeves of my coat together and raise the whole thing above our heads, keeping a firm grip on each side of its makeshift handle..

There's a few bits and bobs kept within the coat itself rather than on my person, heaviest among them the bloodstained claws, but it doesn't appear to be weighing it down too badly.

Unfortunately, it does little to slow our descent; I can feel our trajectory moving ever so slightly in the direction of Sheine's centre, but I have no guarantee we'll come out of the drop with our legs intact.

All I can do is wait as the torrent of rain batters us forevermore, as though the gods themselves are spitting on us on our way to Hell.

I'm too focused on what awaits us to commune with Vega, but he's calmed down somewhat.

If anything, he almost seems... *ashamed* to have been rescued by me again.

Though the rescue party hasn't quite fought its way out of the fire yet.

Several moments pass, and I notice the angle of the moon's reflection is gradually distorting and rising.

Impact isn't far.

Vega's still not in a condition to brace himself for said impact.

Releasing my grip on my coat and making a mental note to reclaim it later, I bring the young man into my arms.

My right hand covers his nose and mouth, while my left hand covers my own.

I straighten my legs, and Vega at least has the capacity to notice and follow suit.

Then our eyes close.

In the next few seconds, we're either the luckiest men in Tenryuu or we're sinking to the bottom of Lake Sheine with more broken legs than lifelines.

Ending up as a bloody splatter on Dias' doorstep would be a preferable fate.

All that remains in that time is the violent rush of wind and rain enveloping my ears, and the shared look of dread in the eyes of the two men plummeting through the tumultuous Tenryuu skies.

...

...

...

SPLASH!

...

...

...

It's... been a few seconds.

We're not dead yet.

I open my eyes to find we're submerged deep in water.

The bed of the lake lies just feet below us.

Were I not already entrenched in some of the murkiest water on this side of Tenryuu, I would be sweating like a madman.

My left hand releases itself from my face as it paces upwards, desperately reaching for the light of the moon above the surface as yet another clock starts ticking.

I can't afford to think anymore.

I can only push onward.

And onward.

And onward...

...

Then right as Vega begins to struggle, threatening to suffocate by my own hand, we at last break the surface.

The tranquil quiet within Lake Sheine's depths erupts into a chorus of maddened breathing and splashing.

It's ugly and tumultuous... but it's an utter relief compared to what we've endured for hours and hours.

I couldn't tell you what the time is.

I couldn't say we're in a particularly good situation.

But with the rain dying down and the feeling of the still wind grazing our faces, with the night sky now untainted by black beasts hauling away our treasures... this ugly ordeal is finally at an end.

That is, Dias' ordeal.

I get the feeling that Vega's ordeal has only just truly begun.

Chapter 22: Farewell to the Languid Land

It's been three days since the Band of the Wyvern attacked yet another idyllic home in pursuit of me. That day started off as ordinary as any other and ended with Mahro hauling me across what felt like half of Tenryuu, both of us waterlogged and exhausted. By the time we entered Dias and I was more or less dumped into the concerned arms of his two daughters, the sky had begun to turn red, as if the sun had been watching our ordeal from behind its comfy horizon and was just now emerging now that the ashes had stopped smouldering.

The last few days have been spent under worryingly familiar circumstances: I've been left alone in Mahro's home to recover, visited every so often and having my wounds tended to by Myra. The one comfort in these dismal times is that she looks at me not as some strange alien but as a trusted confidant. And yet something looks... off about her. Like there's something great weighing on her mind but she's fighting as hard as anybody could to keep such a thing under wraps. It's natural, of course – I can speak from experience that watching your home devolve into violence and turmoil is a hard sight to recover from. I only wish the proceedings were not so convoluted, so I may stand any chance of isolating what it is that ails her mind.

Mr. Entari was also among the fallen, alongside a handful of friends of the Katsuragi family. Myra happened across Loren's body alongside her sister whilst Temperantia, Mahro and I were barrelling through the skies. Needless to say, I've dared not ask about Matra; if she already wanted to wring my neck before now, I dread to so much as be in the same street as her now that my curse has dragged someone of such significance to her into an early grave.

My curse... Myra isn't the only one whose head is heavy with thought. To even think about the amount of people who've lost their lives just for having the misfortune to share a location with me... it's harrowing. It's so far beyond quantifiable by this point that to begin imagining the number strains my mind to the point of physical pain. Even now, as I sit in relative comfort, how long is it until my bastard "family" decides to return? How many more of their pawns lie waiting in the wings, itching to spread their own in pursuit of me?

According to Myra, the rot is already kicking Dias while it's down; whereas most of its living residents are sticking to their guns and trying to make the best of a bad situation, all too many are packing their bags and rushing off to Shigan, Tenryuu's capital city. It's a surprisingly short distance away, and a tantalizing prospect for the downtrodden seeking a new start given Mahro's descriptions of its economic prowess and hospitality. Granted, those descriptions come from well over three years ago; considering the war itself had forced us apart for so long, and my mentor's appraisal of his home country's measures, I have no doubt corners are being cut everywhere. I'm sure many leaving Dias for the shiny utopia of Shigan will be bitterly disappointed.

Not that I have any right to criticize them, or that I necessarily am even doing so; I have no intention to stay here myself. My bloodline has dragged far too many into the depths of misery and destitution. It's as if fate itself is compelling me to walk this path alone. By my own hand, I must somehow return home *and* put an end to my bloodline's scheming. I haven't got the slightest clue about how to do either, but I can figure it out on the way.

For now, I can just make a start.

At the dawn of a new day, as light breaks into the deceptively shiny and untouched room of Mahro's home, I force myself out of the bed I've spent far too many a night in. Myra was courteous enough to return Helbez's glaive to my side, though the rest of his creations were not so lucky; given that many in the village are in the dark as to the Band of the Wyvern's true intentions and were privy only to their plundering, the people of Dias made the choice to destroy Helbez's vast arsenal and reuse their materials for reconstruction, among other purposes. I would rather have seen the man's work in a museum, but it's not as though I have the grounds to contest their ultimate decision. For now, I take the last reminder of his legacy into my hands; if I ever get back home, I'm sure Lyndra will take a liking to the craftsmanship after she beats my face in.

But speaking of Helbez... more than anything else, his passing is what angers me most; I was certain the whims of fate had brought me here to learn from him, and to return home not just stronger but wiser in my craft. Given that he died before ever getting to pass down a definitive word of wisdom... I can't help but wonder why I was ever brought here in the first place. If these are the machinations of Sihan-Perseli, what does she have to gain by taunting me with knowledge I can't claim, and with the company of a trusted but newly burdened mentor I can't return home in the company of, if her goal is not to kill or abduct me? The only possibility that instils greater dread in every pore of my skin is that my puppetmaster is entirely faceless; that the serpentine lady is a mere decoy, and the true architect behind it all takes pleasure in twisting and turning the trajectory of my life like a piece of molten metal between tongs. The events of my life are turbulent and completely incohesive – and I intend to take back some modicum of control over it, even if it kills me.

With nothing else other than the clothes on my back and the feeling that Mahro's home seems strangely empty, I exit the house for what I hope to be the final time.

Walking through the streets of Dias is a sobering experience; everywhere I look, once fine windows are smashed and shattered. Doors remain broken and battered, signs on houses denoting familial losses and funeral dates are as commonplace as they are haunting. Parents who lost their children sit near their front door, expressionlessly gawking at the sky. Store owners trudge along with the arduous task of either rebuilding their thoroughly plundered and vandalized property or deconstructing it in the prelude to a new life, in a new world. The vibrant red that festoons every inch and crevice of the village seems drained of colour, even when otherwise unperturbed by this new Band of the Wyvern's actions.

Above all, what pains most is the piercing eyes; more often than not, as I pass by the languid faces that litter the streets of Dias, painstakingly sweeping away bits and pieces of the carnage, our eyes meet... and I immediately wish they hadn't. The hatred and scorn in their eyes is as transparent as glass; this scruffy, black-haired stranger walked into their paradise, and is strolling away from the aftermath of having watched it descend into a nightmare. I don't blame them one bit. I'm sure the only thing stopping them from ganging up and pummelling the shit out of me is the big pointy stick in my hands.

And after my little escapade with Temperantia, I'm ready to... *cut loose* a little more. Hesitate a little less. If someone is standing between me and the life I so desperately seek to reclaim, and has no intention of moving, I can't *afford* to hesitate anymore, lest I end up on the back of another bird.

Steeling myself against the gazes, I at last approach Dias Village's entrance arch. It'll be tough to leave Mahro and his girls behind without a word, but if I'm ever to become half the man he is, it's ultimately for the best; I have no doubt that even if Mahro wished to accompany me, Matra is certain to dig in her heels, if only to be rid of me once and for all, and he too would be forced behind by her decision. And for as much as I like Myra, it would be horribly selfish to anticipate she too would uproot any attachments she has left to join me on what feels like a doomed quest.

Doomed... I've been trying to avoid the feeling, but it's hard to deny that a great sensation of doom has been festering in my mind for days on end. As soon as my foot leaves the boundaries of this village, the monsters hiding in my shadows will come to life and stalk me, tracking my footsteps like a pack of starving tigers. I may never know a good night's sleep again, dreading that behind every tree lies a knife, beneath every passing stranger is a bloodthirsty assailant, that every path I tread is the wrong one.

Of course, this doesn't factor in my... *guardian*. But she's about as reliable as Ringo after a single drink, and I already have more than enough reason to doubt her intent. I ought not to rely upon or expect her in such trying times – this is a path I'll carve through my own will.

Before I take the final step, I look up at the sky above Dias, one last time.

...

Oh, right.

That Cladio I sent to Altair.

It never returned.

The little beasties are both swift and very good at their jobs; I've been credibly told that they can travel the entire breadth of the world in a week. Assuming the Cladio travelled eastward across the sea, it should have been back days ago. I can't assume the worst just yet – maybe the pup is stuck in some bureaucratic mess or it's waiting for an answer from my brother whilst he's attending to other matters. But I'm not lingering around in a village where I'm not welcome based on a faint hope.

Now then, all my reservations aside, I can finally face my future. With a deep breath, I take the first steps towards my dismal, dreary futu—

GAH!

Why is Mahro hanging upside down from the entrance arch?!

I would say it feels nostalgic but the sudden sight terrifies me so badly I stumble backward and nearly skewer myself on my own weapon.

What a dismal end that would have been.

"*Hohohoh!* Where do you think you're going, little man?!" my mentor asks as he flies back onto his feet, and the earth he walks submits beneath his booming footsteps, "You crash land in my home, eat my food, watch its downfall, and now you walk away from the carnage like your work here is done?!"

I can only close my eyes – from the sound of his voice, I can tell something dreadful is about to happen, and I could never possess the strength to equal Mahro.

"You do *all of that*, and when you finally make good on starting your little quest, you have the *audacity* to not even ask for my company?!"

"I'm sorry! I didn't mean to—to—what?!" I ask in amazement – my eyes open to find Mahro reeling over in howling laughter.

"*Ahahahahahaaaaah!* What, you- you really thought *I* of all people would beat you into next week? *Hahahah!* I thought you knew me better by now, Vega!"

"No not that, I mean... why would you accompany me? You've no obligation to do so whatsoever."

"It has nothing to do with 'obligation', my friend. I've... had a talk with my girls. The three of us came to the mutual agreement that whatever awaits us beyond the cracked comforts of Dias, we'll be better off for it than if we sit around here for all eternity."

Mahro offers his hand to bring me to my feet, and I momentarily stare at it in a daze before I take it.

"I... what do you mean?! I have an entire clan of people with... *talking birds* trying to kidnap me! They pillaged and murdered the good people of this village without remorse or hesitation! To drag not just you but your daughters along on this path... it's cruel."

"Crueller yet are the words you speak. I'm saddened by the loss of Loren and many other good friends within this village, but if I sent you on your way to die namelessly in some forgotten corner of Tenryuu, I would never know a good night's sleep again for the rest of my life. Do you think I've lived my entire life never once asking for help, never calling upon those I've looked up to? I know a failed venture before I see the first footstep in the mud. *Let us help you.*"

My mind struggles to process what he's saying; it's tough to envision Mahro as anything other than an entirely self-sufficient being. I've watched him fight horrors I could never comprehend, lifting worldly weights that would crush any other man I've ever met. His company would be utterly invaluable; a certain failure would transition into an inevitable win purely from his involvement. I can only feel that... I just don't deserve it.

"What about your home…? Do you not wish to stay in your country?" I ask in a desperate final measure to dissuade him.

"I love my girls more than anything in the world, Vega; what rock we happen to live on matters for nothing to me. But even if I felt some lifelong allegiance towards my home country, what's left of it is merely a desiccated husk. I could regale you for years of the prosperity it once knew, of the freedoms the people of Tenryuu enjoyed, but it would be useless. It would only serve to propagate an image of what no longer is. The warmongering bastards that puppeteer this land now can have it for all I care; you still have a home to get to, one that, for all the batterings it's taken, is unmistakably yours. No price is too great to preserve that."

I'm… stunned.

He's as well-equipped for a verbal confrontation as any physical one, and every word that leaves his mouth is vivid with both conviction and contempt. Even if indirectly, I'm responsible for the deaths of his close friends and many other good people, and for demolishing the livelihoods of more or less everybody within these walls. Yet he's as insistent as ever on remaining by my side, insofar as to bring his daughters along on what moments ago was a hopeless suicide mission.

"So… you don't plan to return?" I ask.

"Not at all. There's nothing left for us here. For however long my flame of life may burn yet, I can always start anew in Morosus."

With this answer, I can bring myself to smile for what feels like the first time in years. It's the only tangible outcome of the tangled web of conflicting emotions coiling around my aching mind, and so… I decide I ought to trust it.

"Thank you. I truly mean it. I only hope I won't let you down." I say meekly.

"After more than 40 years in this world, it'll take something ungodly to let *me* down. Don't get your brain in a knot just yet."

"Oi, you!"

Before I can turn around to discover the source of the yell, a rigid arm flies around my neck – it's a strangely enthused Yuna, and… and… *half of her left arm is metallic?!*

"What in the world?! Where... where did you get that?!" I ask, utterly baffled.

Two fingers is something, but... half of an entire arm being replaced?! What madness!

"That glint in your eye, Vega. It's been six years since last we met but to me... why, at this present moment I could mistake it for yesterday."

That voice... can it... can it really be...?

I quickly look behind Yuna to find another woman standing there with her arms crossed and a brown bag held by the inside of her elbow. A hooded cloak with the colour of withering grass conceals a plain grey shirt belonging to a very well-endowed lady.

Then I see her face. The umber hair atop her head is similar in length to my own, though it clearly belongs to a woman at least a decade older than me. An eyepatch conceals her right eye, the socket for which looks strained and damaged beneath the leathery patch, while her left eye is a soothing green. But there's one thing it can't hide: the slight but ever-present pulsation at its core, and I've only ever met one person with such special eyes...

"S-Saki...?"

I struggle to even say her name, in no small part because I can hardly even believe she's here at all.

I mean... she did leave for Tenryuu all those years ago so this shouldn't have been as big a surprise as it was, but... why *now?!*

"I've been attending to personal matters as of a few days ago. But now... it appears I'm free."

As if nothing has changed at all, she's speaking as if she could read the exact concern clouding my mind.

Before any more words are exchanged, she slowly strolls over to me, carefully examining my entire body with her piercing eye and taking the rough metallic appendages grafted in my hands into her delicate own. The creator may be vastly different but the warmth in her hands hasn't changed whatsoever. With an enthusiastic hum, she looks me in the eyes once more.

"Julius certainly got better, didn't he? But why don't we get you home and show him how we *really* do it, for old times' sake?"

"...I would like that."

I'm barely able to construct even that sentence – not just Mahro and his family, but Saki, who I never expected to see again for as long as I lived, is also accompanying me? I'm trying to remain composed considering what we're up against, and the disastrous consequences any grievous misjudgement on our part may incur, but a part of me is childishly gleeful.

"Say, big guy, how long did it take ya to get used to those?" Yuna asks as she swings her new arm around with barely any control.

"About a week for each finger, maybe? Though I'm sure you'll adapt a lot faster than a weak little seven year old." I answer.

"S-seven?!" Yuna cries out, her maw agape, "Even as a baby, you led quite the exciting life. I'm awash with envy!"

"The envious obscure their envy, darling – you're as honest as they come." Saki comments, "And I'm certain that if you saw what kind of life a young Vega led... well, you'd be grateful for the one you *did* lead."

I answer Saki with an affirming nod, and Yuna releases her grip with a disappointed grunt.

"Honestly, now that you're going away I wish you could've told me about all these wacky adventures of yours. Your life is this country bumpkin's ambitions!" Yuna says bitterly.

"I'm a country bumpkin myself. Fate just has it out for me, I suppose." I answer, "Besides, I think fate has already robbed you of enough; I'm terribly sorry about your boss."

"Yeah, that... complicates things. I'm the de facto shot caller now, but... I'm really out of my depth on this one." Yuna answers, approaching something of a frown for possibly the first time in recorded history.

It's at this point that we're interrupted by a series of footsteps – it's Myra and Matra, each carrying a brown bag similar to Saki's with them and with the younger of the two looking far more enthused. Matra is in her uniform while Myra presents herself before us in unfamiliar garments: A white and purple leather shirt that cuts off below her breasts and wraps tightly around them, joined by skin-tight black leggings and an equally dark skirt. Come to think of it, I swear she described one of her mother's outfits in such a way, though it now comes adorned with a light belt to store a pair of daggers and other miscellaneous items. Is she taking her mother's clothes as some sort of... memento?

"*Uwaaaaaah, Milkbaaaaaag!* You're leaving poor little me behind to go on the adventure of a lifetime?! You're a heartless demoness!" Yuna cries as she grabs a stoic Matra by the shoulders and shakes the red out of her hair.

"Peace, my friend. Loren may have passed on, but you have Aster and Moka by your side yet. On the other hand, I cannot remain here; after such a calamity, the spiritual makeup of Dias is no doubt in utter disarray. I do this not for pleasure, Yuna. This is ultimately in my best interests." Matra calmly answers her wailing friend.

"You can just say you're fond of me after all." I say to her with a grin.

"Shut your mouth." Matra answers with a piercing glance.

Ouch... despite her unlikely participation, her heart is as closed off as ever. Will she really last on such a journey?

"Yuna... I'm not sure we'll ever meet again, so in that event, thank you for everything." she says, more or less ignoring my existence.

In contrast to her sharp approach to yours truly, she delivers her farewell to Yuna alongside a brief ruffle of the drained tomboy's hair.

"Tell your mother we wish her a strong recovery." Myra says with a pained smile.

"And feel free to break into our home on the off chance you require something within. It's hardly as though we'll grace it with our presence furthermore." Mahro adds, to which Yuna gratefully smiles.

"And you, Scraggly Hair." she says hastily, pointing at me.

"Uh... what?"

"Yeah, Scraggly Hair. I don't know what this Band of the Wyvern business is all about..." Yuna starts before tightly clasping my left hand with her newly forged own – the mutual touch of steel creates a hopeful clang as they meet, "...but if they still get up your ass, give 'em Hell!"

I smile deviously as our eyes connect, a burning bloodlust shared between them.

"You bet we will."

And with that, our party – Mahro, Myra, Matra, Saki and myself - takes its leave once and for all. Myra and Saki take their time waving and shouting goodbyes to Yuna as she grows ever more distant, while Mahro, Matra and I keep our gazes firmly ahead, facing the uncertain but no doubt tumultuous future.

Beneath the farewells, Matra walks up to my side, though still refusing to meet my eyes.

"Don't make me regret this." She says sternly.

I'm sure she could find *some* way to be disappointed even if we topple our pursuers and return to Ford with the stars in tow, but I'm not about to let such an opinion show on my face.

"I won't."

My promise procured, she at last seems content and re-joins her sister's side.

After a while the farewells die down once and for all, with Yuna becoming a dot on the horizon.

As the sun shines down on all of us, Saki strolls up to my side, swinging her bag hypnotically.

"My, how the time flies when I'm having fun! If only Altair were here too; reliving our days in Ford just isn't complete without him, no?"

I don't look back on such days with the fondness she apparently does, given that it kickstarted the ugly Eden ordeal, but I can't be so heartless as to shoot down her eagerness.

"Either way, I think the two of us have a lot of catching up to do. I doubt your new life in Tenryuu has been free of tumult." I say.

"Aye; I doubt either of us could summon the words to do our tales justice. For life is as beautiful as it is cruel."

How fascinating – our paths in life diverged significantly, and yet our conclusion is the same. All we can do is hope the worst of life's cruelty is behind us.

"So, Vega, as the man in charge, what is our mission?" Mahro asks, and it's a very good question – I haven't put much thought into the specifics, but it doesn't take long to summon a rudimentary plan.

"Altair should be stationed at the border of Morosus. We'll make our way there through Vana, and should he be occupied elsewhere, we'll head for the capital and send word to him from there. In the company of the military, that Temperantia scum and his compatriots shouldn't be able to lay a finger on us, and then we can set ourselves on ending this new Band of the Wyvern once and for all."

"I see... then I shall trust in your plan, my friend." Mahro says with a reaffirming pat on the back, "This path we tread will not be easy, but rest assured; you'll emerge a greater man."

A greater man... if that's what I get to face my family as, then I welcome whatever ordeal the world can throw my way.

Snarl Boy... Temperantia...

Do your worst.

Afterword

So... this is my second time writing this afterword, as well as of course my second time doing this whole "first chapter" thing, and I've gone on an interesting journey over the process of thinking this whole saga up; I went from this simple idea of a boy waking up on a beach and trying to get back home, to an epic clusterfuck where the boy is a prince and there's 93 uncles and aunts to juggle and politics and complicated geography, worldbuilding, contradictory magic systems, and now here I am again, pretty much back at square one (point five, maybe) and I think the story is far better off for it. Even now, I want to use the first volume as a springboard to a more interesting main journey, but I at least want to think I've significantly improved the flow of the whole thing; originally Steph died in the fifteenth chapter rather than the fifth, and half of the way there was a meandering tutor arc that spent way too much time setting up already stupid future events without being at all interesting in their own right. Therefore, I want to use this first part of the afterword to offer thanks: First to my buddy/tank Whirblewind for reading over my drafts and giving some much needed, *very* direct criticism that I firmly believe has made the final outcome a lot better. He's admittedly more well-read than I so the insight proved to be critical. And of course, I want to extend my thanks to Kentaro Miura, the mangaka behind the action-horror masterpiece *Berserk*. His work has had an enormous impact on what I look for in character writing and tone, and I was devastated when the news of his death broke. The whole situation was and still is tragic, but it ultimately served as the motivation to finally get off my arse and start making this whole thing. As well as my thanks, I extend my most sincere condolences to his loved ones.

I guess the first insight I want to provide is about Saki: I've been plotting this story in my head for about two and a half years as of writing and started work on the first draft sometime around July of 2021, and while it's gone through countless iterations, there's one idea that's persisted throughout all of them: "Man, I really want there to be a group of people who see inside bodies and shit with their eye". I brought this up to Whirble a while back while forming the first draft and he mentioned its strong resemblance to the premise of *Saya no Uta*, a game I'd heard rare mentions of but knew nothing about. That conversation resulted in me playing the game over the next few days and absolutely loving it. It's enchanting, beautiful and *absolutely fucking disgusting.* I hadn't decided on Saki's name at the time, and so I chose it as a sort of nod to the main character of *Saya no Uta,* plus I like it as a name in general. All things considered, it's a short story but there's very little else that even comes close to making its villains so compelling. It's very rare that a character's fall into darkness is so effectively communicated with such brevity, and stories of significantly longer length can still fail the landing miserably. I guess my biggest takeaway from the story from a 'learning to write' perspective is that even if there's not much of an 'arc', there needs to be a thorough through-line in why characters end up the way they do; having a dude kill scores of innocents because his mommy beat him feels like a non-sequitur at best and a punchline at worst.

I'm not really sure what else I can say right now so I'll just talk about my future plans a little. This was obviously the first part of a much longer tale. How many instalments there will be I cannot yet say, but I'm determined to bring it to completion no matter what; I've had these ideas in my head for far too long to let them go to waste. That being said, a year straight of working on this first part has taken quite a bit out of me, and I've had weeks-long bouts of zero progress more than I care to admit. So after this, I'll probably work on one of my side projects for a while alongside Part 2; I've come up with an awful lot of ideas I'd love to explore, though how many of them will come to fruition has yet to be seen. Something standalone/pulp would do me well, I imagine. I know I'm still young and many would say I have all the time in the world to explore my ideas, but considering how fast my 20s have already crept up on me, I have a feeling that I'll be pushing 30 before I even realise it.

If you want to know what I'm up to or want updates on my work, feel free to follow me on Twitter at @Kishinjou1 (@Kishinjou was taken). That being said, I write for a mature, *enlightened, <u>adult</u>* audience and my Twitter reflects it; alongside status reports on my next project(s) and unsolicited opinions on videogames and cartoons of Asiatic origin, expect a lot of unsafe for work retweets of anime girls. Mostly Utsuho Reiuji! *Open my page in public at your own peril.*

Printed in Great Britain
by Amazon

20788564R00226